Best [illegible] Bill —
I hope [illegible]
this "Pilgrimage" —

PILGRIMAGE
A Tale of Old Natchez

Louise Wilbourn Collier

Louise Wilbourn Collier
October 8, 1994

PELICAN PUBLISHING COMPANY
Gretna 1994

Published by St. Luke's Press, 1982
Published by arrangement with the author by
Pelican Publishing Company, Inc., 1994

First printing, 1982
Second printing, 1984
First Pelican Pouch edition, 1994

Library of Congress Cataloging-in-Publication Data

Collier, Louise W., 1925-
Pilgrimage, a tale of old Natchez / Louise Wilbourn Collier.
— 1st Pelican Pouch ed.
p. cm.
ISBN 1-56554-064-6
1. Family—Mississippi—Natchez—History—Fiction. 2. Women—Mississippi—Natchez—Fiction. 3. Natchez (Miss.)—History—Fiction. I. Title.
PS3553.047464P54 1994
813'.54—dc20 94-27835
CIP

The people and events in this book are real. In some instances, however, the facts have been adjusted to fit the purposes of the story.

Manufactured in the United States of America
Published by Pelican Publishing Company, Inc.
1101 Monroe Street, Gretna, Louisiana 70053

To my Great-Aunt Ernestine Walworth—
in her memories and my dreams
we often made this pilgrimage,
riding up long winding drives
in a horse and buggy to take tea in the gardens
and galleries of Natchez

Part I

1853-1865

CHAPTER ONE

EVEN the birds were strangely still in the oppressively hot and humid weather which had plagued the southern half of the state of Mississippi for weeks now, but the lawn and shrubs that surrounded The Burn itself had flourished in the tropical atmosphere and were lush and green on this August afternoon of 1853.

The town of Natchez, which owed its existence to its high and healthful situation on the river bluff above the disease ridden swamps where the rich flood lands were divided into extensive plantations, had recently become a very unhealthy place to live. The dreaded Yellow Fever was making one of its recurring visits. No respecter of persons or class, it hit in the meanest shanties Under-the-Hill and in the elegant mansions of the wealthy planters clustered on the top of the hill.

Architecture, borrowing its beauty of proportion from the Greeks and with its craftsmanship suborned from a vast pool of African talent, had combined to create an impressive array of beautiful buildings—buildings which contained the finest materials available and were meant to last forever, as though the builders knew that they were destined to become monuments.

The dignified white frame house that John and Sarah Walworth had built in 1832 was rarely empty, but today The

Burn had a lonesome look about it. All the family including the servants had left it and now it sat waiting for its family to come home. The deadly heat of the afternoon sun was behind it now as the sun started dropping toward the river, which lay a couple of miles away, barely visible from the house because of the thick screening of the trees.

At last the carriages turned in at the gate and pulled slowly up the sweeping semicircle of the drive to the steps leading to the lower of two columned galleries, which jutted out from the center of the house beneath a rather stark Doric portico.

Three children, a boy and two girls, jumped out of one of the carriages. Then the boy turned and helped a tall black woman in a dark gingham dress and bonnet to alight from it.

John Periander Walworth and his wife, Sarah, and their older son, Douglas, were in the second carriage. The young man got out first and his father half-lifted his wife into his son's outstretched arms, where she stood for a second sagging against him.

As the negro woman approached to help, John Walworth said, "Let's put her to bed, Aunt Chloe. She's completely exhausted. She's been through so much these last few days."

"You children must be sure not to disturb your mother," he added as the carriages drew slowly away, and they nodded solemnly.

The youngest, Clara, was especially thoughtful as she watched Aunt Chloe lead her mother off to bed just as though she had been eight years old like Clara. After her father and her grown-up brother, Douglas, had disappeared into the house she seated herself between her older sister and brother, Laura and Ernest, who had taken seats on the gallery steps and begun to fan themselves with their hats.

Clara looked from Laura, who was thirteen, to Ernest, who was twelve. They were blond and blue eyed and beautiful like Douglas and her father. Only she and Lucy looked like their mother with their brown straight hair and gray eyes. She guessed that was one of the reasons she felt so lonesome without Lucy.

Clara had been looking forward to her sister Lucy's eleventh birthday party, counting the days until it would be, when Lucy had gotten sick with the Yellow Fever and the party had had to be called off. Everybody in the house had become busy with important and mysterious things, and Mama never even came out of Lucy's room. Aunt Chloe had taken meals to her there, her dark, blunt-featured face stern, but with tears running down it.

Now, suddenly, just the day after her birthday, Lucy was gone—completely gone—taken away and put down in the ground with dirt on top of her. Only everybody said she was supposed to be in Heaven. How could that be? Heaven was such a strange, faraway place. You couldn't write letters like when Douglas was away at school. Clara didn't want to go to Heaven—very definitely not. And she didn't want Lucy to be there, or down in the ground either. It made her feel very bad to think about it, even though Laura and Ernest assured her that the real Lucy was not in the ground, and that Heaven was supposed to be a very good place to be.

Chloe and Sarah started toward the stairs together, Chloe's arm firmly about the frail woman's corseted waist.

"Mother, let me carry you up," Douglas urged.

Sarah roused herself out of the semistupor into which she had taken refuge from her grief and exhaustion. "No, my dear son. That's not necessary. I'm quite all right. Aunt Chloe will look after me. You stay with your father and take care of him for me."

Douglas embraced his mother, and then as the two women slowly ascended the semispiral staircase which made a sweeping loop in midair, he and his father stood watching.

John Walworth sighed, "I believe she will be able to sleep now. It's a blessing after all that she's so exhausted. Let's go out on the back gallery."

They walked through the open doorway at the end of

the hall and sat down on the gallery. Neither spoke, each preoccupied with his own grief and concerns.

What a nightmare the last few days had been, thought Douglas. His little sister Lucy had suddenly fallen ill and had died of the Fever that was rampant all over Natchez. Added to his shock and grief over that was the terrible fear that his young wife, expecting their first child at any moment, might be stricken with the dread disease. Nobody knew how or why some people got it and others did not. Nobody knew how to protect themselves and those they loved from it except to leave town, and it was probably too late for that. At any rate he had sent his wife to her parents on the outskirts of town when he had received the first word of Lucy's illness. He had known at once that it was the only thing to do, although it had been horribly depressing staying in their new house alone. To see a little sister suffer and die on her eleventh birthday had been almost unbearable for him. He didn't know how his mother and father could endure it. They had already lost three children between him and Laura, and now Lucy. Good God, life was hard!

He glanced at his father. His face was sad, yes, but otherwise inscrutable. What a man! His strength and self-discipline had always awed Douglas and made him feel somehow inadequate. Everyone said he looked like his father. He had the same corn-colored hair and sky-blue eyes, deep-set above high cheekbones, the same straight nose with wide nostrils. But did he have his father's iron? Although he knew that everyone expected him to, he was afraid that he did not.

John Walworth forced himself to count his blessings. He had four surviving children and a wonderful wife. He had his health and he had wealth, which he had earned himself. As a young bachelor on a visit from Cleveland, Ohio, he had chosen to stay in Natchez, working first as a law clerk, then becoming successively a planter, bank president, alderman, and mayor. He had acquired, in but a few years, land, slaves to work it, and a wife of fine character, who was truly the other half of himself. There was much to be thankful for. After all, what right had he or any man to expect to be exempt from suffering and tragedy? It was a part of life. One must accept it and go on. When the first child had died he had wondered if he could. He had found out that he could. The pain mounted within him. He closed his eyes and let it hurt. It would go away eventually.

He wasn't sure just how long he had sat there with his eyes closed, but when he opened them he realized that dusk was creeping up on them. The clusters and spires of the vegetation in the terraced garden that fell away from the gallery had become the dark ramparts and turrets of a medieval fortress, and the leaves on the trees were like black lace etched against the twilight sky. Such beauty was hard to bear when your heart was aching.

"Well, Father, I guess I'd better go home now." Douglas' voice was husky and almost inaudible.

"Why don't you spend the night at The Burn?" John Walworth suggested.

"Thank you, Father, but I've got to get home. Esther's expecting me at Elmo for supper."

"Well, if you really feel you must—but, Douglas, for heaven's sake don't go to Linden. You mustn't try to see your wife until the Fever's done. Even if the baby should come."

"I wouldn't dream of doing such a foolish thing!"

"No, of course you wouldn't. Forgive me."

The children were still sitting on the steps of the front gallery as Douglas prepared to leave. The first stars of the evening shone weakly, and here and there a firefly winked at them. The mosquitoes had come out of their lairs in the thick bushes and Clara slapped at one.

Voices came from the hall.

"You're sure you won't stay?"

"I'm sure, Father. I need to go home."

"Well, I wish you'd have some supper first. I got a little soup for everybody." That was Aunt Chloe.

"Thank you, Aunt Chloe, but Esther has something already waiting at Elmo. Take care of Mother."

"Lord, Mr. Douglas, child, don't you know I will?"

"I do know it, Aunt Chloe, bless you!"

The door opened and Father and Douglas walked onto the gallery, their faces still grim and sad.

"Goodbye, Father. I'll walk over in the morning."

Douglas gave Ernest's blond head a preoccupied pat and put his other hand on Laura's curls. Then he did a very unusual thing for him. Catching Clara up in his arms, he gave her a hard hug, and she was positive she heard a sob as he set her down and hurried away.

How funny, she wondered, and then she understood. She thought, he hugged me because he couldn't hug Lucy! Suddenly she wanted to comfort him and protect him from being hurt as though she were fifteen years older than he instead of fifteen years younger.

Douglas quickly covered the distance from The Burn to Elmo, the stunning Greek temple he'd had built at the north end of The Burn's property for his bride. It was now quite dark, but a half-moon had risen, and Elmo's whiteness gleamed in its soft blue light. Even in Douglas' distraught state, he felt a little surge of pride and satisfaction as he beheld the six soaring Doric columns that supported the high hip roof.

Elmo was as wide and as tall as his dreams and those of his wife. If anything she loved it more than he did. They had copied their favorite house, beautiful and stately D'Evereux, the house of her aunt, Mrs. St. John Eliot, who had graciously lent them her plans. The young couple intended to adapt the plans to their own needs, but in the end had decided that the original plan could not be improved upon, and with Mr. and Mrs. Eliot's approval, built a replica of D'Evereux.

They had moved into the house with the paint barely dry on its walls about three weeks ago so anxious they were that their first child should be born at Elmo. Circumstance had changed all that of course. How empty the new house seemed now with his wife not there. He almost dreaded going into it.

As he crossed the gallery that ran the width of the house, a heavy-set negro man in shirtsleeves opened the wide front door.

Douglas was surprised. He had told Uncle Perry that he needn't wait for him.

"Evening, Mr. Douglas. How is Miss Sarah and everybody over at The Burn?" Uncle Perry inquired, his deep, resonant voice gentle, concern softening the surprisingly Caucasian features of his dark mahogany face.

"All right, I think. Mother's gone to bed, and Father is holding up fine. You needn't have waited for me. Esther can serve me my supper. I don't want much."

"I just wanted to be sure you didn't need me for anything."

Douglas grasped the older man's arm and squeezed it affectionately. "Thank you, Uncle Perry. I do appreciate your staying. It helps not to walk into an empty house, but you go on now. I'll be all right. Tell Esther I'll be ready for supper in a few minutes."

"All right then. Good night, Mr. Douglas. I hope you rest well."

Uncle Perry was a good man, Douglas thought, as he climbed the steps to his room to freshen up before eating his supper. The elderly mulatto had been with his family since before Douglas was born. Loyal and devoted, he was really a member of the family just as Aunt Chloe was, although he would never take the liberties that she did. Actually he was already working in The Burn household when John Walworth had brought Aunt Chloe up from one of their plantations to help nurse Douglas' little brothers during their fatal illnesses. A woman of many talents, she had continued as the nurse for Laura, Ernest, and Clara, helping in the kitchen and eventually becoming the cook.

Uncle Perry had had his share of tragedy. His wife, Marge, who was the cook at The Burn while Aunt Chloe was still the nurse, had burned to death when her clothes caught fire on the stove, leaving him with two sons and a daughter. His daughter had died of Scarlet Fever the following winter and the boys had run away not long afterward.

Uncle Perry had borne these griefs patiently and philosophically, teaching first Douglas and then his brother Ernest to fish and hunt much as he might have taught his own sons.

He had seemed delighted when Sarah and John Walworth had suggested that he go to work for Douglas and his bride at Elmo and he had been with them since they had moved into the house.

Esther, a comely, but unhappy looking, young black woman, served Douglas his supper by candlelight on the back gallery, her ample bosom and hips ballooning above and below a relatively small waist and swaying gracefully with her movements. She had little to say and Douglas was grateful for her silence. He didn't know her very well as she had belonged to his wife's family. She had a reputation among the other servants for being disagreeable, but he hadn't had any trouble with her. He found the trick was to stay out of her way and he did just that. Tonight, although her expression remained typically sullen, she seemed quite solicitous and he felt that in her own way, she, too, was trying to express her sympathy.

Esther was a good cook and had prepared a tempting light meal for him of ham and biscuit, fried custard and sliced tomatoes, but he couldn't seem to eat much of it and after a few minutes he thanked her and left her clearing the table. It was still stiflingly hot inside so he walked through the hall to the front gallery.

The night had turned darker, the moon and stars obscured by clouds. The only light was the dull red glow in the sky from the fires that had been kept burning in the streets ever since the epidemic had broken out.

There was a sudden flash of lightning, but it was just from the heat. Despite the thick clouds there appeared to be slight chance of rain. If only it would rain and turn cooler, the Fever might abate, although there would continue to be some cases until after the first frost.

Something down the road caught his attention. He heard the rhythmic thud of horses' hooves before he saw the shadowy form of the horse and rider turn into Elmo's drive. In a few moments he could see that it was his friend and law partner, Will Martin, riding toward him.

When Douglas had followed his father's footsteps to Harvard, Will, already a successful lawyer, had told him that as soon as he finished school he wanted him to join him in his law firm. And Douglas had done so, although sometimes he wondered if he was really cut out for the law. He had performed well enough, but deep down he wasn't sure he liked it. Perhaps he was lazy, but he hated all the hairsplitting and digging for facts. Will seemed to relish it, and Douglas wished that he could.

The horse stopped at the mounting block beside the gallery, and a man with dark, lank hair, and lively blue eyes, handsome in spite of a vaguely disheveled appearance, dismounted and strode briskly up the steps.

"Will, what in the world are you doing here?"

"Well, my little wife sent me to check on you. We hated to think about your being here by yourself tonight. I thought you might have stayed at The Burn, at least tonight, but I remembered you telling me at the funeral that you didn't plan to."

"It's awfully good of you to come by, Will. I really appreciate both you and Margarette thinking about me, but I'm doing quite well. Esther gave me my supper, and I'll probably turn in early tonight. It's been a strenuous day."

"How are your parents?"

"Holding up extremely well. Mother, of course, is exhausted, but Father is simply marvelous. He's a stoic if I ever saw one. Will you come in and have a brandy with me?"

"Fine. That's a good idea. And then I'll go home and let you get some rest."

After Will had left Douglas sat on the back gallery for a while. He didn't think he could sleep yet.

What a great friend Will was! Well, of course, more than a friend to be exact.

He remembered an afternoon about three years ago. He had ridden his horse over to Linden to see Will and his new bride, little sixteen-year-old Margarette Conner. Linden was Margarette's home, and they were staying there while they built their own house next door. Douglas had been away at school when they were married, and although he knew the Conners and had once been to a party at Linden, he didn't remember Margarette; so he was anxious to meet the spoiled tomboy turned beauty, which was the way she'd been described to him.

Douglas leaned back in his chair and closed his eyes. He often relived this scene.

He had directed his horse into a winding driveway, leading through a spacious grove of moss-draped live oaks, to a white frame house of wonderfully delicate proportions. It was built low to the ground, the bottom story stretching out to a wingspread of nearly a hundred feet. A gallery with a colonnade of slender cypress pillars ran its entire length. This gave Linden, in spite of its Greek pediment, a Spanish look, appropriately enough, as the oldest part of the house dated from Natchez's Spanish period. Linden was not the grand design of any architect. It had simply evolved to meet the needs of its various occupants. By the alchemy of chance, as well as by its owners' taste and ingenuity, it had turned into a harmonious and unique entity. Douglas reined up to admire the unselfconscious grace and charm of this enchanting house.

Suddenly both he and his horse had become aware of the approach of another horse and rider. In a few moments they were joined by a gray sorrel and, seated sidesaddle on his back, a young woman with an abundance of dark hair tumbling loose in curls about the shoulders of her bottle-green riding habit.

Douglas found himself gazing into a pair of large, brown eyes that seemed to look right into his soul. She was as beautiful as everyone said, her features classic in an oval face with a complexion the color and texture of heavy cream. She smiled at him, and he saw what they meant about her sparkle and charm, but there was another quality that he had not expected to find, a serenity. "This girl has been maligned!" he had said to himself indignantly. "She's as sweet and unspoiled as the morning air," and he felt a sharp stab of envy and regret. Lucky Will to have found her!

He returned her smile with a little half-bow. "Good day to you, Mrs. Martin. I'm Douglas Walworth."

Her sudden laughter had rung out merrily and the pure music of it aroused another twinge of envy and regret. He had told himself he must try to conquer those unworthy feelings and rejoice for his friend.

And then she had said, "But I'm not Mrs. Martin. I'm her sister, Rebecca. we look quite a lot alike, and people often confuse us!"

"You are not Margarette Martin?"

"No, I am Rebecca Conner."

"Thank God," Douglas had murmured under his breath, and right then he had known that he never wanted to live without Rebecca Conner. He had married her the following year after his graduation, and now he and Will were not only friends and law partners, but brothers-in-law.

Dammit, the mosquitoes were eating him up. What a nuisance they were!

He decided that he ought to go up to bed. He walked reluctantly into the house, its silence enveloping him, its stillness oppressing him. Perhaps he should have accepted his father's invitation to stay at The Burn, but it might be some time before Rebecca could come back to Elmo, and he might as well get used to the idea of staying here alone. At least at Elmo he could feel Rebecca's presence and be comforted by it.

Down the road at The Burn, Clara lay forlornly in the big bed she had shared with Lucy. She couldn't sleep. She wished Lucy weren't way up in Heaven. If only she could reach out her hand and touch her! Then she thought about the white rose that Lucy and the Scottish gardener who worked for them then had planted a few years ago. Lucy was always so proud of that rose and watered it herself and weeded it, and everybody made a big fuss over it and called it Lucy's rose. Clara had a sudden urge to see it now and touch one of its blossoms.

So she slipped off into the darkness of the garden. She found John Walworth on his knees beside the little rose bush sobbing. She could scarcely believe her eyes. Her father crying? That was the most impossible thing that had happened yet! Somehow she knew that he mustn't know that she had seen him so she crept away, back into the house. She didn't understand all about everything that had happened, but she had learned a lot of things these last few days that she would never forget, she thought, as she crawled quietly back into her bed. The world was more mysterious and frightening than she had ever dreamed, but it was exciting and interesting, too. How glad she was to be alive!

CHAPTER TWO

REBECCA sat beside her mother in a shady corner of the deeply recessed gallery that stretched around the rear of Linden, embracing a formal garden. Nothing but a few hardy zinnias and petunias were blooming in the early September heat and even they looked ragged and wilted.

Nearly two weeks had passed since Lucy's funeral and there had been no new cases of the Fever for three days. Hopes were high that the epidemic might be subsiding. In spite of that, or maybe because of it, she was getting restless. She missed Douglas in so many ways. She felt like half a person without him. Her body ached for his although she knew that things couldn't be the way they were until after the baby came. But, oh, just to be able to talk to him, to hear the sound of his voice with that special softness and huskiness in it when he spoke to her. It filled her with wild longings just to think about it!

And she was worried about him, too. He sometimes got depressed. She wished he had not had to go through the ordeal of his little sister's tragic death without her there to comfort him. She knew he must be worried about her, too, and the baby. The baby, she thought, and could feel it stretching within her. She put her hands with awe on the swollen mound of her abdomen. It was still amazing to her the way this little human being had grown inside her, and she couldn't imagine how in the world she was ever going to give birth to it. Other women did though so she guessed she could too. She glanced at the older woman beside her serenely buffing her nails and felt reassured.

She picked up a small piece of batiste from her lap and began stitching a narrow band of lace onto it. In a few moments she dropped it again, reaching for a folded fan which lay on the table beside her. "It's too hot to sew!" she exclaimed, and flinging the little fan open she swept it briskly back and forth in front of her.

"Well, you've already made enough dresses to clothe twins!" said Jane Conner.

"Yes, I guess I have," Rebecca sighed. "It's just that it gives me something to do."

"I know, my dear. You've been very patient." Jane Conner surveyed her daughter, a thoughtful expression in her penetrating gray eyes. It was really hard for Rebecca to be separated from her husband at this time with the birth of their first child expected at any moment, actually two weeks overdue according to the doctor. Thank goodness it was steady and even-tempered Rebecca and not her mercurial younger daughter, Margarette. Rebecca was so sensible, thoughtful of others, cheerful and pleasant. And it was well she was so when you considered her marriage to Douglas Walworth. Of course Douglas was a fine young man of good family, handsome enough to make Rebecca the envy of all her friends. But there was a brooding quality beneath the surface of his good looks and charm that Jane sensed more than saw and which gave her some concern. She had not shared this intuition with her husband, who liked Douglas well enough and thought the world of his father, John Walworth. She had kept these troubling thoughts to herself.

"Yes," she said aloud, "Margarette would have had the whole household in an uproar with her tantrums!"

"For goodness sake don't ever say that to Maggie, Mother! It will just confirm her worst suspicions."

"You mean that I am partial to you? That's ridiculous!

Margarette has her good qualities and you have yours. I love you both, but I am quite capable of seeing you objectively. I'll admit I may have made a gratuitous comparison." Jane added, "But it wasn't the least unfair."

"Mother," Rebecca said, changing the subject, "I've decided that if the baby is a girl I'll name her for Lucy. I think Douglas would like that and it would mean a lot to Mr. and Mrs. Walworth. You know I had planned to name a girl Jane Frances and call her Daisy, but now I believe the baby ought to be named for Lucy."

Jane smiled approvingly at her daughter. "That's a nice idea. I'm sure Douglas and his mother and father will be pleased. And no doubt in time you can have your Daisy, too."

"It's so hard to believe that Lucy is really gone. Why, only a few weeks ago she and I were sewing like this on the gallery at Elmo! You can't imagine how beautifully that child could sew! Her stitches were so tiny and even, they put mine to shame! I remember I told her that she must have the best dressed dolls in Natchez, and she was so pleased. What a sweet little girl she was! I was awfully fond of her."

"Yes, she was a dear child. She had such quaint, old-womanish ways. I keep thinking of her at your wedding. She was so proud that some of the blossoms from 'her' rose were in your bouquet. Well, it's a tragic loss for Sarah and John. My heart aches for them. What a vicious thing the Fever is!"

Jane rose from her chair, drawing herself up as always to the fullest height of which she was capable. She had produced beautiful daughters, but she, herself, was a rather plain, even severe-looking woman, and she was short with a tendency toward plumpness. She didn't really mind not being pretty, but, oh, how she would have enjoyed being tall and stately. Well, she often thought, one accepted what one was given by the good Lord and did the best one could with it. So she made the most of her meager gifts, dressing with classic simplicity and carrying the dumpy little body, which she secretly detested, as proudly as if she had been a great beauty.

"I'm going inside to wake your father from his nap. It's almost time for tea. Your sister is coming over. She'll be here soon."

The English custom of afternoon tea, which had made its way to India and to Africa, had also crossed the Atlantic and become firmly entrenched in this small American river town. Perhaps it had taken root in the Natchez soil because of the leisurely pace of the plantation way of life where gentlemen seldom worked in the afternoon and there were plenty of servants to free the ladies from household chores. At any rate the gardens and galleries of Natchez provided tea and conversation regularly at four o'clock in the afternoon for invited guests or for any friends who might come to call.

"All right, Mother, I'll wait here for her."

Rebecca folded her hands over her stomach and set the rocking chair in which she sat to moving gently. She could hardly wait to tell Douglas about naming the baby Lucy. Oh, how much she wanted to see him! Their separation suddenly seemed unbearable to her.

"I'm sick of being a prisoner here!" she told herself. "I want to be with my husband! I can't stand to be apart from him a minute longer! I'm going to tell Mother that I'm going back home to Elmo where I belong!"

She sighed. Of course she couldn't do that as much as she wanted to. Even if Douglas hadn't asked her to go to Linden she would have come anyway, and she knew she must stay until it was certain the epidemic was over. She had to take every precaution for the sake of the baby. But, oh, it was hard, so hard!

She loved Douglas so much. The first time she had ever seen him he was sitting on his horse out in front of Linden. He had thought she was her sister, Margarette. She had been attracted then by his slim good looks, his thick, wavy, golden hair, his nicely cut features, and his blue eyes so different from her own, but she had grown to love him for his intelligence and imagination and sensitivity. He was a subtle, a complex, a challenging man, not easily understood. She had longed to make him happy, and she had felt that she could. And she had, too, she thought with satisfaction.

Of course, Douglas worried such a lot about things that other people never gave a thought to. He worried about politics and the differing views of the northern and southern states, fearing that they were irreconcilable, and he even worried about the morality of slavery. He worried about his clients and his performance as a lawyer. He needed more comfort and reassurance than the average man.

She frowned thoughtfully, remembering something that had happened on their wedding day. They had been married not quite a year ago in the parlor here at Linden. Hordes of guests had filled the parlor, the dining room, and the spacious front and back galleries at the reception following the ceremony.

Mr. Adam Bingaman, one of Natchez's leading citizens, a man of enormous wealth and influence, and egotism as well, was bestowing his blessing on them in his expansive way. Speaking in a commanding voice, he had declaimed, "What a glorious time to be young! This country is on its way to greatness, and Natchez will undoubtedly be its greatest city! Do you realize that we have more millionaires per capita than any city in the United States? You and Rebecca won't have to pioneer as your parents and I did. You're inheriting a ready-made kingdom!"

Douglas had had his arm around her, and Rebecca was certain that she felt a shudder go through him. It was almost as though he felt Mr. Bingaman's intended blessing were a curse.

Rebecca didn't really like to think about that incident. It only recurred in her rare moments of depression. She must stop this silly moping! She decided that while she awaited Margarette's arrival for tea she would go and play on the piano in the parlor. Music was one of the great joys of her life and it would help to clear away these gloomy cobwebs from her brain.

But before she could get up to go inside, her sister burst onto the gallery as energetically as a firecracker on the fourth of July.

"Well, hello, Maggie. It's good to see you. Come sit down. How's everybody at Monteigne?"

"All fine, thank God. Except for me, who's dying of boredom stuck out here in the country with nobody but servants and children to talk to. I'm perishing to go to a party and hear some gossip. The only news I've heard for weeks is who's got the Fever and who's died of it. I'll tell you the truth, I don't know whether it's worse to be a victim or a survivor!"

"Maggie, you oughtn't to talk like that!" Rebecca was horrified. "That's like asking the Lord to strike you down."

"Now, Becky, you know I don't mean it and so does the Lord. Mercy, but it's hot today! If only it would rain. A good thunder storm would make us all feel better, and it might wash the Fever away. How are you, Becky? Any signs of the baby yet?"

"Yes. Mammy Martha says it ought to start coming any time now."

"Oh, Mammy Martha! She thinks she knows more than the doctor."

"Well, she's had a lot of experience, Maggie."

"She's just an old black know-it-all, that's what she is, and she'll drive you crazy telling you about it! I told Mother to keep her away from me when my Margaret was born."

"She means well, and I think she knows more than you give her credit for."

"Well, you're her pet so you ought to take up for her. She and I never did get along."

Rebecca fluttered the little fan. "It really is hot this afternoon, isn't it? Not a speck of a breeze."

"The sun is getting into your corner. Why don't you bring your rocker this way?"

"Well, I guess I should." Rebecca rose awkwardly from

her chair. As she straightened up she was aware of a vague discomfort in her back. As mild as it was she knew without any doubt what was happening.

"Maggie," she said, putting her hand to her back, "I think the baby is starting to come."

"Well, praises be!" Margarette leapt up out of her chair. She gave her sister an appraising look and then ran inside the house. "Mother," she called, "where are you?"

Jane Conner called a midwife to assist her daughter, since all the doctors were not only busy, but had been in constant contact with the Fever victims.

Rebecca's labor went on all night, and long after the sun had risen. It was high in the heavens when the midwife, assisted by Rebecca's old nurse, Mammy Martha, delivered the baby, a little girl.

Mammy Martha, a deceptively frail looking old woman, proudly displayed their new granddaughter to Jane and William Conner. "Ain't she beautiful?" she crooned. "And I'm the first to hold her, the very first! Just like with Miss Rebecca."

"She is healthy and she is here, thank God," said Jane.

William Conner peered at the baby through thick, rimless spectacles, a whimsical smile on his round face. "I wouldn't call her beautiful yet, Martha, but I'm sure she will shape up in time," he said, and he held a finger for his granddaughter to grasp. "Lucy," he told her, "you will be the eldest and can boss all your sisters and brothers around when they arrive."

"You don't need to tell her, William. She's sure to think of that on her own. We must send word to Douglas right away."

When the message reached Douglas of the birth of his daughter he was filled with mingled joy and disappointment, not that the child was a girl, though he would, of course, have preferred a boy, but that he had not been there and couldn't see Rebecca, couldn't share this moment with her. But thank God all was well!

He hurried over to The Burn to tell his parents about

the arrival of their first grandchild. How glad he was to be able to take them some good news!

He ran up the steps of The Burn's front gallery and into its spacious central hall. The recently painted portrait of his father which his mother had had hung over the petticoat table caught his eye, and he paused before it. He was a father now himself. It was hard to believe, especially when he hadn't even seen his child. Looking up into John Walworth's stern and confident countenance, Douglas wondered if he would be adequate for the demands of his new role. He hoped he would be a good father and that little Lucy would be proud of him. He would try.

CHAPTER THREE

EVERYONE was thrilled with Douglas' news. His mother's face, so pale above her black voile mourning dress, had lit with pleasure, the first genuine pleasure he had seen on it since his sister had fallen ill. John Walworth had showed less emotion, but his "Thank God!" was fervent enough. Little Clara was very interested in the baby being named Lucy, and Aunt Chloe burst into wild tears, crying, "Praise be to the Lord!" between her sobs, which died away to sniffles as Douglas patted her on the shoulder and John Walworth muttered, "Now, now, Chloe, get yourself together."

Sarah and John insisted that he stay for dinner and they sat on the back gallery of The Burn chatting while they waited for it to be ready.

"Were the servants pleased by the news of little Lucy's arrival?" Sarah asked him.

"Oh, yes indeed. There was much excitement. But Esther was very upset that Anderson brought the message to the office instead of to Elmo."

"Did she think they should have had the news before you did?"

"That wasn't the problem. She wanted to see Anderson. She's told me just now that they want to get married. It seems she begged to go back with her grandmother, Mammy Martha, to Linden with Rebecca. Mammy Martha set her straight of course. But now I see why she's been so out of sorts ever since she's been at Elmo. She's been pining for Anderson. Anyway, I told her the marriage would be all right with me if we could work it out with Mr. and Mrs. Conner. I thought I might offer to swap Thornton for Anderson."

"But isn't Thornton married?" asked John Walworth.

"Well, yes. I guess Bessie would have to go with him. If we can't manage without her perhaps you could bring somebody up from one of the plantations."

Clara and Naomi, the little daughter of one of the servants, were playing at the bottom of the double stairs that led from the gallery down to the garden. The merriment in the children's voices was providing a pleasant background to the adult conversation. However a sudden altercation evidently arose and the subsequent squabbling was less pleasant.

"I ain't going to play with you no more!" Naomi was indignant.

An imperious voice replied, "You have to!"

"Don't have to neither."

"You do, too. My father owns you."

A horrified silence fell on the gallery.

"Yes'm, and he owns you, too."

John Walworth's look of consternation gave way to delighted laughter in which Sarah and Douglas joined.

"Out of the mouths of babes," he chuckled. Then he frowned, adding, "But we can't have Clara saying things like that. Or thinking things like that for that matter. I guess I'd better have a little talk with that young lady right now."

John rose and called over the gallery railing, "Clara, I want to speak to you for a moment. I'll come downstairs, and we'll walk down to the summer house."

John and Clara went together down the brick walk which descended to the third level of the terraced garden, a small flight of steps at each level. At the foot of the garden was a vine-laden square shelter, enclosed with lattice on three of its sides and furnished comfortably with wicker armchairs. John seated himself in one of these and drew Clara to him.

"We overheard your conversation with Naomi just now."

"She was impudent to me," said Clara.

"No, Clara. You were impolite to her."

"I have to be polite to Aunt Chloe because she's older, but Naomi is my age."

"You should be polite to everyone regardless of age," he paused. "Or color," he added. "How can I explain this to you?" He paused again reflectively and then continued, "My dear child, there are lots of things that money will buy. You can buy a man and use him, and you can force him to do a lot of things. But one thing you can't ever force him to do is like you. I hope you never get so lonesome you have to play with somebody who doesn't like you. If you want Naomi to play with you, be nice to her. Remember, I don't own her soul. That belongs to Almighty God."

Something like relief flashed in the child's gray-blue eyes, and she uttered a small sigh. "I'll tell her I'm sorry and ask her please to play with me."

"That will be very nice, but you must ask her to play with you later because I am sure that it is time for dinner now. Run quickly so you won't be late."

Clara scampered off up the path to the house and John followed, walking slowly. The incident had been strangely disturbing to him. Why? He was good to all his negroes and he treated them with respect. Negro labor was a necessity in farming a big plantation. Their strength and endurance made them well suited to the work. And they needed caring for. They couldn't make it on their own. They hadn't the background or the intelligence. Most of them. And they were surely better off than those left behind in the jungles of Africa at the mercy of each other and the wild beasts! Then why, suddenly, did he feel so guilty? It was probably what he had said to Clara about buying a man and using him and making him do things. There was something not right about that. But the system actually worked pretty well. The Abolitionists were impractical lunatics with no regard for the consequences to individuals or society of their irresponsible actions and propositions. After all, the world was less than perfect in many ways and would always be. He would think about it no more.

During dinner, the big meal of the day, which was nearly always served in the early afternoon in Natchez households, Douglas remarked with the new optimism which the birth of his first child seemed to have given him, "I feel we've seen the worst of the Fever. It's been four days since any cases were reported and there's been only one in the last ten days."

"I hope you're right," said John, shaking his head.

"I guess I ought to start getting the school room ready. The children should begin their classes as soon as the quarantine can be lifted," Sarah said. The baby's birth had helped her spirits, too. She seemed almost her old self again.

"But it's still so hot on the third floor, Mother," murmured Laura.

"Well, you can have your classes on the upstairs gallery until it gets cooler," replied Sarah.

"Who is to teach them this year?" Douglas inquired.

"Miss Mollie McLaughlin. You remember she was governess to the young Surgets. Lottie recommended her highly and Emily Dunbar wants to send her children over to take classes with ours so we can share the expense of Miss Mollie's salary."

"I don't want to go to school with that sissy Porter Dunbar," protested Ernest. "He doesn't even know how to shoot a marble, and he'll be the teacher's pet." Ernest continued in an assumed falsetto, "'Oh, Ernest, why don't you have manners like Porter?' 'Oh, Ernest, look at Porter's fine penmanship!' 'Porter, dear, please show Ernest how to work this problem.'" He shook his head in disgust.

Laura and Clara giggled. They loved it when Ernest went into his act.

"He sounds to me like an ideal schoolmate for you,

Ernest," observed John. "Perhaps you could reciprocate by teaching him a trick or two about the handling of marbles."

"I think it will be fun to have the Dunbars," said Laura. Eleanor Dunbar was one of her best friends.

"I want Naomi to go to school with me," declared Clara. "Please, may she?"

"That would not be suitable," answered Sarah. To her utter amazement her husband interrupted, "I don't see anything wrong with that. The child ought to be taught to read and write, and she would be company for Clara."

Douglas wondered if he had heard right. His father was usually so predictable and this position was completely out of character. He supposed it had to do with the children's squabble on the gallery steps and Clara's attitude. It seemed unwise and would probably lead to trouble of some kind, but Douglas felt strangely pleased that his father had made such a spontaneous gesture.

Sarah, who had been sitting speechless, found her voice. "Well, John, I don't know what to say. It would be an extra burden on Miss Mollie. I don't think we should impose on her."

"I will pay Miss Mollie an extra amount of money. I'll talk to her about it. I'm sure it can be worked out."

"What about the other children? It doesn't seem fair to single Naomi out." Sarah was obviously perturbed and bewildered.

John hesitated for a second. He had acted on a sudden uncontrollable impulse. He had been too hasty. He glanced at Clara's glowing little face and knew it was too late to retreat. "I doubt that that will prove a problem. Just say that Naomi is to be a companion to Clara." When the family had finished their dinner Douglas walked over to the kitchen, which was located in a separate building from the main house and connected to it by a covered walk. He wanted to tell Aunt Chloe goodbye and to thank her for the meal.

"Mercy, it's hot in here!" he exclaimed as he entered the

steaming room. How do they stand it, he wondered, but Aunt Chloe didn't seem to mind it at all. He guessed she was used to it.

"I enjoyed my dinner, Aunt Chloe. It's always a treat to have dinner at The Burn. Esther is a good cook, but she can't touch your rolls or your pastry. That apple cobbler was so good it was sinful! It made me remember how you used to feed me cobbler with a glass of milk 'to fill up the cracks.' It's a wonder I didn't grow up as fat as Mr. Bingaman!"

"I never seen the day when you were fat, any of you children, but you sure ate aplenty."

Naomi, a wiry nine year old with a head full of tiny little braids, each one tied with a small bright bow, burst into the kitchen full of excitement followed by Clara, equally excited.

"I'm going to school! I'm going to school!" she cried. "Aunt Chloe, I'm going to school!"

"Oh, you and your foolishness! Go away with you!"

"No, it's true, Aunt Chloe. Naomi's going to go to school with me on the third floor when the quarantine is over."

Aunt Chloe looked skeptical and Clara appealed to Douglas, "Tell her it's true, Douglas."

"Yes, it's true. Naomi is to keep Clara company in the school room this year."

"Well, I don't think much of that," muttered the black woman, "filling her head full of notions, learning to read and write and such, when she ought to be learning something useful. What will a little black girl do with that kind of learning? I tell you Mr. John and Miss Sarah are making a mistake and I intend to tell them so."

"Well, I'd better be going," said Douglas, glad he didn't have to deal with Aunt Chloe's disapproval.

"Tell Miss Rebecca I'm right glad about the baby and I can't wait to see her."

"Neither can I," replied Douglas with a wistful smile.

CHAPTER FOUR

THE calendar that hung on the wall of the office over Douglas' roll-top desk announced that it was December 5, 1858, and in spite of the brilliance of the midday sun it was a little chilly in the office. Most of the fall had been so hot and muggy that this crisp, cold weather was a welcome change and the slatted shutters that stayed closed against the heat all summer were flung wide open to let in the sunlight and fresh air. They let in all the street noises as well, which made it hard to concentrate.

Douglas impatiently shoved aside a thick book with thin pages. It had proved of little value to him in finding a way out of the tangle of liens and easements and disputed property lines that were complicating the settlement of Mr. Lyle Dunbar's estate.

He pulled out the gold watch that Rebecca had given him last spring on his twenty-eighth birthday. It was only fifteen minutes past twelve, nowhere near time to go home for dinner. He sighed and reached for the next book.

"I wish I could look on this as a game the way Will does," he told himself. Oh, well, not many men loved their work. And he had been so blessed in his homelife.

It was hard to believe that it was five years now since the joyful day he had moved his wife and baby daughter from Linden to Elmo. Appropriately enough it had been the week before Thanksgiving. There had been much coming and going between the two houses that week. Douglas had arranged with William Conner to swap Anderson for Thornton and his wife. The jubilant young black drove Rebecca and little Lucy and Mammy Martha to Elmo in the Conners' carriage and then Thornton and Bessie drove it back to Linden. Esther and Anderson's wedding had taken place on Thanksgiving Day in the parlor at Elmo. Douglas gave the bride away and Uncle Perry was best man. Esther's disposition improved greatly for a time but reverted to type during her immediate pregnancy. By the time her little girl, Lessie, was born she had settled into a pattern of unrelieved glumness. Douglas told Rebecca that he shouldn't wonder if Anderson wouldn't like to be swapped back to Linden.

The year following Rebecca's homecoming Douglas' cup overflowed with the arrival of a son, John Periander Walworth II.

Rebecca had suffered a miscarriage in 1856, but last April their second daughter was born, named Jane Frances and called Daisy. She was eight months old now, and Rebecca was expecting another baby in February.

These had been happy years. The sun seemed always to be shining on Elmo, yet Douglas couldn't help being aware that there were dark clouds gathering on the horizon. It disturbed him that nobody else seemed to notice them or take them seriously. He guessed the reason he did was because of his years at Harvard when he had discovered the great chasm that stretched between the thinking in the East and in the South.

He remembered so vividly the condescension of his classmates to the son of a slaveholder from the not-quite civilized, new state of Mississippi. They had deluged him with questions.

How did he feel about owning slaves? Did he approve of the institution of slavery? Had he read *Uncle Tom's Cabin*? Had he ever bought a slave? Had he ever sold one? Had he ever beaten one? Did he have a black mistress? Wasn't it true that all white southerners did?

Their questions had opened up doors and windows in his mind that he had tried to close and now nearly ten years later the doubts still crowded in occasionally.

It seemed like only yesterday to Douglas that a small boy had ridden on horseback beside his father over their cotton and sugar plantations, which lay in the malaria-ridden, swampy country to the south and east of the town.

He remembered going with him to the place known as the "Forks of the Roads" where slave auctions were held. There he had watched with wide and innocent eyes the bartering of black men.

"Father, they took that boy away from his mother!" he demurred on one occasion.

John Walworth shrugged impatiently, or perhaps, it was defensively, it occurred to Douglas as he looked back. "My boy, the world is often cruel, and you needn't expect it to be otherwise. The woman is ill. She won't live much longer anyway. The child is healthy and strong, and old enough to take care of himself. Besides there's always some woman who looks after the stray children. Of course I would never separate a mother and child myself, but he's probably just as well off. You must remember they don't feel the way we do."

Douglas started to ask, "How do you know that?" but decided that this would only irritate his father, and that he would ask his mother about it when he got home.

Sarah Wren Walworth, reared on a plantation south of Natchez, had led a simple and sheltered life, and her heart was as tender as the new green leaves of spring. She often found it difficult to adjust to the more luxurious and sophisticated ways of the city, and she wondered much about the various inhumanities of man to man. However she had grown up with the institution of slavery, seeing it only in its most benevolent form, and she questioned it even less than her husband did.

Douglas asked his mother, "Today at the auction they sold a boy off from his mother. Father said they don't feel the way we do. Do you think that?"

Sarah had looked shocked, then recovered herself. "I must say that I don't approve of taking children from their mothers, but it is true that the negroes are different from us, Douglas. They have very little sense of responsibility. They need to be looked after, and taken care of like children. Their religion and culture are quite primitive. You know how superstitious they are, and in spite of all we try to teach them, their voodoo ways are still just below the surface."

"Even Aunt Chloe?"

"Aunt Chloe is different."

Douglas had decided that he must accept his mother's explanations, and he had tried to shut those doors and windows then against the disturbing winds of doubt, but they had continued to whistle in from time to time.

Years later at the university he attempted to answer the questions and criticisms that came his way. He realized that many of these criticisms were all too true, but many of them were exaggerated, and some of them were downright false. It seemed to him that people in the East were eager to believe anything bad about the South. As he struggled to explain the true situation, he began to realize how complicated it was. It was certainly not as simple as his mother had pictured it, nor as his new associates thought it to be. He wondered if they all really believed it was that simple or if they just wanted it to be.

The idealistic young student, horrified by the political rhetoric of the day, the threats of abolition, secession, and civil war, began to think of himself as a bridge between the two sections of the country. His idol and model became the outstanding moderate statesman, Henry Clay, a frequent visitor to Natchez, whom he met at a party on one of his visits home.

When Douglas, although timid by nature and dreading the thought of public speaking, was selected by the Polymnian Society at Harvard to make an address, he agreed to do it, choosing for his subject, "The State of the Nation."

He attempted in his speech to reconcile the differing interests and points of view of the North and South, concluding his arguments with the ringing words:

Let our prayer ever be: The Star-Spangled Banner, long may it wave, o'er the land of the free and the home of the brave!

His address had been very well received, and he had sent a copy of it home. The letter which his mother had written him about it was one of his greatest treasures. He had read it so often he knew it by heart.

"My dear son," he could still see the graceful, spidery lettering in his mind. "We received your speech and I assure you I was most gratified with it. I am something like your classmates. I did not think you had so much in you, and your father is as proud a man as I have seen. While he was reading it, he could scarcely control his voice. You would have felt yourself repaid for all the trouble and pains you have taken if you could have seen him. His eyes fairly sparkled and he did not find one single fault with it. I met your grandfather on the steps of the church yesterday and he asked me if we had read your speech and I told him, 'Yes,' and he said, 'Well, what kind of a thing is it and what is the reason you did not bring it with you? I want to see it very much.'"

Douglas smiled now as he thought of his peppery and puritanical grandfather, Woodson Wren. The old gentleman was not in very good health now. He ought to go to see him, but his grandfather would be certain to give him the same lengthy lecture he had heard so many times before. The only thing about Woodson Wren that saved the day was that he did have a sense of humor, at least about some things. Well, he ought to go to see him anyway because his time on this earth was certainly growing short.

Douglas sighed. Here he was day dreaming again when he ought to be reading about the case of Young vs. Malone, and trying to find a way to settle Mr. Dunbar's estate. He was fed up with the exasperating case. Maybe he needed to get away from it for a while. It might help his perspective. He decided to go and see his grandfather.

Woodson Wren, a widower for some years, lived with a son and daughter-in-law on his plantation in that part of the Second Creek neighborhood several miles south of Natchez.

Douglas decided if he left right away he could get there in time to have a short visit before dinner, which was never served at The Wren's Nest before half past two, and then he could get home before dark if he rode hard. He would send word to Elmo of his plans. Rebecca would approve. She was always telling him that he ought to go to see his grandfather.

Douglas enjoyed the two-hour ride in the wooded countryside. The road wound through hillsides, still green with here and there a hint of fall color. The cold weather was brisk and refreshing, and the rhythmic pace of his thoroughbred was soothing.

The time seemed to gallop faster than his horse. He couldn't believe it when he arrived at a break in the trees on his left which signaled the entrance of the drive to The Wren's Nest much more effectively than the rough wooden sign which was halfway hidden by the heavy vegetation. A long alley of live oaks led to the modest house where his mother and her brothers and sisters had been born and reared.

Built in the pioneer or plantation French style in 1770, the low-roofed house was set high off the ground and supported by sturdy brick pillars. Inside, the furnishings were sparse and not overcomfortable, thoroughly compatible with the personality of the owner.

His grandfather was so glad to see him that Douglas was ashamed of himself for not having come sooner. The old man was extremely feeble now physically, but the keenness of his mind and the strength of his spirit were amazing.

Douglas' uncle, Will Wren, was out supervising the repair of some fences, and his plump, jolly wife, Susan, was ministering to some sick children in the quarters, so Douglas and his grandfather were able to visit with one another in privacy and in peace.

They sat in matching high-backed, horsehair-covered armchairs on either side of a small fire.

"Do you mind if I put another log on, Grandfather?" asked Douglas, noting that the older man had pulled an afghan over his knees.

"No, certainly not if it seems cold in here to you."

While Douglas tended to the fire, his grandfather asked him about his law practice and about the cases he was working on.

"You like the law, don't you, Douglas?" Woodson Wren was himself a lawyer and had been a justice of the peace for the Natchez Territory before Mississippi had become a state.

"Oh, I like it, Grandfather," he lied.

"That's good. It's most important for a man to be happy in his profession, more important than the money he makes, although that's important, too, especially when one lives as you do!"

Woodson Wren had strenuously disapproved when Douglas and Rebecca had built Elmo right after their marriage. "How do you know you can afford it?" he asked. "You don't know what kind of a law practice you're going to have, or what your income will be."

In a way that had been true, but he was going into a partnership with his brother-in-law, Will Martin, who had an excellent practice. Furthermore, John and Sarah Walworth had given them the land at the north end of their property, which extended some distance beyond The Burn's fenced lawn, and the Conners had given them the money to build the house. Of course, they hadn't really needed such a large house for just the two of them, and at first they hadn't had enough furniture for it, but now it was nearly filled up with children and servants and furniture.

Elmo was but one of the things of which Woodson Wren disapproved. To his way of thinking the Conners were extravagant and frivolous. He had been appalled by the elaborate wedding and reception and the alcoholic punch.

However, he was very fond of Rebecca in spite of everything, and she of him.

Douglas ignored his grandfather's little dig. "How are things with you these days, Grandfather?"

"I won't lie to you, Douglas, but I won't complain either. The only thing worse than old age is the alternative, and when I think of the welcome Satan is preparing for me I know when I'm well off! Tell me about my great-grandchildren. Why didn't you bring them to see me?"

"They're fine, fit as fiddles, and growing so fast you wouldn't believe it. Daisy is eight months old now, you know, and Lucy is five and John, four. I would have brought them, but you and I wouldn't have had much visit if I had. I'll bring them next time, I promise."

"Well, why didn't Rebecca come? You ought to have brought her."

"Oh, I haven't told you our news yet, have I? We are expecting another child."

"So I'm to have another great-grandchild! I certainly hope I'll live to see it. It's such an interesting world. I guess that's why I want to keep on living."

"You might be fortunate not to live to see some of the things that lie ahead of us," said Douglas.

"You mustn't be such a pessimist, Douglas!" Woodson Wren surveyed his grandson in consternation. "That's far too gloomy a remark for a young man like you to make."

"I'm sorry not to be more cheerful, Grandfather, but the political situation looks extremely disturbing to me."

"If you mean all the bickering between the North and the South, that's been going on for as long as I can remember."

"But not the violence and bloodshed that's taking place in Kansas."

"Kansas is a territory. It's new country. There's always a certain amount of violence and bloodshed in a frontier situation like that. Things will settle down."

"I hope you're right," sighed Douglas, "but somehow I don't think the Abolitionists want things to settle down.

They intend to keep the pot boiling. And, of course, you can't really fault them in theory. In a country that professes to be 'the land of the free,' the system of slavery is an embarrassment, and there is something basically wrong in treating human beings as 'chattel.'"

"They filled you full of that nonsense at Harvard, didn't they?"

"They did make me look at the problem more objectively."

"Well, I wish you'd made them look at the problem more objectively."

"Well, I don't know what the ultimate answer is, but right now I think we could all use a little objectivity."

"Promise me you will try to look at life more positively as well, Douglas," said his grandfather.

Their conversation was interrupted at this point by the raucous return of Will Wren from the fields, full of fun and jokes, and then Aunt Sue finally arrived from her errands of mercy in the quarters in time to preside over a hearty but simple country dinner. It seemed to Douglas that every time he went to dinner at The Wren's Nest they served Brunswick Stew and cornbread and had peach cobbler for dessert. He often wondered if they ever ate anything else.

Will Wren also was a lawyer and had practiced for a while in Natchez, but had never cared much for the law and had finally turned to full-time farming. After his mother's death he and his wife and their numerous children had moved into The Wren's Nest with his father. He and Douglas were as different as two men could be, but they obviously shared the same distaste for the law. However, Douglas didn't feel sufficient rapport with his uncle to dream of discussing with him the feelings which he had kept secret from everyone.

After Douglas had gone, Woodson Wren went to his room for his afternoon nap.

He didn't feel so well today, but maybe he was just depressed.

"Almighty God," he prayed, "look after my grandson,

Douglas. I'm worried about him. He worries too much." He added, "I guess he takes after me."

Douglas arrived at home just after sundown. The sky was a Joseph's coat and he thrilled to its beauty as he rode up the drive to Elmo intending to head for the stable, but Rebecca was waiting for him on the gallery. She waved to him and he changed direction, stopping his horse at the mounting block by the front steps. Before he could dismount she came down the steps and stood beside him.

"There's trouble at The Burn. Naomi has run away."

CHAPTER FIVE

DOUGLAS found his parents and Clara sitting by the fire in the back parlor of The Burn, their faces sombre. Although it was growing dark, no one had lit the lamp.

Clara looked up and even in the dim light he could tell that she had been crying. It startled him to see how adult she looked. Of course, she was thirteen now.

"Douglas, I'm so glad you've come!" cried his mother. "Naomi's been gone since last night and we very much fear that she's run away."

"She went to bed with the others, but by morning she was gone. Apparently she took some personal possessions with her which indicates that she intended to leave," John Walworth explained.

"Have you put out the word in town?"

"Well," said John with some hesitancy, "I didn't want searching parties with bloodhounds. However, I took the liberty, with your wife's permission, of course, of pressing Uncle Perry into service, since I felt that his experience with his sons' disappearance might prove helpful. We have done everything that we feel we should. Uncle Perry is still Under-the-Hill making inquiries, but I haven't much hope."

"How is Jessie taking it?"

Jessie, the laundress, was Naomi's mother.

"Well, she is, of course, quite upset. Aunt Chloe is with her now trying to calm her down."

"When did you discover that she was gone?"

"Clara discovered it. She thought it was strange when Naomi didn't come to the classroom for her lessons this morning. So when Miss Mollie dismissed them, she went to Naomi's room to look for her. Naomi wasn't there and nobody had seen her."

While Douglas and her father talked, Clara sat staring into the fire. When she had been unable to find Naomi, and the other children said they hadn't seen her, she had gone to the kitchen to ask Aunt Chloe if she had seen her.

"Aunt Chloe, I can't find Naomi anywhere," she had said. "She didn't come to her classes this morning and she's not in her room and nobody has seen her all day."

Aunt Chloe looked up from the big wooden bowl in which she was mixing a huge mound of dough, and the alarm in her eyes echoed in Clara's heart. It was as if both of them sensed the truth at the same moment.

The black woman poured some water from a tall enameled pitcher into a basin, rinsed her dusty hands from white to black, and dried them on her apron. "I knowed trouble would come of that schooling. I'm just surprised it didn't come sooner. Poor foolish child. I hope no harm comes to her. She don't know what the world's like. She thinks everybody's good like Miss Sarah and Mr. John. Lord, I feel sorry for Jessie, lost her husband and now her child's runned away!"

"Maybe we're wrong, Aunt Chloe. We don't know for sure that she has."

The kitchen door opened and Jessie had burst in. "She's done taken all her clothes and her books and the necklace you give her for Christmas. My child's done gone for good!"

Jessie collapsed into the ladderback chair by the kitchen table, put her face in her hands and began to sob.

"Oh, Jessie, don't cry. At least we know now that she hasn't had some terrible accident or something. I'm sure we can find her, or maybe she'll decide herself to come back home," Clara tried to comfort the distraught woman.

Aunt Chloe looked at Clara over Jessie's bent head, and shook her head grimly. Aunt Chloe didn't think Naomi would ever come back.

"Miss Clara, child, you better go tell Mr. John and Miss Sarah. They'll want to know this right away."

When Clara told her father, he had frowned and groaned, "Oh, my God!"

Her mother cried, "Oh no! Oh, poor Jessie! What in the world got into the child? After all we've done for her, too."

"Do you think we can find her, Father?" Clara beseeched John Walworth.

Her father was silent, and Clara begged, "Please, Father, try to find her!"

"Just wait a moment, Clara. I'm trying to think how we ought to go about it. She must have left sometime during the night so she is most likely far away from here by now. We didn't have much luck with Uncle Perry's boys when they ran away. I believe I'll go over to Elmo and get him to help me. He may know some things I don't about the Underground Railroad."

When her father mentioned the Underground Railroad, the name given to the network of hiding places and secret means of transportation for runaway slaves, Clara suddenly saw the problem in a new light. Naomi was a runaway slave! Her rescuers might not be gentle. And Naomi did not want to be rescued. She must have been unhappy or she wouldn't have run away. Naomi wanted to be free! That was it. But freedom was so dangerous. A fourteen-year-old negro girl out in the world by herself? However, Naomi was no fool. She knew the world would be dangerous, and she had chosen to take her chances in it. Clara had felt a sudden thrill of admiration for Naomi's courage.

She ran after her father and flinging her arms around him cried, "Thank you, Father. Try to find her." Then she paused the barest second and added softly, "But don't try too hard."

"I will, my dear," he murmured. Then, as the import of her words sank in, he gave her a quick, sharp glance.

Slow, heavy footsteps in the hall heralded Uncle Perry's return from Under-the-Hill and betrayed the failure of his mission even before he appeared dejectedly in the doorway of the parlor.

"No luck?" John Walworth's question was more a statement of fact.

"No, sir, Mr. John. No luck at all."

"Well, thank you anyway for trying. Before you go back to Elmo will you go out to the servants' quarters and speak to Jessie?"

"Yes sir, Mr. John, that is just what I was intending to do. I hate what I have to tell her, but it's better she get used to the idea soon as possible."

Uncle Perry left and silence fell in the parlor again.

Then John Walworth spoke. "It is a tragedy for Jessie, of course, and Clara will miss her companionship, but it is probably just as well. I made a terrible mistake in permitting Naomi to go to the classroom with the children. I didn't foresee all the consequences of it. She was acquiring abilities and tastes beyond those of most darkies. I realize now that she would never have been satisfied living with her own people here in Natchez. God knows what awaits her out in the world, but I pray she'll find some happiness there. She is extremely bright and perhaps she will do well."

John had admired the little black girl's spunk ever since that day five years ago when she had so aptly put Clara in her place. He guessed it would stand her in good stead now. He looked across the room at Clara. Had she meant what he thought she had? Did she not want Naomi to be found and brought back? She met his gaze and her eyes told him what he wanted to know. Strength stood before strength. She was his own child. He had always loved her and been proud of her, but he had a new respect for her.

It was cold in her room on that December night, but Clara got out of her bed and went to kneel down beside the window. She looked out into the darkness. Naomi was out there somewhere in the world, and when it was dark and cold would there be a warm bed to crawl into? "Oh, God, take care of Naomi," she prayed. "Let her be free and let her be happy." The tears streamed down her cheeks. She knew she would never see Naomi again. It was as final as death. But she would pray for her every night.

CHAPTER SIX

THE winter months of 1858-59 went by slowly. Clara missed Naomi. The school room was lonely without her friend, and she thought about her all the time and prayed for her every night.

In February there was much excitement over the birth of Douglas and Rebecca's fourth child, and third daughter, Annie.

Little Annie was a beautiful baby, the first girl in the family to have inherited the Walworths' blue eyes. It was the general consensus that she would grow up to look like Laura.

The flowering trees and shrubs burst forth, trumpeting the arrival of spring, and there was the annual family celebration at the blooming of Lucy's rose. By the time the month of May arrived, the weather was so warm it was like summer.

Clara didn't think as much about Naomi now, but she still prayed for her every night. And she often wondered where she was and what she was doing and if she sometimes wished she were back at The Burn. She imagined all sorts of chance meetings that might take place between them in the future. Naomi would tell Clara about the adventures she had had, and Clara would ask Naomi if she was glad she had run away and if she would do it again.

And Naomi would say yes, that her freedom had been worth the danger and the struggle. Sometimes, though, Clara wondered if Naomi was still alive, or if some bad thing had happened to her.

Clara started dancing school, and she made some new friends although she knew no one would ever be as good a friend as Naomi. She enjoyed the dancing. It was fun. And she began to be aware that there was an attraction between boys and girls.

The boys in her dancing class were awfully silly though. She didn't really like any of them.

Her sister Laura went to parties all the time now and had young men calling on her, especially Will McPheeters.

Her brother Ernest had been to dancing school and went to parties, but he didn't call on any young ladies. She couldn't imagine Ernest doing that. He just liked to tease girls the way the boys in her dancing class did.

Clara spent a lot of time at Elmo. She adored Rebecca and enjoyed the children. Lucy and John were fun to talk to and little Daisy was so sweet and cuddly. Now there was the new baby, Annie, so beautiful with her big blue eyes.

And then she was fascinated by Douglas and Rebecca's relationship. When she saw them look at each other Clara got gooseflesh. Even though they were married and had four children they seemed to her like Romeo and Juliet.

One very warm May morning after Clara had spent the night there, the household at Elmo began the day on the back gallery with a breakfast of fried green tomatoes, grits, and sausage with biscuit.

Clara and the children had finished theirs and been excused from the table, and she had organized a game of Chinese school for Lucy and John on the gallery steps. Little Daisy wanted to play, too, and Clara included her in the game in spite of the indignant protests of the older children that she would only spoil the game.

Douglas sat coatless and collarless, his shirt unbuttoned at the neck, reading yesterday's copy of the *Natchez Courier* and finishing his second cup of coffee.

Rebecca, looking cool and fresh in her morning dress of yellow and white striped voile, had brought out her needlework, and the servants were clearing the table.

Douglas lowered the newspaper, gazing thoughtfully off toward the woods that lay beyond the split-rail fence, which enclosed the grounds of Elmo.

"What would you say if I told you that I've decided to run for the state legislature?"

Rebecca did not look up from the piece of flowered needlepoint in her hands.

"Why, that I should prefer you to stay out of politics," she replied in a cool little voice.

"But, Becky, I feel that I must do it." He looked down with dismay on her bent head. Her thick dark hair was parted in the center and pulled severely back into a bun in the fashion of the day, a trying style for most, but quite becoming to Rebecca's classic face.

"I feel that the nation is headed like the shot out of a cannon on a dangerous course, and I want to do something, anything, to change the direction, or at least slow the pace. Moderate voices are so desperately needed." He lifted his cup, but it was empty, and he set it down again with a little clatter.

Rebecca continued to pull a deep purple thread through the design of a violet. "But you know a Whig can't be elected this year."

"I don't have to run as a Whig."

"You wouldn't run as a Democrat!" Rebecca looked up now, incredulous.

"I don't have to run as either. I can be an independent candidate."

She put her needlework aside, an anxious little frown on her usually serene face. "That means you'll be opposed by both parties. You'll make all kinds of enemies. Oh, Douglas, please don't do it!"

Clara, who had listened closely to every word of the conversation, anxiously awaited the outcome of their disagreement. It was plain how strongly they both felt about this issue. She felt the tension growing between them and she observed the distress and disappointment clouding Douglas' face.

"Oh, I'm being selfish! Of course you must run!"

To Clara's amazement her sister-in-law completely changed her position, not grudgingly, but generously and graciously. "Rebecca saw how important it was to Douglas to have her approval," she thought. "How wise she is!"

Douglas jumped from his chair and pulled Rebecca up into his arms. "My darling Becky! I'm such a lucky man! You're the most understanding wife in the world!" He drew back to look at her, tracing the lines of her face with his fingertips. "God made Eve for Adam and you for me."

He bent to kiss her.

While Clara eagerly and furtively watched this tender moment between husband and wife, little Daisy tripped on the steps and tumbled to the ground with a loud wail.

Chagrinned, Clara gathered her up and tried to calm her, but Daisy screamed for her mother.

Rebecca took over, soothing the child and assuring Clara that it wasn't her fault.

"But it was my fault because I was listening to you and Douglas and not watching her," Clara confessed.

"Well, keep what you heard to yourself. Don't mention my running for the legislature to Father and Mother until I have a chance to tell them myself," Douglas cautioned her.

When Douglas went to The Burn that afternoon to talk to his father about his decision, he told Lucy and John that they could go with him.

"May we ride our new ponies?" Lucy wanted to know, and five-year-old John began to chant, "Want to ride my pony, want to ride my pony!"

"All right," Douglas agreed.

They were a charming threesome, the slim little girl with long, dark hair and the little blond boy sitting proud and straight on their new ponies with their handsome, young father riding watchfully behind.

"I love to go to The Burn," said Lucy. "Grandma and Grandpa are so nice, and Aunt Chloe is too."

"She bakes good cookies," agreed John, and his blue eyes sparkled. He turned in the saddle to give his father one of his infectious grins. "Yum, yum!" he said, rolling his eyes and smacking his lips.

"Watch the road, Johnny," cautioned Douglas, but he smiled. Who could help but smile when John did?

"I like Grandpa's stories," said Lucy, her eyes keen and her face alert. She had a very inquisitive mind, and had earned the reputation in the family of being very bright.

"Do you know why The Burn is called The Burn?" she asked John now as they trotted briskly along.

Douglas shook his head. As usual Lucy was trying to show off her superior knowledge. Rebecca said this was a very natural thing for an older sister to do.

"Because it burned up!" declared John.

Lucy gave him a disdainful look. "You don't know anything," she told him. "Grandpa told me that The Burn got its name from the stream of water that runs down back of the garden. 'Burn' means brook in Scotland and we are Scottish, at least partly."

Douglas couldn't help but be impressed by his six-year-old daughter's command of the facts. She really is a smart little girl, he thought.

"But it did burn," insisted John, "it used to have two galleries in front and now it only has one."

"That's true, but it already had its name before the fire happened."

"Why didn't Grandpa put back the other gallery?"

"Because Grandma said they didn't need such a big house anymore with Uncle Ernest ready to go away to school, and Father had his own house, and Lucy that I'm named for had died."

"Oh," said John. Then he called back to Douglas, "Are we riding well, Father?"

"Extremely well," replied Douglas. "Your backs are straight as arrows."

"Which one of us rides best?" Lucy wanted to know.

Oh, Lord, thought Douglas, what a competitive little creature!

Aloud he said, "Well, you both ride very well, but perhaps John rides a little better than you do. After all he is a boy."

Lucy scowled. She couldn't see what that had to do with it.

The children felt quite important trotting up the drive to The Burn. They were especially pleased that Clara was standing on the front gallery watching them. She made the proper fuss over their ponies and their horsemanship, pouring her approval into their eager little hearts.

Douglas, watching, thought what a good mother Clara was going to make some day.

"Are Father and Mother here?" he asked.

"Yes, they're on the back gallery having tea, and so is Laura. Will McPheeters has come to call on her. I'm just leaving to go to Stanton Hall. Mrs. Fitzgerald is having her dancing class there this afternoon."

"You're becoming such a young lady," said Douglas. "Only yesterday you were climbing trees."

"Well, I might climb a tree tomorrow, but this afternoon I'm going to dance," replied Clara.

"I'd rather climb a tree," stated Lucy.

"I think it's fun to dance," John said, flinging himself from his pony and doing a little jig.

Clara and Douglas laughed, and Lucy looked scornful. "I'm going to go see Grandma and Grandpa," she said with a toss of her long hair.

"Well, now tie up your ponies to the hitching post first, both of you," instructed Douglas, "and mind you tie them securely. They're as frisky as you are."

Clara turned to Douglas. "John is so much like Ernest. I remember him acting just like that."

"Yes," agreed Douglas. "In fact he still does."

"Who am I like?" asked Lucy.

Clara didn't hesitate. "You act just like your grandpa. Go

on now and speak to him and Grandma. They'll be so pleased to see you. I'd better dash or I'll be late."

"But I don't have blue eyes like Grandpa, and John does. Mammy Martha says I have cat eyes."

Grandma and Grandpa were indeed glad to see them and after kisses and hugs Grandma took them off to the kitchen to see Aunt Chloe.

"Let me pour you some tea, Douglas." His sister Laura seated herself behind the silver service, looking, it occurred to Douglas, as though she belonged there. She was beautiful in such an elegant sort of way, and that ashes of roses dress with the touches of ecru lace provided the perfect setting for her pink and gold coloring. He saw that Will McPheeters thought so, too. He had a worshipful look about him. Poor lad, thought Douglas, he was so awkward and ill at ease. How difficult it was to be young and shy. He wondered which was harder for the young man, talking to Laura or to her parents.

"Are you still going to be a doctor?"

Will McPheeters started at Douglas' question, cleared his throat, and replied, somewhat hoarsely, "Yes, well, that is, I hope to be. I'm taking a college course now, and I do plan to go on to medical school."

Douglas hoped the young man would be happier in his profession than he was in his. He supposed that his dissatisfaction with his law practice was one of the reasons he wanted to run for the legislature.

When the conversation turned to politics John Walworth said, "I'm afraid the Whig party is finished in the South. It looks as though the Democrats will have a field day in the next election, and conservative and moderate men will have no representation."

"Perhaps someone might run on an independent ticket," suggested Douglas.

"Running and winning are two different things. It's hard enough to get elected when you have a party organization behind you," replied John. "I certainly wouldn't attempt it."

"Actually, I'm thinking of attempting it," said Douglas.

The silence was lengthy and uncomfortable. Finally John Walworth spoke. "Have you considered the amount of your time which would be required to campaign for the office, and should you be successful, the time you would have to spend in Jackson? And do you feel that you can rally sufficient support to oppose experienced candidates with the backing of established organizations?"

He doesn't think I'm capable. Douglas had feared that would be the case. Of course John Walworth hadn't said that, and his expression, as always, was inscrutable, but Douglas knew his father, or thought he did.

He's never had any confidence in me, he told himself now with some bitterness. Aloud he replied, "I don't know the answer to those questions, Father. I only know that I want to try. I feel so strongly about keeping Mississippi in the Union, and working out our problems by compromise and accommodation. After all, should we let the extremists win by default?"

John Walworth shook his head. "No, I guess not," he agreed, although he was filled with misgivings. He very much doubted that his son was cut out for public life, but he seemed determined, almost fanatically so. He sighed deeply, "Well, go ahead and try then. I'll give you all the support I can."

"Thank you, Father. I'll try to justify that support."

Oh, how he would try! As much as anything else he wanted to make his father proud of him.

CHAPTER SEVEN

SHORTLY after Douglas announced his candidacy for the Mississippi State Legislature, he and Will Martin attended a meeting of the Adams County Light Guard, whose activities had heretofore been primarily social. Lately, however, it had become a political forum, and an emotional one at that.

The meeting was long and the discussion heated, ending with the Secessionists and the Unionists in absolute disagreement on everything.

Afterward Douglas and Will stood by their horses talking. A group of Secessionists passed the two brothers-in-law without speaking.

Douglas sighed, "This town is as divided as the nation, Will. Where in the world do you suppose it'll all end?"

The older man shook his head, grinned, and brushed back an unruly forelock, running his fingers through it as he did. "Damned if I know! It's gotten so you can't discuss politics without getting into an argument, and I'd a whole lot sooner get into a fight! I like a good fight. It clears the air. But you take an argument, and what happens? Everybody ends up mad!"

"I'm glad you can joke about it. I can't. The whole thing depresses me. Do we really have to make a sacred cause of slavery? I want to protect my property as much as anybody, and I'm no Abolitionist, but the institution can't be defended morally. I don't really believe in it, or want to perpetuate it."

Will nodded. "Nobody knows what to do about it, but I think most of us realize that the system has got to go eventually, and that we'll all feel a lot better when it does. At any rate I'm certain the majority of this group is planning to support you in the election. We had the majority on most points tonight, you know. Eustace Farr and his crowd are just reacting to the extremism of the John Browns."

"I don't know which group of extremists is worse, ours or theirs. Each one claims to be fighting the devil himself."

"From the wrath of the righteous, good Lord, deliver us," intoned Will, exaggerating his Kentucky backwoods drawl, "especially when they think they are!"

"Well, I guess us unrighteous sinners had better head for home. Looks like a storm coming." Douglas glanced up at a large black cloud, which was moving rapidly across the sky. And as he spoke thunder rumbled distantly.

The storm did not wait, but broke upon him before he was able to reach home or shelter. He rode through the blinding rain, the wind and water lashing him, occasional flashes of eerie light enveloping him, and the thunder cracking sharply, close to him now.

Branches from the big trees lining the road were crashing everywhere. One fell directly in his path, and Douglas' skittish mare rared and whinnied in panic. It was some time before he could calm the frightened horse enough to move on.

He arrived at Elmo soaked and chilled. A hot bath, a glass of brandy by the fire, and Rebecca's presence warmed his body and cheered his soul, and he told himself that it was nonsense to regard the storm as an omen of any kind.

"Will says he thinks the majority of the Adams Light Guard will vote for me," he said to Rebecca, "but there's a lot of increasingly strong feeling for secession. It's very probable that I won't be elected, and even if I am there may be nothing I can do."

When Will arrived at Elmo from the courthouse at four o'clock on the twelfth of October 1860, Douglas knew at once that he had lost the election. It was written all over his brother-in-law's expressive face. Well, perhaps, it was just as well. He almost felt relieved.

"You needn't say a word, Will. I already know the outcome."

"You do," grinned Will. "Then how come you look so sombre? Didn't you want to get elected? I would have sworn you did."

"Then he did win?" cried Rebecca, putting her hands dramatically to each side of her head.

"Douglas Walworth is the newly elected city member from Adams County to the Mississippi State Legislature."

Rebecca let out a little shriek of relief and pleasure. "Oh, Douglas, you did it! You've won!"

The indifference with which Douglas had shielded himself for defeat buffered some of the excitement of victory now. It took a few minutes for the joyful news to reach his heart. He had won!

"Congratulations, Douglas." Will held out his hand and Douglas clasped it.

"I could never have done it without you, Will. Thanks for encouraging me and supporting me the way you have."

"Well, you're certainly welcome. Of course both of us may wish we hadn't gotten you into this hornets' nest before we're done. By the way the *Courier* staff is jubilant. They're already at work putting your victory statement in print. And here's a list of questions that the editor of the *Free Trader* sent you."

The *Natchez Courier*, one of the town's two newspapers, had supported Douglas while the *Natchez Free Trader*, which had by far the largest circulation, had backed his opponent, a Democrat.

"What kind of questions?"

"Well, to begin with they want to know how you classify yourself, as a Democrat or as an Oppositionist."

"They already know I ran as the representative of no party."

Douglas had placed his name on the ballot as "Douglas Walworth, Patriot."

"They also want to know your position on the Southern Plank."

"Why should I have a position on a plank of the Democratic Platform when I'm not a Democrat?"

"Damned if I know, but, their next question is whether you approve and endorse the Democratic Platform."

"Well, I'm certainly under no obligation to do so, nor even to reply to any questions from a newspaper that didn't support me. But it might provide a good opportunity to make myself heard. What do you think, Will?"

"Yes, I think it might. Why don't you look the questions over, and I'll help you draft a reply at the office tomorrow."

"Won't you stay to dinner with us, Will?" Rebecca asked her brother-in-law.

"Well, I'd like to but my little wife has guests coming out to Monteigne for dinner so I'll have to decline that kind offer."

"How are Maggie and the children?"

"All fine and in excellent voice. They manage to keep Monteigne from becoming too serene. How are the young Walworths? Is Lucy still asking those unanswerable questions?"

"Oh, yes," laughed Rebecca, "I've learned to say 'I don't know.' It's the only way to get any peace. Have you a moment to speak to her? You know you're her favorite."

"Well, she's mine, and I'll take a minute to speak to her anytime."

"I believe I'll step over to The Burn and tell Father and Mother about the outcome of the election if you'll excuse me, Will," said Douglas. "I know they're anxious to hear. I'll be back in time for dinner, Becky."

"Goodbye to you now, Douglas. I'll see you in the morning. Give my regards to Mr. and Mrs. Walworth."

"Thank you again for everything, Will. I'll see you tomorrow."

Everyone at The Burn was so pleased and proud of him. His father shook his hand and congratulated him formally, adding, "I'm happy for you, Douglas."

His mother shed a few tears, and as usual, Aunt Chloe shed more than a few. Ernest and Laura looked impressed, and Clara seemed more pleased than anybody.

Douglas had wanted so desperately to prove himself, to make his mark in the world. He had always known that much was expected of him, and he had been frightened and overwhelmed by that knowledge as a child, but he had told himself that it would be different when he grew up. Then when he had grown up he had found things were not as different as he had hoped. Although he made every effort to conceal it, he still felt inadequate and insecure, and uncertain as to what he wanted to do. He knew he would never be able to handle the overseers and field hands on the family plantations with the authority which was so instinctive to his father. He liked to write, but his family would not think that a suitable full time occupation. He had settled on the practice of law, which he had found uninteresting and unfulfilling.

Then he had conceived the idea of running for office. Politics interested him and he would be able to use his talent for putting ideas into words. He had made the decision himself. He, himself, had decided to do it, to run for the legislature despite the initial opposition of both his wife and his father. And now he had won. Oh, it was glorious, glorious!

He decided to show his father the list of questions and John Walworth scrutinized them with the fine disdain which had withered many an adversary.

"They want to know if you approve of inserting the Southern Plank into the Democratic Platform. Since you're not a Democrat I hardly see how that concerns you."

"Well, what they really want to know is whether I'm in favor of congressional protection of slavery in the Territories. Of course I'm against that, as you know, for a variety of reasons."

"They had better let this slavery agitation alone if they have any sense. If Congress can protect slavery in the Territories, most assuredly Congress can legislate slavery out of the Territories. Have they ever thought about that?"

"That's an excellent point, Father. I'll use it in my reply."

"Why should you reply at all? You owe nothing to the *Free Trader.* Why, look here, they ask if you approve and endorse the Democratic Platform of the State of Mississippi. Why should you do that?"

"Because I'm going to have to work with the Democrats. They are the power to be reckoned with in the State Legislature now. Actually I can support most of the resolutions with the exception of the fourth."

"Well you certainly can't endorse that one!"

"No, but I believe I can with a qualification." Douglas drew a piece of paper from the inside pocket of his coat. "Where it says that in the event of the election of a Black Republican candidate for the Presidency, Mississippi will regard it as an act of hostility, I want to insert the clause, 'and in the event of an overt act in disregard of the Constitution and the rights of the South, Mississippi will regard, et cetera.'"

John Walworth surveyed his son with a look very like surprise it seemed to Douglas. He nodded. "I will admit your clause is an improvement. Perhaps you can convince your fellow legislators that the election of Mr. Lincoln in and of itself is insufficient cause for any drastic measures. If you can, you will have served your state and your country well."

Douglas was overjoyed by his father's unusual words of praise.

"Of course, there is very little likelihood that they will agree to any sort of qualification," John added.

When Douglas returned to Elmo he found Mammy Martha waiting for him on the steps of the front gallery. She was holding Annie, the baby, on her lap and watching Daisy frolic in the yard with the latest litter of puppies. She stood up and called to him as he walked up the drive, "Mr. Douglas, Miss Rebecca's done gone to Linden. Brother

Perry, he drove her over in the carriage. Mr. William has taken sick. Oh, Lord, Mr. Douglas, how's Miss Jane going to make it without Mr. William? Why they've always been just close as a coat of paint on a fence!" Mammy Martha shook her head woefully.

"Well, let's not write him off yet, Mammy Martha. Perhaps it won't prove to be that serious. I'll ride on out there. Tell Esther to go ahead and give Lucy and Johnny their dinner. I'll be back later in the afternoon."

"Yes, sir, Mr. Douglas. Give Miss Jane my love. This will be hard on her. Yes it will." The old woman gathered up her charges and disappeared into the house, still shaking her head.

Douglas went directly to the stable. He pulled on the riding boots he kept there, while Esther's husband, Anderson, saddled up his horse for him.

As he galloped along the Linden road his thoughts swung wildly from concern for his father-in-law, to pleasure at his father's recent commendation, to how he should word his response to the *Free Trader.*

In forty-five minutes he was there. He slowed his mare and directed her onto the winding drive.

He always had a feeling of pleasure when he turned into that drive. It reminded him of his first meeting with Rebecca, of course, but there was something so appealing about the house itself, set back beyond the grove of tremendous live oaks, their powerful branches swirling around their big trunks like the arms of an octopus.

When one looked at Linden one was reminded of fresh-washed crystal or new-fallen snow, of a big armchair and a dog-eared book, or a bed turned down with robe and slippers beside it. One thought of a breakfast tray with a rose on it, or a family gathered around a well-laid dinner table. One could hear people calling to each other, a piano softly playing, a negro voice moaning a comfortably melancholy song or erupting in rich laughter. One could smell freshly brewed coffee, the mingled aroma of fine tobacco and leather, linseed oil and beeswax, lemon verbena and magnolia. One saw curtains blowing out of windows in a summer breeze, children playing on the gallery, dogs running in the yard.

He approached the house slowly. Linden had a different look about it today. There was a stillness, a sadness. It was a house of illness and impending death. Instinctively he knew, as Mammy Martha had, that William Conner was dying. In spite of the fact that his father-in-law was almost eighty, it saddened Douglas greatly to think of it. His grandfather, Woodson Wren, had died last spring shortly after Annie's birth, and now the passing of his father-in-law, William Conner, seemed to foreshadow not only a changing of the guard, but the end of an era. His earlier elation at the news of his election gave way now to the deep sense of uneasiness that had always plagued him, and he had a sudden vision of chaos ahead.

CHAPTER EIGHT

DOUGLAS was right. When William Conner died in the fall of 1860, an era passed with him. Although life in Natchez remained unchanged in the following months, certain events were shaping a very different future for them all.

Douglas allied himself with the moderates in the legislature and spoke out frequently, responding to the rabid talk of the Fire-eaters, as the radical Secessionists were called, with pleas for moderation.

To his dismay Abraham Lincoln was elected president in November of 1860, defeating his chief opponent, Stephen A. Douglas. Lincoln had won substantially in electoral votes, but by a close margin in popular votes, actually receiving a minority of the total vote.

Protest meetings erupted throughout the South. Douglas addressed an outraged citizens' group on the river bluff at Natchez, counseling patience: "Let us not be hasty to act. The issue is too serious for precipitous action. Let us leave the decision to Mr. Lincoln. If he loves the Union, as he claims, surely he will not strike the death blow. At any event, let not our beloved state strike it!"

But he told his wife and parents, "I felt as I spoke that I was standing on the last crumbling brink of the Union."

Resentment all over the South continued at fever pitch.

On November 10, 1860, the legislature of South Carolina passed a resolution calling for a convention to meet at Columbia on December 17th to consider secession. On November 13th it resolved to raise 10,000 volunteers for the defense of the state. Governor Pettus convened the Mississippi Legislature into an extraordinary session on the twenty-sixth of November.

In one of the dome-shaped legislative chambers of Mississippi's beautiful capitol building Douglas looked on apprehensively as the majority of his fellow legislators endorsed the principle of secession as a reserved right of the states and authorized the election of delegates to a convention which would consider the question of Mississippi's secession from the Union.

Events had played into the hands of the Fire-eaters, and they had become more numerous as well as more ferocious. He and the other conservatives had been assailed and ridiculed by most of the newspapers. One article asserted that the policy of waiting for an overt act was one of imbecility and disgrace "out of keeping with the spirit of our revolutionary fathers." They were scorned by popular sentiment as cowards and weaklings. However Douglas still had some substantial support in Adams County, and the *Natchez Courier* remained staunchly behind him. After much soul searching, he decided to run for the position of delegate from Adams County to the Secession Convention as a Co-operationist. This meant endorsing secession, but only in unity with the other southern states. Several of the conservative legislators had adopted this approach. If no conservatives were elected, they reasoned, there would be no way to exert a moderating influence over the convention. They had urged Douglas to join them in this effort. Rebecca and Will Martin agreed that he should, although John Walworth had been bitterly opposed to the idea of his endorsing secession in any form. It had been a difficult decision, and he still wondered if it were the right one.

When the election was held on the twentieth of December, Douglas won by a comfortable margin in conservative Adams County, but in the state as a whole there was an overwhelming victory for the radical Separate Secessionists.

"It is all over, but the shouting," Douglas broke the news to Rebecca, who was perched on the canopied four-poster bed in the guest room wrapping Christmas packages. She finished tying a large red bow on one of them, and pushed it hastily aside. "Oh, Douglas, I'm so sorry, but perhaps when it comes to the actual vote, the radicals will back off."

"We are going to be completely outnumbered at the convention and the Fire-eaters have no intention of backing down. I very much fear that this is the last Christmas we will celebrate as citizens of the United States, and God only knows what the new year may bring."

"Oh, Douglas, don't be so glum about it! We have each other and the children, and we'll manage all right and be happy no matter what happens. Secession may not be so bad. It might even be better to be able to lead our own lives without all the wrangling over the territories and the tariffs and the taxes, and being a constantly endangered minority with only a little piece of paper between us and tyranny."

"Becky, that is an important little piece of paper, and I don't like to contemplate life without it. My most ardent hope is that if worst comes to worst we'll be able to form a union with the other southern states and continue to be governed by the same precepts which are written into the Constitution that you and I have been blessed to live under all our lives. But above all, I hope we won't provoke any military action by moving too precipitously."

The next day brought the news by wireless that South Carolina had seceded the day before.

"At least we won't be the first," said Douglas grimly.

The convention assembled on January 7th, 1861, and two days later voted eighty-four to fifteen to secede. Douglas and his friends returned to their constituencies with the one last hope that the people could be persuaded to repeal the ordinance.

The *Natchez Free Trader was* jubilant. "Bring out the cannon and let it roar its loud, reverberating approbation," it exulted.

The secession of Florida, Alabama, and Georgia followed on the heels of Mississippi's decision. Then Louisiana and Texas joined them, and on the fourth of February the secessionist states met at Montgomery to consider the formation of a confederacy. In four days they had adopted a Provisional Constitution, which was based, as Douglas had hoped, on the Constitution of the United States, with a few changes, the primary one being a specific clause on the right to own slaves, although the importation of slaves was prohibited. A few thoughtful changes included one allowing the president to approve a portion of an appropriation bill, or to disapprove a portion, thereby preventing riders tacked on to legislation.

Even John Walworth was impressed by the new Constitution. "This is no radical document, thank God. It's a carefully considered blueprint for a sound and workable government. If we must govern ourselves, it is at least a good beginning. I just pray now that a civil war can be avoided. I would like very much to know what is going on in that oversized head of Mr. Lincoln's."

"His recent speeches have ignored the whole problem," said Douglas, "but our radical friends are going to have a rude shock after he's inaugurated, in my opinion, because I don't think for a minute he intends to let us go without putting up a fight."

"Nor I," replied John. "I remember his campaign speeches too well, and the Radical Republican platform. I only hope that some of the old Whigs will be able to restrain him. I have been corresponding with some of my friends in New York and Ohio as well as our family there, urging them to do all they can. Why don't you write to some of your friends in the East?"

"I doubt that any of them would have much influence with Mr. Lincoln, but I guess it wouldn't hurt anything. Perhaps I'll write to your old friend, Moses Williams. He's a very influential man in Boston and I got to know him rather well when I was at Harvard."

Douglas knew that his father continued to hope for a reconciliation, although it was obvious that two nations existed now. The Confederacy had a Constitution, a president and vice-president, and a cabinet. It was seeking foreign recognition. The machinery of government was in motion.

But whether secession was to mean war still remained to be seen.

Douglas asked himself, what if war does come? What will I do then? How can I choose between my state and my country? He could not bring himself to answer that question.

The situation in South Carolina over the disputed forts in the Charleston harbor grew more tense everyday. One of the forts, Sumter, was still occupied by a federal garrison. It was in desperate need of supplies and reinforcements. Any attempt by the Federal government to reinforce it was bound to provoke an incident since South Carolina had passed a resolution that the forts should henceforth be under the control of the state. Opinion in Lincoln's cabinet was sharply divided on the subject of such an attempt.

On April 11th matters were finally brought to a head when the Confederacy represented by General Beauregard, acting on intelligence that federal reinforcements were on the way, demanded the evacuation of Fort Sumter. The demand being refused, in the early morning hours of April 12th the Confederate army fired on the fort, a bombardment ensued and on April 13th the fort surrendered.

Word of this surrender, which had proved to be a glorious and bloodless victory for the Confederacy, spread rapidly to the far corners of its seven states.

When Douglas arrived at his office on the morning of April 16th he found Will Martin and several of their friends from the Adams Light Guard in agitated conversation.

"Good morning, Douglas," said Will. "Have you heard the latest news?"

"Why, yes, Fort Sumter has surrendered. Is that what you mean?"

"No. That's yesterday's news. I'm talking about Lincoln's Proclamation."

"What proclamation?"

"He's declared that insurrection exists, and he's called up 75,000 militia."

"So he finally dropped the other shoe. I knew he never intended to let us leave without a fight. And now what do we do?"

"That's just what we've been discussing. We're making plans to contact the other members of the Light Guard, and organize ourselves into a troop. It looks as though they may need us."

Douglas was shocked. Knowing Will Martin as well as he did and knowing how strong his support of the Union had been, it was astonishing to him that his brother-in-law could have changed his position so completely in such a short time. It seemed almost a betrayal.

"I know this comes as quite a surprise to you. We haven't been in very close touch lately with you gone so much these past months. We've all been through some agonies of reappraisal. Events are moving so fast these days."

Douglas found his voice. "They certainly are!"

"Douglas, you know how I've always felt about the Union. I wish it hadn't come to this, I most heartily do, but since it has, we have to think about defending ourselves, now that it looks as though Mr. Lincoln has decided on a policy of coercion."

One of the other men spoke up. "When you talk about the 'Union,' remember, Douglas, that we have a new union. We formed a confederacy with the other southern states, and now it's our duty to support it."

"He's right, Douglas," said Will.

"Well," said another, "how about it? Will you join us?"

It was the moment he had dreaded for so long. He couldn't say yes and he couldn't say no.

"I don't know," he replied. "I need some time to think

about it. I—I'll let you know in the morning."

Douglas found the atmosphere in the little office uncomfortable, and he excused himself to go to the post office.

It was a relief to get away from the pressure of such united opinion.

I won't be pushed into this, he told himself. But what else am I to do?

He thought of discussing it with his father, but dismissed the idea. He already knew what he would say. John Walworth was a Union man to the core, and a conservative by nature. He would say, "Wait and see."

Rebecca would be reluctant for him to join up for reasons of her own. There was really no one he could discuss it with. It was his decision, his alone. No one could make it for him.

That night Douglas lay beside his sleeping wife, tense and wakeful, staring up at the elaborate pleating of the pale pink satin canopy that arched above them.

His blue eyes shifted restlessly from the canopy to the shaft of moonlight coming in at the long open window beside the bed, and then to Rebecca, sleeping peacefully beside him. He was tempted to wake her, but resisted the impulse. This time even she couldn't help him.

Whoever would have thought when he was born thirty-one years ago that he would have such a decision to make?

How he wished he were more like his father! The image of John Periander Walworth, strong, self-confident, and decisive, arose before Douglas now like King Hamlet's ghost.

His heart was a battleground of conflicting emotions. He felt that he was being torn to pieces along with the Union.

His wakefulness was making his bed a prison, and he decided to escape it. He rose and drew a dressing gown over his nightshirt, slipping his feet into a pair of soft leather slippers. Then padding quietly through the wide upstairs hall, he went out onto the little iron balcony that hung over the recessed front door. He looked down upon the empty moonlit gallery, his eyes seeing the beauty of the fluted Doric columns and their long silhouettes slanting across the stone floor, but his heart too preoccupied to care.

He wandered aimlessly down the stairs and out onto the front gallery. He sank down on its broad shallow steps and sat for some time looking up despairingly at the sky. And as he looked, sunshine began to push up the night's dark blue curtain. If only some happy solution would come like the sunshine to lighten the absolute darkness of his dilemma! But he told himself, I guess I can't expect any miracles.

He leaned back on his elbows, watching the rapidly spreading pink streaks in the lightening sky, and he was reminded of another man and another dawn, and a ghostly choir in his brain sang:

"O say can you see
By the dawn's early light
What so proudly we hailed
At the twilight's last gleaming,
Whose broad stripes and bright stars
Through the perilous fight
O'er the ramparts we watched
Were so gallantly streaming?
O say does that star-spangled banner yet wave
O'er the land of the free
And the home of the brave?"

The stirring words of the anthem and the picture they evoked of the stars and stripes flung out briskly in the breeze made his heart ache. He was genuinely and deeply devoted to his country. But he kept forgetting. It wasn't his country anymore. He had a new country and it contained his home, his family, and his friends. There was no way he could turn his back on it.

He knew what he had to do. He had really known it all along. He would tell Will tomorrow that he would join the Adams troop to defend the Confederacy.

The day burst upon him, and he realized he was exhausted. He hurried up to bed, relieved to have made the decision, but still hoping in his heart for the miracle that would prevent him from having to carry it out.

The miracle did not happen.

CHAPTER NINE

A splendid ball was held at "Rosalie" in June of 1861 in honor of the departure for Virginia of the Adams troop, which had been organized by Will Martin.

When Douglas arrived in his new uniform, he caused quite a stir amongst the ladies, and Rebecca said that even in her best apricot silk trimmed with gray lace she knew she was not as beautiful as he.

He did cut a fine figure in the dove-gray uniform with its shiny gold buttons and yellow silk cummerbund, his high black boots and silver spurs gleaming. But beneath the sparkling exterior, his heart was heavy, and he found himself completely out of tune with the prevailing gaiety and excitement.

For Sarah and John Walworth, who attended with their daughters, Laura and Clara, and their younger son Ernest, it was also far from a joyous occasion. Civil war had special heartaches for them. John Walworth had close relatives in Cleveland, Ohio, his birthplace, and in New York. Now their first-born was going off to fight in a war in which John's nephews would be fighting on the other side.

When Douglas had informed them of his decision to enlist, Sarah had burst into tears. Now as they rode along in the carriage on their way to the party, she had to press her fist hard against her lips to suppress a sudden new onslaught of emotion, and even John Walworth's stoic face had a troubled expression.

Ernest, at eighteen, a younger and livelier edition of his brother, knew how terribly upset his parents were about the war and about Douglas' enlistment, and he suspected that if he should mention his own desire to join up they would really throw a fit. He hated controversy and dreaded bringing it up. He could hear them now protesting about how he should finish his education. But he had made up his mind he didn't want to go back to school. Before he had left the University of South Carolina at the end of the semester, having chosen to go there instead of following his father and brother to Harvard, he had talked to all his best friends, and they had told him they weren't coming back, and were going to enlist instead. He had decided not to say anything about it yet and how he was going to tell his family was weighing heavily on his mind. He, too, wore a troubled expression.

Laura didn't know which way to feel. Will McPheeters had declared that he loved her and wanted to marry her, and that was quite exciting, but he was leaving with the Adams troop, and she didn't know when she would see him again. Added to that was the fact that she hadn't quite made up her mind how she felt about him. So she was confused and preoccupied.

Only Clara had her mind on the party and she was very thrilled about it. It was her first really big ball. She wished she was as pretty as Laura. She had been staring at herself in the oval mirror of her dressing table a lot lately. Was she pretty? People were beginning to say so, but not quite the way they said it about Laura. In fact Laura was beautiful, all pink and gold with big, blue eyes. And Douglas and Ernest were so handsome with their blue eyes and golden wavy hair. It wasn't fair that her hair was both brown and straight, and her eyes more gray than blue. It wasn't that she was homely, and she guessed she should be grateful for that, but she would like to be more interesting looking.

Nevertheless young men were starting to look at her, and her figure had blossomed out rather nicely.

Maybe some day she would have a real beau like Laura did. She didn't really see what Laura saw in Will McPheeters, though. Oh, he was nice, and her mother and father thought he was wonderful. They liked his family so much, too. But he wasn't what Clara had in mind. She wasn't exactly sure what that was, but at least she knew what it wasn't, and it wasn't any of the young men she knew. When she married she wanted it to be like it was with Douglas and Rebecca. There was something between them that you could actually feel.

She said aloud, "I hope somebody will dance with me Wouldn't it be awful if they didn't? I'm really getting nervous!"

"Oh, don't be silly, Clara! Of course they will, and besides you've always got Ernest," her sister told her.

"No she hasn't either. I've got plans of my own," replied Ernest.

"Well, I don't want to dance with my brother anyway. I'd much rather be a wallflower!"

"Well, here we are," said Ernest as they turned into a torchlit driveway leading to a red brick mansion of epic proportions, impressive even in a town where the climate and the way of life produced houses with ceilings twenty feet high and hallways that were not only big as ballrooms, but often used as such.

Rosalie stood beside the river on the site of an old fort, from which it took its name. Its white-columned galleries looked straight up the oncoming river, which cut relentlessly into the earth at the bottom of the tall, steep bluff. To the right from the upper gallery, the roofs of the city could be seen nestling among the green of the tree tops. The view from this height was superb, and when the ladies went upstairs to leave their shawls, Clara stepped outside for a moment to watch the spectacle of carriages parading up the long avenue to the house. "How tiny they look from here," she thought. "How tiny human beings really are!"

She put her hand with a sudden reverence on one of the great Tuscan columns which supported the roof. "And yet we can build what is so much bigger than we are."

When the ladies came downstairs, a group of young men, who were friends of Laura's, were standing at the foot of the stairs. When one of them claimed her for the next dance, another invited Clara.

While they were dancing she noticed a very handsome young gentleman, whom she had never seen before, watching her, and Clara was glad she was wearing her new white chantilly lace dress with the wide off-shoulder bertha collar, its scalloped tiers of skirt suspended over an enormous hoop. It was a lovely dress, and she knew it so well that she hadn't even minded Ernest's brotherly comment that she looked like a wedding cake in it.

Her brown hair was parted in the center, and caught into a cluster of long curls on either side of her pink cheeks, their rosy glow a result of exertion, excitement, and prolonged pinching before her mirror at home. Her father had suspected that she was wearing rouge, and had ordered her to go and wash her face. Her mother had had to explain that this was what all young ladies did to assist nature. Her father had reluctantly acquiesced, muttering something about why anyone would want to look like a hussy, and her mother had informed him that Clara's dancing teacher, Mrs. Fitzgerald, whom he thought so good-looking, wore rouge without a doubt.

Now stepping lightly to the music, conscious of the intense gaze of the attractive stranger, Clara's cheeks were rosier than ever, and she outdid herself for his benefit. When the music stopped he applauded, looking directly at her, and she felt a sharp thrill of excitement and anticipation.

Moments later Mrs. Dunbar brought him to her for an introduction.

"Clara, my dear, this is Mr. Sanford, our visitor from Atlanta. Ross, this is Miss Clara Walworth of 'The Burn.'"

Clara looked up into an outrageously irreverent little

boy's face under a thick mop of copper-colored curls, and her heart almost stopped beating. She widened her gray-blue eyes, dropped a demure curtsy, and murmured, "How do you do?"

Golden glints of mischief and mockery lit the merry brown eyes that looked down into hers. Did he know her heart had skipped a beat? He smiled. He did know, and he was glad. They were undoubtedly the happiest people in the whole room. No, in the whole world. How could you learn so much in the time between two heartbeats? Clara felt that she had known him all her life, and that there was a country somewhere, and a language, which belonged just to them.

"Miss Clara Walworth of 'The Burn,' may I have this waltz?"

"Mr. Sanford of Atlanta, you may."

They danced well together, their feet barely skimming the floor, and when the fiddlers finally lowered their violins the two were breathless.

Ross offered Clara his arm. "I think what we need is a little fresh air, Miss Clara. Let's go out on the gallery."

This vast breeze-swept area was teeming with other young couples in search of air and romance. Ignoring them, Clara and Ross strolled to the gallery's edge, where they stood side by side looking out in silence into the black velvet, star-bejeweled night, drinking in its beauty and mystery, feeling themselves a part of it, and of each other, experiencing deliciously the ancient and universal attraction of man to woman, and woman to man. For the second time tonight Clara was moved to awe and humility in her awareness of things much larger than herself, but at the same time to the thrilling recognition that she could have a part in them. Forces from within and without were pulling her toward this young man, and toward life itself. Clara trembled at the sheer ecstasy of being alive and in love.

"You dance beautifully, Miss Clara," Ross spoke suddenly in the world's language. "You're beautiful and I love you," he said in theirs.

His eyes sought hers, but she looked away. Those gently mocking, almond-shaped eyes saw too much, and she was afraid of them.

"Thank you, Mr. Sanford. I love to dance, and, of course, it always helps to have a good partner." Her courage returned, and she raised her eyes to meet his. And now she was sure she saw his heart skip!

"There's a good waltz. Let's dance it." He caught her impulsively by the hand and led her back toward the dance floor. On their way through the crowded hall they passed Douglas and Ernest talking to Will Martin.

"My goodness, you look so dashing in your uniform, Douglas!" said Clara as they exchanged a light kiss in greeting. "And you, too, Captain Martin. These gray uniforms are really very becoming. May I present Mr. Ross Sanford of Atlanta? He's visiting Mr. and Mrs. Dunbar. Mr. Sanford, this is Captain Martin, and this is my brother Douglas and my brother Ernest."

"When do you leave sir?" Ross asked Will as the men shook hands, and Clara noticed that he appeared flustered and embarrassed.

"Within a week, if our arrangements work out as planned."

"As soon as that! Well, I wish you every success—I—yes, every success."

"Aren't you dancing, Ernest?" asked Clara.

He gave her one of his brotherly looks. "I have more important things to think about right now," he told her.

"Well, excuse me!" she exclaimed with mild sarcasm. She turned to Ross. "I think we had better hurry if we plan to dance this waltz."

Ross seemed so relieved to get away and Clara wondered why. Perhaps he just felt shy with the older men but then he didn't seem the timid type.

When Clara and Ross had left, Ernest resumed his conversation with Douglas and Will. "But I don't see why I can't go with you just because I've not been a member of the Adams Light Guard."

"Ernie, in the first place, you ought to finish your education, and in the second place, you're not eligible to go in the Adams troop. If you won't take my word for it, you'll have to accept Will's."

"He could make an exception," wheedled Ernest, looking hopefully at Will Martin.

"No," replied Will, "I really couldn't even if I wanted to, and besides, I agree with your brother that what you should do is go back to school."

"I'd probably be the only fellow there."

"Well, you'll get so much the better education!"

Ernest sighed. He could see he was getting nowhere.

"I have the next dance with my wife. I'd better go and find her," said Douglas. He smiled affectionately at his downcast younger brother, thinking how strange life was. He would have given anything not to have to go to war, and Ernest, who couldn't go, was dying to. He put a hand on Ernest's shoulder and gave it a little squeeze. "There are any number of young ladies pining away to dance. Why don't you make one of them happy?"

"I'll think about it. Maybe I will."

Ernest stood watching his brother and Rebecca dancing together. The way they were looking at each other was so, well, so touching. Ernest wasn't the least bit sentimental, but damned if it didn't bring the tears to his eyes! They shouldn't have to be separated, he thought. Why should Douglas go? He doesn't even want to. I'm the one who ought to go. And what's more I'm going to! I don't have to go with the Adams troop. I can enlist on my own. Tomorrow he would tell his father that he intended to do that.

CHAPTER TEN

THE next afternoon John Walworth rode over to Elmo to talk to Douglas about Ernest's determination to enlist. Rebecca shooed the children away and left the two men sitting on the back gallery.

"I don't understand why he feels he must do this. For that matter I've never understood why you felt compelled to enlist."

A troubled silence fell which Douglas finally broke. "No, I suppose you really can't understand because you weren't born here. You didn't grow up in the South. You don't feel that it's part of you and you're part of it. You don't know what it's like to go away to school and have everyone look down on you because you're from Mississippi, to have them ask you how many times a day you beat your slaves, to try to explain that although slavery is wrong, some sort of paternalism is necessary, to be misunderstood, to be unfairly judged, to be the victim of preconception and misinformation, and even hostility. These things tend to intensify a man's natural loyalty. I know we southerners have our faults, but they're not as black as they're painted. Anyway, I know why Ernie feels this need to support the South. We are Mississippians and we can't be anything else—not and be true to ourselves, even if we don't approve of everything Mississippi does. I guess it's impossible to explain."

"No, you've done a very good job. I understand your feelings better, but it doesn't change my opposition to Ernest's enlistment. He should finish his education. There are others who can more conveniently take up arms to defend our state. Besides, I don't hold the view of so many that there will be a quick and easy victory for the Confederacy. In fact, I very much doubt it. The war will probably wait for him."

"I agree with you about that, Father, and I've already told him as much. I think Ernie is too young to go. If you think it will do any good, I'll talk to him again."

John gave him a look eloquent with gratitude, and father and son shared a rare moment of understanding.

"Thank you, Douglas. I feel Ernest will at least listen to you."

John took his leave, and Douglas followed his father out onto the front gallery. He held the horse as the older man swung himself briskly into the saddle.

"The young man who is visiting the Dunbars arrived to call on your sister just as I was leaving to come here."

"Laura attracts men like flies, but only Will McPheeters seems to be seriously interested. Too bad she doesn't seem interested in him."

"The young man came to see Clara."

"Oh! Goodness, it's hard to think of Clara being so grown up. But now that you mention it, I remember that she introduced me to some young man from Atlanta at the party last night. He didn't let any grass grow under his feet, did he?"

"No, he didn't."

Tea was being served at The Burn in a small lattice-walled pavilion on the bottom terrace of the garden. The roses on the tiers above were especially beautiful right now. Every one of them seemed to be in bloom, and their delicate scent hung pleasantly in the warm afternoon air.

A huge silver tray holding the tea service and Sarah's best yellow china tea cups was placed on the round wicker table in the center of the summer house. The Walworths and their young caller sat in comfortable wicker armchairs around it.

"Clara, dear, will you pour the tea?" said Sarah.

Clara wished she had worn her blue and white instead of the green and yellow muslin. She had changed out of it at the last minute and now she wished she hadn't. Laura looked so adorable, just like a Dresden shepherdess, in her pale blue.

Clara clasped her trembling hands behind her. "Yes, Mother."

But how could she with him there only a few feet away? Last night had been another world, another eon. In the daylight it appeared all to have been a dream. Where was that common language they had spoken? This afternoon they were just two young people who didn't know what to say to each other.

But Laura took care of the conversation, chattering away about this and that, and looking ravishing. Clara saw the admiration in Ross Sanford's eyes and felt wildly jealous.

Somehow she managed to pour the tea without spilling any and to hand the cups with only a tiny bit of clatter.

Finally he rose to leave and Clara thought, "But I never said a word to him, not a single word. And now he's leaving and it's too late!"

And then what was her relief, her joy, her ecstasy when he inquired if he might call for her in one of the Dunbars' carriages to take her on the following day to the afternoon tea that Margarette and Will Martin were having to honor the Adams Light Guard?

Seated beside him in the carriage in her most becoming daisy-bedecked straw bonnet, Clara directed Ross onto the road that led to Linden and Monteigne.

When the horses had settled into a steady rhythm, Ross turned to look at her. He smiled and she noticed how his eyes crinkled. "That's a fetching bonnet, Miss Clara. I always say every work of art should have a suitable frame."

Clara laughed, "Oh, how you do turn a phrase, Mr. Sanford! Is that the way they talk in Atlanta?"

"Only when they're madly in love."

Her heart shook and fluttered. Of course he was only joking. He had come to call at The Burn and even after he had met Laura, he had asked her to go with him to the party. He must like her even if she was only just a little pretty and not really beautiful. But madly in love? Hardly.

She changed the subject. "I'm surely glad to get away from home! Things have been in a terrible uproar ever since Ernest told my mother and father that he wants to enlist, too. They were already upset about Douglas going, and it's just the last straw for Ernest to go. They're hardly speaking to him now, or he to them, and none of them is very jolly to be around."

"That's exactly the reason that I'm here in Natchez!" Ross exclaimed. "My father thinks I should go back to the university and complete my education. But I feel that I ought to enlist. All my friends are, and I know everyone is wondering why I don't! It's really awkward for me because I was involved in a plan to free the slaves which got a lot of publicity. Of course, my loyalties lie with the South, but a lot of people don't understand that. I tell you I was right glad to get away from Atlanta just now."

Clara's eyes widened. "What was your plan to free the slaves?"

Ross gazed reflectively down the road. "Oh," he muttered, "it wouldn't have worked. Even then I knew it wouldn't work. It was to be done gradually. First we intended to educate the bright ones, teach them some reading, writing, arithmetic, and citizenship. Then we were going to raise some money to reimburse the owners of those we felt were qualified to be granted their freedom. Of course just the education part was enough to upset everybody. My parents were horrified that I had had any part in it."

"How could there be anything so wrong with educating the negroes?" murmured Clara and she thought briefly of Naomi for the first time in a long time. She could scarcely believe this young man's imagination and daring. Plenty of people, her brother Douglas included, talked a lot about the evil of slavery, but here was somebody who had actually tried to do something about it! Ross was such an interesting and exciting person. "I've heard Douglas and Father discuss it, and I think they both believe that there ought to be some education for them."

"Well, people were afraid that it might encourage an uprising of all the negroes, and maybe it would have. My father says a little education is a dangerous thing. Of course, if it ever had a chance it's done for now."

"There's Linden." Clara pointed through the grove of trees on her right. "That's where my brother's wife lived before they were married. She and Margarette Martin are sisters, and Monteigne is built on some of the old Linden property."

"Monteigne is the French form of Martin, isn't it?"

"Yes, Will's family were French Huguenots and their name was originally Monteigne. The house is rather like Linden, sort of low and rambly and the detail of it is beautiful. I think it's an absolute gem of a house. There it is. Drive around to the back," directed Clara. "That's where everybody will be, and there'll be somebody there to take the horses."

Monteigne, like Linden, stretched galleried wings backward to form a courtyard, and the guests were assembled there. The ladies in dainty pastel organdies and voiles were surrounded by a sea of gray uniforms.

Margarette Martin saw Clara and Ross arrive and came to greet them.

"Mr. Sanford, I'm so delighted that you could come, and I see that you have excellent taste in young ladies. Clara has a lot of sense in her pretty little head. She doesn't just giggle and fan herself! There's tea and punch on the gallery. Do go and have some."

"Are she and your brother's wife twins?" asked Ross as they walked away.

"No, but as you can see they do look very much alike.

In fact when Douglas first met Rebecca, he thought she was his best friend's wife. It was love at first sight, and he thought it was hopeless!"

Ernest made his way through the crowd to join them at the tea table.

"Am I glad to see you!" he said to Ross. "I think I'm the only man here under sixty not in a uniform!"

"Oh, forget about uniforms!" exclaimed Clara.

"But how can we?" replied Ernest.

At the tea all anybody could talk about was the war, the imminent departure of the Adams troop, and all the new enlistments. Clara began to see why Ross and Ernest felt so left out.

Her young girl's understanding of war was limited and hazy, and in her innocence she could not fathom the depths of its horrors, but she did know that going to war was dangerous, that one might be killed. Still she knew that if she were a man she would have felt she had to go, too.

However on the ride home when Ross brought up the subject again she said, "Perhaps your father is right. Maybe you should finish your education. That seems sensible to me."

"Well, I don't know. All I know is that I feel mighty uncomfortable when I see practically everyone else in uniform, and hear all that talk about the war. I feel that I'm shirking my duty, and that people will think I'm a coward."

"Well, I don't think you should worry about what people think."

"That's easy for you to say, but you don't know how it feels to have everyone disapproving of you. And after all why should I let men like your brother Douglas bear the brunt and make the sacrifices so that my education won't be interrupted?"

Clara had no ready answer for that. She didn't want Ross to go to war, but she understood how he felt, and Ernest, too. And she knew that sooner or later both would go.

CHAPTER ELEVEN

ON June 11th, 1861, the Adams troop departed for Virginia amidst hundreds of waving handkerchiefs and hastily stitched Confederate flags. There was band music and shouting, kissing and weeping, and great excitement.

Douglas embraced his father, kissed his mother tenderly, and then turned to Rebecca. They had said goodbye the night before. There was nothing left to say. They exchanged a long look. She held out her hands and he took them in his.

"God keep you," she whispered.

"And you," he replied.

And then they were gone, all the handsome young men on their thoroughbred horses. In the feverish excitement only a few considered that some would not return.

A musical had been planned the following evening at Stanton Hall, and Clara and Ross attended it together.

Stanton Hall was the home of Dr. Frederick Stanton, an emigrant from Dublin, Ireland. His elaborate and costly residence was a replica of his ancestral home. The twin-galleried white brick house was lavishly embellished with ornamental iron, and splendidly furnished with possessions and purchases from abroad. It boasted a spacious interior, and when the doors between the double parlors were opened, a distance of seventy feet stretched between the two wall-sized mirrors, which were inset at either end. A series of fireplaces, their white marble mantels heavily carved with fruit and flower designs, heated the rooms. Double doors led from each parlor into a central hall sixteen feet wide. The rooms were designed to accommodate large groups, and were especially well suited to their present function.

The guests were seated on stiff little chairs which obscured completely the muted gold and rose Aubusson rugs beneath them. Armchairs, loveseats, and tables were pushed against the walls. The evening was warm, and brass fans covered the empty fireplaces.

Clara and Ross started toward some seats which friends had saved for them. They stopped on the way to speak to Rebecca and Margarette Martin, who had come with their mother. The two sisters were as outwardly smiling and cheerful as their husbands would have wished them to be, and looked quite beautiful in their best gowns. Jane Conner was still in mourning, but her widow's weeds were stylish and set off her pearls and diamonds admirably. She exclaimed over Clara's dress, palest pink organdy embroidered with sprays of deeper pink flowers and widely sashed in dark green velvet.

"I just know, my dear, that this beautiful material came from Paris."

"Well, yes," smiled Clara, "that's right. It did."

"The French have a way with fabric that is unmistakable." Mrs. Conner applied her lorgnette for a more careful scrutiny of the embroidery.

"Have you met Mr. and Mrs. Dunbar's guest? This is Mr. Sanford of Atlanta, Mrs. Conner."

"Oh, yes, I believe that I have met Mr. Sanford. I suppose you'll soon be in a gray uniform like all the other young men."

"Well, ah, yes ma'am, I suppose so," Ross flushed and stammered.

"I think we'd better take our seats, Mrs. Conner. It looks as though they're ready to begin. It's nice to have seen you," murmured Clara, thinking how she would like to choke the old crow!

Miss Ellen Montgomery, exquisitely gowned in mauve taffeta, her diamond lavalier sparkling, was first on the program. After a graceful curtsy, she seated herself at the piano, and with a spectacular flourish attacked it. Her fingers swooped wildly over the keys, punching, pouncing, stroking, not always at the appropriate time. She seemed determined to make up for lack of talent with technique.

Clara stole a sideways glance at Ross. He had an innocent expression on his cherubic face. Without moving his head, he rolled his eyes toward her, and an uncontrollable giggle bubbled inside her. When her effort to suppress it failed, in desperation she began to cough. Observing several disapproving frowns, she made as dignified and hasty an exit as possible into the hall, making her way with difficulty through the rows of chairs, strangling and choking all the while. Ross followed close behind. They hurried out onto the front gallery, and ran down the steps and across the sloping yard all the way to the handsome iron fence which enclosed it. Finally out of earshot of the other guests, Clara leaned against a fencepost, and collapsed into a fit of giggles.

"Oh, oh, oh!" she moaned. "How awful! But when you looked at me, I just couldn't help it."

"Well, how in the world do you think I felt? I couldn't laugh, and I couldn't even pretend to cough. You'd already used that!"

Ross released his own pent-up laughter, and they stood there leaning on the iron grillwork, giggling and gasping until exhaustion overcame them. They rested themselves against the fence for several moments in silence. Then Ross reached out and caught Clara by the fragile shoulders that emerged so provocatively from the enormous starched puffs of her pink organdy sleeves. He drew her to him and kissed her tenderly on the lips.

"Oh, Clara, I love you," the words spilled out in youthful ardor to a stunned and breathless Clara, who drew back, half in genuine shock and half in lady-like pretense.

"Forgive me, Miss Clara, I—I forgot myself," Ross murmured contritely. Then a sly gleam stole irrepressibly into his amber eyes and he added, "I reckon I'm really not sorry at all unless you are."

"I'm not a bit sorry," Clara replied, marveling at her boldness, and she thought, I never knew what it was to be happy before—until this moment.

They stood gazing raptly at one another until finally Ross glanced toward the house. "I guess we ought to go back. They might organize a searching party."

"Yes, they might," agreed Clara, sighing and accepting his offered arm. "I'm afraid they might."

John Walworth was in the hall waiting for them.

"Are you all right, Clara?" he asked.

"Oh yes, Father," replied Clara in confusion, nervously touching her pearl choker, "I just got a tickle in my throat."

John Walworth's face was impassive. "Well, I see you were well taken care of. Do you want to risk going back?"

"Oh, no, Father, I believe it will be better if I just sit here in the hall," Clara whispered anxiously. She would rather have faced a live dragon breathing fire than make a reappearance in those parlors.

Clara couldn't sleep a wink that night. When they were getting ready for bed Laura had confided to her that Will McPheeters had asked her to marry him before he left, and that she had sent him off without an answer.

"I just couldn't decide what to do. I do like Will a lot, and I know Mother and Father do. But I don't know if I want to be married to him or not."

Clara gave her sister a searching look. "Are you in love with him?"

Laura sighed, "I don't know."

"Well, if you were you'd know it."

"How do you know I'd know?" snapped Laura. "Oh, you're just too young to understand!"

Clara said nothing. Poor Laura not to have this feeling, this wonderful glowing, tingling feeling.

But now, turning and tossing restlessly after Laura had gone to sleep, she began to wonder. The glowing feeling seemed to be bursting into leaping flames inside her. Did Ross feel the way she did? Will had asked Laura to marry him. He loved Laura, but Laura didn't love him, at least not enough. Ross had not asked her to marry him. She wondered if he had thought her too bold and unladylike in showing her feelings so plainly. He had said he loved her, but did he love her as madly, as passionately, as she loved him? Oh, she couldn't bear it if his love for her was not as fierce and consuming as hers for him!

Several days after the departure of the Adams Light Guard, John Walworth found a note propped up on the table in the hall. It said:

My dear father,

Forgive me, but I am doing what I feel I must. I know that you and Mother will be quite distressed, and I regret that very much. After talking to Douglas, I really tried to make up my mind to go back to school. But the more I thought about it, the more I knew I could not do that. Farrar and I are going together to Memphis and we will enlist there. I will keep you posted on all developments.

I do love you and Mother very much and am sorry to leave without saying goodbye.

Love also to Laura and Clara.

Your devoted son,
Ernest

Clara was surprised at how calmly her parents accepted Ernest's unceremonious departure. She thought, they must have known all along, as I did, that he was going to go.

However, that afternoon her mother stayed in her room, having developed a headache. Her father walked over to Elmo in the afternoon to break the news to Rebecca, and Laura was invited to have tea with Will's parents. To Clara's delight she was left alone to receive Ross when he came to call.

She felt awkward and tongue tied again, though, and it

seemed to her that Ross was behaving strangely.

"I hear that Ernest has left," he said.

"Yes, that's right. That's why my mother has a headache and my father isn't here. He's gone to tell Rebecca about it now. Actually they're taking it much better than I would have thought."

"I wish I knew what to do," Ross sighed. "I have to go back to Atlanta in a couple of days, and I dread it. It will mean I have to make my decision."

Clara felt as though someone had thrown a glass of cold water on her. Of course she had known Ross would be going back to Atlanta. But so soon! The cold water seemed to be seeping into her heart. He was going to leave, and that would be the end of it.

"That isn't the only reason I hate to go, Clara."

Hope sent sparks all up and down her.

"I don't want to leave you," he said.

Then don't! she cried out in silence. Take me with you!

"Of course I know it's impossible right now," he added, "but as soon as we can, I'd like for us to be married. Oh, Clara, would you wait for me?"

But why is it impossible? her heart cried out again. But she knew that it was. They were so young, and the war had made everything so uncertain. Neither of their families would approve of them marrying now. Ross was right. They must wait.

"Of course I'll wait. Forever if I need to."

"If only everything weren't so unsettled. I don't even know how to ask your father's permission for us to be engaged."

"Well, don't tell him that you're thinking of enlisting," warned Clara.

The day before he left, Ross called upon John Walworth at The Burn. Asking a man for his daughter's hand was unnerving, and Ross was uncomfortably conscious of the moistness of the palm of his hand when he took John Walworth's graciously extended one.

The older man was formal and reserved, but cordial. His

handsome face had stern lines, especially about the narrow mouth, and his blue eyes pricked Ross like a sword.

"I guess you may have some idea why I'm here, sir," Ross began, and waited hopefully.

Was there a flicker in the blue eyes, and a tiny curve to the grim mouth?

"I am not given much to speculation."

Ross squared his shoulders, swallowed, and manfully began again. "Well, sir, the reason I am here is to ask your permission to marry your daughter, Clara, whom I love very much."

"I see. That is most interesting." Now there was definitely a very small smile.

"I feel that I should tell you something of my prospects, and what sort of life I can hope to offer Clara. Of course, I know we'd have to wait until after the War, and until I finish my studies. My father owns some land near Atlanta, which will be mine someday. He's already given me a piece of it. However, I plan to pursue a legal career as well, and I have a deep interest, which I feel every educated man should, in politics."

As Ross set forth his financial position in detail, John Walworth listened, a pensive expression on his face. Ross paused, and John said, "Well, sir, you do appear to have good prospects, or you would have, if it were not for the War. I wonder how much any of us can count on in the future. Even if God grants us a speedy victory we will have problems. The South has no industry, and we've already incurred some heavy debts to finance this war." He sighed, "Well, we must hope for the best. You seem to me to be a young man of character and ability, and will no doubt do well whatever your circumstances may be."

Ross' face brightened perceptibly.

John continued, "But you and Clara are both quite young and should not consider launching into marriage until your prospects have become certainties."

"Oh, no, sir. Of course not."

"Furthermore, you would be asking my daughter to

leave her family and friends here in Natchez and Clara has not even met your family. I would consider it most important for all concerned that they should become acquainted with one another before any definite plans are made."

"Oh, yes, sir. I plan to have Clara come for a visit as soon as it is possible. If it were not for the War, I should have already asked her to come. I know my parents would love her, sir, as I do, and I would always do everything in my power to make her happy."

"I feel certain that you would, and that you must have a fine family. The Dunbars have assured me that this is so. But marriage is a serious and lifetime affair. Young people should know as much as they can about one another before taking such a big step."

"Oh, yes, sir. I agree, and I know that my family would feel the same way about it."

John Walworth held out his hand. "Mr. Sanford, when Clara has had the opportunity to meet your family, and they to meet her, and when you are in a position to marry, I should be most happy to have my daughter marry you."

The news of Clara's engagement came as something of a shock to Laura, who had sent Will McPheeters off to war without a definite answer.

"But Clara is too young to be married!" she protested to her mother.

"Now, Laura, she isn't going to be married. She's just engaged. Mr. Sanford is in no position to marry yet, nor will he be for a long time. Who knows what may happen in the meantime. They may never marry. You and Aunt Chloe can both relax."

Chloe was beside herself at the news. Although she had gradually become the full-time cook for The Burn household, she had begun as the nursemaid for Sarah's children, and in a real sense they all belonged to her, too. Clara was her baby, and Chloe simply could not adjust to the idea that she was a young lady now.

"Miss Clara, married! You must be joking! Why, she don't even know how to keep her room straight. And to that boy with his baby face! He can't take care of her! I don't know what Mr. John is thinking about. I really don't't!"

When Sarah explained to her that an engagement did not necessarily mean a marriage, and that in any event their marriage would be very far in the future, Chloe muttered indignantly, "Well, I should hope so."

The first letter came from the University of Virginia. John Walworth brought it home from town, and when the family gathered in the dining room at the two o'clock dinner hour he said to Clara, "There's a letter for you on the table in the hall. It has a Virginia postmark, I believe."

Her cheeks felt on fire and her heart thumped madly. How was she supposed to sit there at the table and eat her dinner when a letter from Ross was only a few feet away? And that was what she was supposed to do. Dinner was a family ritual and she wouldn't dream of asking to be excused from it. But how could she possibly wait?

Her mother and father and Laura were discussing the letter that had not come from Ernest.

"Well, the mail is abominably slow now, and although it is easy to understand why, it is frustrating nonetheless," John said, and then began to devote his entire attention to carving the fragrant lamb roast which had just been placed before him.

"I do hope Rebecca has heard something from Douglas. I believe I'll send word over to Elmo for her to come to tea this afternoon," Sarah said, her face wearing a worried little frown.

"Clara, pass the mint sauce, please. Dear, the mint sauce."

Would they ever stop talking and eating? Clara found that a few bites were all that she could swallow, and she could not keep her mind on the conversation.

Finally dinner was over. She walked as rapidly as she could with any kind of dignity into the hall and picked up her letter from the table. Holding it in both her hands, she walked sedately out the door to the back gallery, then she ran down the stairs and down the garden walk to where there was an ancient live oak with a little wooden bench around it. She sank down onto the bench and leaned back against the tree's huge trunk. She held the letter first against her heart and then against her cheeks. Next she gazed at the address, Miss Clara Walworth, The Burn, Natchez, Mississippi. What a beautiful handwriting he had, so bold and masculine! She rubbed her fingers over it. Then she opened it very slowly. Now that she had it in her hands she wanted to make this moment last as long as possible.

The letter began:

My darling Clara,

Each morning I awaken to a thrilling thought, that you exist, that there is a Clara Walworth, and this thought remains foremost in my mind all day. When the night comes I begin to dream of you before I go to sleep, and I could not sleep at all if I did not know that I could take you with me into my dreams. I am without doubt the most happily haunted man in the world! It is difficult, my dearest sweetheart, I can assure you, to keep my mind on my studies, and it would be impossible if I did not keep reminding myself that each completed subject brings you closer to me.

Clara caught the letter to her heart. Oh to be close to him! When? When would that be? But he loved her, he missed her, he dreamed about her! She looked up at the limbs of the old tree arching above her. As a child sitting here she had often thought how they seemed to bend over her in a kind of benediction. A squirrel ran up the trunk of the tree now and several startled birds flew off. Oh, it was such a beautiful world!

More and more letters came filled with hopes and dreams and plans. Clara read them over and over, and she slept with them under her pillow at night.

Then the letters began to mention the recent developments in the war and Ross' increasing feeling of frustration with his role of spectator, and finally one of them said, "As it now appears that we may have a sudden end to the war, and I should very much regret not having had the opportunity to do anything for our cause, I have decided to enlist."

CHAPTER TWELVE

THE Confederate victory on July 21st, 1861, at the first battle of Bull Run, in which Douglas' Mississippi Regiment participated, relieved some of his misgivings, and fighting for the "Cause" helped to strengthen his belief in it. He and so many like him were forging new loyalties on the battlefields, as they fought side by side against a common foe, an invading enemy, whom it would become ever easier to hate and fear.

As the first year of the War ended successfully in Virginia, disturbing news reached Douglas of the Confederate defeat at Shiloh, which left vulnerable the whole undefended area that lay to the south of it. The Mississippi Valley, of which Natchez was a part, was now threatened from above.

Douglas became obsessed with fear for his family. He discussed the situation with his brother-in-law. "Will, the river is vital to us, and they want it. They'll be headed straight to Natchez now. I don't like being so far away. If anything happened, we couldn't get home. We'd be completely cut off from our families."

"Shiloh was a setback, not the last word in the West. They'll recoup. Natchez is 300 miles south of there anyway. It's not in any imminent danger."

"Well, I don't like it. My year's enlistment is almost up, and I think I'll get a discharge and go home. I'll re-enlist somewhere closer to Natchez."

Douglas applied for a discharge, and shortly thereafter the news of the surrender of New Orleans to Admiral Farragut confirmed his worst fears. He was now quite frantic to get home.

On April 30th, 1862, Douglas received his discharge and set about procuring passports and transportation. In three days he was on his way, but the trains were crowded and slow, and there was no direct route. He arrived in Natchez at 9:00 P.M. on May 13th, the day after the mayor and council of Natchez had surrendered the city to Admiral Farragut. Although the town was not occupied, the presence of Yankee gunboats on the river gave reality to the formal surrender.

John Walworth, who was a selectman on the City Council, explained to his son, "We had no choice. We had no forces, no fortifications, absolutely no means to defend ourselves. We do have a good position on the bluff, but Governor Pettus appears to think Vicksburg is a better place to defend, and Jefferson Davis doesn't seem to care about either city! You'd think the importance of the river would be more recognized by our leaders. At any rate, Palmer's demand for our surrender was gratuitous, as we told him in our reply. At least they didn't get any of our cotton. We saw to it that was burned. It was a painful sight, too, the whole riverfront ablaze with the only real currency in the South, all of it going up in smoke!"

"I'm sure there were some reluctant arsonists," Douglas murmured.

"Well, it did sometimes take the point of a gun to get a match to strike!" John Walworth told him.

When Douglas read the official reply of the mayor and the City Council to the demand for surrender, he couldn't help but smile. He thought he knew who had composed that reply. Its tone of icy disdain was so typical of his father. He felt a twinge of sympathy for Commander Palmer and Admiral Farragut.

The reply stated:

"An unfortified city, an entirely defenseless people, have

no alternative but to yield to an irresistible force or uselessly imperil innocent blood. Formalities are absurd in the face of such realities."

In a few days the gunboats moved on, and Natchez sighed with relief.

Several days later an unexpected visitor arrived at The Burn's front door. It was Ross Sanford. Like Douglas, the disaster at Shiloh and the war on the river had filled him with apprehension so he had decided to apply for a leave and go to Natchez to see Clara.

However, with the gunboats gone, the town was going about its business as usual, and the War seemed very far away.

"I can see that spring is here," said Ross as he and Clara walked hand in hand through the garden. Late blooming azaleas, mingled with roses, peonies and early lilies, wrapped the terraces that descended the hill behind The Burn with brilliant ribbons of color. Birds fluttered from bush to tree calling joyfully to one another. The lattice walls of the summer house at the rear of the garden were bursting with yellow jasmine, and pendulous clusters of lavender wisteria hung over the fence behind it.

A pair of squirrels chased each other merrily around the bench beneath the garden's big tree. Then they sprinted madly up the trunk into its hospitable branches, where sudden rustlings of leaves indicated that the game was still in progress.

"Oh, spring has been here for over a month, but it didn't come for me until you got here!" Clara looked up at him, her small heart-shaped face aglow with her happiness.

Ross stopped and faced her. "You are spring to me, Clara," he said seriously. Then his impish humor broke through and he grinned, "Why, you're the prettiest little flower in the whole garden! You know in that white dress you look a lot like this rose!" He plucked a blossom from the white rose bush beside him, and handed it to Clara.

"Oh," she breathed, "that's Lucy's rose. How strange that of all the flowers in the garden, you should pick this one!"

"Who's Lucy?" asked Ross.

"Lucy was my sister. She died of Yellow Fever when she was eleven years old. This was her rose. She and our old gardener planted it together, and she always took care of it herself. She was very proud of it, and we always called it 'Lucy's rose.' You can imagine how much it means to my mother and all of us."

"Give it back to me, Clara. Pin it to my uniform—right here over my heart. It'll be a talisman, reminding me of you. I'll always keep it with me. When I come back, you'll find it there."

"It will shatter all to pieces," laughed Clara. All the same she was quite pleased and touched with the idea.

"No, it won't. I'll keep it in my breast pocket. You'll see. I'm going to keep it forever."

Ross left at the end of the week to return by way of Atlanta to his regiment in Virginia.

He mentioned to John Walworth the possibility of the Walworths coming with Clara to Atlanta to stay with his parents in case of any further trouble from the gunboats.

"I deeply appreciate your kindness and concern and that of your parents, but I'm sure we are all quite safe here. The surrender was a mere formality. I think they've done with us."

"Well, I sincerely hope so," sighed Ross. He wanted so much to ask John Walworth to give him permission to marry Clara and take her with him, but he knew that was impossible. It was best for Clara to stay with her own family until the War was over. But when would that be? It might last another year. And suppose something happened to him? Of course, in that case he knew it would be better for Clara if they were not married. He mustn't be selfish.

Clara could hardly bear it for Ross to leave. She had hoped so that he would ask her to marry him, but he hadn't. She had almost suggested it herself, and then had been too proud to do it. Now it was too late. But surely the War would end soon and then everything would be all right.

The river war was far from ended. Throughout the month of June the newspapers were filled with accounts of the siege and repeated bombardments of the fortified city of Vicksburg. July came, and still the siege continued.

Douglas and Rebecca often walked over from Elmo in the late afternoon to have tea with the senior Walworths at The Burn.

On one such afternoon they sat in the summer house in the garden. Sweet peas and morning-glories climbed on the back fence now behind beds blooming profusely with hollyhocks and roses, and every color and variety of summer annual. The heat of the day was letting up, but not even the smallest breeze disturbed the leaves of the big oak.

"Do you realize," John Walworth asked suddenly, "that here in our garden we are within range of guns from the river?"

A thoughtful silence fell over the little family group while they digested that interesting piece of information.

"I'm thankful Natchez wasn't chosen for a role like Vicksburg's," muttered Douglas.

"It's simply awful to think what they must be going through there. My heart goes out to those people, their homes and businesses destroyed, their city, an armed camp, and the streets filled with rough soldiers!" Sarah's face was transfigured by her ardent sympathy. Plain as she was, she had a way of looking beautiful at times.

"Well at least they're our soldiers, Mother. You know if Vicksburg falls, Natchez could be occupied by Federal troops, something I fear almost more than the bombing. I don't like to think of my wife and sisters at the mercy of enemy troops."

Again a silence fell. Foremost in all their minds was Order Number Twenty-eight, recently issued by General Butler in New Orleans: "Hereafter, when any female shall by word, gesture, or movement, insult or show contempt for any officer or soldier of the United States, she shall be regarded and held liable to be treated as a woman of the town, plying her avocation."

"Have you heard any more about the *Ram*?" Feeling that

her son had been indelicate to mention such matters in the presence of ladies, Sarah deliberately changed the subject.

Rebecca suppressed a smile. Grandma Walworth was a dear, but she was also a hopeless prude.

The *Ram*, about which Sarah had inquired, was the *Arkansas*, a huge iron-clad gunboat. Along with a sister ship, the *Tennessee*, it had been under construction in Memphis before the Confederate naval defeat there. The Rebels had set fire to the *Tennessee* to prevent her falling into the Yankees' hands, but the *Arkansas* had been floated down the river to safety before the battle. Rumor had it she was now at the mouth of the Yazoo. Carpenters and engineers, and blacksmiths and their forges, had been borrowed from the surrounding towns and plantations to complete the construction. Many had gone from Natchez.

"Well, I heard in town today they're recruiting men, and that they're not being too particular about their qualifications," said Douglas.

"It sounds as though they're ready to send her out, then," said John Walworth.

"The word is that she's ready to go, but that the main channel is blocked by a half-sunken raft, which is quite large. They figure it will take at least a week to remove it. Since the water is falling so fast they're afraid that by then the ship won't be able to make it out of the Yazoo. They say Captain Brown is not a man to give up, though, and the betting is he'll do it somehow."

"Well, if he doesn't do it soon, he won't do it this year. The Mississippi won't wait for him," said John Walworth. "If he lets the river fall too low, he'll just have to sit there until spring or, more likely, until Farragut decides to come and blow him up!"

Sarah looked up toward the house on the hill above them. "Here comes Clara. She got a letter from Ross today, and she's been in the clouds ever since. Laura hasn't had one from Will McPhecters in over a week. She's at tea with his parents now. The girls just live from letter to letter."

Rebecca murmured, "I know how that is!"

"Speaking of letters, I wish we'd get one from Ernie," said Douglas.

"Well, you know Ernest said in his last letter for us not to expect to hear from him again soon. He said his division is kept constantly on the march circling around the mountains of west Tennessee. "

"Is that the one he signed 'D. Boone'?"

"You know," said Sarah, "to read his letters you'd think he was just off on a lark to have some fun. He never lets on that he takes any of it seriously."

"Yes," sighed John Walworth, "everything is a joke to Ernest." Secretly he admired his debonair son's lightheartedness.

Before they left, Douglas drew his father aside to discuss the secret plans he had been making to become a volunteer aide to General Clarke.

"Have you not yet told your wife?" his father reproved him.

"No, not yet. I don't want to upset her unnecessarily. I want to be sure it's going to work out before I say anything. I've talked to Major Kimmel and Colonel Clarke, and arrangements are being made for me to meet the general in Jackson at the first opportunity. I do hope he'll accept me. I hate leaving Rebecca and the children, but if I could serve on General Clarke's staff I'd be close to home. If some danger threatens, I should be able to get back. At any rate I'm going to lend whatever support I can to regaining control of the river. I think that the safety of us all depends on that."

When goodbye kisses had been exchanged all around, Douglas and Rebecca began to walk arm in arm down the road that led from his parents' home to theirs, Rebecca chattering of this and that. Suddenly she stopped and looked up at Douglas. "You haven't said a word since we left The Burn. What's the matter?"

He hesitated, "Well, I—didn't want to say anything until things were more definite, but it looks as though it's going to work out for me to become an aide to General Clarke. I can't just go on doing nothing, and serving on his staff I wouldn't be as far away from you and the children."

Rebecca turned pale and shut her eyes for a second. She took a deep breath, looked up at him, and then away. "I knew you'd be leaving soon, but I've tried not to think about it. I didn't want to spoil this time we've had together. I've treasured every minute of it. I know you have to go, but I didn't know I'd mind this much. Oh, Douglas, do you really have to go?"

"Becky, I don't want to leave you, but a man can't shirk his duty however hard it may be. You wouldn't really want me to!"

"Oh, Douglas, why did we have to live in times like these?"

"Not a day goes by that I don't ask myself that question, and I can't help but feel that worse lies ahead."

"We mustn't talk this way. Worrying about the future and moping about the present won't do us a bit of good. I'm ashamed of myself for being such a cry-baby and I promise I won't be anymore, but you must promise me something, too, Douglas."

"That I won't be a cry-baby?"

"No, silly, that you will be careful, that you won't try to be too heroic."

"I think I can safely promise you that I won't be a hero."

CHAPTER THIRTEEN

WHEN Douglas arrived in Jackson on horseback on July 25th, 1862, he had already heard the news of an event which had taken place on July 15th, but he was anxious to get a firsthand account. In shirtsleeves and mud-caked boots, his gray pants stained with sweat and splattered with mud, he sat in General Clarke's hotel room listening intently while the general and two of his aides told him what had happened.

On July 15th, the sitting duck, which Admiral Farragut and his fleet had assumed was safely penned up in the Yazoo, had made its way down the Mississippi with incredible speed, cumbersome, homemade monstrosity that it was, ploughing through the midst of two Federal fleets, numbering about thirty-seven vessels in all. Taken completely by surprise, the Yankee gunboats could not get up sufficient steam to maneuver, or to pursue their attacker. The *Arkansas* charged upon them, an unseemly knight in a suit of armor forged from wagonloads of assorted iron objects and painted a muddy brown to blend with the river. With her ten guns firing into the surrounding enemy ships, the *Arkansas* cut a swashbuckling path, receiving some damage, but inflicting far more. Straight through the stunned Union fleets to the sheltering arms of the Vicksburg batteries, the *Arkansas* had steamed in triumph!

"Imagine the heat in those engine rooms in mid-July! They say the temperature was 120 degrees or more! It took a lot of steam to move at such high speed."

"How did the men stand it?" Douglas wondered.

"Brown ordered the crew replaced every fifteen minutes."

"I heard Captain Brown was seriously wounded."

"Yes, he may lose one of his eyes. He was shot in the head, and fell unconscious on the gundeck. They thought he was dead but he revived and resumed command."

"His reputation for determination was evidently not exaggerated."

"When they got to the Vicksburg wharf, they were met by a crowd of cheering spectators. They say Brown just stood there on the deck with the blood running down his face, and when he took off his cap you could see the hole in his head. They say he said, 'Boys, I never was under fire before, but I am not so scared as I expected to be.'"

"He doesn't sound like the sort of man who'd be scared of anything! Were there heavy casualties?"

"Not so many as you might think, although I heard when the crowd rushed on board to congratulate Brown and his men they were stopped cold at first sight of the deck. They say it was a ghastly scene with heaps of torn, bloody flesh, arms and legs and torsos, all over the place. But there were only ten killed and fifteen seriously wounded according to the official report."

Douglas shuddered at the graphic description. The price that must be paid for victories was so awful. He was glad he had not been Captain Brown.

"But the latest news, which you probably haven't heard, is that Farragut has pulled up anchor, and gone downstream. The siege is lifted! They're dancing in the streets of Vicksburg."

"The whole fleet's gone?"

"The whole fleet. All their attempts to destroy the *Arkansas* failed, and with the water falling so fast, and their coal supply so low, they really had no choice but to withdraw."

"Of course this is splendid news for us, Captain Walworth," said General Clarke in the crisp voice that was one of his qualifications for command.

"This frees the *Arkansas* for action. We are, as I believe you know, soon to join General Breckinridge in an attack on Baton Rouge. With the *Ram* to protect us from the river, we should recover the city without much difficulty. It will be an important step in regaining control of the river."

Douglas nodded. "The presence of the *Ram* will make our job much easier." A thrill of anticipation ran through him. Another brilliant victory seemed certain, and he would be a part of it!

"I've made plans for us to go to Vicksburg tomorrow. We've been invited to dine on the *Ram*."

At dinner in the captain's cabin on the *Arkansas*, they discussed the coming attack on Baton Rouge and the role they wished the *Ram* to play in it. Captain Isaac Newton Brown was not present. He was in the hospital at Grenada, and had been replaced in command temporarily by Henry Stevens.

Captain Stevens was hesitant about committing the vessel without Captain Brown's approval.

"I'm really just the caretaker until he gets back," he protested. He turned to the slim, young, black man who was serving them. "A little more claret, please, Jim."

"How long does Captain Brown plan to be on leave?" asked Douglas.

"It depends on his health. He's been through enough to have killed an ordinary person."

General Clarke drained his wine glass and smiled at the waiter who refilled it. "Thank you very much, Jim." Then he addressed the group with compelling decisiveness. "He's proved himself to have courage and coolness under fire. But he doesn't own this ship. And he isn't the only man who can operate it."

"Let me point out to you, sir," said the young captain, "that the *Arkansas* has some wounds herself. Her engines were badly damaged in that collision with *The Queen of the West*."

"We'll give you time to repair them," said General Clarke, "but we must have your support. It will make all the difference in the success of our effort. Your big guns will give us the protection we need."

Captain Stevens stared into his glass of claret. He saw that General Clarke was not a man to be denied.

"Well," said he finally, "I'll tell you what I'll do. I'll wire Captain Brown, and see what he says."

That was the only commitment they were able to extract from the acting commander of the *Ram.*

"We'll just have to apply a little pressure from above," General Clarke told Douglas later. "I'll confer with Breckinridge and Van Dorn. Van Dorn is most anxious to retake Baton Rouge. We can count on his help."

And so, although Captain Brown wired in reply to Captain Stevens that the ship should not be moved until he returned, Van Dorn ordered the *Arkansas* to move down the river to aid Breckinridge in the coming attack on Baton Rouge, and work was begun on the damaged engines. Repairing them was complicated by the fact that the chief engineer was still in the hospital along with most of the crew. Nevertheless, on August 3rd the *Arkansas* headed south, her engines working satisfactorily, and nearly a full crew on board, most of them wearing bandages.

Meanwhile Douglas was marching through the swamps and bayous of Louisiana with General Clarke on their way to Baton Rouge. Douglas knew the miseries and dangers of that country well. The Walworth plantations were located in it. From mud and mosquitoes to quicksand and malaria, it was all familiar to him, and he had dealt with alligators and water moccasins before. The difficult part for him lay ahead when he would be expected to shoot or slash at other human beings, and to ignore cries for help from wounded men. He devoutly hoped that a blast or two from the *Arkansas* would bring forth a white flag from the enemy forces.

On the night of August 4th they were still ten miles from Baton Rouge. General Breckinridge and General Clarke and their staffs held a council of war, and decided to make a night march to the city.

The entry for August 5th in Douglas' diary read:

> *"The battle commenced at daylight. A terrific day. We drove the enemy to the river. The gunboats played up on us so severely we could not hold the town. General Clarke severely wounded and captured. Came back to camp."*

They had reached the river in triumph, eager to see their guardian angel the *Ram*, running like children to a mother's skirts. All they could see were enemy gunboats, pouring fire on them.

Douglas and his fellow officers attempted to hold their ground in spite of the raining shells, wondering what had delayed the *Arkansas* and praying for her sudden appearance. Then as more and more men fell around them and panic threatened, they began to retreat, fighting through the streets of the city.

General Clarke fell from his horse, wounded. A Yankee cavalry officer quickly dismounted and, lifting the wounded man onto his horse, swung back into his saddle and galloped away with his prize. In the desperate man-to-man fighting in the town's narrow streets none of his men were able to reach the general in time to prevent his capture.

Not until Douglas returned to Natchez a week after the whole misadventure did he learn what had happened to the *Arkansas*.

The *Ram* had never reached Baton Rouge because her engines had failed as she was headed to attack the suddenly encountered gunboat *Essex* and three other Union vessels. Completely helpless, she had drifted toward the riverbank. Henry Stevens ordered most of the crew ashore. With the help of those remaining, he broke up the ship's machinery with axes and hand grenades. Then cartridges and loaded shells were scattered over the deck, and the guns were loaded. Fires were set on board, and Stevens and the men left her.

The Ram drifted toward the Union fleet, all her guns

discharging. Puzzled, and suspicious, the enemy vessels scurried out of her way.

On floated the gallant ship, as Stevens later said, "fighting the battle on her own hook." Finally, a few minutes after noon, she blew up into fragments with a great explosion.

Nearby at the time was Isaac Brown, desperately trying to reach his ship. He had reached Ponchatoula, the nearest railroad approach to Baton Rouge, when his ship blew up, ending her short and spectacular career of twenty-three battle-filled days, all the hopes she had raised with her triumphs exploding with her. Regaining control of the Mississippi was no longer possible, and its valley lay helpless now before the unchallenged might of the Yankee gunboats.

CHAPTER FOURTEEN

AFTER the futile attack on Baton Rouge and the capture of General Clarke, Douglas found himself again without a position. While he considered what to do next, he resumed his life at home, almost as usual. He and Rebecca attended church and went to tea, and he rode horseback with his little son, John. He also found himself in charge of the fortifications, which the citizens of Natchez had prepared on their own for the purpose of repelling an attack. These consisted of some breastworks and two or three small cannons.

Douglas drilled the little band of citizens who had volunteered for militia duty. The group was made up of those either too old or too young for battle, their ages ranging from nearly ninety to one young lad of nine. The Silver Grays, as they called themselves, took turns patrolling the river.

On the first day of September the dark squat shape of the *Essex* loomed on the river. The gunboat came to the Natchez landing Under-the-Hill, and a raid was made. Hay, rice, and hogs were seized there and from across the river they took a supply of coal and some negro workers.

The next morning Douglas rode into town to get the mail and the newspaper, and he stopped by the fortifications to be sure they were adequately manned.

When he returned to Elmo it was almost two o'clock,

time for dinner to be served. Clara had come to dine with them, and she and Rebecca and the two older children were waiting for him.

"What does the *Courier* have to say about the Yankee plundering?" Rebecca asked.

He unfolded the newspaper and pointed to a headline. Rebecca took the paper from him, and read the article aloud:

The Naval River Thieves

The correspondence of General Breckinridge with the Federal commander at Baton Rouge charges the Federal Army and Navy with violating the rules of civilized warfare. Any doubt about the truth of such charges was relieved by the depredation at the Natchez landing on September 1. These officers deserve to be hunted down by every shotgun and rifle in the river district.

She returned the paper to Douglas. "Well, I must say I agree!"

"If I had a gun, I'd shoot them all," declared little John and everybody laughed.

Douglas seated Clara on his right and Rebecca and the children took their places. A blessing was said and Uncle Perry began to serve the dinner. The serenity of this domestic scene was disrupted by a sudden clattering of horses' hooves outside. Douglas and Rebecca exchanged anxious glances.

In a moment two young boys from the Silver Grays burst upon the family group. One of them spoke excitedly to Douglas. "Captain Walworth, those Yankees, they're leaving the boat again. They're coming up the bluff! What should we do? Should we fire on them? We don't know what to do!"

Douglas had hoped fervently that this wouldn't happen. He really hadn't thought the problem through yet. Nevertheless he was in charge, and he knew that he must act quickly and positively. He rose, and laid his napkin beside his plate. "Becky, will you please excuse me? This is a matter that won't wait."

He turned to Uncle Perry. "Uncle Perry, will you please bring my horse around for one of these men? I'm going to take one of theirs. I must get to the bluff right away." He turned to the young man who had spoken. "Let's go."

Rebecca sat silent and stunned, more frightened than she had ever been in her life, not for herself or the children, but for Douglas. The look on his face was what alarmed her so. His mouth had been so grim and there was a wild look in his eyes. What was he going to do? She thought of the article in the *Courier,* and what she had said about it. She wished she had had time to tell him she hadn't meant it.

Clara observed her sister-in-law's concern and wanted to tell her not to worry, that everything was going to be all right, but the words stuck in her throat. She was worried, too.

"What's Father going to do?" asked John.

"He's going to defend the city from the Yankees!" cried Lucy, and Rebecca thought that look in her eyes is just like her father's.

"Let's go up to the roof and see what we can see," suggested John.

"That's a wonderful idea!" Lucy was out of her seat already. "Oh, Mama, may we?"

"Yes, let's all go." She jumped up, and led the way, running up the stairs, clutching at her long full skirts to lift them.

Elmo's high hip roof like D'Evereux's was crowned by a small observation tower surrounded by a bannistered path called a widow's walk and from there the river could be seen.

Rebecca clung to the little guard rail, breathless from her hasty climb up two long flights of stairs, and dizzy from the height at which she found herself. She had a sudden horrible urge to jump. I must get hold of myself, she thought. With a surge of will power she calmed herself.

"John," she said, "go get your father's field glasses. We can't see very well at this distance. Clara, can you see? Are the men still coming up the bluff? Do you see any of our men? Look out, Lucy! Don't lean over the rail."

"The people look like ants from up here. I can't tell who's who, Mama," cried Lucy.

"I can't figure that out either," said Clara, shading her eyes with one hand and holding on to the rail with the other.

Suddenly several sharp reports rang out. Rebecca's heart stopped beating, and then began to pound frantically. She glanced at Clara and their eyes met in mutual alarm.

"The shots were headed towards the river. Father must have told our men to fire!" Lucy was swaying back and forth in her excitement, and as Clara grabbed her by the wide sash of her starched white pinafore, Rebecca said sternly, "Lucy, you will have to stay perfectly still, or I will send you downstairs."

A few more shots rang out, and then all was quiet again.

Rebecca shivered. "I hope that's the end of it."

John arrived, puffing and panting, with a pair of binoculars. "What happened? Who fired the shots? Did I miss it all? Why couldn't Lucy have gone for the glasses?" He was disgusted to have missed the action.

Rebecca adjusted the binoculars, and trained them onto a small boat which was drawing alongside of the *Essex*.

"There seems to have been only a small party of them. I wonder what they'll do now?" Rebecca lowered the glasses, her big, dark eyes still filled with apprehension.

After several more minutes of quiet, Rebecca turned to Clara. "Well, that seems to be all there is to it. Let's all go down now and finish our dinner."

"It appears to be over," Rebecca told the servants, who had been hovering near the foot of the stairs.

Mammy Martha was sitting on the bottom step, the two smallest children clasped to her bosom, rocking back and forth, humming a hymn with a mournful melody.

"The Lord has delivered us!" she cried now. "Praise be the name of the Lord!"

"Amen!" cried the servants.

"Amen!" cried the children.

"I guess we'll try to eat our dinner now," said Rebecca.

"Won't none of it be fit to eat, Miss Rebecca," protested Esther. "It's all stone cold."

"Oh, just warm it up. We don't care. I doubt if I can eat anything anyway, but the children must have some dinner."

When they had reassembled at the table, John asked his mother, "Shall we say the blessing again?"

"Why yes, John. It would be very fitting to offer thanks right now. Will you do it, please?"

They bowed their heads, and a screaming noise above made them all look up at once.

It was followed by a dull thud, and the sound of the china on the table rattling as the ground beneath them reverberated with the impact.

As more screams and thuds followed, they began to occur simultaneously. Uncle Perry appeared in the doorway of the dining room, his handsome mahogany face furrowed with fear. Rebecca and Clara turned pale, and the children were wide-eyed. Nobody spoke a word for several long moments.

Rebecca put Douglas in God's hands with a brief, silent prayer, and then she didn't permit herself to think of him again.

"Let's get everybody to the cellar, Uncle Perry."

With Clara's help, they shepherded the children and the other servants and their children down the narrow winding stairs. Everybody was calm but Mammy Martha, who was verging on hysteria.

"Hush, Mammy Martha," said Rebecca more sharply than she meant to.

At this the old woman took offense. "Who are you telling to hush? I raised you with better manners than that. To think you would ever speak to me that way! To think you wouldn't show an old woman more respect!" she wailed indignantly.

Uncle Perry came to the rescue, taking her by the

shoulder and giving her a stern look. "Calm yourself, Sister Martha. Think of the children. You should set an example." The steadiness of his rich, deep voice was reassuring.

"I apologize, Mammy Martha. I didn't mean to be disrespectful to you. I guess my nerves are a little on edge." Rebecca sent Uncle Perry a grateful glance and he raised his eyes eloquently upward and shook his head, as they followed the frail, and suddenly silent, descending figure of Mammy Martha.

The cellar was much quieter, though the shrieking and booming could still be heard.

The adults set themselves to entertain and distract the children, who soon accustomed themselves to the situation and began to enjoy it.

Uncle Perry took out his knife and began to whittle a piece of kindling into the shape of a pig, and then a whole menagerie, while Mammy Martha, in better spirits now, rendered her famous version of the story of the Great Flood and Noah's Ark, complete with vivid impersonations of all the animals.

The liquid eyes in her small wrinkled face, which looked so much like a prune, commanded the absolute attention of her audience. Mammy Martha was a born storyteller, and years of practice had made her an artist. The children had heard her tell this story many times, but she usually added something new, and they could never hear enough of her animal talk. Most of her animals were indigenous, pigs, cows, coons, rabbits, opossums, or chipmunks, but also included were some exotic beasts. An outstandingly ferocious lion and a prissy, mincing giraffe were part of her repertoire. Today she introduced a horse with the hiccups, and he was an instant success.

When the Lord had given the rainbow as a sign that never again would He send such a flood, there was an outburst of spontaneous applause, which Mammy Martha received with a regally restrained nod of her head.

John was quick to follow her act.

"This is our Ark," said he, "and we, each of us, have to be an animal. I bid the horse."

In spite of the ensuing arguments, this game proved to be a successful timepasser, and it was not until their third hour in the cellar that the irritations of confinement began to mount.

The little children became fretful, complaining of being hungry and thirsty, and the older children became bored and began to tease each other and to fuss.

Halfway into this third hour the noise outside suddenly subsided. The little group in the cellar at Elmo sat waiting, afraid to believe the bombing had stopped, and not daring to leave their refuge.

A few minutes passed, and still all was quiet.

The children began to beg to go upstairs.

"Not yet," Rebecca told them. "I think we should wait about an hour before going up."

They were still there when Douglas ran into the house shouting, "Becky, where are you? Is everybody all right?"

Rebecca flew up the steps, Clara and the children at her heels. "Oh, Douglas, thank God!"

He hugged her against him. "Yes, thank God! I was so frightened for you all. I had to sec if you were all right. I've got to go back and help. We don't know how many people may be hurt. There's a good deal of damage. Most of it is Under-the-Hill. What a terrible thing this is! How can they war on women and children? I still can't believe they did it. What a ghastly revenge for a few shots fired at men in uniform who were stealing from us!"

He left without speaking to any of the rest of them.

Clara sighed, "Well, I guess it's really over now. Douglas is safe, and we're all right. We can be thankful for that."

"But we don't know about your parents and Laura, or my mother and Margarette and her children. You must go home to your family right now, Clara, and see about them and tell them that we're all right. I don't want to leave the children, but I'll send Uncle Perry to see about Mother and Margarette. And, Clara, I'm so glad that you were here with me. You've been a big help."

"But I didn't do anything," protested Clara.

Rebecca smiled at her. "You're cool under fire, my dear, and you helped me to stay that way."

Clara gave her sister-in-law a little hug. "Douglas is lucky to have married you, and I'm lucky he did, too!"

Douglas returned at dark. Rebecca was waiting for him on the gallery. Wordlessly he pulled her into his arms and leaned his cheek against her soft brown hair. Then he began to sob, choked, silent heavings which finally burst into sound.

Rebecca held him and waited until he was able to speak.

"A child was killed. Her name was Rosalie—Rosalie Beckman. She was a beautiful little girl. They killed her! They killed her! Oh, God, I killed her!" He began to sob again.

"Oh, Douglas, no. You mustn't say that. You mustn't think that. You aren't to blame because those monsters decided to take their revenge on a defenseless city."

"Without warning," moaned Douglas, "without the slightest warning! If they wanted to punish the city, they could have given us time to evacuate the women and children. Why couldn't they have done that? How could they not have done that? The mother . . ." He broke down again. "Becky, you should have seen the mother! It was terrible, terrible!"

The ultimate cruelty to the conscience of a sensitive man was hurled onto the front gallery the next day. Wrapped around a brick, the message was inscribed in bold, crudely executed letters: *MURDERER.* It struck one of Elmo's pillars, but the wound was to Douglas' heart.

It was true, he thought. No matter what anybody said, he could not deny that the responsibility for the tragedy of the child's death rested upon him. And although the newspapers and most of Natchez's leading citizens had supported him and approved his action, what had he accomplished with it? Destruction and death were the price of it, and the enemy had lost nothing.

But he had tried to do what was right, or had he just been too anxious to be a hero?

All these thoughts ran endlessly through his mind.

He and Rebecca attended the child's funeral, an ordeal made more excruciating for Douglas by the whisperings and mutterings which he heard around him: "So unnecessary!" "It's a mercy we weren't all killed." "Such a stupid thing to do." "The idea of a defenseless city taking on a gunboat!"

But more terrible than these irresponsible criticisms, or even the note accusing him of murder, was his father's dry comment, "Well, there's no use to cry over spilled milk." Here was the failure he really could not bear. He longed so desperately for his father's approval, and John Walworth had not the eyes to see his son's need.

Douglas found himself now most anxious to get away from Natchez, but Jefferson Davis, to whom he had written after the battle of Baton Rouge regarding a new appointment, wrote him at last in reply that operations were winding down with winter coming on and that he should wait until spring for his orders.

CHAPTER FIFTEEN

IN March of 1863 both Douglas and Will became a part of the newly formed Army of Tennessee in one of its cavalry divisions. Will, the organizer of the Adams troop which had served under General Jeb Stuart of Virginia, was given the new rank of brigadier general and placed in charge.

After they had left to fight the war in Tennessee, some unfortunate events took place back in Mississippi. On July 4th, Vicksburg surrendered, and shortly after that Natchez was occupied by the enemy.

Margarette wrote to Will telling him about it:

Linden
Sept. 27, 1863

My dear husband,

On Monday, the 13th day of July, at 1 o'clock p.m. our usually quiet little town was thrown into the greatest state of excitement and alarm by the arrival of the Yankees, and no wonder, for their arrival was unexpected and several regiments came up the hill screaming and whooping like wild Indians. In less than an hour pickets were stationed at our front gate and the yard filled with soldiers.

I went over to spend the night with Uncle and Aunt Eliot at D'Evereux, returning in the morning after breakfast to find John and the rest of the negroes completely demoralized.

Before I got there a Yankee officer had paraded all through the house while a soldier played Yankee Doodle on the piano for the benefit of the negroes, who were invited to take seats on the sofas. He concluded his visit by writing an insulting note in my own room, leaving it on my dressing table for me to read.

I spent the day at Monteigne but went that night to Linden. The next morning I returned to Monteigne to find Adeline and Amelia gone and the house broken open and robbed by them and Federal soldiers. Amelia broke open your desk in which was my key basket. Knowing where everything was she had no difficulty in making her selections and stripping me of all my valuable clothing as well as the children's, all the house linen, mattresses and pillows; all my children's shoes, hats, and bonnets, your tools and willow baskets. All the medicine she wished, such as quinine, paregoric, peppermint, calomel, and camphor. All the sweet soap, perfume, and cologne and all the groceries.

It was a wholesale business and when the keys could not conveniently be found, the axe was used. My dressing table and your wardrobe were both broken up.

I cannot describe to you my feelings when I entered the house that morning and saw such a scene of confusion as presented itself to me, for the few things that were left were scattered about promiscuously, beds pulled to pieces and furniture split. I was near beside myself than anything else.

In the midst of the confusion J. M. fortunately made his appearance. I stated the case to him and carried him all through the house. He seemed to be very sorry for me and said he would immediately report the case to General Ransom and try to get my things back.

Fortunately Amelia had not gotten her stolen property further than the bridge. The Yankee soldiers carried it that far for her and when J. M. passed the bridge she was still there with our valuables, waiting for a conveyance to carry them to town. J. M. asked the picket stationed there not to let the articles be removed as they were stolen goods and that he was then on his way to report the matter to General Ransom.

Amelia, hearing this, left her plunder, all except what she could carry in her arms, and that was a good deal.

A Lt. Doane, one of Ransom's aides, came to see me and ordered the picket to see that all of Amelia's stolen property be returned to me. So I succeeded in getting all of my clothing, except that worn by Amelia, Adeline, and their children.

Among other things stolen was the silver tea set and that I got back. The bonnets, hats, shoes, tools, and medicines I have never seen.

Lt. Doane was polite enough and I thanked him for he did more than I could have expected from any of them.

Uncle Wood insisted that Amelia be arrested and made to return the balance of my things. She was arrested and carried before Major McRee, the Provost Marshal. To him she gave you and particularly me, a most undesirable reputation for brutality, etc. Said we starved and half-clothed our servants and worked and beat them to death. She also swore she had nothing of mine. All this done publicly in the Court House. Well, she was released without even a reproof!

The day after the stealing I was at home again and standing on the back gallery when who should make his appearance but faithful (?) John accompanied by a great, rough, red-faced, brutal looking man in his shirt sleeves. John walked immediately up to me, the man close beside him, and demanded of me your saddle which was upstairs in the house. I very foolishly ordered him to go for it and while up there he stole your oil cloth coat. The Yankee all the time staring in the most impudent and insulting manner. I did not speak to him as I believed he came there for the express purpose of insulting me and I was never more frightened in my life.

I had the satisfaction of seeing your saddle carried to the stable and put on one of the carriage horses which John mounted and the other horse was mounted by Captain Smith, the Yankee, and both rode out of the yard as though the place belonged to them.

That day I made up my mind that Monteigne was not a safe place for me so I moved over all my clothing to Linden and only go home occasionally for a little while.

About ten days ago a message came from Hardy that half a dozen soldiers had broken open the house. My furniture and many valuable things were still there and I insisted upon going over so Mother said she would accompany me. When we got there, sure enough, there were seven or eight Yankees strolling around, making themselves quite at home. Mother did all the talking. My heart was too full for me to speak.

She asked them the object of their visit. What was my horror to be told that they intended taking our home for a hospital for the negro regiment encamped at the Forks. A General Gresham now commands this place and I understand he is a humane man and a gentleman. A negro regiment has been formed at the Forks of the Roads, each company commanded by a white man. The negroes are well armed and dressed in uniform and drilled daily. Whenever a citizen is to be arrested and whenever there is one of our soldiers around and the Yankees hear of it, a squad of negroes is always sent to arrest them. This, I suppose, is done to humiliate the people.

This arming of the negroes is a terrible business and is very hard to bear patiently. The negroes are dying very rapidly in the camp and they are making a graveyard in General Quitman's enclosure.

It is said twenty thousand negroes have come to the Yankees at Natchez. A colony of negroes has been formed Under-the-Hill, extending several miles above Brown's Saw Mill. All the able-bodied men are put into the camp at the Forks of the Roads, and the old men, women, and children are put Under-the-Hill. We hear they die there sometimes twenty a day. Many of the negroes have become dissatisfied and returned home. Now to return to Mother and my visit to Monteigne.

Mother talked to the man in a most dignified manner. Finally he said, "Well, we will put a poor man's family in here and take his house for a hospital." And in an hour Mr. Crane and his family were established in our room and in the nursery.

I have moved all of the furniture to Linden and the house looks desolate indeed. I should have told you that Major McRee was perfectly polite and gave me permission to order all negroes off of my place, even if Colonel Smith did send them.

Now my dear husband, I have given you some of my experiences since the Yankees came. Do you not think my trials have been many and bitter?

The Yankees think you, with a command of 4,000 men, are only 15 miles from Natchez. Some negro has told them that you occasionally spend a night here and for three days D'Evereux and our house have been closely guarded and we think they are watching for you. A number of men are at the front gate, one at the greenhouse, a number in the bayou and some near the stable. I can't bear to go home now. I am so unhappy after a visit to that dear spot, once the happiest on earth to me.

I received yesterday your letter giving an account of that terrible battle at Shelbyville. Oh, how grateful my heart felt to a merciful God for protecting you in the midst of such danger.

The Federals are now fortifying the northern part of the town and The Burn will be inside of the fortifications. I feel so sorry for Mr. and Mrs. Walworth, the labor of years to be destroyed. I understand the Yankees take great credit to themselves for not burning your house down long ago.

When you write please be very cautious in what you say. The Yankees are very vigilant and capture a great many letters. If you can send a letter by the person who takes this out to you, you can say what you please. It is getting late and I must close this long letter. Oh, my darling husband, I cannot tell you how dear you are to your loving "Little Wife."

Margarette

While Margarette was sitting at a small Sheraton writing table at Linden pouring out these troubles to Will, Rebecca sat at Elmo at a pompeiian red spinet, hand painted with sprays of flowers. When she played, she could forget everything but the music. This little spinet was her most cherished worldly possession. It had belonged to her great grandmother Gaillard, having been brought on a flatboat all the way from a plantation on the Santee River in South Carolina to the Natchez Territory. Its range was limited, but the purity and delicacy of its tone more than made up for that as far as Rebecca was concerned.

"I'm afraid I'll be consigned to hell for loving this heavenly music too much, and that my punishment will be an eternity without any music," she had told Douglas. And he had reassured her, "How could it be a sin to love heavenly music?"

She was caught up now in the exquisite ecstasy of a Bach fugue when a small hand was placed urgently on her shoulder. It was John.

"Mama!" he cried. "Grandpa Walworth is here to get a

wagon to take back to The Burn to put their things in. They've got to move in an hour."

Rebecca rose, and soothingly brushed back the wavy blond hair from her son's finely featured face, now all flushed with excitement. "Well, where is Grandpa? Why must they leave in an hour? What's the rush? The Yankees couldn't possibly expect them to get their things packed in an hour."

"Grandpa and Uncle Perry have gone to the stables to get the wagon and the horses. They told me to tell you."

Rebecca ran from the house out to the stables in back where she found the two men hitching up the horses to the largest wagon. Her father-in-law, in a cold fury, but controlled as always, gave her the facts. "They say they told us that our home would be inside the fortifications, and they say we must vacate it in twenty-four hours as they need it for a hospital."

"Oh, twenty-four. John said an hour! But couldn't they give you a little more time? It seems so unreasonable."

"I will not beg favors from them," replied John Walworth, and Rebecca knew that that was the end of it.

When Uncle Perry returned with the first load of furniture, bric-a-brac, and clothing, Rebecca, the other servants, and John and Lucy were waiting on the gallery to help unload.

Rebecca asked Uncle Perry, "How is Grandma Walworth? She isn't trying to do too much is she?"

"Miss Laura and Miss Clara and Sister Chloe, all of them, is trying they best to keep her from overdoing. They set her down in a chair on the front gallery to direct us, but she keeps jumping up and running around. Doesn't anybody really know what to try to take, and everything's mighty confused. Don't you reckon if Mr. John had asked for more time that Yankee officer gentleman would have let him have a little longer to move?"

Rebecca said with a small sigh, "Pride can be an awful burden, can't it?"

"Yes'm," he replied, thinking how sensible she was. Rebecca had a good rapport with all her servants, but she and Uncle Perry understood each other especially well. Diplomatic, pragmatic, and easy going, they moved through life and its vicissitudes with much greater ease than most people, and they often wondered what all the fuss was about.

On the other hand, others and in particular her sister, Margarette, could not understand why Rebecca got all the good and faithful servants while their own were so good for nothing. In fact it had always seemed to Margarette that Rebecca was luckier than she about everything, excepting in husbands, and she had never been able to see how Rebecca could put up with Douglas' moods.

Elmo absorbed The Burn household remarkably well. It was a spacious house, and with a little rearranging and doubling up everybody was fairly comfortable.

However the senior Walworths were devastated by the loss of their house. Their children, with the exception of Douglas, had been born there and three of them had died there. They had rejoiced and they had suffered within its thick, sturdy walls, which had sheltered them from the weather and from the world. But the house represented more to them than a beloved shell of the life they had lived within it. It was a part of them, an expression of their hopes and dreams, the symbol of what and who they were.

Sarah had supervised the planting of every tree and shrub and flower in The Burn's garden, nursing them through mercilessly hot summers and unexpectedly cold winters, through washing rains and parching droughts. Now her plants were at the mercy of strangers, enemies even, who didn't care. And, above all else, what would happen to Lucy's rose? Sarah could not bear to think about that.

Clara felt the agony of her parents, and she shared her father's sense of outrage. How dared anyone order you out of your home! She had fantasies of standing on The Burn gallery declaring to the Yankees that she had no intention of leaving it, that they would have to kill her first.

There had been no way to move all their furniture to Elmo, those beautiful things that were family treasures or that had been acquired over the years. There was little reason to hope that they would ever see them again. They would be looked upon as the spoils of war.

They all kept thinking of precious things they ought to have brought with them, but the time allowed for them to move had been so short and there had been so much confusion.

The servants adjusted to their new arrangements very well for the most part, but a problem arose between the two cooks, Esther and Chloe, a couple of generals, neither of whom had the slightest intention of being second in command. Of course, as everyone tried to point out to Aunt Chloe, it was Esther's kitchen, but she felt that her obvious seniority both in years and service entitled her to greater privilege. Even Rebecca, with all her tact, seemed unable to resolve the situation. The kitchen became an armed camp.

John Walworth observed in his dry way, "The bloodiest battle of the War is going on out there in the kitchen."

Mammy Martha, who was of a peppery temperament herself, had nevertheless given up years ago trying to control her wayward granddaughter, Esther, and she and the affable Uncle Perry steered as clear of the skirmishing as they possibly could, secretly sympathizing with Chloe.

Another conflict took place between the oldest member of the family and the youngest. Four-and-a-half-year-old Annie was given to violent temper tantrums, of which her grandfather strongly disapproved. One day as she was launching into one he seized her by her little shoulders, and fixing her with his icy stare, said in his sternest voice, "Young lady, you will be silent!"

Annie blinked her big, blue eyes, swallowed a large gulp of air, and fastened her little pink lips firmly shut. She didn't make a sound.

Everybody was very impressed, but no one else was ever able to have the same effect. Annie continued to have tantrums but not around Grandpa Walworth. And five-and-a-half-year-old Daisy added a new sentence to her vocabulary: "I'll tell Grandpa!"

CHAPTER SIXTEEN

ON October 26th, Margarette wrote again from Linden to Will:

Linden
October 26, 1863

My dear husband,

I am running some risk smuggling letters through the lines. Well, if they should be captured, and I called to account for it, I will tell the Commanding Officer, himself, that though the laws were bloody as were the Spartans, I would undertake the same thing.

Natchez is nobly sustaining its reputation for being a good old Union town. You remember you suggested the Federals would be entertained in Natchez? Well, they have been entertained, by some, in great style. It is surprising how many good Secessionists have become warm Unionists.

There was a dinner party on a gunboat last week. Among the ladies who attended were Misses and Mrs. E. M. and Mrs. M. As they went aboard a most terrific report was heard and lo! It was a cannon. Powder was wasted on that occasion.

You know young ladies like to have beaux and there are none here now except those wearing the cloth, brass buttons and riding stylish looking borrowed horses. Borrowed as you borrowed the mules on the last raid. For two Sundays past Mrs. M. has had in her pew, with herself and daughters, two sons of the famous General Thomas.

Mrs. J. O. has been seen several times riding with the officers. I should not think her Rebel husband would enjoy such proclivities in his young wife. Miss C. is also very partial to the Yankee officers. She was such a strong southern girl before the Yankees came, especially whenever a handsome young Confederate officer was present. All Yankees who have any sense of honor must be disgusted. I did hear that one of the Federal Generals here said he had much more respect for the man who had buckled on his armor and gone to fight for what he supposed to be a right cause than for him who stayed at home, assisted the Rebels as much as he could before the Federals came, and now, out of policy, had become such a wonderfully good Union man.

There has been a large fire in Natchez—Mr. Reddy's, Stanton and Stockman's, all now occupied by Yankees, have been burned to the ground. The store of Myers is still a shoe store, is owned in partnership by Mr. H. Nutt and a Yankee. Between the destruction of property, in and around Natchez, by the Yankees and fires, there will soon be very little left of a once beautiful and prosperous town.

In the Provost Marshal's office, in the Court House, is a card headed: "A Warning to all ladies—Miss M. B. and Miss E. M. were ordered to leave Vicksburg and the Federal Lines on twenty-four hours notice for leaving the Episcopal Church when Lincoln was to be prayed for." I think those ladies should have said their prayers at home.

I have only been in the carriage twice since the Federals came and then I went to church. On both occasions it was filled with our enemies, but they behaved very well and do not go into private pews unless asked. The minister is not afraid to pray for our absent soldiers, notwithstanding the church is crowded with Yankees.

It is said there are several cases of Yellow Fever in Natchez.

Now, my dearest husband, I must close my letter. I pray for you unceasingly.

Accept all the ardent love of your "Little Wife."

Margarette

The Union soldiers, an annoyance and an inconvenience to the town's people, were nevertheless, for the most part, remarkably well behaved during the first year of the occupation.

There were families whose homes and lives remained almost undisturbed, most of these being openly friendly to the enemy. Some had always been Unionists, but as Margarette commented in her letter to Will, there were those who had been turned by the occupation from "good Secessionists" into "warm Unionists."

The Federal officers were lavishly entertained in many of the Natchez homes. One of the grandest of these was that of Mr. and Mrs. Frank Surget, Clifton, which was located near its sister mansion, Rosalie, on the highest point of the river bluff, a red-brick, white-columned palace filled to overflowing with priceless pieces of art. Bluecoated officers often strolled about its elaborately landscaped grounds at afternoon garden parties, took tea on the private dock on the river, or sipped vintage wine from the Surgets' well-stocked cellars as they admired the original paintings and sculpture of world-renowned artists.

John Walworth had little patience with such fraternizing. "I think the Surgets are behaving like fools. Even if their sympathies are Unionist, they shouldn't flaunt them," he observed to his wife.

"Well now, John," protested Sarah, "I feel sorry for Lottie! I really do. I'm sure Frank makes her do it."

"That's just what Mrs. Sessions told me," said Rebecca. "She said Mrs. Surget is quite distressed about the reputation they're getting. She says she can't bear to go to church because of all the looks and whispers. I do feel sorry for her."

A few days later Rebecca was in the pantry arranging a bouquet with some of the fall flowers she had just gathered from the garden. She was absorbed in her task when she suddenly became aware of another presence in the room. She looked around and standing at her elbow was Lessie, one of Esther's children. The little black girl was watching her, her small face serious and intent.

"Well, hello, Lessie. Do you like flowers?"

A nod.

"Well, how do they look? Did I make a nice bouquet?"

Again a nod.

Rebecca stood back to survey her work. Then she picked up another flower. "I think it needs something else right here," she said.

A small black finger pointed to another spot. "Here," said Lessie.

"Oh, well, all right, let's try that. Why, I believe you're right, Lessie. That's exactly what it needed. You have a very artistic eye."

The small face lit up, and the full, soft lips curved with pleasure.

"Lessie, Lessie, where are you anyway? I can't never find you when I need you. You are the most good for nothing child I ever did see," Esther's impatient voice came from the kitchen and Lessie's happy smile gave way to a guilty look. Esther was much too hard on the child, Rebecca thought, but she was her mother, and one didn't like to interfere too much.

"Here she is, Esther. She's helping me," called Rebecca and Lessie gave her a dazzlingly grateful smile.

"Oh, yes'm, I'm sorry, Miss Rebecca. I was just trying to get dinner ready. It's 'most two o'clock."

"Is it really that late? It must be time for Mr. John to come home. Maybe he'll have a letter from Mr. Douglas today. I must go and see." She smiled at Lessie. "Thank you for helping me. I'll get you to do it again."

John Walworth had brought no letters from town, but he did bring a story, which he repeated to his family at the dinner table.

"There's a rumor circulating that Clifton is to be destroyed to make way for a Federal fort."

"Clifton?" everybody cried out together in amazement.

"I heard it from more than one source. I imagine the rumor was started out of spite. The Surgets have made so many enemies lately. Anyway it's all over town. Nobody can talk about anything else."

"But when the Surgets have wined and dined the Yankees like royalty why in the world would they destroy Clifton?" protested Rebecca.

Margarette Martin had more information to impart when Rebecca and the Walworths arrived at Linden late that afternoon to have tea with her mother and sister. Sarah and John came in their carriage with their two older grandchildren while Uncle Perry drove Rebecca and her two sisters-in-law in her carriage.

After one of the hot, muggy days, which was not unusual in October, a sudden shower had come up. The big oaks in their grove in front of the house dripped now with rain as well as moss. A yellowish gray sky thinly veiled the setting sun, letting through just enough of its rays to give the world an unearthly glow.

A pair of birds calling to each other made a melancholy music like the cries of woodwinds, and the low rumble of distant thunder provided an accompaniment of muffled drums, it seemed to Rebecca, as the two carriages crunched slowly through the wet gravel of the drive. The glistening black trunks of the trees stood out from their ghostly surroundings like sturdy pieces of reality, and were somehow comforting. They were something solid that one could hold to. The atmosphere of unreality was disturbing to Rebecca. Her whole life seemed so unreal to her lately. It seemed impossible that she was living through a war, that Douglas was away fighting it, and that Natchez was an occupied city. Three years ago she would not have believed that any of these things could happen. What would the next three years bring? She knew that nothing would ever be the same again.

Clara sat beside her dreaming her own dreams, but they were happy ones. Soon the War would be over, and she and Ross would marry and live in Atlanta. She had his last letter tucked in the bosom of her white voile shirtwaist where the feel of it warmed her flesh and her heart. The rain-drenched grove looked appealing and romantic to her. The birds calling to each other through the mist were lovers, who would soon be reunited just as she and Ross would. The thunder was the War, a menacing undercurrent, but she brushed that thought aside. It had no place in a young girl's dreams.

Laura gazed out of the window on her side thinking similar thoughts.

The three young women were so wrapped in their reveries that when the carriage pulled to a stop at Linden's front steps, nobody moved.

"Come, come, young ladies, Uncle Perry is standing in the rain waiting for you," called John, resting his dripping umbrella in the large stand by the front door.

"As much as we need this rain, couldn't it have waited until after teatime?" Jane Conner stood in the door greeting her guests, who were busily shedding their rain gear. She had aged rapidly in her years of widowhood. Her hair was completely white now and her face deeply lined.

"I believe it's about to stop now, though, so let's sit on the gallery. Margarette, would you ask Thornton to bring the tea out there?"

"All right, Mother, but don't you dare say a word about Clifton until I get back."

"What about Clifton?" Laura and Clara asked in chorus.

"Some gossip Margarette heard at D'Evereux today when she went to dinner there. Sarah, dear, I do hope you're feeling better than I am. This weather is so dreadfully bad for our joints. I don't expect to feel well again until June!"

Lucy and John scampered off with their little Martin cousins, and the adults seated themselves in the cane-bottomed rocking chairs that were placed in a line well to the back of the deep gallery, out of reach of the driving rain.

The remains of the fall roses were scattered all over the ground.

"How lovely roses in the rain smell!" Clara drew a deep, ecstatic breath, wriggling her straight little nose with pleasure.

"Well, enjoy it to the fullest because you won't be smelling any more roses until next spring," said John Walworth.

Margarette joined them, followed by Thornton carrying

the huge silver tea pot and another servant with a tray full of tiny sandwiches.

"Maggie," said Rebecca, "what is it you know about Clifton?"

"We've heard it's going to be demolished," said Laura.

"It's true! The Yankees are perfectly serious about destroying Clifton," Margarette replied, eager to tell her tale. "They're going to dynamite it! They gave the Surgets twenty-four hours' notice. It will be done tomorrow morning."

"I just can't believe it!" Rebecca exclaimed.

"Nor can I! I never heard anything so shocking! Clifton is practically a museum. Why would they do such a thing?" asked Sarah. "And to the people who have done so much for them!"

Jane Conner shook her head. "Clifton may be ideally situated for a fort, but it's certainly not the only spot they could use."

"Well, if they must have the perfect spot, it seems to me they should have chosen Rosalie. It's on the exact site of old Fort Rosalie, and it has an equally commanding view of the river, doesn't it, John?" Sarah turned to ask her husband, who had had nothing to say on the subject.

"All I can say is I'm glad I didn't count on Yankee gratitude."

"You haven't let me finish," said Margarette, quite shamelessly enjoying herself. "Mrs. Surget told Mrs. Linton that the order was personally signed by the chief engineer, whom it so happens she forgot to invite to that dinner party last week!"

"So there's the reason for the fort!" cried Sarah.

"Nonsense. This is a war, my dear, not a tea party. I will not believe an officer of the United States Army capable of being motivated by such trivia!" John Walworth dismissed the idea summarily.

The ladies were not so sure.

"If it isn't true, it's quite a coincidence, John," said Jane Conner. "Nothing about it makes any sense. They don't have to blow up that beautiful house to build a fort. There's plenty of room for both."

"I don't think we've heard the whole story," said Rebecca.

"And what's more, we never will," added John Walworth.

He was right. The mansion was dynamited to bits the next day, and for some reason the fort was never built.

CHAPTER SEVENTEEN

THE creation of the Military Division of the Mississippi and the transfer of the popular General Gresham brought a new order to the occupied city of Natchez, or rather a new disorder. There was little visiting about or going to dinner or tea at one another's homes by the town's folk now. Under the new regime there seemed to be no interest in protecting the persons and property of the citizenry. Theft and arson were common and went unpunished. Jeers and insults were directed at anyone who ventured out of their homes. The younger black men, including Esther's husband, Anderson, had either been conscripted, or had run away. Rank and file soldiers and the black men, who were put into uniform, roamed the streets, drunk and disorderly, answerable to no one. In addition to the vandalism, theft, and arson, there were ominous reports of rape.

Clara, Laura, and Rebecca became prisoners, never leaving the grounds of Elmo. And even there they were not completely assured of safety. Soldiers often came up to beat on the door and demand food or whiskey. It was better for young and attractive women to stay out of sight. All any of them lived for these days were the letters that came from time to time.

Clara sat on the steps that stretched across the front of Elmo waiting for her father to come back from town. In spite of the dangerous conditions, he went into town every day to visit with friends. Since the newspapers had been shut down, there had sprung up a grapevine of news of a hearsay quality, which was better than nothing, and there were certain sources who smuggled letters in and out of the lines.

She knew she wasn't supposed to be out in front of the house, but she couldn't help it. If she saw any blue uniforms, she would scurry inside.

As soon as she saw the unmistakable, erect figure of her father, tiny in the distance, walking up the road toward Elmo, Clara ran all the way to the gate to meet him. Behind her came Sarah, Rebecca, and Laura, all of whom must have been watching from the house. Of course there was only a slight possibility that any letters had gotten through.

"I do wish he would walk a little faster," murmured Sarah.

"Look," cried Rebecca, "he's holding up a letter! Oh, my goodness, I think there are two of them!"

Clara was already unlatching the gate, and she and Rebecca ran ahead to meet John, who handed one of the letters to Clara.

"I'm afraid there was nothing from Douglas this time," he said to Rebecca, "or from Ernest," he added.

The light went out of Rebecca's eyes, and she gave a small sigh. Then she smiled at Clara. "Well, I'm happy for you, and I guess the other one must be for Laura so that's good news for her."

Clara took her letter to the only spot in the crowded house where she had found she could have absolute privacy, the little crow's nest on the top of the house, which had become her secret hideaway.

She seated herself in a corner on the bench inside the railing, and only then did she glance at the envelope. It said, "Miss Clara Walworth," but it was not Ross' handwriting, although it was quite similar. She slit the envelope open with her fingernail, and drew out a single sheet of stationery. The letter began:

My dear Miss Clara,

It is my painful duty to inform you that our son, your fiancé, Ross, was killed last July during the battle of Gettysburg. We have just now received word of it. It is an unspeakable loss to us all, and I extend to you the sincerest sympathy from our grieving hearts. It is, I think, no small comfort that he died in the service of our Cause.

Clara sat staring at the words, her heart rejecting them, refusing to let them sink below the surface. How odd, she thought, my whole life is over, but it doesn't hurt at all.

In a few minutes it would be time to join the family at dinner. They would ask her about the letter. What would she tell them? There was no way she could say the words. And she wanted no words of sympathy from them. She wanted only to be left alone. She wanted not to talk about it or to think about it.

She heard them calling to her. Calmly she walked down the steps and into the dining room where they were all gathered. She handed the letter from Mr. Sanford to her father without a word, then she ran all the way back up to her rooftop refuge, the protective paralysis of her shock at last penetrated, exposing a raw grief that was cataclysmic and total. She was attacked by tidal waves of agony that washed over her, battering her with ever-increasing force. She was amazed and almost pleased to know that she was capable of such intense feeling. But how, how can I stand it, she thought? Suddenly her heart took refuge in disbelief. It was a horrible mistake. It was untrue. She would not believe it. It had been months since Gettysburg; Ross couldn't have been dead when she was writing to him every day! She had even received some letters from him in those months. It was absolutely impossible. No, she would not believe it. But her mind would not let itself be fooled. It spoke now sternly to her heart. It is true, and you must accept it.

And so she tried to face the truth, but it was no good. She would not believe it. Maybe later she would believe it, but not now. Now it was necessary to think of nothing, to feel nothing. She could scarcely exert the energy to breathe, and it hurt when she did. She must just stay completely still and think of nothing. And even then the huge, aching lump inside, which was her heart, would not stop hurting.

John Walworth sat holding the letter which Clara had handed him. He had no need to read it. He knew what it must contain. Somehow they all knew. Even the children, little Lucy and John, knew to keep quiet, that something serious had happened. Uncle Perry stood like a statue holding the platter of food he had brought from the kitchen.

Sarah broke the silence finally, her voice trembling a little. "What does the letter say, John? Is it from Ross?"

"I—I haven't my glasses." John handed the letter to Rebecca, who was seated beside him. "Will you read it for us, my dear?"

Rebecca took the piece of paper from him as carefully as if it had been a poisonous snake, and in an even, expressionless voice she read the letter to them.

"Oh, my! Oh, my poor baby!" Sarah moaned softly. "How will she take this? His letters have become everything in the world to her. This is going to be so hard for her. She's too young to face this kind of tragedy. Oh, how I hate this war!"

Laura looked down at her plate. Suppose my letter had said that, she thought, instead of that Will has gotten a leave and is going to try to get through the lines and see me somehow?

"John, I think I should go to her," Sarah said uncertainly.

"Give her a few moments alone first, Mother Walworth," urged Rebecca.

"Rebecca is right, my dear," said John. "I don't think she wants to see anyone right now. Let's go ahead with our dinner and later on you can offer help and consolation."

"Well, all right, I guess you're right. I just can't bear to think of her having to face this." Sarah sighed and glanced toward Uncle Perry, who came forward at the unspoken signal, and began to serve the dinner, his solemn bearing and demeanor conveying his sympathy and concern.

It was one of the children who finally discovered her. After the difficult dinner had been gotten through and Uncle Perry had carried out the plates of half-eaten food, Sarah had gone to the room, which Laura and Clara shared, looking for Clara, and when she had not found her there the family had begun a search, which Lucy and John had joined in with enthusiasm.

I know where she might be, thought Lucy with sudden inspiration, and she ran up to the tower. She found Clara there sitting on the bench, pale and strangely calm.

"Aunt Clara, everybody's been looking for you everywhere. Are you all right?"

"Yes, Lucy, I'm all right. I'm sorry everyone's been worried. I just needed to be by myself for a while. Tell Grandma I'm going to be all right, and that I'll be down in a little while."

After Lucy had gone, she had another little visitor, a black one. It was Lessie, one of disagreeable Esther's children. The child stuck out her hand awkwardly. In it was a piece of cake, half-wrapped in a napkin.

Clara found this gesture oddly comforting.

"Thank you, Lessie. What a kind and helpful thing for you to do!"

With a shy smile Lessie vanished, leaving Clara wondering what to do with the cake. Since she could think of no other absolutely safe means of disposing of it, she ate it, forcing it down crumb by crumb.

In the weeks that followed, Clara found that she was able to go through the motions of living. After she had cried once in her mother's arms and once in Rebecca's, she had kept her tears to herself, but as the days rolled relentlessly by she came to know an even more terrible sorrow. Unlike the violent anguish of those first hours, it was quiet and deep, a sorrow which no amount of tears could dispel or soften, the pain of which relaxed its grip only when she was exhausted. And there was nothing to cure it. The eagerly awaited letters would never come again. The mischievous brown eyes that she had loved so much would not tease her anymore. No laughter would ever delight her heart as Ross' had. No mind could be so in tune with hers. The sparkling spirit which had danced her to the very gates of paradise was gone where she could not follow. Or, could she? There was a thought!

She continued to seek sanctuary in the crow's nest, and one day the thought of ending the painful and hopeless succession of interminable days that her life had become seized her imagination and she thought how easy it would be to fling herself off of the roof and put an end to it all.

She recoiled in horror from the dreadful and sinful thought. But after all, why not? There was nothing for her to live for. Then she saw the agonized faces of her mother and father as plainly as if she had done the deed. She knew she could never deal them such a blow. And, oh, even if it were not for them she guessed she could never destroy herself because, well, because there was beyond everything else a duty to life itself, to the creator who had given her her life. Whether I'm happy or not doesn't matter. As hard as it is, I guess I must go on living.

In spite of her brave words Clara did not go up to Elmo's tower again.

CHAPTER EIGHTEEN

CHRISTMAS in Natchez in 1863 was a generally sad and dreary affair. The men couldn't get through the lines to be with their families. People hesitated to venture very far from their homes for any reason, exposed as they were to humiliation, robbery and possible physical harm.

Uncle Perry and John Walworth put up a tree at Elmo for the children, and some handmade gifts were exchanged, but none of the adults had the heart for much celebrating. Clara said to Rebecca, "Thank goodness for your children! What would we do without them?"

They did go on Christmas Eve to a family party at D'Evereux, the home of Rebecca's Aunt Anna and her husband, St. John Eliot.

The children were invited, too, and they were thrilled to be included in a nighttime party. Rebecca dressed them in their velvets, which had to be let out as far as the seams and hems would allow. There was no money to spend on new ones, and anyway there was very little material in the stores, certainly nothing so fine as velvet. Daisy and Annie, who had grown the fastest, were stuffed into their dresses with all the buttons straining, and Daisy had complained that she couldn't even breathe, but they felt very grand.

Clara surveyed her wardrobe and decided that there was really nothing to wear but her red taffeta. She was not officially in mourning, of course, and it wouldn't have been proper to wear black. But red? Oh, what difference does it make, she asked herself? Perhaps it would make her look more cheerful. At least it looked like Christmas.

Laura hadn't heard anything from Will McPheeters in weeks and neither had his parents so she, too, was quite depressed. As she and Clara were dressing she said to her sister, "I wish we didn't have to go to this party. There'll be nobody there but old people and children anyway!" Then she saw Clara's face and felt terribly ashamed of herself. She knew she ought not to act that way when she at least had the hope that Will was alive!

The Walworth carriages drove up to the St. John Eliots' stately white house looming grandly in the moonlight. Clara thought, "We might have gone in a circle and come back to where we started from. D'Evereux is exactly like Elmo. I wonder if Mrs. Eliot really liked having Rebecca and Douglas copy her house. I guess it was a compliment, but I wouldn't want to have a house just like somebody else's."

The doorway and the iron balcony above it were festooned with ropes of boxwood, and light streamed from the long windows. The Eliots were noted for their beautiful and elaborate parties when D'Evereux was always illuminated by hundreds of candles. Of course tonight's party was only a family gathering and would have to be much less lavish anyway on account of the War.

Mr. and Mrs. Eliot stood in the hall greeting their guests. They were a handsome and dignified pair, both tall and silvery haired, austere, but gracious in manner.

Clara had often heard both her father and Douglas speak with admiration of St. John Eliot. He had been a great supporter and friend of the famous statesman, Henry Clay, and Henry Clay had always stayed at D'Evereux when he came to Natchez.

His wife, Anna, was the sister of the late William Conner. She was childless and so was his other sister, Margaret Conner Wood, the wife of Spencer Wood. The Woods lived in the country near Natchez on their plantation, Black Hawk. The two couples were devoted to their sister-in-law, Jane Conner, and her children. Rebecca and Margarette had spent almost as much time growing up at D'Evereux and at Black Hawk as they had at Linden.

Both St. John Eliot and Spencer Wood had opposed secession, and Spencer Wood had quietly remained loyal to the United States throughout the War. Too old to go to war himself and having no sons to send, he had not been forced into the position of having to declare himself. He and his wife had stayed at Black Hawk until just recently, when the unrest generated among the negroes by the occupation of the surrounding area had convinced him that it was not safe for his wife to stay by herself at the plantation when he had to be away from the house so much. His negroes had remained loyal, however, and he was still attempting to farm his land in spite of the surrounding chaos, so he brought his wife to D'Evereux to stay with her sister, while he, himself, commuted back and forth through the lines by means of a special permit.

Anna Eliot sent the excited children to select packages from under the tree and directed her older guests to the dining room where her sister, Margaret Wood, was presiding over a magnificent silver punch bowl filled with frothy clouds of egg nog.

When they returned to the parlor they found Jane Conner and Margarette Martin in agitated conversation with Spencer Wood.

After greetings had been exchanged, Anna Eliot explained, "Jane and Margarette have had trouble at Linden."

Jane Conner elaborated, "I had to discharge Thornton for insolent conduct, which is most regrettable as it leaves us nothing but a household of women at Linden."

"Did you and Margarette and the children drive over here by yourselves?" asked John Walworth.

"Yes, Mr. Walworth. We drove over before dark with the hope that somebody will follow us home. I told Mother that I refused to let the Yankees make me a prisoner on Christmas Eve!" said Margarette.

"I think you ought to stay here tonight. We'd love to have you," urged Anna Eliot.

"But our presents are at home!" cried one of the little Martins in dismay.

"Thank you, Anna, but I believe we'll be all right at home," said Jane.

"I think we'll be all right tonight, too," agreed Margarette, "but I've made up my mind now that I want to leave Natchez. Mr. Martin has been trying to persuade me to move out to a small town in Alabama called Evergreen. Some friends of ours from Vicksburg have gone there, and they know of a family who could take us in. It's out of the Federal lines, and I could not only hear from him frequently, but I could write to him without being afraid of my letters being read by our enemies or of me being arrested for the crime of writing to my husband! And I should even be able to see him occasionally." Margarette glanced at her mother. "But Mother doesn't want to go, and I certainly can't leave her at Linden alone."

"My dear," exclaimed Anna Eliot, "that is no problem. Your Uncle Eliot and I would love to have your mother come to stay here at D'Evereux with us."

"Thank you, Anna, but I really couldn't do that. You don't need another refugee." Jane Conner was quite adamant.

St. John Eliot frowned and shook his head. "I really don't like the idea of you women and children alone at Linden. It's too isolated, and there's been a lot of trouble out that way. I think it would be a very good plan for you to come here and stay, and let Margarette go to Alabama if Will wants her to."

"What do you think of my going to Alabama, Uncle Wood?" Margarette asked Spencer Wood. She had always been his pet.

"Well, when you first spoke of wanting to leave Natchez I thought it was a rather drastic and unnecessary step, but I find I'm changing my mind about a lot of things these days. It may be that it's the best thing for you to do."

"I would hate to leave my house sitting empty, and at the mercy of vandals, like Monteigne," demurred Jane.

"It seems to me your safety is the most important thing," said John Walworth, and Rebecca added, "Indeed it is, Mother. I hope whatever you decide to do, that you and Margarette won't continue to stay at Linden by yourselves."

"Promise me that you will give this some serious thought, my dear Jane," said St. John Eliot.

"All right," agreed Jane reluctantly. "I'll think about it. I don't want to stand in the way of Margarette and the children leaving if they want to go, and I know that General Martin is most anxious that they should do so."

"Well, now, we must forget the War, and all our problems, and remember that it's Christmas Eve," said Anna. "Rebecca, will you play some Christmas carols for us so that we can sing?"

They gathered around the ornately carved grand piano, a troubled group, the candlelight flickering on their anxious faces. Then as they began to sing the familiar songs with their messages of hope, it lifted their hearts a little in spite of everything.

CHAPTER NINETEEN

JOHN Walworth sat in the library at Elmo in the tall leather wing-back chair that had become "Grandpa's chair." He was reading Douglas' letter again. It had been written in March. Here it was May and they had just received it. The letter was addressed to him. Douglas spoke of a visit he had just made to Margarette Martin and her children in Evergreen, Alabama, where they seemed so happy and pleased with their arrangements. He went on to urge his father that they all leave Natchez: "From what Margarette tells me, Elmo is no place for any of you, particularly ladies, and more especially sisters. I do most earnestly urge you to consider some asylum for all of you outside of Natchez, but if you cannot agree with me I beg of you to make an effort to send Rebecca and the children. Perhaps she can raise the means by the sale of furniture or jewelry or anything else she may possess to enable her to come out with the children to join Margarette in her location with Mr. and Mrs. Miller. I assure you she can live cheaply and happily there."

John Walworth sighed heavily. It was true. The situation in Natchez grew worse every day. It was completely out of hand. The women of his household didn't dare go out of the house and even he hesitated to venture on the streets now. It was a miserable way to live.

But leave Natchez? Uproot his frail little wife again, leave their familiar surroundings, set out on a long and arduous journey under no telling what sort of conditions, to go to a strange place where there very probably would be few comforts? It was one thing for young people to do that, but entirely another matter for people of their age.

He supposed Rebecca and the children should go since Douglas wanted them to. They could go to Evergreen and stay at the Millers' with Margarette and her children. Perhaps Laura and Clara should go with them. Douglas was right that Elmo was a very dangerous place for young ladies now. Its proximity to the fortifications meant that soldiers were always about. The girls couldn't even walk around the grounds without encountering them. Of course many of the Union troops were undoubtedly fine young men, who would mean them no harm. But this was not always the case and some of the incidents which had taken place lately went beyond mere unpleasantness to more serious and even criminal acts.

John looked thoughtfully out of the window which was beside his chair. The library was at the back of the house and the window commanded a view of Elmo's sloping grounds and the woods that lay beyond, lacy and green now that spring had been around a good two months.

Something was moving in those woods! John felt a coldness seeping through him. He had an intuitive knowledge that a man and not an animal was out there. In the next moment he saw that he was right. Oh, good God, it was a soldier! The man slipped under the rail fence and ran in a furtive darting fashion to a hiding place behind one of the out buildings.

John had rehearsed this moment in his own mind many times. He knew just what he should do. His pistol was in the locked drawer of Douglas' desk. John kept that key with him at all times, and he unlocked the drawer now and took out the pistol, which he kept unloaded because of the children. Quickly he slid some bullets into the empty chamber. Then he went to look for Uncle Perry. The kitchen was connected to the house by a covered walk and with the gun concealed inside his coat he strode out onto the back gallery and toward the kitchen. The soldier remained in his hiding place.

Uncle Perry was polishing some brass andirons. Aunt Chloe and Esther were busy ignoring each other as usual. John spoke to them casually and then said to Uncle Perry with a long, significant look, "We have a visitor, and I need your help. Bring the andirons. They don't need any more polishing."

"Yessir, Mr. John." Uncle Perry followed John back to the house, an andiron in each hand.

As they stepped inside the central hall John turned to Uncle Perry. "I saw a man in uniform run from the woods out back to behind the spring house. We'll wait for him in here. I don't want any trouble if we can help it."

Uncle Perry took a deep breath. "Yessir, Mr. John."

Clara stood frozen at the head of the stairs. She had just started to go downstairs when she heard her father tell Uncle Perry about the soldier. With sudden inspiration she turned and tiptoed to the flight of stairs that led to the crow's nest. She ran as quietly as an Indian scout up to the top of the house and on her knees, she peered through the balustrades of the "widow's walk." The soldier was slipping across the lawn, coming toward the house. Her heart gave a lurch. He looked so familiar somehow. He looked like Will McPheeters, that was who he looked like! But he had on a blue uniform.

Clara flew down both flights of stairs, startling her father and Uncle Perry, who were both standing, grim and tense, watching the blue-coated figure slithering across the back gallery.

"It's Will McPheeters! Don't shoot him! I'm sure it's Will McPheeters! At least I'm almost sure," she whispered breathlessly to them.

"Who is out there?" John called out.

"It's me, sir, Will McPheeters. I've come to see Laura."

John laid his pistol on the petticoat table in the hall. Uncle Perry stood holding the andirons. "Thank the good Lord," he murmured.

Will walked in somewhat sheepishly, and John Walworth said, his voice shaking a little, "Well, I must say this is a most unusual way of paying a call."

Clara was already running up the stairs to get Laura.

Will had managed to get through the lines in his borrowed blue uniform. He had already seen his parents and had persuaded them to move out beyond the lines. They had some relatives in the country who had told Will they would be happy to have them come and stay with them. He wanted Laura to come with them and marry him.

Will had always been so shy that the family found it hard to believe he had done such a dashing thing, least of all Laura, but she liked his new masterful personality and felt quite swept off her feet. When he said, "Do you want to come with my family, Miss Laura?" she looked back at him, her lovely blue eyes shining with her pride in him as well as her love for him, and answered, "I do."

Clara thought, it's almost as if they're getting married right now.

"May I have your permission to marry Laura, Mr. Walworth?" Will asked with some apprehension.

"How do you feel about all this, my dear?" John asked Sarah.

"Oh, she must go, John," cried Sarah. "She must go!"

"There is your answer," John turned to Will and smiled. "You have my permission and my blessing," he hesitated and added, sighing, "and my prayers."

Clara's face registered sudden alarm. "I believe I hear horses."

Everyone heard them now. Laura uttered a little shriek and then clapped her hand to her mouth.

"Oh, John, what shall we do?" cried Sarah in panic.

"Everyone go upstairs. Take Will and hide him somewhere, anywhere. Let me handle this." John looked them over and catching Clara's eye, added, "Clara, I'm placing you in charge. You decide what to do upstairs. Now go! As fast as you can!"

When everybody had vanished up the stairs at his command, John peered out of the front window. Just as all of them had feared it was a Union officer. Accompanying him was the usual black man in a blue uniform. They were hitching their horses to the post.

Moments later boots thumped heavily up the steps and across the gallery and the door knocker was banged several times.

John was gripped by the same deadly coldness he had felt earlier, and he suddenly remembered the pistol he had left lying on the hall table. He reached for it, but it wasn't there. Maybe Will had seen it and taken it with him. He certainly hoped so.

The knocker was banged again and John steeled himself to face whatever awaited him. He opened the door.

"I believe this is the home of the rebel, Douglas Walworth," began the insolent young officer. "Is that a true fact?"

"This is the home of my son, Douglas Walworth, and I am John Walworth," responded John in his iciest tone.

"Well, we're here to inspect this place for the United States Army and see as to its suitability for a negro barracks." It seemed to John that the young officer took an obscene pleasure in delivering this message, and that the black man was leering at him all the while. He had never needed his self-control more than he needed it now.

He stood carefully and disdainfully to one side. "I see that you feel the need of no invitation."

An inspection of the house was the last thing they needed right now, but John was smart enough to know that any resistance would provoke increased determination and perhaps suspicion. The best thing that could be hoped for was a wide-ranging but superficial inspection.

He put from his mind for the moment the implications for the future of this unwelcome visit.

The tour went as John had expected and hoped. They

never even went upstairs. A great deal of time was spent in the kitchen, and the officer came back to report to John.

"We'll need your house, sir, in about twenty-four hours. I suggest you start packing up. We'll also need your man, Perry. He is to come with us. I've sent him to get his things. And now good day to you."

"Are you taking him against his will?" asked John.

"Why not?" asked the officer. "That's a strange question coming from a slave owner!" He walked out the door, slamming it behind him.

John went to the kitchen, not even stopping to tell them upstairs that the danger was over. Indeed he wasn't sure that it was yet.

He found Uncle Perry with tears streaming down his mahogany cheeks, utterly distraught.

"Mr. John, what am I going to do? They want me to work in the hospital. They tell me I have to go. They're waiting for me at the gate."

John put his arm around Uncle Perry's shoulders. "I'd sooner part with my right arm than you. I'll try to appeal this to the military court. I guess you'll have to go now, but we'll see if we can't work something out."

John had an uneasy feeling that he was making a mistake, that he ought to insist that Uncle Perry not leave, but he couldn't risk a scene just now, not until Will got safely on his way. At least, he told himself, Uncle Perry would be in a safe place at the hospital. He would have enough food and decent living accommodations unlike those poor run-aways who were quartered Under-the-Hill.

Here he was wasting time on regrets when there were so many things to be done! He sprang into action.

"Clara," he called to his daughter, and she appeared instantly at the top of the stairs. "They've gone. All they wanted was Elmo and Uncle Perry. Tell Will to get on his way. We've got to start packing."

Good Lord! What have we come to, thought John Walworth, when I'm relieved to hear that what they want is to take my son's house for a negro barracks!

CHAPTER TWENTY

AFTER Will was safely on his way the family gathered in the parlor to discuss their plight.

"Where in the world can we go?" Sarah tried to keep the quaver out of her voice. "Will and Sue haven't any room for us and my sister has been put out of her house, too. And there are so many of us!"

"Well, you don't have to worry about me," said Laura. "The McPheeters will take care of me!"

"Yes, thank goodness," sighed John Walworth. "I suppose you can just pack up your things and go straight there."

"Well, I guess the children and I will go to Alabama and join Margarette as soon as it's possible," said Rebecca.

"I think we should all go there," said John. "There is nothing to hold us in Natchez any longer, and we might as well get out of the Union lines where Douglas and Ernest can write to us and visit us, and we can have some peace of mind. I never want to see another Union officer!"

"But we can't just go to Alabama," remonstrated Clara. "We have to go somewhere first."

"That's true," said Rebecca. "I'll have to write Margarette and see if the Millers still have room for us. They may have taken in some other boarders. But I'm sure she can find something for all of us. Although I don't know how expensive another place might be. Perhaps we should sell some of our furniture if we can get it out in time."

"Oh, my dear!" Sarah looked shocked.

"Well, we might as well sell it as leave it here," sighed Rebecca.

"I have my jewelry. We can sell some of it if we need to." Sarah was not to be out-sacrificed.

"We have a little money and we can borrow some," said John. "Let's not act hastily."

"But we do need to hurry and pack up what we can here so we must decide where to go first," said Clara.

"You're absolutely right. That is the problem we must deal with now. Has anybody got any ideas? I don't seem to have any."

"Perhaps we could open up Linden," suggested Rebecca.

"No," Sarah spoke up firmly. "Jane has boarded it up and laid it to rest. I don't want her to have to go through all that again."

"Let's talk to Uncle Eliot and Uncle Wood and see what they can think of. There's a guest wing at D'Evereux. They might be able to take all of us there, at least until we can make arrangements to go to Alabama," Rebecca said to John Walworth.

"As much as I hate to impose on them we may have to do that. I'll go and talk to them while the rest of you begin to pack up. We don't have much time, you know."

John Walworth left, and the women began to deal with the problem of evacuating the accumulations of two households.

"I don't know where to begin," said Rebecca. "I guess first of all we need to notify the servants." She turned to her mother-in-law. "Mother Walworth, would you attend to that? Mammy Martha is upstairs with the children now so I will break the news to them. Laura and Clara can begin to get their things together. After we get everybody's clothes packed we can decide what to do about the household things, and about our silver and our most valuable possessions."

The suitcases and trunks were lined up on the front gallery of Elmo when John Walworth returned with the men servants and two wagons from D'Evereux.

"Anna and St. John Eliot have insisted that we come to D'Evereux. It is most gracious of them, and I see no other recourse, but to avail ourselves of their generosity," John told the women, who were busily engaged now in wrapping the fragile china and crystal. Noticing this he added, "They also said to bring what we could of our valuables and they will store them for us."

Rebecca looked up from her wrapping. "There's only one thing that I really care about, my Grandmother Gaillard's little spinet. I can't bear to leave it."

"It would be very difficult to take," said John.

"Oh, I know," sighed Rebecca, "and there's so much that we have to take."

"Maybe we could hide it somewhere," suggested Clara.

"Well, we couldn't put it in the cellar. The dampness would ruin it."

"We could put it in the upstairs storeroom and pile furniture and books and junk around it. It would be out of the way there, and it's not the sort of thing anybody can easily walk off with," said Clara.

"That's true," agreed John. "They're more apt to damage it than they are to steal it. Let's try that."

Clara was so glad they had been able to do at least that much for Rebecca.

John drove Laura to join the McPheeters after a brief but emotional farewell which left Sarah quite undone.

Rebecca and Clara decided that Sarah and Mammy Martha and all the children, including those of the servants, should go ahead to D'Evereux while the wagons were being loaded. It was then that Esther's absence was finally noticed. Neither she nor any of her younger children were anywhere to be found. An interrogation of her eldest daughter, little Lessie, resulted in the information that Esther had taken her children and run away to the Yankees. "Mama done gone away with those soldier men. I told her I didn't want to go. I told her I wanted to stay with my Grammy Martha and go wherever you go," she told Rebecca.

"Well, you certainly shall," promised Rebecca, gathering the little girl to her in a comforting embrace.

The last wagonload pulled away from Elmo. Only Aunt Chloe, John, Clara, and Rebecca were left now to ride in the carriage. John assisted Chloe into it and turned to the younger women. Clara, glancing toward her sister-in-law, held up a warning hand.

Rebecca stood at the foot of the gallery steps gazing at the house that she and Douglas had built, a look of infinite sadness on her face. Behind Elmo's proud facade with its lofty columns and sublime proportions the whole of her happy married life had been lived. So much living and loving had taken place within its walls. How could she leave it? The tears welled suddenly in her eyes and she thought, I may never see Elmo again. As she stood looking at the house her imagination played a weird trick on her. Elmo seemed to be going up in flames. She uttered a little cry and John and Clara were instantly at her side.

"My dear, are you all right?" asked John.

"Yes, yes, I'm fine. I don't know what happened to me. I thought I saw something. It was nothing. I'm perfectly all right. I'm ready to go now. Let's go right away."

Rebecca left without looking back. The image of her house in flames kept coming back, but she willed it away.

The carriages and their restless horses stood waiting at the front steps of D'Evereux to take the Walworths to Jackson, where they would board the train headed to Selma, Alabama. From there they would have to arrange transportation to Evergreen. It was early in the morning, the sun just rising, and a fresh, dewy quality was in the air. It was a beautiful time of day, but nobody had a moment to notice it. Instead everybody was very cross and preoccupied. Had they remembered everything? Where was the suitcase with the children's clothes? What about the medicine kit? Where was there room for the lunch basket and the water jug? Little John wanted to bring his stamp collection. Lucy needed to go back into the house for an important errand. Mammy Martha's voice was getting higher pitched with every second. Aunt Chloe was rearranging the luggage and muttering to herself. Sarah was as pale as a ghost. Daisy and Annie were fighting over their seats. John Walworth was standing on the gallery in serious conversation with St. John Eliot and Spencer Wood, while Rebecca and Jane Conner exchanged last minute messages and a tearful farewell.

Amid the furor Clara observed the little black girl, Lessie, standing by herself near the carriages. "Goodness what a hullabaloo! Come on, Lessie, hop in!" She gave her a boost up into one of the buggies. Poor little thing, but plucky little thing, too!

At last they started on their way. Anna and St. John Eliot, Margaret and Spencer Wood, and Jane Conner stood on the gallery waving goodbye, looking quite small and insignificant beside the tall columns.

The carriages swayed and bounced and finally D'Evereux disappeared. Little John and Lucy sat on the seat with the driver singing "Oh Susannah," but when they reached the part, "I come from Alabama," they substituted, "I'm gwine to Alabama!" They regarded the whole affair as a great adventure and were in the highest of spirits.

Listening to the music of their merry little voices, Clara thought again as she had at Christmas, thank goodness for the children!

Then she felt suddenly overcome with the realization of what was happening to them. They were going into exile. They would never be able to return to the Natchez they had known. If they ever came back, everything would be different. They had left Natchez behind and she hadn't even had time to say goodbye.

CHAPTER TWENTY-ONE

DOUGLAS' family had been settled in Evergreen, Alabama, for some time before he was able to come to see them. The war in Tennessee had been raging at a furious pace, and every man had been needed. Actually he was still needed, but he was not in shape for any more battles and neither was his horse. Will Martin, who had been promoted to major general following his courageous leadership against overwhelming odds at the Battle of Shelbyville, had insisted that he take a month's leave.

"Go rest some and be with your family, Douglas. You won't be any good to us if you don't. You're a sick man. You've never gotten over that last round of chills and fever. I'm going to take some time off, too, as soon as I can. I'll be joining you before long. Tell Margarette I'm fine and just need her to tell me off good and proper a few times to be completely happy."

So Douglas had begun his journey to the Alabama refuge that was now the only home he had. Travel was exhausting. The destruction of the railroads left gaps that had to be covered on foot or, if one was lucky, by wagon. Such trains as ran were both unpredictable and crowded to capacity.

When he finally reached Selma, he luckily was able to obtain a wagon ride all the way to Evergreen, a three days' journey.

A few hours later he reached the comfortable country house of the Millers. In minutes he would see his family. He realized that he felt nothing, no elation. He was completely numb inside. His deep exhaustion had been building for weeks, and was of the spirit as well as of the body. Suddenly he could go no farther. He sank down on the top step of the gallery, leaned back against a square wooden pillar, and closed his eyes. Clara found him there sound asleep, and when she realized the strange bearded man was her brother, she ran into the house to get her sister-in-law.

Rebecca rushed down from upstairs where she had been tending her children, all in bed with colds and fever, but she stopped in her tracks at the sight of her husband slumped against the post, so thin and pale and seedy that she hardly knew him. She tiptoed to his side, and knelt down, her hands clasped tightly together, her big beautiful eyes fastened on him in tenderness and anxiety. She couldn't bear to wake him. She stayed there beside him, perfectly still, until he stirred, and then started and opened his eyes. With a little cry she threw herself on him. He caught her to him, and they clung together in silence for a long time. Then Rebecca drew back and looked him over. "I must put you to bed right away. Can you make it up the stairs, do you think, or shall I get some help?"

"Oh, I'm all right. Just pretty tired. That's all. I do need a few hours' sleep."

"You certainly do. Let's don't waste any more time."

"Are Mother and Father and Clara here, too?" he asked as she helped him to his feet.

"Clara is here with Margarette and me and all the children. We've put the boys in one room and the girls in another. Mammy Martha and Lessie have their own quarters here. Your mother and father have rented a room in town and Aunt Chloe is with them. She's a great comfort to your mother." She did not tell him that his mother had been quite ill and that his father had aged shockingly. There was time enough for him to find out those sad things.

"Do you like Mr. and Mrs. Miller? I thought they seemed good people."

"We like them both. He's solid as a rock, a man of few words, but so kind and friendly, and she's a hearty, chatty, motherly soul. They both work all the time from dawn to dark, and we lead separate lives here under the same roof, sharing the same kitchen. It suits us all that way."

Douglas' last words before he drifted back into an exhausted sleep, which was almost the moment he sank into the softness of a real mattress with clean sheets on it, were a mumbled, "Then you are glad you came—you're happy here, Becky?"

"Very happy, Douglas. We're all so glad to be away from Natchez."

Douglas slept until noon of the next day, and when Rebecca offered to bring him his breakfast in bed he did not refuse.

He had not seen the children and now they tiptoed into his room, John proudly bearing the breakfast tray, followed by all the girls dressed in their night gowns, their throats wrapped in liniment-soaked scraps of flannel.

"You'll just have to look at them," Rebecca shook her head firmly as Douglas held out his arms. "I made them promise not to go near you and give you their colds. That's the last think you need."

"Just one hug apiece," pleaded Douglas.

Rebecca weakened. "Well, if they turn their faces away."

Lucy and Daisy ran to embrace their father, but Annie hid behind Rebecca, clutching at her skirt.

"Why, Annie!" remonstrated Rebecca.

"It's all right. She doesn't know me with my beard," Douglas laughed, and a feeling of release came over him. How long had it been since he had been able to laugh?

Reassured by his laughter, Annie peeped around Rebecca's skirt at the bearded man propped up in bed, and then she sidled to him, and he caught the little golden-haired girl up into his arms.

John stood gravely by the bed, waiting with the tray.

When Douglas had put Annie down, he placed it carefully on his father's knees.

"Did you get your promotion?" he asked.

"I did. Kindly address me as Major Walworth from now on."

John was beside himself with delight. "Yes, sir, Major Walworth," he replied with a snappy salute. He grabbed up his father's coat from the chair where it lay.

"I haven't had time to do any sewing I'm afraid, John."

"Just hand it here, little Johnny. Mammy Martha will sew the major's stripes on," a thin, whiny voice came from the door where Mammy Martha stood, as pleased and proud as John.

Rebecca sent the children out and sat beside Douglas, watching him devour his breakfast.

"I had no idea I was so hungry. Where in the world did you get this coffee? I don't know when I've had any real coffee!"

Rebecca smiled, "We save it for special occasions. Douglas, have you been ill?"

"No, not really. My hard ride on Wheeler's raid rather broke me down, but there's nothing seriously the matter. Nothing that a good rest and being with you won't take care of."

He reached out his hand to her, and when she took it he pulled her down onto the bed with him, upsetting the breakfast tray, which fortunately now held only empty dishes.

Rebecca told Douglas later as he was trimming his beard, which he had decided to keep, everyone having assured him that he looked so distinguished with it, and that it befitted his new rank, "I know Clara is anxious to see you. She shares this room with me, you know, and when she found you on the gallery yesterday afternoon she packed up her things and moved in with the girls. I don't know where she slept, most probably on the floor. She has been a great help to Margarette and me now that Mammy Martha is getting so feeble. When Daisy and Annie had such terrible temperatures one night, Clara bathed one little head while I bathed the other. Actually Mammy Martha, who I thought would be of no use to us at all, although, of course, we couldn't leave her behind, has been a help, too, with the meals, such as they are, and with the washing and ironing, as well as with the mending. Of course her stitches wander about wildly, but who cares? I do wonder what your coat will look like."

"It doesn't matter. The Rebel army strives more for warmth than style these days. Mammy Martha will make a perfectly adequate tailor. How is Clara? Still heartbroken about that young man?"

"Yes, I'm afraid so, although she tries hard to be cheerful, and I think that keeping busy and being with the children are good for her. Laura's marriage must have been difficult for her. I'm sure she couldn't help but compare their situations. I don't mean that she begrudges Laura and Will McPheeters their happiness, just that it was such a vivid reminder of all she has lost."

"Well, she must get over it. She's too young to take this so seriously."

"War ages people in a hurry, Douglas," replied his wife. "Clara's grief is very real and very deep. It would be a mistake to make light of it in any way."

Then she told him about his mother's illness and his father's sudden decline. "I hate having to tell you these things, but I feel I ought to prepare you, so it won't be such a shock when you see them. Thank goodness they have Aunt Chloe with them. She's as good a nurse as she is a cook. There seems to be no end to her talents."

"Yes, Aunt Chloe has always had a liking for nursing. She's picked up a lot from listening to doctors' instructions, and asking intelligent questions. Then, too, she knows about the medicinal uses of herbs, something she learned in her childhood on the plantation."

"Well, she's a wonderful woman. I respect her judgment as much as that of anyone I know."

"She is a wonderful woman, and so are you."

She put her arms around his neck, lifting her face to his. "I'm awfully glad you think so!"

Even though Rebecca had warned him about the changes he would find in his parents, Douglas was horrified to see the extent of their deterioration. His mother walked as though a feather could knock her down, dark circles ringed her eyes, and she seemed a little vague and forgetful. Of course she was just recovering from the ever-prevalent chills and fever, he told himself, but he wondered if she would ever be her old self again. His father certainly wasn't himself. He had an air of seeming not to know what to do next that was quite unlike him.

"Well," Douglas observed pensively to Rebecca, "I guess the War is changing us all. I know it's changing me. I've learned such a lot I never wanted to know, I've seen things I never wanted to see, and I've done things I never wanted to do. And there's no way to forget them or undo them. I suppose I'll just have to live with them."

Her first sight of Douglas had shocked Clara, and as the days went by she noticed how quiet and melancholy he had become. Thank God for Rebecca, she thought again and again. She's the only person who seems able to cheer him up, outside of maybe John or Annie, who do seem to be able to coax a little laugh out of him every now and then with their roguish ways.

Clara was discovering that Rebecca had become very important to her as well. Her sister, Laura, now married and living with the McPheeters in their refuge in Jefferson County, Mississippi, was inaccessible to her, and she had all but lost her mother as a confidante, feeling toward her now almost as a mother instead of as a daughter. Their roles seemed to have become reversed. Even her father's personality had changed with age and stress. He was no longer the tower of strength he had always been. It was especially disturbing to see him uncertain and helpless, a victim of events beyond his control.

If it had not been for Rebecca and Aunt Chloe, who never seemed to change, Clara would have felt very lonely indeed. How strong they are, and wise. I want to be like them, she told herself.

She had also grown deeply fond of the child, Lessie, Mammy Martha's great-granddaughter. Although she was John's age, and a year younger than Lucy, Lessie seemed much more adult in so many ways, and she spent most of her time after her chores were done with Mammy Martha or with Clara or Margarette, or most often with Rebecca, whom she obviously adored. She followed her everywhere and imitated her in many touching little ways. Rebecca and Lessie were always gathering wild flowers and making really spectacular bouquets with them.

Clara, remembering her own friendship with Naomi, wondered why Lessie didn't seem to want to play with the other children. Of course she was the only black child in the group, and Lucy and Margaret and Emily Martin were all older than she and thick as thieves, while John and the Martin boys had their own boyish pursuits. It was no wonder that Lessie felt shy and that she didn't fit in.

Clara had been impressed by Lessie's determination not to leave Elmo with her mother, Esther, and her younger brothers and sisters. True, Esther had often been harsh with the child, but nevertheless it couldn't have been easy for a ten-year-old girl to make such a decision and to take a stand against a domineering parent.

Late one lovely fall afternoon Clara paused beside the Millers' gate on her way home from having tea in town with her mother and father. The sun was setting beyond the stretch of brown fields across the way. She waited there, watching until it dipped out of sight below the rim of the horizon. Then she started up the walk to the house. Lessie was sitting on the steps, her chin cupped in her hands, looking up at the multicolored panorama of the sky as though somebody had just hypnotized her. She didn't even seem to see Clara.

How that child loves beauty, Clara thought. There's poetry in her if she could just express it. Clara looked back at the blazing sky. God's canvas, she thought. The sunsets had been gorgeous lately. She enjoyed their beauty, although it was painful to her, too, because the color of the setting sun always reminded her of Ross' radiant hair.

Sometimes Clara dreamed such vivid dreams of Ross that she awakened certain that he was still alive, and sometimes she pretended that he was. She imagined him appearing suddenly at Evergreen, sweeping her off of her feet and into his arms in a crushing embrace, kissing her again and again and again. When they could finally talk he would explain that he had gotten lost from his division and been captured and put in a Yankee prison from which he had just made his escape. Then they married in a simple ceremony under the big pecan tree on the Millers' front lawn, and drove away in a mule-drawn cart to spend their honeymoon in Greenville, the nearest city, or sometimes they went to a little cottage in the town of Evergreen. These fantasies gave her some escape from the stark realities of her life, but she was careful to remind herself that that was what they were, fantasies.

She tried not to think at all about the future. It was too depressing to bear. She had learned to live in the moment. She tried to keep busy and to be useful and somehow she got through the days. The nights, without hope, were the hardest part for her, and she invented all sorts of games to occupy her mind through the long sleepless hours.

Douglas' visit had been very good for their father, Clara noticed, and she told her brother so. "He needs man-talk. He's been so surrounded by all us women."

The two men spent long hours discussing the military situation.

"We get so little accurate news here. Tell me what you feel to be the truth about our position, Douglas," John said to his son.

"Well, Father, we may be wearing them down. They've taken some terrible losses in Tennessee, that's certain. Hood's army is well in the rear of Sherman, and he's destroyed his main line of communication, the railroad, very effectively. We're all hoping for good results from that bold move. The general opinion is that Sherman will either have to cut his way out or surrender."

"And what do you think he will do?"

"Well, most of us believe that he'll surrender."

"My God, I hope so." John Walworth's words were a prayer, not an epithet.

"General Beauregard is in command of our whole department now. His name is a talisman to us, and a terror to the enemy. As you know he fired the first gun, and we like to think that he'll fire the last as well."

"God grant it," said John, "and that this horrible carnage shall cease."

Doubt and dismay surged through Douglas in the silence that fell between them. He didn't really believe his own optimistic words. No, he didn't believe them at all, but he had to pretend that he did.

CHAPTER TWENTY-TWO

NEWS of the evacuation following the Battle of Atlanta reached them in Evergreen with surprising speed. It was a disaster of horrendous proportions. The worst had happened, and they all knew it, although nobody put it into words. There was nothing to be gained by saying it, and it was much too terrible to talk about.

Clara longed to know what had befallen Ross' family. She wondered if their home had been in the path of Sherman's destruction. Since it was outside of the city perhaps they had been able to stay there. She hoped so. Although she had never met them, she felt very close to them. Ross formed a bond between them even more in death than he had in life.

Douglas rejoined Wheeler's cavalry, now a tiny, tattered remnant, numbering about twenty-five hundred men, and when Hood set out from Georgia following the Battle of Atlanta on a campaign to recapture Tennessee and the psychological advantage, he left Wheeler and his men to guard Sherman. This guerrilla force was the only deterrent to Sherman and his 68,000 men when they set out on the brilliantly conceived, triumphant "March to the Sea." For days Douglas and the other hardened Confederate veterans, on their gallant, overworked and underfed horses, played a delaying game, nipping here and there at the heels of the giant centipede, which crawled relentlessly and inevitably to its destination at Savannah.

Douglas wrote in his diary:

Two new recruits joined us today, and we will soon have them saddled and put to work. It is distressing to me to see mere children such as these subjected to the travail and hardship of camp life, and especially to the demoralizing influences which encompass a soldier. It is the hardest blow to our country that the best in the land should be reared in such a school.

We are in close proximity to the enemy now, constant cannonading and skirmishing going on. The lines skirmish all night, and there is scarcely an instant in the day or night that the rattle of the small arms is not heard. The booming of the cannon echoes ceaselessly, and screaming shells go crashing and tearing through the woods.

Another entry began on a more cheerful note:

We had a most delightful windfall this evening which I make haste to record, as in the midst of so much bad news I am happy to be able to report anything of a pleasant nature. Our division was heatedly in pursuit of a division of Yankee cavalry all day. Late in the evening we came suddenly upon some landscaped grounds and a very fine house, so recently visited by the enemy that a cloud of dust still lingered behind their route of escape. We were so tired and near starved that we determined to stop for the night. We found a delicious supper, hot and waiting on the table. The Yanks had ordered it prepared for them. Our charming hostess, a Mrs. Bradley, assured us that the change in her guest list was not unwelcome, and we had a very merry time of it, enjoying every bite of the Yankees' supper. We even had a little blackberry wine.

I find I am too tired to write any more. I will just add that being in such a home, sitting at a table properly set, graced by a lovely woman, has made me long so for my wife that I almost wish we had not stopped here.

When Sherman reached the south Georgia coast, and sent his famous wire to Lincoln, presenting him Savannah as a Christmas present, he settled his men down there to rest out the winter, and Douglas and Will returned on their horses to Alabama.

It was a long, sad, difficult journey home through the desolated countryside. Finally they left behind the ravaged fields and charred ruins, but not the refugees, many of whom had fled to western Georgia and Alabama. Wagonloads of hungry, ill-clad children were a common sight along the road. Seeing them filled Douglas with an overwhelming sorrow. The bewildered, but trusting, little pinched faces lingered obstinately in his mind long after he had turned his eyes away.

When Douglas and Will finally arrived at Evergreen, Douglas was treated to an unexpected and joyous reunion with his brother, Ernest. Quite a few unashamed tears were shed, and the two brothers talked into the night, as tired as Douglas was, trying to catch up on everything that had happened in the long months since they had seen each other.

Ernest had much to tell. He had met a young lady named Mary, had fallen in love with her, and wished to marry her. He had no money and no prospects, but at this point who did? Mary lived in Kentucky just over the Tennessee border, and he was leaving in a few days to go there. Dared he ask her father's permission for them to marry? Look at Laura and Will McPheeters, and for that matter at Clara and her fiancé, Ross. Shouldn't one take what happiness one could in this uncertain world?

Douglas, thinking how differently he would have answered Ernest a few years ago, replied, "If the young lady is willing, marry her, Ernest. You certainly have my blessing, if that means anything."

Even John Walworth gave his blessing, and Ernest made ready to leave for Kentucky, but first a belated Christmas was celebrated in Evergreen.

Somehow in the eye of the storm there was not only calm, but an aura of warmth and love, of a strange sort of peace and happiness in the moment with no thought of past or future.

The family gathered for a ceremonial dinner at the Millers' house. Mr. and Mrs. Miller had thoughtfully declined the invitation to join them.

"Lord, honey, thank you, dear, but Mr. Miller and I will just go in town to my sister's for the day. You folks need to be together without no one else about. We had our Christmas dinner on Christmas day, Mr. Miller and me, and we will just leave you to yourselves," Mrs. Miller had said to Rebecca when she and Margarette had invited them.

The dinner was surprisingly delicious and bountiful, as Margarette commented, "Sort of a loaves and fishes affair." The men had shot a wild turkey and some quail, which Aunt Chloe's culinary art had rendered golden brown, tender, and juicy, and with them they had sweet potatoes, the ubiquitous cornbread, and even a little blackberry wine. Then a festive fig pudding awaited them for dessert.

Rebecca and Lessie, who seemed to be always at her side, had decorated the table with spicy evergreens heaped in baskets.

"I never saw a more Christmasy table," said Clara, and everyone agreed as they seated themselves around it.

"The cedar and pine smell so Christmasy," said Lucy.

Aunt Chloe placed the huge platter of game before John Walworth, and his grandson, who had shot two of the quail himself, said with obvious pride, "What about the way the turkey and the quail smell?"

Sarah, who was gradually recovering some strength, beamed at him. "Yes, Johnny, I can hardly wait to taste that quail you provided us with. It wouldn't have been much of a Christmas dinner without the birds you men brought us."

John Walworth rose, the family noted with a twinge of sadness, a little slowly and carefully. He was beginning more and more to show his age.

He held out his hands to them. "Let us offer thanks to almighty God." All heads bowed, and John prayed, "Our gracious, heavenly Father we offer Thee our praise and thanks for all Thy blessings, for this Christmas dinner, and for the great joy of being united with so many of our family, and we ask Thy special blessing on those members who are absent from us today. We thank Thee for the safe return of those who have been in such grave danger and who have endured such great hardships, and we pray that Thou wilt keep them safe through all future peril. Above all we thank Thee for Thy gift to us on that first Christmas, Thy Son, our Savior, Jesus Christ. Amen."

John's blessing left the group a little tearful, so Ernest, who detested tears, was quick to cheer everyone up with a toast. "To blackberries, bless their juicy little hearts!" he cried, raising his glass. They all laughed and took a sip of the wine, and John Walworth began to dispense the turkey and the quail.

There was much curiosity about Ernest's intended fiancée, and now Sarah asked him, "What is Mary like, Ernest? Tell us about her."

"Well, Mother," said Ernest, "to tell you the truth she's a little overweight, but she has such a temper I don't dare mention it to her. However I feel sure that after we're married she'll be so happy that the situation will soon correct itself."

Sarah looked, by turn, alarmed, relieved, and finally chagrinned. "Ernest, you are wicked to tease your poor old mother so! Now tell us what she's really like."

"Well, she's not the least bit overweight, but she does have a little bit of a temper, and she is utterly adorable when she's angry!"

Douglas shook his head. "Well, I hope you'll always think so."

Will grinned. "I expect he will."

"What does she look like?" asked Margarette Martin. "Now don't tell us that she can't smile because she's lost all her teeth, and that she wears a wig because she's bald as a billiard!"

Ernest smiled ecstatically, "She has beautiful white teeth, a dazzling smile, a little tilted nose, and the loveliest . . ." he glanced suddenly at Clara, paused and finished rather lamely, "blue eyes."

"What color is her hair?" little Lucy asked. "You didn't tell us that."

"It's red with glints of gold in it." He hated having to say it.

The silence was difficult, and Clara broke it. "She sounds beautiful, Ernest."

"Oh, she is. I'm as good a judge of womanly beauty as I am of horseflesh, if I do say so myself!"

"How are you on character?" John Walworth asked with a small smile.

"Oh, she's got plenty of that, too, and she's very quick and intelligent, and," and Ernest paused again, this time for emphasis, "I love her."

"Which," said Rebecca, "is what matters most, and if you love her we will, too."

She really means that, thought Clara, admiring Rebecca's always open, generous spirit. She wished she could be like that, but she doubted that she could ever feel quite that way about everything. Anyway she could try to behave that way and perhaps the feelings would follow. She had found that she did feel more cheerful when she acted cheerfully.

"Do you think it's time for the pudding?" asked Margarette. And all the children shouted, "Yes!"

CHAPTER TWENTY-THREE

AFTER dinner the men settled down to discuss the War. Will, because of his exalted rank as major general, a remarkable feat for a man with no previous military education or experience, was the central figure in the discussion. Both Ernest and John were anxious to hear his views on the progress of the campaign and the men and the strategy behind it.

During the discussion Will brought out his journal to check on a disputed point, and Ernest asked him, "Have you been keeping a pretty complete record of your activities?"

"Yes, I've tried to, although I don't make entries on any regular basis. I just try to write whenever I have the chance."

"Have you got anything on the battle at Shelbyville?" John Walworth inquired.

"Lord, yes, I wrote at length on that miserable episode! I was plenty peeved about it, and I had to get it out of my system some way."

"Read it to us," urged Douglas. "I know Father and Ernie are anxious to hear all the details, and as a matter of fact, so am I. You remember I had a bad case of bronchitis and got left out of it. I've never really heard the straight of it either."

"I would greatly appreciate your sharing some of your observations with us," John Walworth added his persuasion.

"I may have gotten a little long winded. I doubt you'd want to listen to all of this."

"Let us be the judge of that," said Douglas.

So Will began to read:

Trenton Co., July 19, 1863

Such has been the constant movement and excitement prevailing in my command and such the wearying, provoking labor that has devolved upon me that I have not been able to write anything for weeks.

This is Sunday and Dr. Bryson, a chaplain from Fayetteville, Tennessee, is to preach at 11:00 today. Although always anxious to hear preaching, this will be the first sermon I have heard since March last. The sermon is to be preached under the trees near my quarters.

I am camped near a little village called Trenton in the extreme northwest corner of Georgia. On the east, but 1½ miles distant, is the Lookout Mountain. I am getting my command ready to move down the valley toward Jacksonville, Alabama, in the valley of the Coosa River where I hope to get forage and rest and to collect together the fragments of my scattered division.

Our army is now south of the Tennessee River. General Bragg's headquarters are at Chattanooga, 18 miles northeast of this place. Our army is in force along the river and upon the railroad towards Bristol. Forrest is in East Tennessee, Morgan in Indiana, Wharton at Reynold and Rome. Reddy at Tuscombia and thereabouts. And along the river we have cavalry pickets. Hardee has gone to take Pemberton's place. D. H. Hill takes Hardee's corps here.

The army is generally not injured by the retreat. The infantry had no fighting at all. Stragglers and deserters number probably 4,000. Men and officers regret that it was necessary to leave Middle Tennessee. All that has been written in the papers about surprises of cavalry at Harris and Liberty Gap being the cause of the retreat is simply nonsense. Bragg did not intend to hold the gaps. If he had he would have made provision to do so. Wheeler's Cav-

alry was surprised and the infantry did fight in skirmishing for a day or two and then the retreat began.

The principal fighting by chance fell upon my division. I had been saying that I should be relieved from picket duty. My command was tired to death, almost—my horses, nearly starved. I had four wagons which I had to fight for and haul forty miles. I could only give my horses ½ rations. The men only rested one day in three. At last on the 21st of June, Wharton began to relieve me. That day I was asked to my astonishment to cook 3 days rations and be ready for a raid in rear of Murfreesboro with all my horses that could travel. One third of my horses needed shoes. I could take only 1,750 men, tired and but indifferently armed, riding horses just able to travel. Before Wharton finished relieving me I had only 10 days rations left.

On the 23rd I began a march toward Chapel Hill. As I passed below Reunionville, I heard firing on the lines above that place and sent to the officer in command proffering aid. But getting no answer in time, I massed to get in rear of the enemy and wished at once to charge on 250 led horses, guarded by only 2 squadrons of Yank cavalry. General Wheeler insisted on reconnoitering and giving the enemy a chance to find out I was there and in what force. If he had let me alone, though I had only 600 men and 2 guns, I would have captured the horses and the holders, about 80. The delay enabled the Yankees to recall their troops.

I ordered a charge by 150 men and killed some Yankees and captured 15 horses with their equipment. I lost 2 men, captured, and 2 horses, killed. But I could not push forth since I found some 2,000 men suddenly confronting, the men who had been miles away when I first proposed a charge, so we heard from citizens and so the Yanks said themselves. This was my first experience on the field with Wheeler. At all events the Yankees were forced to abandon their attack on the picket lines and retired.

That night I camped with my command at Chapel Hill. The next morning the rain came down in floods. I protested that my command could not make the proposed raid, but Wheeler ordered me on out to Spring Hill, sending off 200 men whose horses were lame and broken down. I continued the march with 1,500 men. It rained all day and we made only 14 miles. It rained all night.

Next day we marched to Spring Hill, between Columbia and Franklin. My rations were out. No forage could be had. I sent down to Columbia 150 more men, unfit for duty by reason of uninvincible horses. The enemy then moving on Bragg's right, I was ordered by him to return to Chapel Hill. Through rain and mud, back we went and reached that place about sundown on the 26th. No rations or forage to be had. I then received an order to move to Middleton, 16 miles off to the right to be ready for a fight at daylight. And so, all night, on rocky, muddy roads and swollen streams, wet, hungry, and tired we were ordered to move by the march route to Tullahoma. That route would be through Shelbyville where I hoped to get some cornbread and bacon.

At 12 my exhausted command reached the suburbs of Shelbyville and was halted. I had gone in advance to General Wheeler and represented my condition and got his order for corn and rations. I had had the command inspected. Only 1,000 horses were fit for duty. As my men had but few cartridge boxes, nearly all the ammunition, carried in pockets, was destroyed. Only 5 rounds to the man. I had marched 56 miles without sleep. The horses had had no forage for 48 and the men no food for 36 hours. Yet I was ordered to move out and hold 7 miles of entrenchment against almost the entire mounted force of Rosecrans' army. I moved out and soon was attacked at all points. I reported my ammunition exhausted in 2 regiments. Still Wheeler, who was in command, would not permit me to withdraw.

Soon the Yankees charged and I was driven by them into town with a loss of 100 men. By my artillery for 2 hours I checked the enemy and again remonstrated against the effort to hold the town with 900 men against 8 or 10,000 when we had not on an average one round of cartridges.

As Will's story grew more exciting the women and children gathered around to listen, too.

At last Wheeler gave me permission to retire and I was passing my column over Duck River by the Tullahoma Bridge when I was ordered back. I resumed my position in part, not having time to post all my men when the Yankees charged down on us on four streets. Wheeler had heard by some stragglers that Forrest was in rear of the enemy and about to charge.

Duck River is close to the town and was swimming and has steep banks. There are two bridges near town. Our retreat would of course be over these bridges.

Now the enemy came on at a charge, men and officers maddened by liquor. My artillery could not stop them, my men had no ammunition, and the Yankees had revolving rifles and pistols and sabres. I had only long guns—then ensued a disaster such as I wish never again to witness. The men dashed for the Tullahoma Bridge—it became jammed by horses and artillery. The Yankees dashed in behind the rear of the column, killing and wounding and capturing—three out of four pieces of artillery were captured and our 400 (guns)—12 were killed, 22 drowned, and 50 or 60 wounded. When the bridge became jammed hundreds plunged into the river. Some drowned, some escaped losing horses. Some were wounded and captured on the banks. Many swam safely on. I had sent Minor with an order to the bridge. He could not cross it and swam his horse over and was captured, unhurt.

When the Yankees charged I was in rear of the main column and tried to stem the torrent with a few bold men, but they fell and I turned with Farrar and 3 others off the main road and back from the river to a point where I had posted a small force, intending to use this body to charge in flank of the main body of the enemy going towards the bridge. There I found 50 brave men and General Wheeler and staff and a few others joined us. I led the charge and brought the firearms back. We reformed, but my force was now only 20 or 30 men. Again we charged and ran the enemy back. Once more we formed and I led 10 or 12 men into the final charge. Out of it Farrar, one other officer, two wounded men and I alone came. The others had been killed or unhorsed. One man fell dead from his horse across the neck of my horse. Here, Perick Smith, who acted most gallantly was unhorsed and I think was captured. I am not certain. He may have been killed. In this fight as at Rome he was at my side and as cool as a veteran. I hope sincerely he was not hurt.

In the meantime General Wheeler and his staff discovered a column of the enemy coming in behind us and had left. I was made desperate by the occurrences of the day and cared very little whether I escaped or not. Farrar urged me to leave and tried to dissuade me from trying to cross in the presence of the enemy. I told him to plunge in. His horse would carry him over. He dashed away to try the bridge. I hesitated an instant as there were several of my men jumping in and I did not wish to drown any of them. The head of the Yankee column swept round a wall and was on me. One man caught me by the sabre scabbard or belt. The officer leading the charge presented his pistol at me from the other side and demanded my surrender. My own pistol was in my hand but concealed by an open loose coat. I saw just then an open space of water, threw up my pistol, fired it in the officer's face, putting spurs to my gallant gray, and down we went 10 or 12 feet into the river. There such a hailstorm of balls greeted me! Across I went and up the steep bank and away. Wheeler swam high up and escaped with me. I do not know how it was possible for me to get away. The officer I shot was killed and I seemed to be the target for hundreds of revolvers and carbines, but not a shot touched me or my horse. The enemy has my sabre with my name on it. Several of my men tell me that Farrar got to the bridge and was surrounded, but was captured firing his pistol. I had a message which purported to come from him through a citizen that he was at the house of a Dr. Lipscomb in Shelbyville, wounded in the leg, but doing well. I have since learned that no officer was killed near the river or was drowned. So I think Farrar is a prisoner. One of my surgeons who was left behind says no officers' bodies were found in or near the river.

Will paused, "And, of course, I later learned that both the message and my surmise were correct. He was treated by Dr. Lipscomb and he is a prisoner. Well, that about wraps up the action at Shelbyville."

"Let us hear the rest of your comments. I find your observation most interesting," said John Walworth. "We know so little of what is really going on. I want to hear every word."

"So do I!" exclaimed little Lucy, who thought her uncle Will Martin was the next thing to God.

"Well, all right. There's not much more."

This day's work has satisfied me that Forrest was right when he told me Wheeler was a clever little fellow, but not fit for command. He is as fit for his post as one of our drummer boys. The whole affair was his. He was in command and never listened to my representations or suggestions. He is merely a stubborn boy. I was never so much disappointed and grieved. My division was broken in pieces, injured in strength and reputation. My officers and men all understand the matter perfectly and are very anxious I should get away with an independent command.

The next day I went with my shattered command to Tullahoma. I was sent for by General Bragg. I noted all the facts and said, "If any blame whatever is attached to me or my command I wish a court of inquiry." In the presence of Generals Polk and Withers he said, "No blame is attached to you or your command. Your conduct was all that I could have desired and your men were not in condition to fight." I told him if we had a chance I would show him that my men could and would fight. He said, "You shall have it."

So on the 2nd of July we did have this chance with 600 men from 7 A.M. to 4 P.M. I held Elk River against 10,000 men trying to put bridges over the swollen stream. With little loss I inflicted heavy loss on them. The water fell and at 4 P.M. several columns, preceded by artillery-firing grape and sharp shooters, waded over and I fell back fighting, having no supports, but I had alone all that was desired, the army having passed on in safety. Falling back I reached a wide open field, the ground rising gradually in my rear to quite a hill. Back over this field I retired in lines, fighting with a chance of the fortification of our army on the hill. I was fighting Inchin's Brigade, 2,000 strong with 650 men. He had a line of infantry in tight behind him. My men fought as if in drill. Not a straggler, no precipitancy or flurry but cooly and steadily. The enemy several times formed to charge, but my line was too steady and firm. At last the enemy halted and I was ordered to retire and my lines came out of the fight as if on parade. As we moved back, the troops we passed cheered me and my men. Staff officers of General Bragg were present and reported the field fight as the handsomest cavalry fight seen in the west. It put to rest all questions of the fighting qualities of my division.

My little sorrel was twice wounded, but slightly. I lost a little of my pantaloons only.

Walworth, who had not been with me since the 22nd, joined the next day. He had been quite sick and was sent off to the rear when we commenced the march. We then followed the army back across the river.

I am distressed that Vicksburg and Port Hudson have fallen. We have lost arms, 27,000 men, and prestige. The black clouds like those that followed Donelson once more are over us. The campaign has been a badly managed one, but it is useless to grumble. We must get ready to fight the harder.

I did not like the invasion of Penn. That and the fall of Vicksburg and Port Hudson will, I fear, enable Lincoln to carry into effect his Conscript Act and add 300,000 men to the Yankee army. I believe that if Lee had remained in Virginia and we had finally repulsed Grant and Banks the war would have been virtually at an end.

To have accomplished this it was only necessary to do one of two things, which I had hoped and believed would be done. After the battle of Chancellorsville we could have sent a corps to East Tennessee to join Buckner and move into Kentucky while Bragg followed Rosecrans and pushed him across the Ohio. This was feasible. It was easy, I think, of accomplishment. The other plan was to have sent forward from the army of Virginia a corps to replace one to have been sent to Wheeler from this army and to have pursued the investment of Vicksburg. We will not succeed until we concentrate large armies and quit the system of small, independent armies.

I am for myself most heartily disgusted with the management of General Wheeler and his staff. Only a strong sense of duty keeps me where I am.

I am distressed about Margarette and the children. I fear the narrow belt of country, hitherto untouched above and below Natchez, will be devastated and my wife and children will be saved from starvation by being recipients of rations from the benign government of the United States. The thought is somewhat maddening. But what right have I to claim exemption from what has befallen so many thousands? I can only ask God to protect and shield my loved ones.

By General Hardee's aide I sent forward the last letter I expect to reach home for some time to come. He promised to get it through. It will relieve Margarette, who is no doubt in great trouble about me as well as Farrar. I got a dispatch through to the effect that I was well and Farrar and Minor captured.

I will stop writing. What a long, ill-natured diatribe!

"Well, that's all of it." Will snapped his journal shut.

"How grateful I am to be under a man like General Kirby-Smith! Has General Wheeler improved any?" Ernest wanted to know.

"Not a bit!" replied Will. "And it looks like I can't get loose from him. He's my albatross."

"One wonders why we haven't long since lost this war. I suppose the only thing that's saved us is the equal stupidity and inefficiency of our enemy," said John Walworth.

"Uncle Will, weren't you afraid when you shot the Yankee, and had to swim across the Duck River with everybody shooting at you?" asked little John.

"Of course he wasn't!" cried Lucy indignantly. "Uncle Will isn't afraid of Yankees, and neither am I! I wish I were a man and could go to war!"

Will put an affectionate hand on his fiery little niece's dark brown, flowing hair. "It's not much fun to kill a man, Lucy. Be glad you don't have to." Then he turned to his nephew. "No, John, I can't say that I really was afraid. I did feel sort of shaken up when it was all over, but at the time I guess I was just too busy to be afraid."

"Your Uncle Will is being modest, John. He was very brave, and he thought more about his men and his responsibilities than about himself. That's what heroes are made of," Douglas told his son. He would have liked to be a hero himself, and he felt a small stab of envy.

Ernest left the next day to go to Memphis, but Douglas and Will spent the entire month of January at the Millers'.

It was close quarters for the two families. Douglas and Margarette occasionally found each other irritating, and they both found Mammy Martha irritating.

"I don't wonder that Margarette and Mammy Martha don't get along," Douglas told Rebecca one day after a spat had erupted between them. "They're both rotten spoiled."

"Well, I think it hurts Margarette's feelings that she likes me best and says so, but I don't see what I can do about it."

"Well, there's one thing for sure. You can't stop Mammy Martha from speaking her mind, and that voice of hers would put a screech owl to shame!"

In spite of these minor difficulties January was all too short, and when Sherman headed north in February with his sights set on South Carolina, orders came for Will and Douglas to go up with the army of Tennessee to join with Hardee's 20,000 troops and state militia in South Carolina.

"Heaven help South Carolina because I'm afraid we can't," said Douglas to Will.

"Yes," said Will, "we've come full circle, haven't we? That's where it all began."

"That's why I believe it will be a target for an even worse destruction than in Georgia."

"Yes, after all Sherman didn't burn anything there that didn't get in his way!"

Douglas and Will departed together. Clara and their wives and all the children followed them down to the gate. The air was charged with all the unspeakable things in their hearts. There was no longer any serious thought of victory, there was just blind loyalty. The ship of the Confederacy was sinking, and they would not desert her now.

Douglas had said to Rebecca the night before, "You know there is no hope. There's nothing left but honor."

Rebecca nodded, her heart overflowing with the tears she didn't shed.

Douglas embraced Margarette and Clara and each child briefly and ceremoniously. Then he kissed his wife and swung resolutely into the saddle. He gathered the reins up in his hands, looking down on the little group as if he were trying to memorize every detail of the poignant picture they presented. John and Lucy, touchingly protective, stood beside their mother, while Daisy and Annie hopped up and down with innocent excitement on either side of Clara, who held each firmly by the hand.

Rebecca had never been more beautiful, he thought.

She was wearing one of her silk party dresses, her everyday ones being all worn out. This one, made with a deep *V* neck and big puffed sleeves, had once been jonquil yellow, but now it was the color of straw. Faded and limp, and ridiculously dressy for the occasion, it was nevertheless exceedingly becoming, but he did not notice that at all, and she had certainly given no thought to what she would wear, as she had four long years ago when he had left to go to war for the first time. What Douglas saw now as he gazed down at them, storing the memory in his heart, was the love and concern in her eyes, and the courage in her smile.

The suffering they endured at being separated seemed to grow greater with every parting, and each time Douglas wondered if he could really ride away.

"Take care of each other," he said, and then he and Will galloped off.

CHAPTER TWENTY-FOUR

SPRING came to Evergreen, and it was time to plant the vegetables that enriched the staple diet of the wartime South—cornbread and bacon. It was also time to plant the feed corn for the stock. As there were no hands left on the Millers' place, all the able-bodied adults, and even the older children, Lessie, Lucy, John and their Martin cousins, helped with the planting. It was hard work, but they took turns, and Clara rather enjoyed it, going gratefully to her bed at the end of each day, her muscles aching, and her spirit at peace.

Rebecca fainted in the field one day. It was soon determined that she was with child, and that the baby should be born about the first of October. She was retired from the field, and the work went on, planting giving way to hoeing and chopping weeds.

Rumors were flying that Lee had surrendered, and that Selma and Montgomery had been captured, but nobody knew for sure that any of it was true. In mid-May Confederate soldiers straggled into Evergreen with the news of General Taylor's surrender to Canby at Citronelle, Alabama, on May 4. Then they heard that General Kirby-Smith had surrendered at New Orleans, and the next thing they knew Ernest was in Evergreen, telling them that it was all true, that the War was over.

It was wonderful to hear that the War had ended, but it didn't seem to make much difference in their lives, which went on just as before, and there was no sign of, or word from, either Douglas or Will.

Of course they were profoundly grateful to have Ernest safe and with them, although they knew that his stay would be brief, as he was anxious to return to his bride. Mary had accepted his proposal, her father had given his approval, and they had married in January. They had had one week's honeymoon, then Ernest had rejoined his regiment, which had wound up surrendering in New Orleans.

In a few days Ernest was on his way. Still no word came from Douglas and Will. Margarette and Rebecca were beside themselves with apprehension. John Walworth kept assuring Sarah that there was no way they could be expected home from South Carolina yet. In Evergreen they had no easy access to casualty lists. All they could do was wait and hope and pray.

Laura had written that she and Will were expecting a child in May. They hadn't heard from her lately and Sarah was wild with worry about her, too. Finally word arrived in a hand-delivered letter written by Will McPheeters that Laura had given birth to a daughter, that both mother and baby were doing well, and that the baby had been named Sarah.

But Sarah and John could not rejoice properly over this good news when they were so anxious about the safety and whereabouts of Douglas and Will.

Rebecca's condition was an additional worry for Sarah.

"Aunt Chloe, I'm so concerned about Miss Rebecca," she confided. "There's no competent doctor anywhere near us to look after her. Promise me that when the time comes you will deliver the baby yourself. Get a good midwife to help you if you can, but don't let that old drunken fool, Dr. Morrison, anywhere near her. I want your solemn word on it."

"Yes'm. You has it, Miss Sarah. I won't allow him near her, and I promise to be right there. Don't you worry none. Everything's going to be all right."

When Douglas and Will returned it was already the second week in June. The anarchy and confusion that now reigned throughout the South had, of course, delayed them. Will had waited until all of his men were either hospitalized or able to leave to go home, and Douglas, now his chief aide, had waited with him.

Now that the War was over and all of the men safely back, the problem for the family was what was going on in Natchez. No letters had come through from there, or for that matter from anywhere, for months. It would be very risky, especially under the prevailing conditions of travel, to launch out with Sarah and John and the small children, much less Rebecca. There was no sense in attempting to go home until they knew what awaited them there, so the family remained in Evergreen, while Douglas and Will went on a scouting expedition. They made the journey to Natchez to see what the situation was, returning on July 2nd.

They found Elmo and The Burn still in Union hands. The Burn, in its capacity as a hospital, was full of wounded soldiers, and Elmo, which had first been used as a negro barracks, now housed a negro school. Douglas had been unable even to obtain an interview with any responsible person regarding the restoration of their property, and there seemed to be no hope of the return of their houses for the foreseeable future. There was no way they could go home.

Will had found Linden and his and Margarette's home, Monteigne, boarded up, the fences down, and weeds waist high. But with the help of Uncle Perry, with whom they had been joyfully and tearfully reunited, he and Douglas had opened up Linden and put it in shape for Jane Conner to return to. Will planned to take Margarette and their children back to Linden to stay with Jane while Monteigne, which had had serious structural damage wreaked upon it, was repaired.

The news that they could not yet go home was a bitter pill for the Walworths. Evergreen had been a welcome haven for them, and they had even managed to find some happiness there, but now that the War was over it began to seem unbearable—an exile instead of a refuge.

Sarah yearned to see her daughter Laura and all her old friends. Although she had recovered from an attack of malaria, another strange and unidentified malady was now sapping her strength and making her feel wretched. Perhaps it was old age, but she was not well at all. She had the feeling that if she didn't go home soon she might not make it at all.

John Walworth, although he never gave expression to it in any way, was more homesick even than Sarah. Outside of his family and his farming, Natchez had been his life. He had spent years of his life and hours of his time serving the city and he loved it. Evergreen had been stultifying and arid for him, and he shared Sarah's sense of not having much time left. He wanted his house back and his land. From the moment he had learned the War was over, he had been thinking about the plantations. What shape would they be in? The swamps and forests of the primitive country in which they were located were always just one step behind you, ready to swallow you up if you missed a step. There were a lot of missed steps in three years! The cabins would all have to be rebuilt, and the levees, and the labor—scattered like dandelion fuzz—would have to be reassembled somehow. A Herculean effort lay ahead, but he could hardly wait. Thinking about it made him feel ten years younger! And now, unable to go home and get started, he felt all of the frustrations of these past years, of his forced inactivity, swelling inside of him until he thought he might burst.

Rebecca wanted desperately to get home and have her baby there. She had not said so, but she was worried about herself and the baby. She would like to have a doctor on hand, someone other than old Dr. Morrison, who didn't draw a sober breath. She would be better off with just Aunt Chloe than with him.

Clara wondered why she should care so much about going home. There was nothing there for her. Oh, of course, she wanted to see Laura and her friends, but suddenly she wanted to see The Burn. She wanted those wounded Yankees out of there. She wanted to wake up in her old room, she wanted to have breakfast on the back gallery, she wanted to sit in the summer house and have tea. She wanted to sit under the big oak tree and feel its branches blessing her. She wanted everything back just as it had been. She smiled at her own foolishness. That was one thing that would never be, because change was a part of life. The War had taught her that. You might not want change, but it would come anyway whether you made it happen or it happened to you.

Douglas, too, was chafing to return to Natchez and by the end of the month he decided to go back again to see what he could do about regaining possession of their houses. This time he was successful in obtaining a promise that The Burn would be returned to his parents by the first of September. Dealing with the hatchet-faced, dedicated, Yankee school marm at Elmo had proved more difficult and he had decided to let that go for the time being. He would clearly have to go over her head, but he wasn't sure just who to go to about it. The army claimed they had nothing to do with it. At any rate half a loaf was better than no bread at all. Jane Conner had insisted that they could all stay with her at Linden while they made The Burn fit to live in again, and while Douglas made arrangements for the return of Elmo.

Douglas hurried back to Evergreen. Although they could not even get possession of The Burn until the first of September, Rebecca's condition made it imperative that they start on the strenuous trip home as soon as possible.

He arrived at the Millers' feeling feverish, he had several hard chills during the night, and by the next morning he had to face the fact that he had malaria.

Dr. Morrison was called for the simple reason that they were out of quinine and hoped he had some. He did, but his supplies were limited. There were a lot of cases of malaria in and around Evergreen. He gave Douglas what he could, but Aunt Chloe said he needed more.

John Walworth decided that he ought to drive up to Greenville, Alabama, to get some more quinine. It did seem the only thing to do, but the women were worried about him undertaking such a long hard drive alone.

"I'll go with him," Clara volunteered, and insisted when her father protested that it wasn't necessary.

He could never have made the trip without her. It had taken much longer than they had thought. The roads were in terrible shape, and the Millers' mule was slow and obstinate. They took turns driving, but John's old bones couldn't rest very well in a jostling wagon and he was close to exhaustion when they got to Greenville. They spent the night in the town's best hotel, which gave Clara the shivers. The linen on the bed looked dirty and she couldn't sleep on it. She sat on her suitcase until dawn, and then she woke her father. They went to see the doctor, whose name Dr. Morrison had given them, and he let them have some of his quinine. He was reluctant to part with it, but somehow they touched his heart, this pair, the elderly father, obviously tired and strained to the breaking point, and the young girl so concerned for him and for her brother. Clara told him their story, the old people, the little children and the expectant mother, their anxiety to return to Natchez, their disappointments, and now this new delay. He could not say no.

Back in the wagon John gave his daughter an admiring glance. "I'm certainly glad you came. He wouldn't have given it to me."

That's true, thought Clara. Father never has known how to persuade. I guess he's never had to.

It was September before Douglas had his chills and fever under control, and Rebecca was expecting their child in a month now. Douglas, well aware how bad the traveling conditions were between Evergreen and Natchez, feared the consequences of such a journey for Rebecca at this time.

"I think we should probably wait now until the baby comes," he told his wife reluctantly. He knew how much they all wanted to go home, how hard all the delays and disappointments had been not only for Rebecca, but for his parents and Clara and the servants as well. The children didn't seem to care.

"Oh, please, Douglas." The tears welled in Rebecca's brown eyes, the most beautiful eyes that he had ever seen or ever would. "Please, please, I want to go home. I want to have the baby there. I want to see my mother and be with her. We can all stay at Linden now that Margarette and Will have moved back to Monteigne. If we don't go before the baby comes, we'll have to wait for the baby and me to be able to travel, and in the meantime the bad weather will set in, and it will be months before we can leave. Besides, the medical care I can get in Natchez is so much better than what's available here. I want to have the baby there. Please, Douglas, please."

In spite of his misgivings and those of his mother and father, he could not deny her. They would leave for Natchez as soon as he could hire a couple of carriages to take them to Selma, where they would take the train to Jackson, and when they got there he could get somebody in Natchez to come and get them. Maybe Uncle Perry would be able to.

Long before they got to Selma Rebecca realized that she had made a mistake, but there was no way to turn back now, and maybe it would be all right. She mentioned to no one the pains that troubled her. They were not the regular pains of labor, but they were not a good sign.

CHAPTER TWENTY-FIVE

IT was the middle of the night, but Linden was ablaze with light. Fires burned in the fireplaces and all the lamps were lit.

The travelers had arrived after dark. Uncle Perry brought the first carriage to the front steps and jumped out. He reached up to receive the writhing, moaning figure of Rebecca from Aunt Chloe's arms. Douglas, who had ridden on horseback ahead of the carriages to summon a doctor, ran from the house and pushed him frantically aside. Taking his wife into his arms he ran into the house with her and into the dining room where the elegant table had been covered with blankets and then with sheets. He laid her tenderly on the table and turned to the doctor. "Help her doctor! Oh, God, please help her!"

"I will, Mr. Walworth. I will indeed. Wait outside please." The doctor was gentle, but firm, and reassuring, and Douglas did as he was told.

The sliding doors closed behind him as he stepped into the hall. Everybody was coming in now, Mammy Martha carrying Annie, and Clara with Daisy. Both little girls were sound asleep. Jane Conner directed them to the bedrooms upstairs and turned to greet Lucy and John, who ran to her waiting arms and clung to her, sobbing.

Aunt Chloe and John followed with Sarah, who was pale

as a ghost and barely able to stand. "Go to Rebecca. Chloe, please, please, go to Rebecca—you promised me—go to Rebecca." She slumped against John, and Douglas went to her. He lifted her up into his arms, and Jane Conner looked up from the children to direct him. "Take her to the front bedroom above the parlor." Then she said to Aunt Chloe, "Please do go to Rebecca, Chloe, and come back and tell us how she is when you can."

Jane drew away from Lucy and John. "Now you must get yourselves together and be as brave as your mother is. It will soon be over. You must go and see if you can help with the little ones, and I must see to your grandfather."

When Lucy and John had gone upstairs on tiptoe, their faces sombre, Jane and John Walworth stood looking at each other. "How is my daughter?" Jane asked him.

John shook his head wearily. "I don't know. She's been in terrible pain. I—I don't know. We should never have left Evergreen."

Douglas walked into the hall in time to hear John's last sentence and it cut through him like a knife. A shriek from Rebecca followed, a stab far worse than the thrust of a bayonet.

"Come," said Jane, "and let's sit in the parlor. I'll get you both some brandy, and I think I'll have a little myself."

Clara, on her way down the stairs, met Lucy and John, trudging sadly up, and her heart went out to this plucky pair, who had endured the whole miserable journey without one word of complaint, and helped in every way they could.

"I know you children must be starved," she said, suddenly remembering that they had left Vicksburg in the early morning hours and had had nothing but water and some biscuits all day. "Come with me to the kitchen and we'll make some tea or some hot chocolate. We need some nourishment."

Clara put her arms around their hunched shoulders and gave them a smile so full of love that it warmed their hearts and made them feel that maybe everything was going to be all right in spite of the screams that kept coming from the dining room.

Clara stuck her head into the parlor and was relieved to see Jane Conner ministering to her father and Douglas. Her heart had ached for her brother, when Rebecca had begun her labor on the road between Vicksburg and Natchez. Somebody had had to go ahead to get a doctor, and Douglas was the only one who could make that ride fast enough. Uncle Perry could drive a carriage, but he wasn't much good on horseback. Douglas had had to leave his wife in her perilous circumstances, trusting her to Aunt Chloe and the rest of them, and Clara could see that it devastated him to do it. But Rebecca had made it to Linden and the medical attention that they were all so anxious for her to have.

"Mrs. Conner, may I take Lucy and John to the kitchen for some supper? We'll just help ourselves with your permission."

"Oh, yes, my dear. Please do that, and I thank you." She turned to the men. "Do you want anything to eat?"

They shook their heads. Neither could bring themselves to say a word.

I believe I'll fix them something anyway, thought Clara.

They found Lessie in the kitchen sitting at the table, her head buried in her arms, crying as though her heart would break.

Clara caught the shaking little figure up in her arms and held her. "Now then, Lessie, it's all right. We're all safe and sound and here at Linden at last. And the doctor is taking good care of Miss Rebecca. I expect what we'll be hearing next is a baby's cry."

Lessie's sobs subsided, and she wiped her eyes with the handkerchief that John solicitously offered.

"Now let's see what we can find for everybody to eat."

The screaming died away, and was replaced shortly by a little mewling cry.

"Thank God!" The brandy glass crumbled in Douglas'

hand and bright red streaks appeared. He drew out his handkerchief, and Jane efficiently tied it around his hand, hardly thinking about what she was doing.

After a few moments had passed the doors slid open, and Mammy Martha, who had joined the proceedings in the dining room, appeared with the baby in her arms. "I'm the first to hold her," she declared proudly, "just like all the others!"

Even at this moment of unbearable concern for his wife Douglas felt a hot burst of irritation at Mammy Martha's self-centeredness, but he choked it back. "How is my wife?" he demanded, his voice hoarse and harsh with emotion.

Mammy Martha's old prune face clouded. "She's done had a bad time. The feet was first. It was a bad time for my baby." Mammy Martha did not refer to the baby wrapped in her arms, but to Rebecca herself.

Now as she thought about it, she began to cry, and Jane Conner, from years of experience in dealing with Mammy Martha, decided that she must be got rid of as quickly as possible for the sake of everybody's sanity. "This baby is your responsibility now. Take her back to my room. There's a crib there for her." She spoke in a voice so full of authority that Mammy Martha vanished like a puff of smoke before their eyes. Nobody had even looked at the baby.

Douglas and Jane and John stood anxiously in the hall waiting for further word of Rebecca's condition. The longer they had to wait, the worse they knew things must be.

Finally the doors opened again, and the doctor came out, a grave expression on his face. Their hearts sank to see it.

"Mr. Walworth, your wife is very ill. It was a breach birth. The hemorrhaging has been," he paused, "considerable. I think we've checked it now, but she has lost a lot of blood, and she is quite weak. The colored woman, who's with her now, seems very capable, but I will stay the night in case she starts to hemorrhage again."

"May I see her?" Douglas' face had turned to stone.

"You may, but remember she must not waste any of the strength that's left her."

"Go, Douglas," said Jane Conner, "she'll want to see you. Give her my love. I'll wait until she's stronger."

Douglas stooped to kiss Rebecca's cheek and was terrified by its coldness, but her eyelids fluttered open, and the beautiful eyes gazed at him with recognition, and there was a spark of tenderness in them. "Becky, I love you," he whispered, and she smiled.

"The baby," she murmured, and he told her the baby was fine. He even remembered that Mammy Martha had referred to it as "her." "We have another little daughter and she is fine. Mammy Martha is looking after her."

"It was supposed to be a boy, a brother for John. I told Ernest that the baby was going to be named for him. He was so pleased. I'd like to name her Sarah for your mother, but Laura has a Sarah now. What about Sarah Ernestine? And we'll call her Ernestine."

"Of course. That's what we'll do. Now go to sleep. You need to rest. When you wake up your mother wants to see you."

Rebecca's eyes had closed before he finished. He sat beside her through the night. When morning broke the bleeding began again, and this time it did not stop.

Clara stood by her sister Lucy's grave at Rebecca's funeral. The small grave reminded her of that other funeral. She had been just a child then, but it was surprising how much children could feel and understand. She glanced at Douglas' children, standing forlornly between their grandmothers. She had been so concerned about her brother, knowing all too well the agony he was undergoing, that she had not thought enough about them, four, no five now, motherless children. What was going to become of them?

Her gaze returned to the small grave at her feet. "Lucy," she whispered, her heart yearning for her, memories of her childhood flooding back, memories of two little girls playing in a garden. Both were gone now but both would always live in her memory. So would the young woman who lay in the coffin which was being lowered into the earth. And so, too, would a young soldier with red-gold curls and laughing eyes. The pain came rushing back, but she almost welcomed it, and she knew suddenly that even when it hurt it was good to be alive.

Part II

1869-1870

CHAPTER ONE

A small lamp glowed softly in one of the big bedrooms of The Burn, casting a dim circle of light on the ceiling, which seemed higher than ever at night. Beneath it a huge four-poster stood out from the surrounding shadows. A slight figure with long brown braids knelt beside it, and within the voluminous folds of its feather mattress another little figure squirmed and twisted, bright yellow curls in disarray.

"Daisy, stop that praying, and come to bed. I'm sleepy, and God must be tired himself. Why don't you leave Him alone?"

The kneeling figure remained motionless.

Annie sighed hopelessly into the silence and wriggled herself from back to stomach in the billowy bed. Daisy's prayers got longer every night.

"Annie, you ought not be irreverent!" A small head lifted at last and Daisy's big brown eyes were reproachful.

"Girls, aren't you in bed yet?" a voice called from the doorway, and a young woman in a long full nightgown stood framed in it. Her pale bronze hair gleamed in the flickering light of the candle that she held in her hand. It seemed to form a halo about her face, which emerged from the background of the darkness with the spirituality of a Rembrandt portrait.

"We're going to sleep right now, Aunt Clara!" cried

Daisy, clambering hastily into the big four-poster.

Aunt Clara smiled, and her blue-gray eyes came suddenly to life. Their sparkle was electric, communicating spontaneous and pleasant warmth instead of the scolding they had expected.

"Settle down now." After a quick kiss for each, and a smoothing of the covers, she blew out the lamp by the bed and glided away into the darkness, the wavering light of her candle gradually fading.

The children snuggled together. All the disagreements of the day were laid aside in their need for one another in the mysterious, black world of creaking noises that was night.

"Father will be home tomorrow," whispered Daisy.

"I know. And I'm glad. That means we'll have a good dinner for a change. Do you know, Daisy, I've been hungry the whole time he's been at Fawnwood?"

In the Reconstruction South of 1869, although many tables gleamed with highly polished silver and sparkling crystal, the food, served on the finest china plates, was sometimes limited in quantity and variety. Garden vegetables were plentiful in season, of course, and chicken and pigs were raised, but many commodities were scarce and expensive.

"I hope we have roast beef," agreed Daisy, "and that Aunt Chloe'll make corn pudding and rolls, and I hope Father brings lots of quail from the country."

"And I hope he won't be drunk!" added Annie.

"Annie!" Daisy's whisper was a gasp.

"Well, you know he drinks like a fish—no, he doesn't either—he drinks like two fish!"

"But, he only does it sometimes, Annie, and he's our father, and you shouldn't speak disrespectfully of him."

"He does it most of the time and you know it! And he's very mean when he does, too—I hope you put it in your prayers that he'll be sober."

"I did," said Daisy.

In a room down the hall Clara knelt beside her bed, her hands folded in prayer, her eyes open and staring into the darkness. "And please, God," she whispered, "let my brother be sober."

She rose slowly to her feet and stood looking down into a crib, which was close by her bed. In it lay a child about four years old, a tiny, elfin creature, blissfully asleep.

"Ernestine—such a long name for such a little girl," she murmured, and stooped to place a tender kiss on Ernestine's untroubled forehead.

It was a fine day. The early summer weather could be delightfully cool at times even as far south as Natchez, and today was that kind of day.

The household at The Burn was humming with activity in preparation for the return of its master. Aunt Chloe was elbow deep in dough, and full of important orders.

"Maybelle, Miss Clara done told you, Mr. Douglas, he like that dark curly lettuce. Look what you brought me!

"Brother Perry, it's liable to be cool tonight. You better get some fires laid.

"Lessie, see there's no dust in Mr. Douglas' room, and that there's clean linens on his bed. And we'll be using the yellow china tonight. Mind it's fresh washed."

The gray-bearded negro man started out the door, but turned back when the two young women left.

His face was solemn. "I hope things ain't been too bad for Mr. Douglas in the country."

"Lord, so do I! It makes him take to drinking and puts him in one of his moods. It's hard to see how one man can be so different, one time so good and kind and then another, so mean and hateful. It's like there are two people under his skin."

"Well, his nerves have been bad ever since Miss Rebecca died."

"He always did have those moods. Even when he was a little boy. Miss Sarah used to worry about him so, and right before she died she said to me, 'Chloe, look after my boy for me.'"

"Mr. John worried about him, too. He didn't say so, but

he was always asking me about the whiskey."

"Well all this talk don't help none. Go lay those fires now, and let me get on with my baking."

Out in the garden Clara stood, scissors in hand, surveying her roses which were blooming gloriously. She sighed with satisfaction. She loved the garden, not only for its beauty, but for its aliveness. She relished not just the fragrance of the flowers, but the smell of the earth, and the feel of it under her fingers. It gave nourishment to her soul. She loved making things grow. Each plant seemed like a child responding to her love and care, and she was endlessly amused and fascinated by the other inhabitants of the garden as each of these went its own resourceful way. She guessed she enjoyed the flowers because they depended upon her, and the creatures because they did not.

This morning the garden sparkled in the sunshine. The air was filled with the spicy scent of the flowers, their colorful masses spilling out of the neatly laid out beds as if in protest of their primness. To the unpracticed ear its silence was interrupted only by an occasional bird call, but Clara could hear the rustlings in the leaves and grass of the busy hordes who lived there.

She went from bush to bush gathering blossoms, pausing at a white one to touch the petals of one of its blooms in a caressing gesture.

"Aunt Clara?" a voice recalled her to the world of humanity.

She turned. "Yes, Lucy?" It was her eldest niece, sixteen now, a tall girl with a direct manner and a neat appearance. Lucy's long, dark hair was pulled away from her high forehead and tied with a small piece of ribbon. Clear, gray-green eyes looked out on the world inquiringly from her alert face.

"Aunt Clara, I know that we're having our dinner tonight to celebrate Father coming home, but will it be all right for me to pay a call this afternoon? I'd like to visit the Shields. I want to return some of the books Dr. Shields lent me."

"Yes, certainly, Lucy. I wish I could go with you, but I've invited your Aunt Laura to come to tea this afternoon. She's stopped accepting invitations to social gatherings because she's expecting the baby in two months, and she craves a little companionship. Yes, of course. You may count on going. Just don't be too late getting home."

Clara watched Lucy going up the walk that led to the house and wondered at the role in which fate had cast her. Lucy looked to her as a mother, but there were not nearly that many years between them. She had been just about Lucy's age when the War began. Her life had certainly turned out quite differently than she had expected it to then. Turning her gaze to the white rose bush beside her, she drew in her breath slowly, as though the outside air might stir up some inside hurt, then let it out again with a little sigh as she bent to clip some of the delicate blooms. She added them with difficulty to a big willow basket which was filled to the brim already, and then she picked it up, slipping its handle over her arm carefully so as not to catch the full sleeve of her shirtwaist on the prickly stems.

A whisper of a breeze rustled gently through the leaves overhead, and she stood for a second, allowing her senses to experience to the fullest the pleasure of it.

Then with her free hand lifting her long full skirt, a purple cotton field abloom with vertical rows of tiny pink roses, she went up the path to the house, where she was met on the back gallery by Lessie, a mature young woman for her fifteen years. She wore a handkerchief tied bandana style about her head which she held as gracefully as a giraffe's on her long slender neck. A crisp white apron and a brightly printed calico dress neatly covered most of her trim figure, and contrasted pleasantly with the deep black of her skin.

"Lessie, will you put these in some water for me?" asked Clara, noting with a smile her eager response. She liked arranging flowers herself, but she knew what a special joy it gave Lessie.

Lessie lifted the heavy eyelids that gave her small face a

sultry look, and her full, soft lips parted in a wide smile as she took the basket from Clara. "I'll see what I can do with them, Miss Clara," she murmured.

The Burn sat comfortably back on its haunches in the afternoon sun. Annie and Daisy were perched on its front steps waiting their turn for a bath.

"I'll wear my blue, I think. What are you going to wear, Daisy?"

"My lawn with the yellow rosebuds in it."

"Here comes John!" Annie jumped to her feet.

A slender, fair-haired boy of fifteen vaulted over the gate, and ran up the long curving drive. "How do you do, ladies?" he removed his cap with a flourish and made them an elaborate bow.

The girls giggled. He gave Annie's curly head a pat and one of Daisy's braids a tweak, and vanished, whistling, into the house, the echoes of his joyous nature remaining behind with the two little girls, who adored their brother.

John proceeded jauntily through the hall out onto the back gallery, where his sister Lucy sat copying passages from the books she was about to return to Dr. Shields.

She had met him a few weeks before at a party at Green Leaves, the home of a mutual friend. That attractive *U*-shaped house was built around a live oak, beneath which, legend said, the Natchez Indians had held their pow-wows. An exquisite, formal garden had been laid out in the court that surrounded the historic tree, and here the guests had gathered in the cool of a late spring afternoon.

"Lucy," Clara had said, "this is Dr. Ramsay Shields, an old friend of your grandfather. He and Mrs. Shields have just come back to Natchez to live. They've been in China for thirty years. Dr. Shields is a physician and an ordained minister. Father used to say, 'Ramsay Shields is one of the few brilliant men I've ever known, and one of the best.'"

Lucy was several inches taller than the wizened, sallow-faced man who stood before her, his ears standing out like a pair of wings from his small head. He was, she thought, a really ridiculous looking person. However, there was such a provocative blend of shrewdness and kindness in his almost cavernous eyes, that Lucy knew at once that she was going to like him.

"It's a great pleasure to meet you, Miss Lucy." His voice was high pitched and nasal. Lucy thought the poor little man sounds even worse than he looks. Thank goodness he has a good brain.

"Your grandfather and I were boyhood chums. He and I were very fond of one another." He smiled, tugging at one of his ears. "But I'm afraid your Aunt Clara here has just given you the wrong impression. Perhaps it was because I was so far away, buried as it were among the heathen, that your grandfather said anything so nice about me. What he used to say to me was, 'Ramsay, I know you must be smart because I can't understand a thing you say.' He knew how to shut me up!"

Lucy and Clara laughed, and Lucy asked, "Did you like living in China, Dr. Shields? It must have been very interesting."

"Oh, indeed it was, Miss Lucy! China is a fascinating country, full of mystery and contradictions! It's a place where one can find the greatest wisdom and the greatest ignorance."

Clara smilingly observed her niece's ecstatic face. "You two will enjoy each other, I think."

"You mean the young lady is a good listener?"

"No, not especially, but I believe she'll like listening to you."

Lucy soon discovered that Dr. Shields was a good listener. He and his wife had come to tea at The Burn shortly after the party at Green Leaves, and then Lucy and Clara had gone to call on them. He asked Lucy a lot of questions that made her think and listened with great respect to her opinions.

He had lent her these books about the religions of the world. She didn't want to keep them too long so she had decided to copy down some of her favorite passages.

". . . I make and I unmake this Universe:
Than me there is no other Master, Prince!
No other Maker! . . ."

Lucy was completely absorbed in her task, her forehead lined with the intensity of her concentration, occasionally reading aloud a passage which she found especially interesting:

". . . That man alone is wise
Who keeps the mastery of himself!"

"The soul of the ungoverned is not his,
Nor hath he knowledge of himself: which lacked,
How grows serenity? and wanting that,
Whence shall he hope for happiness?"

"Whence indeed!" exclaimed a gaily mocking voice behind her.

Lucy started. "John! You scared me!"

"What's this?" John picked up the book from which she was copying.

"It's a translation by Sir Edwin Arnold of the *Bhagavad-gita.*"

"You don't say! I'm forced to admit that I haven't the slightest idea what the *Bhagavad-gita* is."

"It's a Hindu poem from their holy book, the *Mahabharata.*"

"Well, where did you get it and why are you copying it?"

"Dr. Shields lent it to me, and I'm copying some passages from it because it's interesting. The ethics and theology are on a very high spiritual plane. The religions of the East have a lot of good aspects. Just listen to this:

"But thou, want not! ask not!
Find full reward
Of doing right in right.
Let right deeds be
Thy motive, not the fruit
which comes from them."

John shook his head. "They'll never get people to be good that way. I always suspected the Hindus weren't very practical. But, you know, there's something rather attractive about impractical people, isn't there?"

Lucy held up her hand and read another passage.

". . . Hard it is
To pierce that veil divine of various shows
Which hideth me; yet they who worship me
Pierce it and pass beyond.

"I am not known
To evil-doers, nor to foolish ones,
Nor to the base and churlish; nor to those
Whose mind is cheated by the show of things . . ."

"Are you thinking of becoming a convert?"

"No, I've decided the Eastern religions are too negative for me." Lucy ruffled through the papers before her and handed one of them to John.

John cast a quizzical glance at his sister and began to read:

"'Neath scorching suns,
Mid filth and stench,
And poverty and pain,
Buddha's Brahmins meditate
With eyes that see not,
Ears that hear not,
And hearts that care not.
Peace they seek and safety,
Safety from the anguish born of life,
Freedom from the burdens of mankind.
Then when the soul denies its own existence
The goal is reached; Nirvana is attained!"

"That's obviously not from the *Bhaghavad-gita.*"

"No, I wrote it."

"Well, I'm glad to know you haven't been converted. Is this supposed to be a poem? It doesn't have any rhyme. Tell you what let's do, Lucy. Let's tell Aunt Clara and Father that you want to become a Hindu." John's blue eyes held a wicked gleam.

Lucy gave him an icy look. "Yes, that would ensure plenty of pleasant dinner conversation, wouldn't it? Father thinks I'm just apt to do something like that, you know."

"Well, you are sort of a wild goose."

"Oh, hush up, John! Hasn't Aunt Clara told you if you haven't anything pleasant to say, not to say anything? It's time for me to go. I've got to return these to Dr. Shields. Do you want to come with me?"

John grinned

"Oh, no. I would only spoil your afternoon. Go along and talk to Dr. Shields about the religions of the East. I'll just stay here and meditate. Isn't that what they do? And where is it they want to go? 'Ye take the high road, and I'll take the low road, and I'll be in Nirvana afore ye.' See, I'm almost there now." John leaned against a column, and closed his eyes.

"You idiot!" laughed Lucy. "Can't you be serious about anything?"

"Well, yes. I'm serious about my law class with Judge Harris, which is where I'm supposed to be right now."

"Goodbye then. See you at dinner."

"Yes, heaven help us! The family celebration is tonight, isn't it?"

CHAPTER TWO

LAURA arrived at The Burn for tea bringing with her her oldest child, a daughter, named Sarah but called Sallie. She was just a few months older than Ernestine and Laura was most anxious that the two young cousins should be good friends. So far they hadn't seemed to hit it off very well, but after all they were only four years old.

Ernestine's young nursemaid, Maybelle, took the children off to play and the sisters seated themselves on the back gallery of The Burn.

"'I hope you feel as well as you look. Motherhood certainly becomes you, Laura." Clara told her blue-eyed, blonde sister, who looked glowing and beautiful despite the shapeless gown that concealed her bulky figure.

"I'm glad to hear it since I seem to spend most of my time in this condition! I saw John leaving to go over to Judge Harris' as we were arriving. He told me Lucy had gone to call on Dr. and Mrs. Shields. He said Lucy and Dr. Shields were going to discuss the religions of the East. Do you think that's a suitable interest for a young girl to have? I must say I think Lucy reads too much, Clara. I do hope she won't end up being an eccentric—," Laura paused and Clara supplied the words that were too awful for Laura to utter: "old maid."

"Well, now, Clara, I didn't mean—"

"Well, Laura, I don't think that just because Lucy has some intellectual interests that she'll be an old maid. Intelligent men should prefer intelligent women it seems to me."

"Well, I don't know about that. By the way I heard the new minister's wife is a pretty little doll with no brains, and that he is quite brilliant."

"Oh, so they've arrived?"

"Yes, they arrived several days ago. He's to preach his first sermon this Sunday."

"Well, what is he like besides being brilliant?"

"They say he's divinely handsome, that he has black wavy hair and dark blue eyes. He also has a slightly beaky nose and a rather prominent jaw."

"What do 'they' say about his inner attributes?"

"I hear he's very charming, but that he has a sort of a determination about him that some people are concerned about."

"He has a difficult role to fill with so many people to please. I feel sorry for him. Especially if his wife has no brains."

"Well, I can hardly wait for Sunday. I guess it's still proper for me to attend church."

"As far as I'm concerned it should never be improper to attend church."

"Of course I wouldn't consider going anywhere the last month."

"Why don't you and Will come by to dinner after the service on Sunday? Douglas will be home from the country this evening and I know he'll be anxious to see you."

"We'd love to. Poor Douglas, I'm sure he'll be glad to get back to civilization."

"Yes. He doesn't enjoy going to the plantation the way Father did, and, of course, everything is so difficult now. It is hard on him having the responsibility of handling Fawnwood. And, Laura, I am quite concerned about him. His drinking is becoming a very serious problem."

"Oh, I know. You've said that before. I'm sorry to hear it,

but I guess he needs to relax and let off steam with all the pressures on him. I think you just have to understand that, Clara."

"It's more than that, Laura. When he's drinking he seems to become a completely different person, and he is desperately unhappy."

"I'm sure he is. He's never gotten over losing Rebecca and I suppose he never will. Of course, he blames himself which makes it worse. Really, Clara, I think you will just have to forgive him for these little lapses."

Clara sighed. She guessed there was no way to make Laura understand. In the first place she didn't want to understand. And Douglas was always on his good behavior around her and Will. Well, there wasn't really anything they could do about it anyway she supposed. Still it would help to have a little sympathy and support.

"I wonder how the planting went," said Laura. "I hope we'll have a decent crop this fall and make enough money to have some left over for us after we make the payment on the mortgage and pay those awful taxes. My Will works night and day, but of course he never gets paid anything for it. He says nobody has any money for anything, much less to pay a doctor with."

"Your Will is a wonderful man, Laura. He's one of those people that the more you know the more you like."

Laura was obviously pleased by Clara's words of praise for her husband. "That's the way I feel about him myself. I'm so lucky to have married him. I almost didn't, you know," she admitted candidly.

"It was his daring visit to Elmo in that borrowed blue uniform that won you over," laughed Clara.

"It was when I suddenly realized the danger he was in that I discovered how much I really cared about him."

Sounds of the children's laughter, and Maybelle's, child-like, too, joining in, drifted up from down in the garden.

"Maybelle is such a wonderful nurse. She loves children and really enjoys being with them. She's rather like a child herself. I find it awfully hard to believe that she's Naomi's sister. Of course they had different fathers, but they are just such totally different people. I wonder whatever became of Naomi."

"So do I."

"I used to think she might come back to see us after the War, you know, the way Esther did."

"I always knew she would never come back."

"Those were happy days, weren't they, when we all went to school on the third floor. Miss Mollie was so horrified when Father told her that Naomi was coming to school with us, and then Naomi did so well she became the teacher's pet."

Clara smiled. "Naomi did do well, and she was so thrilled about it. I used to get mad at her because all she wanted to do was study. I remember I told her once, 'It was all my idea for you to go to school, and I wish I'd never thought of it!' Goodness, but I missed her after she ran away. She was my closest friend."

"It was probably a lucky thing that she did run away. It would have been difficult for both of you when you got older."

"Yes, I suppose it might have. I don't know. I don't know how it would have been for me. I know Naomi must have thought it would be impossible for her. By the way a letter came yesterday for Douglas from Ernest."

"Good! We haven't heard anything from him in ages."

"He isn't the world's best correspondent. I remember Father said once that Douglas' letters were too long and Ernest's were too short. You remember how Father was always comparing us children, and how that used to upset Mother. Ernest and Mary seem quite happy and I believe they like Memphis. It's a good halfway point between her parents and us."

"Clara, Will and I went out to the cemetery last Sunday and it looks to me as though the ivy on Father's grave needs replanting. It's never done as well as that on Mother's."

"I know. I've been meaning to attend to that, but the

weather is too hot now. I guess I'll just have to wait until the fall."

"How long has it been since Father died?"

"Two years now it must be, because he died a year after Mother, and she died the summer after we moved back into The Burn."

"Time really flies. I didn't realize it had been that long."

"How is Mrs. Conner? You said she hadn't been well."

"Oh, that was just a little indigestion. She's quite well now. She's a very vigorous woman for her age."

"I remember how reluctant she was to give up Douglas' children after she had kept them for so long at Linden while he was getting himself together after Rebecca died."

"The main reason they stayed at Linden so long was because we were getting The Burn together after the Yankees moved out of it. Oh, yes, she had come to feel that they were hers, and it was very difficult for her to let go of them. I'm not sure she has 'til yet. Not completely."

"Well, after all, she is their grandmother."

"Oh, of course she is. And it is quite natural that she should feel they belong to her. At first it was a little hard to handle her constant interference, well meaning though it undoubtedly was, but it doesn't upset me anymore. I've even grown genuinely fond of her. She's a very remarkable woman. I've always admired her."

As Laura was leaving to go home, she paused at the doorway to the parlor. "How shabby the parlor is getting, Clara! It makes me feel sad. Mother loved this room so. How distressed she would be to see it looking like this!"

"Well, I'm afraid it will have to stay this way. It would cost a fortune to replace the draperies or to recover the love seat and chairs; and in case you've forgotten, the Walworth fortune is as lost as the War."

"Oh, I do hate to be poor! I count my blessings though. I guess I'm luckier than most."

When Laura and little Sallie had gone, Clara went into the parlor and stood looking about her. It was true, she thought. It did look shabby, her mother's golden room. The yellow silk damask draperies, the brocade upholstery, and the rose and gold carpet from Paris which had so beautifully set off the darkly gleaming rosewood and mahogany furniture, were faded and worn. The tall pier glass mirror, framed in ornate gold leaf, which stood between the two long front windows, still reflected a setting for grace and gaiety at night when the etched glass lamps of the bronze chandelier were lit and the firelight danced up over the delicately carved mantel. But in the uncompromising daylight, the room, like an aged lady, showed its every line of living.

"But it doesn't make me as sad as it does Laura. It's like a person who's lived a lot. You can tell this room has its memories. I even think it's interesting now that our house was filled with wounded Yankee soldiers although I certainly didn't think so when we first got it back!" she thought.

Clara would never forget the shock and revulsion of that first visit with her father to their ravaged house. The departing invaders had not bothered to clean up behind themselves and the empty rooms were strewn with litter. Ink and blood spattered the boot-scarred floors. Unpleasant odors hung heavily in the air and rats and roaches had taken the kitchen and pantries.

John Walworth had said not a word, but the look on his face was terrible to see. That was another thing Clara would never forget.

"Our furniture," she had said when she was able to speak, "where is all our furniture?"

They had found it, most of it, piled in an upstairs room and in the basement. Many things had been broken; many things they never found.

Then Clara and John Walworth had walked down through the tangled jungle of The Burn's terraced garden. The little pavilion was still there at the bottom, overgrown with vines and listing a bit to one side, but there. The wooden bench still circled the big oak tree and Clara led her father to it. "Let's sit here and rest a minute, Father."

They sat in silence, their hearts heavy and their minds numb.

"We'll put it all back together," Clara assured her father. She hadn't the slightest idea how, but she had to tell him that they would. "It's all here. It just needs to be reassembled."

"We mustn't let your mother see it like this."

"No, I'll bring Aunt Chloe and Uncle Perry, and we'll clean it up and sort things out. Of course it will probably take months to restore The Burn completely. We will have to leave Linden long before it's done. We can't impose on Mrs. Conner much longer, but we can at least clean it up before Mother sees it."

John looked up at the arching limbs of the tree. "How grateful I am to find something that's just as it was."

"Yes," agreed Clara, "I've always loved this tree. It seems to be welcoming us home, doesn't it? It looks as though its branches are blessing us, that they're sending down grace and mercy, and—and peace to us."

"It's our Tree of Benediction," said John. He sighed, "I don't know how I'm going to tell your mother that we couldn't find the white rose."

"Perhaps it will come back next spring," said Clara. "It's most likely been beaten down beneath so many Yankee boots and horses."

And that had been the case. To their incredible joy she and her mother had found the little rose thrusting new shoots out of the earth the following spring.

Clara had finally gotten the house and garden back into shape. If only she could have done the same for Douglas, she thought.

Devastated by Rebecca's tragic death and blaming himself for it, Douglas had gone through a long period of depression, wandering about the house, more ghost than man, morose and preoccupied, seeming to care about nothing.

His chief occupation was walking over to Elmo, which

had never been returned to him and still housed the negro school. He had asked a thousand questions of the hostile administrators, but nobody seemed to know or care what had happened to Rebecca's portrait or the little spinet which had been so precious to her. Nevertheless he clung to the hope that they were somewhere in the house, and he kept trying to get permission to search the place.

One day after he returned from one of his obsessive visits to Elmo, Clara, who was just coming out of her room, saw him rounding the curve of the stairway. His face above his beard was as rigid as granite. A filmy substance clouded his eyes, and he did not appear to see her.

"What is it, Douglas? What's happened?"

The stony face did not change expression, and the veiled blue eyes stared through her without the least flicker. He walked past her into his room, quietly and carefully closing the door behind him. It was obvious that something terrible had happened. Clara had a panicky urge to follow him, which she resisted, remembering her own need always to face grief alone at first.

A short while later John Walworth returned from town, pale and distraught, with the dreadful news. Elmo had burned to the ground during the night. No one knew how.

Clara shut her eyes, and prayed silently and desperately, "God, help my brother!"

She was stricken with a terrible fear. What was happening, what might already have happened, behind that closed door? There had been no gunshot, but he might have hung himself, or taken poison. Anything was possible.

Douglas would admit no one to his locked room. He remained there for several days. Trays were sent to him, and he finally began to eat. When he emerged from his retreat, he had built an invisible and impenetrable wall around himself, and he never spoke to anyone of the tragedy.

In fact, he rarely spoke at all. He spent most of his time in his room with the door closed, sunk in a deep depression, and he began to drink more and more heavily.

Rebecca's mother, Jane Conner, wanted to bring the children back to Linden and that roused him temporarily out of his nightmare world.

"They are my children, and I will rear them." He had been quite firm about it.

Then the sudden death of John Walworth shocked Douglas out of the total depression which had enveloped him for so long and he began to lead a normal life again, at least on the surface. His father's death forced him out of his shell to handle the estate and to take over the management and operation of Fawnwood. With Ernest living in Memphis there was no one else to do it.

Clara had thought that having to assume this responsibility might be Douglas' salvation, and at first it had seemed to be, but he didn't really like or understand farming. He had no feel for the land or handling labor. Worst of all was the isolation of Fawnwood. It was bad for Douglas in his depressed state of mind to be alone down there for weeks at a time. It certainly encouraged the heavy drinking which he had begun after Rebecca's death. Or had it begun before then, Clara sometimes wondered when Douglas referred, as he did occasionally, to the demoralizing influences which war had on men? Perhaps his drinking had started then when he was away from home for such a long time, living through no telling what horrors.

Of course everybody was always blaming everything on the War, but sometimes they might be right.

She was still standing in the parlor when she heard footsteps on the front gallery. Then, her brother Douglas walked through the front door into the hall.

CHAPTER THREE

DINNER was far from the happy celebration that had been planned. Douglas had been drinking and the family and the servants were filled with foreboding. Everyone was trying desperately to avoid provoking any unpleasantness, and there was an uneasy atmosphere.

He was exhausted, Clara thought. They should not have delayed dinner for him. He would have been much better off with a solitary supper. But it had been his idea. Since he had to spend most of his time in the country now, he hadn't seen enough of the children, he said, and he had asked her before he left for Fawnwood to plan a family meal for his homecoming.

Fawnwood was the only one of the three Walworth plantations that still belonged to the family, and it was heavily mortgaged now. After their return from their wartime refuge in Alabama, her father had assessed their economic situation. They had not a penny amongst them, and were actually in debt to Spencer Wood, Rebecca's Unionist uncle. They had had to borrow money from him in order to go to Alabama and then borrow some more to get themselves home again.

So they had needed money to pay their debts, money to live on and to repair The Burn, and money to pay taxes on the acreage of three large plantations. They also needed money to reclaim these neglected tracts from the swamps and wilderness, which had overtaken them during the war years, to buy the necessary stock and tools, and to feed and clothe the labor.

After a heart-breaking and exhausting inspection tour of his land, John Walworth had decided what had to be done. The two plantations across the river in Louisiana must be sold. They could expect to get for them only a fraction of their true worth. There could not be a worse time to sell. Still it was the only means they had of raising the money they so desperately needed, and furthermore there was no way to handle the restoration of all three places. Fawnwood was the best located of the plantations. About twenty miles downriver from Natchez, it could be reached by land, a big advantage, as going by steamboat, while an easier trip, was usually much slower because one had to wait sometimes for days for the boat. Fawnwood could be reached in a day's ride in good weather.

So the Louisiana plantations had been sold for even less than John had anticipated, and he had concentrated his efforts on Fawnwood.

He had bought at grossly inflated prices wagons and plows and mules. He had gathered together some of his old hands who were gradually drifting back with their families, and he had bought the cows and hogs and chickens to feed them. He had rebuilt the cabins and the fences and started work on the repair of the levee. With great difficulty and expense he planted a crop of cotton in 1866 which failed. And then as if the South hadn't been through enough already, there was another crop failure the next year. John Walworth died at the end of that summer. Douglas had begun his management of Fawnwood by mortgaging it. The crop of 1868 had gone to pay taxes, interest on the mortgage, and to finance the next year's crop. Now in 1869 they were waiting to see what this year's outcome would be. A bumper crop was almost imperative.

They were short on hands at Fawnwood, too. So many had left for a better-paying job when things got busy, afte

Douglas had fed and housed and clothed them all winter. This was a situation that her father and his generation had not had to deal with.

The confiscatory taxes were another problem that seemed to get worse and worse. The southerners were at the mercy of the carpet-bag government, whose absolute power had led to the usual corruption and abuse. The farmers in Louisiana and Mississippi had formed something called the Tax Payers League to protest the taxes and Douglas had joined, although he was doubtful that it would accomplish anything.

Clara knew that Douglas had all these problems, as well as many others, and she truly sympathized with him, but why, she thought now, oh why did he have to add drinking to them?

Douglas had a sick feeling of self-disgust. He had left Fawnwood early this morning perfectly sober. He had ridden hard all day and he hadn't touched a drop. Then when he had gone to his room to freshen up for dinner with his family, he had felt so tired and nervous that he had poured himself a drink. Just one good drink would make him feel better. Then why had he poured himself another, and how much had he poured? Too much, he realized now as his thoughts struggled through the fog of his drunkenness and the distortions of his bitterness. Although he was making the greatest effort not to betray himself, he saw what he was sure was an accusing look in his sister's eyes. Anger flared suddenly inside him. What right had she to accuse him, to disapprove of him? Had she any idea what he had been going through down there in that hell hole? Did she know how it felt to be so bone tired? Somehow he seemed to be always in the wrong, always on the defensive. And he was fed up with it.

"Douglas," said Clara, "Uncle Perry is offering you the spoon bread. Will you have some?"

"Thank you, no."

Her tone had been polite enough, but he was acutely aware of her disapproval, and his own feelings of guilt were torturing him mercilessly so he struck out at her. "That's right. Sit there in your smug way and act superior!" He hurt inside unbearably and he wanted someone else to be hurt, too.

"Isn't Clara Walworth a wonderful woman though?" he spoke in a heavily sarcastic tone, a little sneering smile on his lips. "She just lives for others, taking care of her brother and his children. Living for them, that's all she wants. What a little saint she is!" He added savagely, "That's what you like everybody to think, isn't it? Is it really necessary to make such a martyr of yourself?" He paused like a snake coiling, and then struck his victim with a question. "Caught a beau yet, Sister?"

Anger ignited into a sudden blaze in Lucy's eyes. "It's a very lucky thing for you, Father, that she's chosen instead to shoulder your responsibilities!"

And now his child was attacking him, his first born!

"Well, listen to Miss Lucy, always ready with an impudent opinion! You think you're so intelligent! It isn't becoming in a woman, either. You really should have been a man!" Douglas spoke contemptuously to his eldest daughter, infuriated by her intervention.

She looked straight into his eyes and spoke in a deliberate and level voice. "I wish I had been, Father. At least, at this moment I do!"

"What an unbelievably self-righteous little prig you are! And I'll tell you something else you ought to know. You've got a heart like a rock! That is, if you've got one at all!"

Douglas had gotten into the habit of telling the "truth" to everyone for the benefit of their souls. He was often unjust, but his thrusts usually had enough truth in them to hurt. These made Lucy wince, for those virtues she found it hardest to come by were humility and compassion.

Uncle Perry arrived from the kitchen with a dish of butterbeans. As Douglas served himself he spilled some of them onto the tablecloth.

"What's the matter?" he demanded of Uncle Perr "You're shaking like a leaf! Look what you've made me d

What in the world's the matter with everybody tonight? I've come home from a hard month in the country, and what do I find? Criticism and disapproving looks, disrespect and inefficiency, and incredible clumsiness! I have problems enough to drive a man crazy! And then I have to come home to this sorry state of affairs!" By now he was shouting.

Clara rose. "We'll have our coffee, Uncle Perry. Daisy, you and Annie say good night to your father and go to your room. It's time you began to get ready for bed."

The little girls, after hasty good-night kisses, scuttled away in great relief. Ordinarily they would have hated to be banished from the adult ritual of after-dinner coffee in the parlor, but tonight they were only too glad to get away.

As Clara resolutely poured coffee, Douglas fidgeted, standing restlessly before the fire. Lucy brought him his cup, and he muttered, "Thank you," setting it on the mantel without a sip. John sat in sorrowful silence. He understood that his father was suffering more than any of them.

Douglas suddenly cleared his throat and addressed his sister. "I had something important to say to you before I was interrupted," he glared in Lucy's direction. "It's entirely wrong for you to sacrifice yourself for these thankless children." Again he glared at Lucy. "Do you think you can live forever on a package of letters tied with white ribbon? Can you? Well, can you?"

It was Clara's turn to wince, and she did, turning pale, but keeping her indignation well in hand. This was the one subject she could not bear for him to bring up.

"Father, let me tell you about my class with Judge Harris." John's attempt to divert the conversation succeeded only temporarily. Douglas had his sister's spinsterhood on his mind, and, relentlessly, he resumed that subject. "Have you no interest in marriage, or do you really like to play the martyr, the faithful sweetheart?"

"Douglas, when you marry again, perhaps I'll marry, too!" said Clara.

This remark outraged him, and he shouted, "I can't

believe that you would dare to compare our situations! You hardly knew that young man!"

"I'm tired, Douglas, and I believe, if you don't care for more coffee, I'll go up to my room."

"Yes, why don't you go up and read your letters?"

CHAPTER FOUR

THE morning brought another beautiful day. When Douglas did not appear at the breakfast table, Clara sent breakfast to his room. She sat now in the back parlor at the mahogany secretary, which served as her work desk, going over her household accounts. She pondered wistfully over the ledgers, wishing that somehow she might find enough money to buy material to make new draperies for the front parlor.

Well, no new draperies, I guess, she sighed, but dresses for Lucy, who really must have some clothes for her parties, and some for Daisy and Annie, though Annie can wear Daisy's old ones, much as she hates to! Ernestine is too little to care yet that all her "new" dresses come from the attic, and a good mending session ought to take care of me. Oh, dear, there I go again! What would Douglas say? Maybe he's right. Perhaps I am making a martyr of myself. Why shouldn't I have a new dress? Am I really, as he claims, hiding behind my letters? But from whom am I hiding? Clara smiled ruefully as she paraded the eligible young men of Natchez through her mind. They could be counted on the fingers of one hand. The others lay on battlefields scattered throughout the South, not only the one she had loved, but the ones she might have loved.

Gone forever were the days when the morning mail

brought handsome envelopes with *Miss Clara Walworth, The Burn* written on them in flowing script, summoning her to dances and garden parties and receptions, or simply inviting her to go for a drive in some young gentleman's fashionable carriage.

And gone forever were the days when her prized letters from Ross Sanford had come regularly, first from the University of Virginia, and then from a succession of camps. Why hadn't they married when Ross had come to see her on his leave that spring in 1862? She had asked herself that question so many times. They should have had what happiness they could. But Ross had not suggested it, and her pride had prevented her from doing so. Of course at that point the War had seemed only a brief delay in the ordered unfolding of an inevitable happy ending. Miss Clara Walworth of The Burn could envision no other.

When Mr. Sanford's letter had come informing her of Ross' death she had thought her life was over, too. She had even been tempted to end it herself.

Then during those long months in Alabama, the last year and a half of the War, she had discovered the satisfaction of being needed. And after their return to Natchez and Rebecca's tragic death she had felt more needed than ever. Taking over five motherless children had not been easy especially with her brother sunk in a deep depression, her mother dying of some strange malady and her father, broken hearted and feeble. A stroke left the children's nurse, Mammy Martha, paralyzed and speechless, and the baby, frail from birth, fell victim to a raging fever. The Burn had become a hospital once more. Since her mother seemed to prefer Aunt Chloe's nursing, Clara had taken over the baby. Mammy Martha's great-granddaughter Lessie cared for her. The three nurses, old and young and black and white, had discovered the deep kinship of humanity. Life became reduced for them for a time to its purest essence with all the temptations, affectations and perversions of the world shut out.

Clara had learned that tragedy need not be without value. Human suffering was one of the great mysteries of life. It was, in a way, a gift. It wasn't to be had for the asking and it certainly must never be sought, but if one didn't become embittered by it, one could be infinitely richer for it. Clara found it impossible to regret the experience of it. After all, wasn't it suffering which gave life dignity and significance? Did it not raise man above his pettiness? If there were no dragons to slay, would there be any heroes?

Sarah Walworth and Mammy Martha finally received the release which was so welcome to them both, and the baby recovered, although she wasn't yet as sturdy as Clara would like for her to be. Little by little the children had become truly Clara's. More and more they looked to her as a parent. That had been difficult for Jane Conner to accept.

She had come one morning to call at The Burn. Clara remembered descending the stairway one morning and hearing Jane Conner's positive voice coming from the front parlor. "Daisy, not bare feet! I'm shocked! Go and put on some shoes at once. Lucy, you are never to go without a petticoat, even at home. No lady does."

Clara paused, and gripped the stair rail. She had told Lucy that she might go without a petticoat in the mornings in hot weather. With so many sick people in the house, the laundry was a problem. Beyond that, there was the principle of the thing. Mrs. Conner had not yet accepted the fact that the children were no longer her responsibility.

Clara mustered all her courage and joined the children and their grandmother in the parlor.

Jane Conner sat erectly on the edge of a large high-backed chair. Her stout, but diminutive, white-haired figure was clad entirely in black with jet lace ruffles at her throat and wrists. She sat with both her hands folded upon a handsome mahogany cane topped by the silver head of an eagle. Although her rheumatism was painful at times, she didn't really need the cane for walking, but it had belonged to her husband and she was sentimental about it. Clara suspected that she also liked the effect of it. She used it as a queen might a scepter.

"Mrs. Conner, how nice to see you."

"How are the sick?" Jane Conner never wasted words.

"Ernestine is much better every day now. I want you to come up and see her. I'm sorry that the children weren't dressed for company, but we have so many extra duties, and so much less help. I told Lucy to leave off her petticoat in the mornings."

"Oh, I see. I should be happy, as you know, to take the children back to Linden. I've always thought that under the circumstances it would be the wisest thing. I'm afraid you have more here than you can handle properly."

Clara understood well enough that part of the circumstances included her unfitness to rear the children. She thinks I'm too young and inexperienced. But if I'm too young, it's equally true that she's too old, Clara thought. And it's time to get this matter settled.

She took a deep breath, and spoke as gently as she could, but deliberately. "Douglas has decided that the children should stay here. I know I may not always do exactly as you think best, Mrs. Conner, but I will promise to do my best to rear them properly."

Jane Conner raised her eyes to meet Clara's level gaze. The shrewd old eyes did not falter before it, and Clara read in them a grim acceptance of the inevitable, and perhaps a little grudging admiration. She suddenly realized how difficult it must be for Mrs. Conner to let go of the children. She knew she must stand her ground, but she resolved that the children would always keep in close contact with their grandmother.

"Oh, I'm sure you'll do a fine job, my dear," said Jane. "I do want to see Ernestine very much, if I may."

"Of course. Let's go up."

As they started toward the stairs, Jane, her tiny, dumpy figure somehow regal, turned to look up at Clara, who was not very tall herself, and said, "Perhaps I could take Lucy's petticoats home with me and have them done up."

Ye Gods! Clara had said to herself with mingled irritation and amusement. Does she never give up?

"Good morning, Sister."

Clara looked up from her reverie, startled to see Douglas, freshly bathed and dressed, his beard neatly combed, a dignified and impressive-looking man, standing hesitantly in the door.

"Good morning, Douglas."

He stood there for a moment, and then began to speak with resolution, "I—I've come to apologize to you for the things I said last night. I know I shouldn't have spoken to you as I did. Please forgive me."

Clara sighed. Such a sincere apology deserved forgiveness, and yet she knew from experience that his repentance would not prevent the same thing happening again. But what could one say that had not already been said so many times before? She had warned him that he was placing his relationship with his children in jeopardy. His management of their family finances, already shaken by war and military occupation, was bound to be affected by his drinking. His whole life was being ruined. Yet he would not, or perhaps could not, change.

"I forgive you, Douglas."

He thanked her humbly, and strode out onto the back gallery. He knew he could not forgive himself.

A few moments later Lucy appeared in the doorway, a determined look on her face.

"Aunt Clara, I've checked on my dresses and I'm sure they'll all do just fine. I don't really need anything new. You get something for yourself."

"Oh, I may do that, Lucy. But you must have something to wear to parties. Now I thought that a white de soie with a little dark green ribbon insertion like one I saw in *Godey's Lady Book* would look cool and become you. I'll order enough material to make the little girls some dresses out of it, too."

"You know Father is right, Aunt Clara. You don't think enough about yourself." Lucy's appraising eyes allowed no escape.

Why don't they leave me alone, Clara asked herself impatiently. What is there left in my life but my family? Why shouldn't I think about them? And why shouldn't I cherish my letters? They're all that's left to me of a "life of my own."

She wanted to cry out to Lucy, leave me alone! But she couldn't help but be touched by her niece's concern for her.

"Lucy, I appreciate your thinking about me and worrying about my happiness, but let me assure you that my life is quite filled with all of you. I went to lots of parties when I was your age before the War. I've had my turn. Now to get back to the dresses. Let me show you the one that I thought would suit you especially well." She picked up the latest copy of *Godey's Lady Book.* "I put a marker at the page. Here it is."

Lucy realized the firmness of Clara's intention to close the subject, and with a wisdom she didn't always show, she let the matter go, thinking, however, that Father was right about another thing. Aunt Clara had a very hard head.

"That does look very pretty," she said. "Thank goodness it hasn't any ruffles. I don't like frills and furbelows. Oh, yes, Aunt Clara, the Shields have invited me to come back to tea this afternoon so that Dr. Shields can show me his collection of Oriental art, and they said for you and Father to come, too, if you could."

"The St. John Eliots have invited us to D'Evereux so I'm afraid we can't go. Why don't you take Daisy and Annie along with you? I think they would find that interesting."

"Well, all right. I'm not sure they'll appreciate it properly, but I'll take them anyway. I'll see if they want to go."

After Lucy had gone to look for her sisters, Clara closed up the ledgers and put them away in one of the long serpentine drawers of the mahogany secretary. Then she went to find Uncle Perry to take her letters to the post office. Her next stop was the kitchen, where she exchanged a few words with Aunt Chloe regarding dinner. Lessie was there helping to clean the quail that Douglas had brought from Fawnwood.

"I'm going out to the garden. I'll get us a few roses for the table," she said to Lessie.

"Yes'm, we needs some fresh ones. Most of yesterday's is shattered."

Like all our dreams, thought Clara, a small, wry smile tugging at the corners of her mouth. I guess that's what we need, some fresh ones!

CHAPTER FIVE

UNCLE Perry started to the stable to hitch up the horse and wagon. He had Miss Clara's letters to mail and he also had an errand to do for Mr. Douglas. He was to buy some denim and calico for the hands at Fawnwood and send it by the boat which would be leaving in the early afternoon. He stopped by the kitchen on his way, where he found Lessie helping Aunt Chloe strip the feathers off the little bobwhites.

"I reckon I need you worse than Sister Chloe does. Mr. Douglas done got me buying yard goods for the folks on the plantation. Come along and help me, child."

Lessie's face lit at the idea of a shopping trip, and Aunt Chloe grumbled good naturedly, "Well, go ahead if he can't handle such a hard job as that all by hisself. I'll get Maybelle to come help me."

Lessie undid the handkerchief that bound her neat little head and discarded her apron. "I'll meet you at the stable. I just have to get my bonnet. Thank you, Aunt Chloe."

The store was fascinating. Lessie loved to go in it. It even had a good smell to it. She admired the lace and embroidery and the bolts of material with all their different designs: the stripes, the plaids, the checks and the flower-sprigged muslin and calico. She wished Uncle Perry hadn't come back from mailing the letters in such a hurry.

Now they headed down Under-the-Hill, the place where

the steamboats and flatboats docked. It was a different Natchez from the one on the hill with its big houses and beautiful gardens, its clean, quiet streets, its dignified court house, its churches, its genteel people in their elegant, faded clothes with their voices like velvet and their manners like silk. It seemed fitting that this Natchez should be situated on the lofty heights overlooking the river, while the other should lurk beneath.

But Under-the-Hill was exciting. It had hardware and feed stores, blacksmiths and buggy shops, and taverns and billiard parlors. Gypsy fortune tellers advertised their places of business by means of large, colorful signs with crystal balls painted on them, or else the palm of a huge hand. Most of the buildings were set up on pilings to protect them from the river's rampages. Some of them had shutters that were always closed, and she had heard that they were wicked places. In the daylight though they looked innocent enough.

Silver Street, the main street, was teeming with people, buggies and wagons, and horses and mules. It was dusty and bustling and noisy. The roustabouts were loading and unloading the barges, and shouting at each other, adding to the general confusion.

Lessie sat waiting in the wagon, observing the scene around her, while Uncle Perry went looking for the captain of the barge. It was taking a long time, and it was hot in the midmorning sun, so she decided to get down out of the wagon. She hitched the horse up in front of a nearby feed store and started to sit down on a bench on the porch. At the other end of the bench sat a fair-skinned negro man. He had a piece of board lying across his knees and he was drawing on it with a small bit of charcoal. Curious, she moved as close as she dared and tried to look at the drawing without seeming to. It was a sketch of the river scene before them, clusters of barges and boats against the bacl ground of the curving river bank.

Without ever looking up he quite suddenly said, "Wel what do you think of it?"

She jumped and blinked, feeling like a rabbit caught munching in the garden, but she couldn't run away so she just sat there.

He was looking at her now, his strange, blazing eyes boring holes through her. She felt an odd excitement mounting inside of her. She was aware of danger, but she was intrigued by it.

"Well, now, tell me what you think of it," he insisted, shoving it into her hands. But she had lost interest in it. All she could think of was him.

She had to say something so she murmured, "Oh, I think it's very good. Yes, it sure is good."

"I've got lots more. This one ain't right yet. I've got some ones of people. I like to do people best. In fact," he squinted his eyes at her and reached out a finger to lift her chin and turn it to the side, "I'd like to draw a picture of you. You got a different look about you."

Lessie was amazed. How could all this be happening to her? It was like nothing she had ever dreamed of. It was like there was another Lessie that she hadn't even known was there.

"Well, how about it? Will you let me draw you? Will you now?"

She saw Uncle Perry striding toward them so she spoke quickly, her voice soft and trembly. "I'll ask Miss Clara to let me off for the afternoon one day."

"Any day this week is fine. Or next. The next week I'm taking out. Just ask for Sam. They know me 'round here."

"All right, Sam, I will. Goodbye." She spoke without looking at him, and hurried off to join Uncle Perry. She knew he wouldn't approve of her having anything to do with this man.

What had ever possessed her to say she would come back and see him again, this stranger with those eyes that made her shiver inside? But she wanted to see him again and somehow she knew that, no matter what, she was going to do it.

When the calling hour arrived in the late afternoon,

Lucy and her little sisters set off on foot to visit the Shields. The doctor and his wife lived in a modest cottage just down the road from The Burn. The road was dusty, but they had worn their boots in preparation for it.

Lucy carried a dainty parasol to keep the afternoon sun from marring her complexion, which was smooth and white. She walked at the measured pace required of a lady, but her sisters scampered ahead, still free from such restrictions. They skipped along hand in hand, drinking the cup of life, alive to every sight and sound and smell. The smells of the road, dust, horse manure and all, they found particularly exciting, for these spoke of a big wide world which began here and led who knew where.

Within minutes they had arrived at the Shields' tiny cottage. It was nestled in the midst of a veritable jungle of shrubs and flowers of every variety. The iron fence that surrounded the yard was loaded with climbing roses and honeysuckle so thick that it was difficult to get the gate open.

"I'll knock!" cried Annie, pushing ahead of Daisy, who stood back with a great show of dignity befitting her year's seniority.

"Well, you needn't knock me down!"

"I didn't!"

"Well, you almost did!"

"Must you girls argue about everything?" Lucy lowered her parasol, and ascended the steps to the narrow gallery which stretched down one side of the cottage. She had to duck her head to avoid the limb of a very large oak tree which dominated the small yard and stood guard over the house.

A lean, stooped man, whose clothes looked much too big for him, opened the door at Annie's knock.

"What good fortune! Three Misses Walworths come to call!" His deep-set, colorless eyes sparkled with pleasure.

"Come in, come in, young ladies. Look, my dear." He addressed a homely lady, wearing a kind smile and an unbecoming dress, who entered the room from another part of the cottage. The awkward rectangle of her long, thin face was topped by a pile of gray hair, which seemed to have a mind of its own, although she had obviously made an earnest effort to control it. "We have callers from The Burn."

"Lucy, Daisy, Annie! How simply wonderful to see all of you! I've just put on some tea. It ought to be ready soon. Sit down, girls. How is that precious little aunt of yours? I wish she had come too. Tell her my yellow rose is blooming now, and she must come to see it."

"Where are the paintings?" asked Annie looking about the room.

"Annie! Do hush!" Lucy whispered.

"Well, quite right she is. I was going to show you my paintings, and I have them right here." Dr. Shields tapped his bony fingers against a flat, red lacquered box which was placed on a low chest, heavily carved and handsomely fitted with brass in the Oriental style.

There was, in addition to the chest and the box of prints, a tiny teakwood table with a fat Buddha sitting on it. On the mantel stood a graceful statue of the Buddhist goddess of mercy, Kwan Yin, and several little carved figures of animals in various kinds of jade.

Over a Victorian love seat, which sat against the wall facing the fireplace, hung an impressive scroll. It depicted the events of Dr. Shields' life, the largest scene showing his arrival by steamship in China. It had been presented to him by his Chinese friends as a token of their appreciation and affection.

When they were all gathered around, Dr. Shields reverently opened the red lacquered box. As he showed them the pictures, he explained the type of art and artist which each represented. There were delicate silk prints of fruits and flowers, which the girls exclaimed over with delight, and some scenes with elaborate and intricate detail, which told a story.

"Ah, here's a good one," said Dr. Shields, holding up a print of a fierce-faced man in cumbersome clothing, brandishing a sword and apparently whirling about. "This is a

Japanese woodcut of an actor dancing. It has a lot of style."

"But he's so ugly!" said Annie, widening her blue eyes. "I thought art was supposed to be beautiful."

Dr. Shields smiled. "Well, Miss Annie, I guess it depends on your definition of beauty."

"What is your definition of beauty, Dr. Shields?" asked Lucy.

"Oh my! That's the hardest question I've ever been asked. You'll have to let me think a moment."

A respectful silence followed. The girls waited, and the doctor looked thoughtful.

Finally he spoke. "I guess as far as I'm concerned—and, of course, beauty is a personal sort of thing—it results from a combination of honesty and harmony and proportion. But not absolute honesty, harmony, or proportion. There needs to be a discordant note somewhere, an imperfection. Otherwise beauty could get to be a bore. Have you ever noticed how one never finds perfection in nature? If it isn't imperfect, it isn't real. It seems to me that we ought always to strive for something far grander and less limiting than perfection. After all, isn't it absurd for us human beings to assume that we can ever understand what perfection is? But to get back to our subject, physical beauty often reminds us of the unseen things we love and admire, and when we appropriate it to represent these things, we add a new dimension to it. One could talk about beauty for hours and not exhaust the subject, but I know two little beauties who would rather have some tea and cake, don't you think, my dear?"

Mrs. Shields nodded. "It should be just ready, Doctor." She left the room, returning in a moment with the tea in a brilliantly colored Chinese tea pot with a bamboo handle. She served the steaming beverage to her fascinated guests in diminutive Chinese rice bowls. It had an exotic aroma which the girls inhaled with zest.

"It smells so good!" said Annie.

"And tastes so good!" said Daisy.

"Dr. Shields, I think we would all agree that this cake is

beautiful," said Lucy nodding at the tall chocolate cake which Mrs. Shields had just brought in.

"Absolutely. The everyday things of life are the most beautiful of all." Dr. Shields' affectionate gaze rested on his wife, an ungainly figure in her rusty black dress with her hair escaping its pins and looking wilder by the minute.

"But is it true, do you think, that beauty is a personal thing? You don't mean, do you, that it exists only in the eyes of the beholder?"

"Oh, no indeed. I didn't mean to say that. I believe that beauty is a reality in itself. It's our idea of it that is subjective."

While Lucy and Dr. Shields debated the ultimates of life, Mrs. Shields entertained the little girls. She gave them each a thick slice of cake to go with their tea and told them about her native state, Virginia. In all the years spent in a foreign land she had never been able to vanquish her homesickness. It helped to talk about it, and when she had willing listeners she would go on and on.

"It's a beautiful place, children, the land always rising and falling, the trees so green in spring and so magnificently colored in autumn. My mother used to tell me the trees were putting on their party dresses. The maple was always the queen of the ball. And in the foothills where I lived, the clouds were so close you often walked through them, and you thought if you jumped high enough you could touch every one of them. You know, children, I hope that when I die perhaps the Lord will let my soul float over those hills on its way to heaven."

There was a rapt expression on the girls' faces as they pictured Mrs. Shields' soul floating like a cloud over the foothills of the Blue Ridge Mountains of Virginia.

"And speaking of Virginia," continued Mrs. Shields, "I've been told your Aunt Clara was engaged to a gentleman from Virginia, who was killed during the War. I've hesitated to ask her about it, but I wonder if I might have known his family."

"I think he was from Atlanta, although some of his letters did come from Virginia. I'm not sure. I don't even know what his name was. Lucy probably does. I've just seen his letters in Aunt Clara's desk," said Daisy.

"Yes," added Annie, looking longingly at the crumbs on her plate. "And sometimes when she comes out of her room, Daisy and I think she's been crying."

"Annie, we weren't sure," said Daisy firmly.

"There's a stack of letters this tall," continued Annie eagerly, ignoring Daisy's warning glance, "and they're tied up with white ribbon." She sighed, "I'd love to know what they say."

"Annie wanted to read them, and I wouldn't let her."

"Daisy, I only said, 'Wouldn't it be fun to?' I didn't really mean to do it. I know it isn't right to read anybody else's letters."

"Girls, we must go!" exclaimed Lucy, glancing at the tall clock by the door. "I always forget the time when I'm visiting here. Aunt Clara will be having a conniption fit." She turned to the Shields. "Thank you for a lovely afternoon. Such delicious refreshments and such stimulating conversation! And the pictures were exquisite, a real treat!"

"It gave me great delight to show them to you," said Dr. Shields. "You know the real pleasure of owning things is to be able to share them."

"Goodbye now, girls," said Mrs. Shields. "We'll see you Sunday at church, I suppose."

"Oh, yes," replied Lucy. "We're all so anxious to hear the new minister."

"He seems to be a very fine young man," said Dr. Shields. "I had the pleasure of meeting him the other day and I think we are most fortunate to have him in Natchez. I hope he will have a happy and fulfilling ministry here. I'm afraid this is a rather difficult time to start a new ministry."

CHAPTER SIX

THERE was much excitement in Natchez over the arrival of the new minister. For as long as Clara could remember Dr. Gordon had been the pastor of the church with the clock tower, and the Walworths worshipped God there each Sunday from their family pew. Dr. Gordon was much beloved by his parishioners, who considered him very spiritual. And indeed he was. Clara smiled at the memory of the dear old man. He had a habit of standing silently in the pulpit for minutes at a time, his eyes raised heavenward, his head cocked just to one side. He looked, she had often thought, as though he were getting his instructions directly from above.

He had passed on to his certain reward, and a young man from Wilmington, North Carolina, had been found to take over the ministry of the church.

Eliot Watson's arrival with his wife and three children was received with reservations by a flock unused to, and suspicious of, change.

The broad-shouldered, stockily built young man of God was good looking enough, the ladies said. They admired his wavy black hair and the thickly lashed, dark blue eyes which smoldered excitingly beneath the wings of his high arching brows. The beaky nose and jutting jaw were less to their taste, but Clara thought these gave his face strength.

Although he was friendly and modest in manner, some of the critical sensed an inner dedication which was so apt to lead to trouble.

As for Mary Watson, it was agreed that she had an unfortunate penchant for overdressing, being a shade too plump for any sort of style. She also appeared slightly deficient in brains or schooling, having an annoying habit of using French phrases incorrectly. However, it was said she seemed to be a devoted wife and mother, and certainly she was a pretty little thing.

Everyone wanted to hear Eliot Watson's first sermon and that Sunday the church was filled to capacity. Its stark white walls were unbroken except for a succession of narrow, plain glass windows. The aristocratic assembly, suited and gowned in their prewar finery, sat stoically on cushionless seats in their straight-backed pews, having left the elaborately furnished Greek temples in which they lived to worship the Puritan God of their forebears.

All eyes focused on Mary Watson as she took her seat in the front pew. She wore a light blue dress, the yoke and full sleeves trimmed with scrolls of darker blue passementerie. Her honey-blonde hair fell in long curls from a tiny flowered hat. The blue eyes were wide and innocent in her smooth and serene face as she settled into her seat.

There was a murmur behind Clara. "The dress calls for a plain hat and the hat calls for a plain dress."

Clara was annoyed at the petty criticism. Then observing Mary Watson's complacent expression, she thought, well, at any rate she seems to be pleased with the way she looks!

The June day was sultry, the humidity unrelieved by any movement of air except that stirred by the myriad tiny fans waved by the ladies who patted their faces and throats with wisps of linen and lace while the gentlemen mopped their brows unabashedly.

The opening hymn was sung with great dignity and little fervor. Prayers were said and scripture read, and at last Eliot Watson mounted the steps to the white paneled pulpit.

A hush settled over the congregation. Even the ladies' fans were folded.

Beads of perspiration shone on the young minister's brow as he stood erectly, almost rigidly, in the pulpit, the blunt fingers of his strong square hands just touching the polished mahogany top rail. Clara felt the high tension of his nervousness and his eagerness to be liked and she found herself anxious for him. Oh, I do hope he'll do well and that people will like him. Surely they will. He's certainly won me over already.

In the absolute stillness which surrounded him, Eliot Watson lifted his hands from the rail and sought among the folds of the black cassock that he wore his trousers' pocket, from which he drew a handkerchief. Wiping away the perspiration, he smiled disarmingly. "You know, nobody told me it got this hot in Natchez. I can see that I will have no need to describe the fires of Hell to you. Not that I don't appreciate the warmth of this welcome. I believe it's the warmest I've ever received."

These playful words brought relief and laughter to his audience. A minister who could joke about hell fire was not going to be too unreasonable.

Then Eliot launched into a comparison of religion and architecture, likening the building of the Kingdom of Heaven to the building of a house. When he referred to the excellence of Natchez architecture, the congregation exchanged pleased glances. This new preacher was obviously a man of superior taste and discernment!

"Our architect," continued Eliot Watson, "has provided us with a set of blueprints, which we call Holy Scriptures, and He has given us a model in the Life and the Person of His Son. But, to our shame, there has been so much disagreement in the interpretation of the plan that there has been endless delay in the execution of it. Sometimes all building has ceased because of bitter dissension among the workmen. We have even killed each other because of our differences!" The indigo eyes beneath the heavy brows sent sparks, and Eliot Watson's voice rang out sharply. "And the shocking truth is that most of these differences arise over the details." He drew his handkerchief across his forehead again and continued.

"A young man, burning with zeal to change the world and make it a better place, approached me recently. He asked me if I could explain why Christianity had failed. 'That is easily explained,' I told him. 'It has never been tried.' But on a more optimistic note let me add that to the extent to which it has been tried, it has improved the world. It has had a great influence upon it. Our concern for our fellow man, our unwillingness to leave him to his fate, is espoused by the humanists, but it was born of Christianity. The justice, however imperfect, which our governments now dispense, is not the harsh justice of the pre-Christian world, untempered by mercy.

"There is a very fine orphanage here in Natchez, which I was privileged to visit the other day. This is a Christian undertaking and is one of many charitable endeavors sponsored by the Body of Christ throughout the world.

"The missionaries returning from heathen lands—" Clara glanced across the aisle to where the Shields sat. The doctor hunched in his pew, arms folded, listening intently with an inscrutable expression. "—can tell us what it is like to live where Christianity has not been.

"Notwithstanding we must admit that, although we profess Christianity and call ourselves Christians, we equivocate, and we fall short both in faith and deed. But our Kingdom's Architect is loving and forgiving and ready to help us make a new start. My friends, let us begin without delay!"

Clara was much moved by the sermon. Dr. Watson spoke with authority and conviction, and she felt his deep sincerity.

"How do you like him?" she asked her brother as they descended the long flight of steps from the church to the street.

Douglas flicked open his watch and, glancing at it, said, "Well, he's off to a good start with that short sermon. He ought to be very popular." He added, "He seems to be a nice fellow, straightforward and easy to follow, goes right to the point; and I was especially pleased to detect a glimmer of humor in him."

All the comments she heard were favorable, even enthusiastic. Clara felt so relieved. She didn't know why she should care that much, but she was so glad that everybody liked Eliot Watson.

CHAPTER SEVEN

A few weeks after the Watsons' arrival, Douglas and Clara decided to have a dinner party for the new minister and his wife. They invited Rebecca's sister, Margarette, and her husband, Will Martin, and the Austin Conners, who were cousins of Rebecca and Margarette's and old friends of the Walworths. They would have had Laura and her husband, Will McPheeters, but Laura was not going out in public now because of her advanced pregnancy.

Clara said to Douglas, "I'd really like to have the Shields, too. They're such dear people, and I think Dr. Watson and Dr. Shields would be very congenial."

"Well, I think you're right. Why don't you ask them? I understand she's very homesick for Virginia. Perhaps we can cheer her up."

Clara laughed, "Well, that's what she says, and I'm sure she would rather have settled there when they came back from China. But Dr. Shields had all those estate problems here, what with the carpet-bag government and that insane nephew of his, that they almost had to come to Natchez. At any rate I think she loves it here now. Virginia is just her 'pie in the sky someday'!"

On the night of the party Clara put on her one good dress, a smartly cut jade silk, which turned her blue-gray eyes to green, and fastened a double row of pearls about her slender throat. She had arranged her light brown hair high on her head, a style becoming to her piquant face with its wide forehead, pointed chin and high cheek-bones. Her reflection in the oval mirror above the walnut dresser resembled the cameo brooch that was pinned at the *V* neckline of her dress.

She adjusted the things on the dresser, gave the room a searching glance to be sure of its neatness, and, lifting her skirts, headed for the suspended stairway, which was such a feature of The Burn. Its path made a breathtaking turn in midair, an eloquent feat of engineering providing enjoyment to the eye, and inspiration to the soul. She rounded its hairpin turn and ran down the straight sweep of it to confer with Aunt Chloe and to check the dining table.

All was in good order out in the kitchen, which was steaming hot and full of succulent smells.

"Don't you worry none, Miss Clara, everything's fine. The rolls is rising just lovely, and the charlotte russe ain't never tasted better if I do say it myself! Go along now, and enjoy your party. My, don't you look handsome!" Aunt Chloe stepped back, raising her long black arms into the air and shaking her head. "I just wish your mama could see you." The gaunt and stooped old woman's pride and pleasure in her young mistress' appearance was beautiful to behold.

In the dining room the table, with extra leaves inserted, was longer than a Chinese dragon. Covered in snowy white damask to the floor, it was set with the yellow china and Lessie's centerpiece, a cascading, fan-shaped bouquet of all the flowers from the garden. Tall beeswax candles rose regally from the many-prismed crystal candelabra on either side. Everything lay in still perfection, awaiting the kiss of candlelight to bring it to life.

Clara joined her brother on the gallery to wait for their guests. The children appeared one by one, dressed in their best, to greet the company before they went up to bed, except Lucy and John, who were to be included in the party.

Lucy wore her new white de soie with the dark green ribbon insertion. It did become her well, Clara thought. Although Lucy was too rawboned to be pretty, she had a lot of elegance and style about her.

"There's a full moon tonight," announced John, leaning against a pillar and scanning the sky. He was wearing one of his grandfather's frock coats which had been cut down to fit him. He looked exceedingly handsome in the pale gray coat, his blond hair bleached, and his fair skin bronzed, by the god of the Natchez Indians. He and Douglas always acquired heavy suntans in the summer in spite of their fair complexions.

"Why, of course there is!" said Clara. "I ordered it myself."

"Oh, I should have known you would have thought of that. How very foresighted of you, Aunt Clara!"

Dr. and Mrs. Shields arrived first, both as badly dressed as usual, and the children clustered around her, for she was one of their favorites.

They were all still standing on the front gallery when the Watsons' carriage arrived. Uncle Perry, stylish and immaculate, in a much-mended claret-colored coat with a black velvet collar, helped them out, greeting them in his easy, courteous way. Then he spoke gently to the nervous horse that had brought them, and led him away to the carriage house.

Clara held out her hands to the minister and his wife as they came up the steps.

"Welcome to The Burn," she said, smiling and reaching down to take Mrs. Watson by the hand.

Mary Watson, pretty and curvaceously plump, in pale blue organdy, flowered bonnet, and lace mitts, responded with effervescent friendliness.

"How nice of you to have us, Miss Clara. We've heard so much about The Burn's hospitality."

"Miss Clara, you look stunning tonight," said Eliot Watson as she held out her other hand to him, and she flushed with pleasure at the compliment and the frank admiration in the charcoal-blue eyes which accompanied it.

Margarette and Will Martin arrived next, followed by the Austin Conners.

It was a congenial group, and the conversation flowed smoothly through several delicious courses of Aunt Chloe's cuisine. No wine was served in the presence of the minister, who was expected to be a teetotaler.

As they left the table for coffee on the back gallery, the men were discussing the new State Convention to adopt a constitution. The first one that had been proposed had contained articles so objectionable that, even with all active supporters of the Confederacy excluded from voting, it had been rejected. This time it was hoped that each provision could be voted on separately. Until a constitution was adopted, Mississippi could not be readmitted to the Union and must continue under martial law, so the issue was urgent. It was also controversial, and this small group reflected the mixed opinions about it.

Will Martin had returned to his law practice and was taking as active a political role as he was permitted, attempting to bring Mississippi back into the Union. He was speaking now on a subject which he had tactfully refrained from bringing up while Uncle Perry and the negro girls, Lessie and Maybelle, had been serving them.

"The section on the right of negroes to testify against white men is one that I feel very strongly should be left in. They ought to have that right."

"Oh, now, what jury would believe them, anyway? It would just cause trouble, Will." Austin was of the traditional view.

"Do you remember the Baylor Wynn case?"

"Of course I do, and that was unfortunate, but Baylor Wynn was unquestionably a negro. It's too bad it couldn't have been proved that he was. Then there wouldn't have been any problem."

Clara, who sat next to Eliot Watson, explained the facts of the case to him in a brief aside. "Some years ago a negro barber, William Johnston, a freedman, who was highly respected and well liked, was murdered. He was extremely light skinned, the type we call 'a man of color.' A young negro boy, who had witnessed the murder, accused a farmer named Baylor Wynn, who was also supposed to be 'a man of color.' But Baylor Wynn claimed he was white, which meant that the boy's testimony against him would be inadmissible as evidence since a negro couldn't testify against a white man. No proof could ever be found of Baylor Wynn's negro blood. General Martin, who was the district attorney at that time, did everything he could to bring the man to justice. Everybody said his three-hour address to the jury was brilliant. But there just wasn't sufficient evidence without the boy's story, and so the murderer went free."

Meanwhile Will responded to Austin Conner, "You mean in that case there wouldn't have been any problem. But suppose Baylor Wynn had been a white man. Anyway, what's important is the right of every man to be heard in his own defense, or to get reparation if he's abused. Don't forget that 'free' negroes are not going to be under anyone's protection."

"Aha, now there's the real problem, isn't it? This damned freedom business! Will, you know perfectly well the negroes don't understand the first thing about our Common Law and its traditions! They don't live by the same set of morals that we do! It's fine to talk about equal justice, but are you really going to apply our laws to them? It's impossible, and you know it! Good Lord, man, the negroes have been living as savages for centuries while the rest of the world has become increasingly civilized! In all this time they haven't changed themselves. Why do you think we can change them now?"

"Austin, I agree that, as a practical matter, there does have to be some compromise with the ideals of absolute justice. This world isn't the Garden of Eden. Paradise was lost long ago. Perfect equality doesn't exist and never will, and perfect justice won't either. Anyone with common sense knows that. But the right to be heard in court is so basic, it's a thing that I feel shouldn't be compromised, and I intend to fight for it."

"Well, I happen to have had a little personal experience with negro testimony myself, Mr. Martin, my love," began Margarette, who had scarcely been able to contain herself during this conversation between her husband and Austin Conner.

"Now, Little Wife," murmured the general.

"Now Little Wife nothing! Of course, you weren't here during the occupation to see how the negroes behaved, stealing and destroying property, and deliberately insulting everyone! But can you have forgotten how the day the Union troops took Natchez, Adeline and Amelia made off with all our things, and then told terrible lies about us to the provost marshal all under oath in the Courthouse? Is that the kind of testimony you're so anxious to obtain?"

"Well, now, because Amelia lied doesn't mean that all negroes do. I know she acted badly, and that a lot of the others did, too, but don't forget there were many who didn't. What about some of our distinguished white citizens, whom I recall you said behaved so shamefully? I'm afraid humanity's frailty is more than skin deep!"

Lucy's glowing eyes reflected the hero worship she felt for her Uncle Will. She had once said about him to Dr. Shields, "He's not always consistent in his ideas, or at least he seems not to be, but then I always think he's right."

Dr. Shields had replied, "Well, you know, Miss Lucy, as Emerson so rightly said, 'A foolish consistency is the hobgoblin of little minds.'"

Will continued, "And actually, Austin, I'm not sure that, although the negroes came to us from a primitive civilization, they haven't the capacity for a higher degree of it. Climate and isolation might account for their lack of development. Training and education do seem to improve them."

Austin countered, "Well, Will, granting for the sake of argument that the negroes, through education, can eventually become civilized as we are, although I don't for a minute agree that they can, you'd still have the problem of controlling them until that time should come. And the idea of illiterate, semisavage men participating in the making and enforcing of our laws is ridiculous! Even Thomas Jefferson, radical as he was, didn't suggest that. Why, just take a look at the Natchez Indians! They had, comparatively speaking, an advanced civilization, but there sure wasn't any democracy or equality in their system. It takes centuries to develop anything like that. The president knows that. Congress knows that. We're just being punished. That's what it really amounts to."

All other conversation had ceased, and attention was focused on the exchange between these two respected citizens of Natchez.

"I grant you, Austin, that democracy is an advanced system of government, depending for its success upon the education and sophistication of its electorate, and I'm as opposed to the negro having the vote as you are. They aren't ready for that."

Dr. Shields turned suddenly to Eliot Watson. "What place, I wonder, does the negro have in this Kingdom we're to build?"

The young minister looked uneasy and startled by the question. "He's one of God's children, a—well, a fellow laborer," he replied.

Clara decided that this was a good point at which to let the argument rest. She refilled their cups and invited the ladies upstairs, leaving the gentlemen to indulge in cigars and storytelling.

When the ladies rejoined the party, Clara proposed that they go out to the garden. "The mosquitoes may have gone to bed and left it for us to enjoy."

"Well, let's hope they've had their supper anyway," was Eliot Watson's smiling rejoinder, as he offered Clara his arm.

The other guests followed them down the shrub-bordered walk with its flights of steps that led to the garden level, the moon, at its fullest, illuminating their descent.

The garden by moonlight had a hushed and holy beauty which refreshed the spirit. The white flowers shone here and there amidst the shadowy shapes of the vividly colored ones that gloried in the daylight, and their mingled fragrances sweetened the night air. The cape jessamine was so poignant that it reached right into the heart. Silence fell on the little group, and for a moment they were as one, united by their reverence and appreciation.

Since human beings can bear only so much of the ethereal, Margarette Martin broke the silence. "Just look at the old white rose! It's always so beautiful by moonlight."

"Everything is beautiful in the moonlight. Does it cloak the truth, or reveal it, would you say, Miss Clara?" asked Dr. Shields.

"Anything so beautiful must be true!"

"The moon's a charming liar, and one mustn't believe it," Douglas disagreed.

"The moon doesn't lie, Douglas. Everything it says is perfectly true," protested Clara.

"But it doesn't tell the whole truth," Douglas insisted.

"And neither does the daylight. I believe that moonlight reveals a more important kind of truth."

"What is that?" asked Lucy, fascinated by the philosophical turn the conversation had taken.

"It shows us the beauty in everything, which most of us don't see in the daylight. It actually reflects the true shape of things better, because it eliminates all the distracting and superfluous details."

Lucy took over the idea with enthusiasm. "I see what you mean. It doesn't just mirror the facts, it interprets them!"

"And," added Eliot Watson, joining the game, "it helps to make us aware of the unseen. When we assume that what we see in the brightness of the daylight is the only reality, life not only loses its magic and mystery, but truth itself is lost along with faith."

Lucy had been eager to talk to the minister all evening, and now, as the guests began to seat themselves in the summer house, she took a chair beside him.

"Dr. Watson, what effect do you think Darwin's theory of evolution will have on our Christian belief? Won't it cause people to lose their faith?"

The winging brows knit together. "Well, Miss Lucy, perhaps some of them, but then there have always been doubters. And, of course, it is, as you rightly say, only a theory. He has no absolute proof that he's right."

"Well, if scientific research does produce some evidence contradicting what the Bible says . . .?" Lucy's face was earnest.

"I don't think we should worry about that happening. The scriptures often contradict themselves, you know, Miss Lucy." With these simple, but meaningful, words he conveyed a more liberal view than any she had ever heard, or hoped to hear, from anyone but Dr. Shields. It was an enormous relief to her. She felt deeply grateful for his response to her need to let her thoughts fly freely.

"It isn't necessary to close your mind when you open your Bible," he added. "Of course we human beings can never know more than a part of God's truth, either spiritually or scientifically. As St. Paul says, 'We know in part and we prophesy in part,' but I think it's our right, even our duty, to keep trying to find as much of the truth as we can, and that we shouldn't ever be afraid of it."

Lucy glanced at Dr. Shields, who was puffing furiously on the pipe he had just lit. He looks as though someone has just given him a wonderful present, she thought.

Eliot Watson's bold words struck a responsive chord in Clara, too. That was just the way she, herself, felt about faith, and she was grateful for the comfort he had given her intellectually curious, and often rebellious, niece. She was glad, though, that certain of her friends were not present to hear Eliot Watson's comment about the Bible contradicting itself. Even though it might be true, they wouldn't want it to be said.

After the last guest had gone, the family sat on the back gallery for a while in the moonlight discussing the evening, which they all agreed had been a great success.

"Of course, Lucy was good enough to turn the preacher's silly little wife over to me so she could monopolize him," John grumbled amiably.

"Well, I didn't want to spend the entire evening talking to her. Her conversation is about as stimulating as a page of *Household Hints*!"

"Now, now!" interrupted Clara. "I think you should both be ashamed to talk that way about our guest. I liked Mary Watson. She may not be brilliant, but she's pleasant and sincere, and you must admit she's very pretty."

"She's an awful bore," Lucy insisted.

John, who had a marked talent for mimicry, began now mischievously to conduct an imaginary conversation between his sister and the minister's wife, rendering with remarkable accuracy Mary Watson's breathless little voice and Lucy's crisp one.

"Mrs. Watson, do you approve of Colonialism?"

"Why, I don't know much about architecture, but I think so."

"I never would have thought of calling Empire building architecture, but I suppose one could."

"Oh, Miss Lucy, you are so clever!"

"Yes, thank goodness."

"Do you do much needlework, Miss Lucy?"

"No more than I have to."

"Then you must like to cook. Do you have any luck with soufflés?"

"Mrs. Watson, have you ever read *The Decline and Fall of the Roman Empire*?"

Douglas, who had been in excellent spirits that evening, laughed until he was forced to wipe his eyes with his handkerchief. John was the one person who never seemed to provoke him even when he was in a black mood, and he took great delight in his son's irreverent humor.

Even Lucy was forced to laugh. "I'm afraid you sound more like me than I do myself, John, and you're an absolutely perfect Mrs. Watson!"

The servants were gathered on the balcony of their quarters above the building which housed the kitchen, seeking respite from the heat. The night air was cool now, but the heat of the day was still trapped inside their rooms.

With the tree frogs clamoring in the background, Aunt Chloe was holding forth on her favorite subjects. The old woman had always valued herself and her own opinions highly, and now, with a successful life behind her, she was unshakeable in her convictions.

The others listened tolerantly, having heard it all before.

"Mr. Douglas is a worrier. He's really more like Miss Sarah, though he puts on ways like his father. Old Master, he didn't worry none. He just did the best he could. And he ran a good plantation. I can tell you that. He bought me and my mammy and three brothers from off another place when I was about Miss Daisy's size. He worked his field hands hard, but he didn't stand for no fighting amongst them. You know, you gets all kinds in the fields. He told them first one cut somebody's throat he'd cut theirs. He meant it, too. And they knew he did. There was some hacking around after sundown, but nobody got killed. I didn't live there too long. Mr. John brought me up to work for Miss Sarah, and we took right to one another. She was what you call a saint, bless her soul! You know, she was such a little bit of a thing, and sickly most of the time, losing all them babies, but she never did complain. Then the War came, and that really killed her. When she took sick at the last, you remember she wouldn't let nobody nurse her but me, and all she could say when she was laying there suffering was how much trouble she was, and I told her, 'Nothing I ever done for you was trouble, Miss Sarah.'

"And she kept saying what a shame Miss Clara have to take over Mr. Douglas' children, and her just a child herself, and she ain't able to help her none. And she said how she ain't never been able to do much all her life. I told her, 'Miss Sarah, it ain't what you done in this world, it's what you been, makes everybody love you.'

"I was with her when she died, and the last thing she said was, 'Take care of our children, Chloe.' And I mean to do just that.

"During the War one of them Union soldiers asked me didn't I want to be free, and I told him, 'What do you mean free?' He said, well, didn't I want to call my soul my own? I said I always had called my soul my own, and it didn't take no war to do it. He said he was fighting to free me, and I looked him eye to eye, and I said, 'Young gentleman, just you go on home to your family, if that's all you got to fight about.' Now the War's over, and we are free, and will you tell me what's different, except we're all poor instead of rich, and black and white trash is running loose all over the place acting high and mighty?" Aunt Chloe paused in her soliloquy to catch her breath.

Maybelle smiled and spoke shyly, for Aunt Chloe was a positive woman, and one did not lightly disagree with her whether one was black or white. "I know it's not much different, but I like the idea of it, to be free to do whatever you likes."

"Hmph," snorted Chloe, "ain't nobody that free, child."

Lessie was perched on the railing, her arms wrapped around one of the narrow wooden pillars of the gallery. She had been staring out into the moon-drenched night, savoring its shining serenity, holding her heart open so that the moon could pour its beauty into it. The unearthly light fell full on her upturned face, revealing its softness and its seeking.

Aunt Chloe's practical words brought her back to earth now, and she joined the argument, giving the squelched Maybelle an encouraging smile. "I know what Maybelle means. It's nice to know you don't have to belong to nobody else, and—and to have a choice where you'll work, or live. If you want to change your job, and go someplace else, you can."

"Who wants to be floating from place to place?"

"Suppose your folks are mean? Suppose they beat you?"

"Ones I seen beat should have been."

Lessie smiled, and let it go at that, but she knew that she and Aunt Chloe had been luckier than most, and she also knew that she was very glad she was "free."

"Sister Chloe," said Uncle Perry, tactfully changing the subject, "what do you think of the white folks' new minister?"

"He's a good man, Brother Perry, and I can tell he's been raised right. Did you notice how he come out to the kitchen after dinner to tell me how he enjoyed it? He's got a straight look about him and a firm hand shake. How did he converse during dinner?"

"Impressive enough. It seemed to me he knowed what he was talking about, and Mr. Douglas and the general listened to him real careful."

"He's a hearty eater. I noted his plate. I like that in a man."

"Well, he's a fine, godly man no doubt. He's young though, and, for all his jokes, he takes life mighty serious."

"If 'young' is all that's wrong with him, I reckon time will take care of that," laughed Chloe.

"Well, now, time can change folks both ways, you know," Lessie teased. "It don't always improve them." She ducked the old woman's playful cuff and continued, "I thought Mr. Watson was nice, too. Seems like he understands how people feel and like he cares about them. I think Miss Lucy likes him a lot, and Miss Clara, too."

CHAPTER EIGHT

THE next morning Clara was in the dining room putting away the china, crystal and silver that had been used for the party and checking the tablecloth and napkins for any stains before they were laundered.

She was humming happily to herself. She had enjoyed the party, especially the conversation in the garden. Eliot Watson was such an interesting person to talk to. Whatever had made him marry anyone as unimaginative and dull as Mary? Oh, it wasn't kind to call her that just because she wasn't scintillating in a group! But it did seem a shame for a man so intelligent and subtle to be wasted on someone who couldn't fully appreciate him. I'll never admit that to Lucy though, Clara told herself with a mischievous little smile.

Lessie came in to take the linen to be laundered, and Clara explained to her about the spots.

"Miss Clara," said Lessie shyly, "could I have the afternoon off today? I know I've taken right many lately, but I won't take any next week."

"Yes, certainly, Lessie. That will be all right with me. Everyone needs a little time for themselves."

Lessie carried the tablecloth and napkins down to the paved area beneath the back galleries where the big wash tubs were. She could hardly wait to see Sam again!

She had gone back. She knew she shouldn't have, but she couldn't help herself. She wanted to know more about Sam. He sketched her, and she went back again because he wasn't through. It was then that it had happened, what she knew she shouldn't have let happen, but she didn't care. Sam had opened up her narrow world. There was so much beyond it that she had never known enough to dream of, and she could not turn back now. Let it lead where it might. She was not afraid, but she did have an occasional nightmare in which her mother or Mammy Martha or sometimes Aunt Chloe stared at her in disapproval. Well, maybe she was a little bit afraid, but that just made it more exciting.

Sam showed her some of his other drawings. He did all kinds. He drew pictures of people that looked like them, but made them look silly. If a man had a big nose, he made it bigger. If his teeth stuck out, Sam made them stick out further. These drawings of his weren't pretty, and they were sort of mean she guessed, but they could really show up some stuck-up folks. She could see that. Sam said all pictures weren't meant to hang on the wall and look pretty. Sam worked on the steamboats, drawing sketches of the passengers, not the mean kind though. Those he kept to himself. Anyway he made his living with his sketching and then, too, he gambled, but Lessie soon discovered that he lost a lot more gambling than he won.

He left the end of the following week on the *Creole Belle*, which had come from New Orleans and was headed upriver to St. Louis, but he said he'd see her when he got back. After he left, it seemed like she just couldn't be happy. She felt all empty inside and the days went dragging by.

Sam had told her that it would be a whole month before the boat was back in Natchez. It had been over a month now and Lessie had been checking for days to find out when it would arrive. It had been expected for several days and surely it would come today, and then she would be with Sam this afternoon!

What, wondered Clara, did Lessie do with all this time off? She never volunteered any information, and Clara didn't like to ask. It worried her though somehow.

Annie wandered in, a forlorn look on her usually merry little face. "Aunt Clara, what can I do? Daisy's talking to the trees and she won't play with me."

"Talking to the trees" was what the family called Daisy's habit of walking about the yard talking to herself. This was an era when such eccentricity was not viewed with alarm, and Daisy spent many happy hours by herself weaving stories.

John stuck his head in the door. "I'm off for a ride, Aunt Clara. Father said Thundercloud needs some exercise."

"Oh, take me with you!" begged Annie, her face brightening.

"Well," John hesitated, "I don't really—oh, all right, come on. We'll ride over to Linden to see Grandmama."

"Oh, thank you, John! Thank you, thank you, thank you!" That would show Daisy.

Clara chuckled, "John, your heart is easily touched. Take this little mess along with you then. I'm certain Mrs. Conner will ask you to stay for dinner so I won't expect you back 'til evening. Don't be late for your class with Judge Harris."

John mounted the eager black horse and reached down for Annie. "Jump," he commanded, and as she did, he swung her up in front of him. "All right, Thunder." He gathered the reins in one hand, holding Annie with the other. "Go, boy."

Thundercloud snorted and tossed his head. They trotted briskly down the drive and out onto the road. The trees on either side reached out to one another, their branches intermingling, forming an arching roof of green lace above them through which the bright blue of the sky could be seen. Annie looked up with pleasure at the rapidly changing patterns of leaves and sky.

How heavenly it was, she thought, to be bouncing along in John's arms on Father's beautiful and prized horse, and as if this were not enough, their destination was Linden, and she would have Grandmama all to herself without Daisy or any of the cousins.

The road ran east from town to Linden. It was a quiet country road, bordered by fields and woods, and perfect for a good horseback ride. John put Thundercloud into an easy canter, and they rocked along together in contented silence. Finally they passed one of the few houses of the countryside, Monmouth, and moments later had left the road, and were galloping up through the grove of splendid old trees that led to the mounting block and hitching post of Linden.

The long matching wings that had been added to the front of the house looked, as Father so often said, like arms stretched wide in welcome! She slid down onto the mounting block, jumped over the two shallow steps which ran the whole length of the many-columned gallery, and ran into the front hall, calling, "Grandmama, Grandmama!"

Jane Conner, impeccable and elegant as always in a black skirt and tucked white shirtwaist, came from the back gallery into the hall, her eagle-headed cane tapping lightly and briskly over the broad planks of the highly polished floor. Tiny as she was, her erect carriage made her an imposing figure, and even Annie didn't forget to curtsy before delivering a dutiful kiss on the tissue-paper cheek. "Well, Annie, this is a surprise, a very nice one, too. Who brought you?"

"John rode me over on Thundercloud."

"Hello, Grandmama." John entered the front door.

"Well, you two are a welcome sight. You'll have to stay for dinner. Annie, run and tell Aunt Mary that you and John will be here. Come on, John, let's sit on the back gallery. It's so pleasant out there this morning."

John followed his grandmother out to the gallery. "Annie wanted so much to come that I brought her along. May I leave her here with you while I put Thundercloud through some paces?"

"Why, of course. I'll be delighted to have her. Just be

sure you stay away from town and you won't run into any trouble. Aunt Mary will have dinner ready when you get back. How was the party? Didn't you have the new minister and his wife to The Burn last night?"

"Yes, we did. The dinner was delicious, and the guests were very pleasant. A little wine would have improved everything though."

"You sound like your grandfather Conner. William didn't like to be deprived of his spirits, although he was actually a very temperate man. I remember when your mother and father were engaged, your great-grandparents had us to dinner at the Wren's Nest. They served not a drop of liquor all evening, being mortally opposed to the use of it. William was so outdone. When he came home he kept fuming about it, and I remember he said, 'That pious old puritan claims he's a descendant of Sir Christopher Wren. How I longed to inform him that Sir Christopher was a bachelor! I should certainly have enjoyed his dilemma!' Of course your grandfather knew as well as you and I that Mr. Wren said he was descended from a brother of Sir Christopher's."

John laughed, "Well, you'll have to admit it was an amusing idea!"

"What's the news at The Burn aside from the party?" asked Jane.

"Well, none really, although Aunt Clara and Father are a bit concerned about Lucy. You see, she wants to become a Hindu."

"A what?" Jane Conner's usually disciplined face registered her utter horror.

"Yes, she's been talking about it with Dr. Shields, and he feels that, perhaps, it's the right thing for her."

Before his grandmother's building wrath could explode, John began to laugh. "Grandma, you should never believe anything I say. You know that."

"Well, John, you really carry your joking too far sometimes. I don't think one's religion is a suitable subject for comedy."

"I'm sorry, Grandmama. I sometimes get carried away." John composed his finely modeled features into a contrite expression.

Annie, just returned from the kitchen wing, thought, he isn't one bit sorry.

Grandmama wasn't fooled either. "Don't die of your grief," she said drily, and turning to Annie, "Did you ask Aunt Mary to set places for you and John?"

"Yes, Grandmama. She said it was always a pleasure to have us. She says John and I are her favorites because we're so jolly."

"Well," said John with an innocent air, "it's nice to be appreciated. Annie, I'm going to exercise Thundercloud while you and Grandmama have a visit."

Annie took a seat beside her grandmother, smiling as broadly as the Cheshire cat. "That'll be just fine. Good-bye, John."

"Don't be in such a hurry for me to leave. It hurts my feelings, Annie. Do you and Grandmama have any secrets?"

"Oh, we have lots of them, don't we, Annie?"

"Well, I'll see you later. Don't talk about me unless you say something very nice."

"Now," said Annie, "he's gone, and here we are, just you and me."

"You and I."

"That's right."

"What was Daisy up to? Didn't she want to come?"

"Oh, she was talking to the trees. When she does that she doesn't know what anybody else is doing—or care."

"Well, Annie, what shall we talk about?"

"Mama."

This was a subject about which neither of them ever tired of talking.

"Tell me again how she looked. I try so hard to remember and somehow I just can't."

"That's not surprising. You were such a little girl when she died, and it's been almost four years now. Well, you know, everyone said she was beautiful, and of course she was to me. She looked so much like your Aunt Margarette that people often mistook them for twins. You resemble her, too, except for your coloring, which is like your Grandfather Walworth's, but Daisy has your mother's eyes. I do wish at least one of you children could have inherited her talent for music. Rebecca was never happier than when seated at a piano. That's why I gave her your Grandmother Gaillard's little spinet. It was one of her greatest treasures. After she married your father and moved to Elmo, I used to miss the sound of her playing so. Even now I often think, if only her music could fill these rooms again." And then a rare thing happened. Jane Conner's eyes filled with tears, but she blinked them away so quickly that Annie never saw them.

"I do remember her playing on the spinet," said Annie. "I used to sit beside her and watch her fingers, and I remember she taught me to play some tunes with one finger."

"She used to call you her little sunbeam."

"Your mother died when you were a little girl, too, didn't she, Grandmama?"

"Yes, although not so young as you were. My mother died when I was ten, but I was only two years old when my father died. My three brothers were much older. We lived in Pennsylvania, but then my brothers, who were all doctors like my father, came to Natchez to practice because they had heard about the great opportunity for young men here. After Mother died I was sent down the river on a flatboat to join them. I was scared to death and I didn't want to go to Natchez. I was sure I wouldn't like living here. I cried all the way. What a silly girl I was!"

"What was your mother like, Grandmama?"

"Well, Annie, your mother always reminded me of her, not only in appearance but in temperament as well. They were both very happy in their dispositions."

"Do you remember anything about your father?"

"No, but my brothers talked about him all the time. He led a very interesting life. Do you want me to tell you about him?"

Annie settled eagerly back in her chair. This was just what she had hoped for, one of Grandmama's stories.

"Well, his great-grandfather, Augustine de la Tacquy, was the son of a French Huguenot refugee. He was born on the Isle of Jersey, which is a tiny island just off the coast of France. It became a refuge for the Huguenots after the revocation of the Edict of Nantes, and Augustine's father had fled there. When Augustine grew up, he joined the Merchant Marine, and eventually came to this country, where he settled at Falmouth, Massachusetts. He americanized his name, and when he died in 1719 his will was signed *John A. Gustine.* Augustine's great-grandson was my father, Lemuel Gustine.

"Father had an adventurous spirit, and so he went to the Wyoming Valley of Pennsylvania, which was just being settled, and he lived the life of a pioneer in the wilderness. He studied medicine under a surgeon who happened to be there, and eventually married and had a daughter named Sara. Then when the American colonies declared their independence and the fighting with England began, Father entered the Continental Army as a surgeon. He took his wife and their three-year-old daughter Sara to a settlement known as Forty Fort, but his wife died soon after, leaving her little daughter motherless. Sara was even younger than you, Annie, when her mother died. I'm sure she couldn't remember her at all.

"Then on July 3, 1778, there was a battle! The British and some Indians attacked the fort. Just imagine, Annie, those Indians in their war paint, and the British troops, resplendent in their scarlet coats! They must have presented a colorful sight, and a formidable one, too, to the little ragtag army of settlers gathered at Forty Fort! But our men marched bravely out to meet them. The doctors went out, too, on their horses to look after the wounded, and during the battle a bullet went through Father's hat. Your Great Uncle Stephen still has that hat. You must ask him to show it to you sometime. It was a narrow escape for Father, and for us, Annie! Just think! If he'd been killed, you and I never would have been born!" Jane paused and Annie looked thoughtful.

"Well, Annie, to get on with my story, we were outnumbered, and they were slaughtering us, so our men finally turned and fled for their lives!

"Father went with the commander of the fort, Colonel Dennison, to arrange for the terms of surrender. The agreement that they finally arrived at stipulated that the inhabitants of the fort were not to be molested in persons or property.

"Then the next day about two o'clock a party of drunken Indians came into the fort and began taking things and insulting the women. Father, who was a very strong man, wrestled with one of them and managed to throw him to the ground. The other Indians were much entertained by this, and they threw him a rope, pointing at their friend, and crying, 'He's a dirty dog. Tie him.' Father was not only brave and strong, but clever too, and he decided to organize a wrestling contest among the Indians to distract them and keep them occupied. This proved so successful that he was able to slip away, and go to see the British commander, Colonel Butler, about the violation of the terms of surrender. When Father told him what had happened, Colonel Butler just shook his head, and said, 'I'm sorry. I promise that I'll do everything I can to protect you, but you know as well as I do that I can't control these savages. I think for your safety you should leave here.'

"When Father got back to the fort, he found that the Indians had gone, and that most of the settlers had already left, too, escaping into the wilderness, where there was little hope that they could survive. There were only about a dozen people left, most of them wounded. Father and one of the ladies pulled boards from the cabins and built and launched a flat-bottomed boat in nine hours! Then they loaded all the people into the boat with their possessions, which they had packed, as best they could, in trunks and boxes and bundles. Father held little Sara in his arms, and they pushed off into the Susquehanna River. What a trip that must have been! The river gets narrow and crooked and its currents are treacherous, and it's full of rocks and rapids. The boat was tossed about and flooded and all the able-bodied refugees had to take turns bailing water. Of course, they were still in danger of Indian attack. The Indians were being incited by the British, and even the tribes which had always been considered friendly were now attacking the American colonists.

"Think how afraid they must have been, Annie! But they were pioneers and had encountered all sorts of hardships and dangers before. They didn't expect life to be easy, and they had the will to survive.

"Late the next afternoon they arrived at a settlement where they took supper and considered spending the night. After a lot of discussion they decided, tired as they were, to go on. It was well they did. Weeks later they heard the news of an Indian massacre which had taken place there that very night! Finally they arrived in safer, more settled, territory. Some of the groups stopped in Middletown, but Father and little Sara went to Carlisle. It was there that he met my mother, Rebecca Parker. I named your mother for her."

"Oh, Grandmama, what a wonderful story! I never knew you had a sister. What happened to little Sara?"

"She was married and gone from home before I was even born. I never really knew her. I was born quite late in my father's life. As I told you, all my brothers were much older."

"Well, how'd you girls get along without me?" Even if she hadn't recognized his voice, Annie would have known who it was. John was the only person in the world who would have addressed Jane Conner as a "girl."

"Oh, we've had a marvelous time. You should hear the story Grandmama told me! Tell it to John, Grandmama. I want to hear it again."

"Annie, you're insatiable," said Grandmama. "I'm sure John has heard that story, but, if he hasn't, I'll tell him at dinner. I know Aunt Mary is ready for Zeke to serve us. Run and tell her that John is here. Oh, there's Zeke now. We're coming, Zeke." Grandmama rose. "Thank you, John." She took his offered arm with the air of one bestowing a great favor, while with her other hand she clasped one of Annie's. Jane Conner never forgot that she was an important person, and neither did anyone else.

They went into the lovely dining room where the Gustines and Conners looked down at them from their portraits and a carved wooden punkah hung over the table. The purpose of the punkah was to cool the diners, and to shoo away the flies.

"Isn't anybody going to pull the punkah?" asked Annie.

"I don't think we need it today, Annie," smiled Jane.

"Let me go get Little Brother to pull it, Mistress." Zeke hated to disappoint Annie.

"All right, Zeke, see if you can find him."

Zeke returned in a moment with a grinning little barefoot boy, the color of chocolate, which may have covered a multitude of sins. He was not dressed for this impromptu job, and his clothes were as dusty as he probably was. He was as excited about the punkah as Annie, and Jane and John and Zeke exchanged smiles. Zeke brought the Dubarry china soup bowls, filled with mounds of fluffy rice, and Grandmama served crabmeat gumbo from the big matching tureen.

Little Brother pulled, and the huge, white punkah swept gracefully to and fro.

"This is a wonderful way to cool your soup," said John. "I'm glad you insisted on the punkah, Annie."

Annie smiled blissfully, not taking her eyes off the punkah. "This has been such a good day. I'm going to always remember it."

CHAPTER NINE

LESSIE could hardly dry the dinner dishes her hands were so trembly. The boat was probably already in. She had arranged with a friend of Sam's to pick her up down at the curve in the road where she could wait for him out of sight behind some bushes. Just as soon as everything was put away she could leave. She would just quietly slip off and hope Aunt Chloe wouldn't notice. So far she hadn't except for one time and Lessie had made an excuse that seemed to satisfy her. She hated going behind Aunt Chloe's back, but she knew that Aunt Chloe would raise a big fuss and try to stop her. A person just couldn't reason with Aunt Chloe. She was too old and too set in her thinking.

The thing that was most troubling to Lessie about her relationship with Sam was what Miss Clara would think. She admired her so, and since Miss Rebecca died she was the person Lessie had tried to be like. But there was no use in a black person trying to be like a white one, she told herself. Everything was just too different. If she tried to act like Miss Clara everybody would only laugh at her. And there was no way Miss Clara could understand the way she felt about Sam. Miss Clara wouldn't ever have feelings like that. She wished she could have talked to her about it, though. She couldn't talk to Aunt Chloe, and poor Maybelle didn't have much sense, and she really needed to talk to somebody.

"Watch out, child," warned Chloe, "you nearly dropped that plate. Don't be in such a hurry. A person would think you had to catch that boat that folks have been waiting for down Under-the-Hill."

If she only knew how close she was to the truth, thought Lessie and she giggled nervously.

When the dishes were all done and put away, she hurried off to the room she shared with Maybelle in the servants' quarters. Maybelle was taking an afternoon nap. She lay on her cot sound asleep, a chubby little cheek resting on a chubby little hand. She looked so peaceful that for a brief moment Lessie almost envied her. But then she thought how never in a million years would Maybelle know the kind of feelings she had known.

She washed her face and changed to her Sunday dress, pushing her bonnet into the bodice to hide it. She fastened the buttons of the dress with difficulty over the bonnet, and her full little breasts strained at the buttons. She suddenly ached for the feel of Sam's hands, all gentle with love for her. But soon, she thought, soon she would be in his arms again! And he would have so many interesting things to tell her! She loved to listen to him talk about his experiences. He would probably have some new pictures to show her, too.

She glanced back at the sleeping Maybelle and then she slipped quietly out of the room, intending to cross underneath the back gallery so she could head for the road on the other side of the house from the servants' quarters. The sky had clouded up, and you could already smell the rain. There was a loud clap of thunder and the wind swirled the branches of the trees. She stood for a few moments in hesitation. There was going to be a storm. But she would go anyway. She had to.

Just then Aunt Chloe burst out of the quarters. "There you are, child. I been looking for you. Let's get this linen off the line before the rain comes." She headed to the clothesline where the tablecloth and napkins swung, tossing and flapping wildly in the strong wind. Lessie's heart sank. If she didn't show up before the storm began, Sam's friend might think she wasn't coming. She considered for a brief moment ignoring Aunt Chloe and running on off to her appointment, but she decided she couldn't do that.

They rescued the tablecloth and napkins minutes before the deluge began and rehung them in the basement. It was a cruel disappointment but Lessie told herself that Miss Clara would understand and let her have her afternoon off tomorrow instead of today.

The storm spent itself quickly however, and Lessie decided she should try to go on, but she couldn't get away from Aunt Chloe. The old woman kept puttering around her.

"I think I'll go for a walk, Aunt Chloe, now the rain's quit and it's so much cooler," she said finally.

"A walk where, child?" asked Chloe quietly.

She knows, thought Lessie, or at least she suspects something.

"You been acting mighty strange lately, slipping off in the afternoons and maybe the night for all I know. Then you been moping around for a solid month. Now you're as excited as if you was six years old and it was Christmas Eve! What is going on I'd like to know?"

Lessie sighed. There was no use to keep on pretending. Anyway it would be a relief not to have to anymore.

"I—met this man named Sam, Aunt Chloe, and I like him and he likes me, and, well, I, I'm going to see him. He's just come in on the boat. He's been on that boat that's come from St. Louis."

"What kind of a man do you have to slip around to see?" Aunt Chloe had the fiercest kind of look on her face.

It was a hard question to answer. How could she possibly explain Sam to Aunt Chloe, either the kind of a man he was or the way she felt about him?

"Aunt Chloe, I have to go now because his friend is coming to take me to see him. I'll tell you about him later. He's a good person, really he is."

"Who are his folks?"

Lessie knew that Aunt Chloe didn't mean his relatives, but what white family he belonged to.

"He ain't got any."

Not only that, but Sam had a bitter resentment against all white people. It was a shame the way he hated them. But he just didn't understand. He had never met any white people like Miss Clara or Mr. Douglas. She had tried to tell him about them, but he didn't really believe her.

"Well, what kind of trash is he? What does he do? Where does he belong?"

"He works on the steamboats, Aunt Chloe. He draws pictures, really good pictures, and people pay him for them."

"Hmph! I don't like the sound of it. He's trash, that's what he is, and you ought not to have nothing to do with him! How long has this been going on?"

"I met him about two weeks before the boat left and it's been gone a month."

"Has he had his way with you?"

Lessie couldn't answer and her silence betrayed her.

Aunt Chloe was hopping mad now, and she exploded, "I'm surprised at you! You're acting like a field nigger! You ain't been raised to act like that. Your ma was spiteful and good for nothing it's true, but your Grammy Martha was a moral woman. She'd be shamed by you, she would!"

Lessie hung her head. "I'm sorry, Aunt Chloe. I—I just can't help myself."

"Hmph! Don't want to is more likely."

Lessie raised her head and faced Aunt Chloe. "I'm going to go anyway. I can't explain why, but I have to go. It ain't that I don't respect you, but I have to go."

"Mark my words, child. You'll wish you had listened to me."

Lessie almost wavered. Then she turned and ran as fast as she could, Aunt Chloe's words still ringing in her ears.

CHAPTER TEN

ELIOT Watson stopped by The Burn one afternoon to leave Lucy a book which he had promised her.

He was finding Natchez an interesting place, provincial, but at the same time surprisingly cosmopolitan. Its civilization was a tiny island in the midst of the fields and swamps and forests which surrounded it, but the little city had always had direct contact with the mature culture of Europe through its inland port facilities on the Mississippi River. He had learned since coming here that before it was ceded to the United States the Natchez territory had at one time or another been under the rule of France, Spain, and England. He could see the influence of all of these in the names and the natures of its people, in the architecture of its houses, and in its customs. Roman Catholicism bloomed side by side with puritanical Protestantism. A rather prim moral code flourished along with horse racing, drinking, and gambling.

Natchez' contradictions were nowhere more evident than in its physical setting. One either arrived by boat at the landing Under-the-Hill, an unattractive, squalid, even dangerous spot, or one rode from the equally dangerous narrow sunken path between steep banks of jungle-like foliage, which was the Natchez Trace, into the town. There, suddenly one would find beautiful homes and well-groomed gardens with the harmony and serenity which man had imposed upon his surroundings.

The worshippers of nature never gave man enough credit, Eliot told himself. They didn't realize that nature without man was cruel and meaningless. And the worshippers of man didn't understand that, without God, man himself was meaningless.

His thoughts returned to this fascinating city which had become his new home. He had discovered that at least half of its population had probably lived in the northeast as recently as one generation back. It was strange that they were so bitter now against "Yankees." Well, not really. He guessed it was understandable when you considered how all the South, and especially this part of it, had suffered during the War. Fathers, sons, husbands, lovers had been killed and wounded, property confiscated, vandalized and destroyed. Natchez had been invaded and occupied, and even shelled once by a gunboat. And, although the War had ended four years ago, martial law still ruled the town. Until just recently black men in uniform commanded by Union officers had paraded through the streets, and now groups of negroes roamed about causing trouble. The carpet-bag government of the state exploited the situation economically, feasting and fattening on the South's carcass like so many greedy buzzards.

However, in spite of bombardment, invasion, and occupation, Eliot reflected, Natchez had been fortunate enough to weather the War with most of its splendid mansions intact. He was really glad of that because clustered here in this small area were some very fine pieces of architecture. He was very interested in architecture. He had almost become an architect, probably would have if he had done better in math.

He had noticed, also, that many of the beautiful houses lacked the proper furnishings to do them justice. Of course many pieces of fine furniture had been destroyed and many had been sold to pay taxes. No one now could even consider anything so extravagant as new upholstery or draperies. Consequently there was a rather shabby look to the interiors which was a little sad, he guessed, and yet he thought there was something comfortable and unself-conscious about it.

It occurred to Eliot that the surviving houses were rather like the people, unchanged on the outside, but with inner wounds. He longed to heal these wounds, but he was young and inexperienced. Moreover he knew he needed to gain the confidence of his new congregation. Still he felt he should do something to help, and it was much on his mind.

He walked slowly up the wide semicircular driveway of The Burn, thinking what a lovely house it was and enjoying the classic balance of its Greek Revival architecture. It sat in simplicity and dignity, like a small white jewel in its setting of hollies and boxwood, its long shutters echoing the dark green color of their leaves.

As he knocked at the carved, paneled door, Eliot's eyes traveled in appreciation from the leaded glass squares that framed it to the half-round fluted columns and pilasters on either side. In the next moment the mistress herself opened the door. Clara stood at the threshold of the cool dark hall, a dainty little figure in a mustard-colored cambric dress, its yoke and short, puffed sleeves of white dotted swiss outlined with the same black braid that decorated the skirt. A circle of golden leaves set with diamonds was pinned to its narrow ruffled collar.

"Good afternoon, Miss Clara."

"Dr. Watson, how nice to see you! Do come in."

"Thank you. I told Miss Lucy that I'd bring her this book we were talking about the other day. I think it might be of interest to her."

"How very kind of you. Lucy will be so sorry to have missed you. One of her beaux has taken her for a drive. Will you have a cup of tea with me?"

"Thank you, Miss Clara, I should be delighted."

"Let's take it in the garden." Clara led the way down the broad hall which divided the house. When they reached the back gallery, with its splendid view of the terraced grounds, she turned to Eliot. "Wait here just a moment while I ask Lessie to bring the tea to us out there."

Clara walked swiftly across the covered pathway that led to the kitchen wing, the long, full folds of her skirt sweeping behind her.

Eliot leaned against a column and looked down at the luxuriant beauty of the vista before him. The heavy fragrant air moved from time to time in little soft gusts like sighs of contentment, as though the earth were well pleased with itself. The debilitating heat of the deep South's early afternoon had passed, but there was still a languor in the air, and Eliot's blood coursed thickly and sweetly through his veins. He felt relaxed and happy just to be alive, and singularly unambitious. The Southern temperament was undoubtedly affected by the temperature, he thought. Although he was a Southerner himself, his home was on the coast of North Carolina where the climate was less enervating.

When Clara returned, they descended one of the twin stairways to the garden walk. The raucous squawking of two mocking birds heralded their arrival in the garden.

"Silly birds, we don't want your babies!" protested Clara, laughing. "Let's sit here," she added as they reached the summer house.

Clara seated herself in one of several white wicker armchairs filled with plump chintz-covered cushions and gestured to another. "Why don't you sit there, Dr. Watson?"

"How inviting this is! Your garden is just as beautiful in the daylight as it is by moonlight!"

"Thank you. I love my garden. I'd rather be in it than anywhere else, and I'd rather work in it than do anything else. I'm afraid my hands show it. They were my mother's absolute despair." Clara smiled at him as she held up her hands, and Eliot discovered the electricity in her eyes. She continued, "You know, Dr. watson, Lucy will feel quite cheated when I tell her you've been to visit. She does so enjoy exchanging ideas with you. John will be sorry to have missed you, too. He studies Latin with Judge Harris in the afternoon. Judge Harris has taken quite an interest in John. He says he has a good mind and such a way with words that he's bound to make a fine lawyer."

"Is Mr. Douglas in the country now?"

"Yes, he has to spend so much time on the plantation now. There are so many problems there these days."

Lessie arrived with a tray bearing the small silver tea service and a plate of wafer-thin molasses cookies.

Clara poured some tea into a fluted china cup, hand-painted with sprays of yellow flowers and a broad band of the same sunny color.

"Will you have lemon or milk?"

"Lemon, please, Miss Clara, and a little sugar."

They settled back with their tea cups, and a comfortable silence fell.

"What a fine tree!" said Eliot, nodding toward the garden's stately oak.

"We call it the 'Tree of Benediction.'"

"Of course! It's quite obvious that it's blessing your garden!"

Clara was pleased that Eliot Watson didn't think it was silly to name a tree.

"Your garden is filled with sentiment, isn't it? General Martin's wife told me a very touching story at your dinner party the other evening about the white rose that was planted by your sister."

"Yes, that's one of the reasons the garden means so much to me."

"Well, it is one of the most beautiful gardens I've ever been in. And The Burn is one of my favorite houses. It has such pleasing proportions, and an integrity and a simplicity of line. You know, Miss Clara, at one time in my life I thought I wanted to be an architect. I guess I've never completely gotten over it. I've enjoyed being in Natchez. There are so many interesting houses here." Eliot looked up toward the house. "Your architect situated The Burn very cleverly on the hill there with its gentle slope to the front and such a steep fall on the back side. Seen from the garden here the house appears Louisiana Colonial in style."

The Burn's columned back gallery rested on square brick pillars above the ground-floor area and was reached by a double stairway. It did indeed look Louisiana Colonial.

"The descending terraces of your garden heighten the overall effect of the architecture, too. It's a nice bit of landscaping."

"My parents had a Scottish gardener who did the terraces and the original planting. I love this view of the house, too."

"And then, of course, your spiral stairway simply transports me," Eliot smiled, "as I suppose every stairway is, after all, meant to do!"

Clara laughed, "It has transported a good many people through the years. And there's been some tumbling down it, too. My brother Ernest tried to ride its bannister once and ended up with a broken arm!"

"It would be a tricky ride. Where is your brother Ernest now?"

"In Memphis working for a printing company. He and his wife like Memphis, and I don't believe he'll ever come back to Natchez. Douglas handles the farming for us all, although he really doesn't care for it any more than Ernest does. It takes so much of his time he had to give up his law practice. I don't think he misses that too much although he once had dreams of a political career. Of course that's impossible now."

"How long has your brother been a widower, Miss Clara?"

"His wife, Rebecca, died when Ernestine was born. It was just after the War ended. Our family spent the last two years of the War in Alabama when Natchez was occupied by the Yankees. After the War was over it was months before we could get possession of The Burn. After Douglas finally got them to agree to return The Burn to us and came back to Alabama to bring us home, he got malaria, which delayed us still more. By the time he had recovered everyone felt that it was too late for Rebecca to try to make the trip, but she wanted to come home, and so we did. It proved to be a serious mistake. It was a terrible experience for all of us. We did get to Natchez and Ernestine was born at Linden, but Rebecca developed complications and died the day after."

A shadow crossed Clara's expressive face. "Douglas reproaches himself for the whole thing because he agreed to let her make the trip."

"That's a great pity! Grief is enough of a burden for a man to bear without adding guilt to it. We all make mistakes and perhaps it would have happened anyway."

"That's true. He really shouldn't blame himself, but Douglas is an extremely conscientious and sensitive person. Rebecca's death was a great tragedy for him in many ways."

"There were five children, left motherless, too, but I see you've taken over that job quite successfully."

"Well, it was my duty, but it's become my joy," Clara smiled with a touch of pride. "They are most satisfactory children! Of course, there are times when I do feel inadequate, especially with Lucy and John, who really aren't much younger than I."

"I think you're the most adequate person I've ever known," said Eliot, and the depth of feeling in his voice surprised them both.

Their eyes met in startled understanding, and something joyous in her awoke. For the first time in years she felt really alive!

"Will you take a little more tea, Dr. Watson?" she deliberately broke the spell that held them with her question.

"I guess not, Miss Clara. I really must be going, but it has been most enjoyable visiting with you."

He rose from his chair slowly like a man waking reluctantly from a pleasant dream.

"Tell Miss Lucy I do hope the book will be of some value to her. I found it quite thought provoking. Thank you so much for the tea."

When the big front door of The Burn finally closed behind Eliot Watson, Clara stood motionless for a full minute. She felt dazed and shaken by the impact of their sudden soul-to-soul encounter. As she struggled to get in command of her chaotic emotions, she told herself, of course, there can never be anything more between us, but I will keep that moment in the garden in my heart forever.

CHAPTER ELEVEN

THAT had been an easy resolution for Clara. At the time the moment was all she had needed. For days after, it warmed and sustained her. The memory of it, the knowledge of it, gave her the keenest joy and the deepest happiness.

She looked forward eagerly to Sunday when she would see Eliot again. Then she ran into him by accident at the Orphanage on one of her regular visits there. The sight of him sent her blood racing and her heart pounding furiously. The calm and lovely feeling she had been cherishing since the moment in the garden seemed to burst into flame! But they spoke quite formally to each other, and there was a disturbing awkwardness between them instead of the comfortable rapport they had enjoyed. Our friendship is ruined now, thought Clara, and all the joy went out of her.

She did her best to respond to the eager greetings of her favorite little orphans, but her heart felt frozen. She went through the motions, wishing she were a better actress, and left earlier than usual, promising to come again soon.

Uncle Perry was waiting for her in the carriage. The Orphanage was only a short walk from The Burn and she would have welcomed the exercise, but ever since the War the downtown streets had become unsafe for ladies. It was better now that the negro troops had been withdrawn, but there were still so many negroes who refused to return to their jobs on the plantations. They hung around the Freedmen's Bureau and were hostile and insulting to white people. And notwithstanding the protection of Uncle Perry, she was conscious of rude stares and sneers from a group congregated at a road crossing. It was distressing, but today she was even more distressed by her brief encounter with Eliot. All the way home she agonized over the lost relationship, which had meant so much more to her than she had realized.

Oh, she thought, if we could only forget the silly moment and be as we were!

She spent a sleepless, restless night. Then by the morning's light she began to feel that she had exaggerated the whole affair.

After all, she said to herself, what really has happened between us? Nothing. What he said to me was highly complimentary. That's all. Everything is the same as it was.

But on Sunday the sight of Eliot, the sound of his voice, stirred her deeply. When she spoke to him at the church door the awareness in his eyes told her without any doubt that he felt just as strongly as she the attraction between them.

In the days that followed, Clara found herself tossed from heights of ecstasy at the fact of her own feelings and the intuition she had of his, to depths of agony at their inability to acknowledge these feelings and to fulfill them.

She kept discovering new and wonderful qualities in Eliot Watson. He spoke from his pulpit one Sunday morning with great eloquence about the ever-rising tide of bitterness toward the North. It concerned her, too, this passionate resentment that was so all pervasive and that fed on itself. Of course it was not surprising. The punitive nature of the Reconstruction measures taken by the Congress over President Johnson's veto had added to the suffering and the humiliation of defeat. The humiliation, thought Clara, that was it, that was the worst part of it all for such a proud people to endure. But they had lost, and they had to live with that fact and try to make a new start. All that animosity was getting in the way. It wasn't healthy. And that was true of the fear and hatred between the white people and the black people as well.

As Eliot spoke on his theme of love and forgiveness, Clara, looking about her, saw backs stiffening and lips tightening.

"The most unfortunate victims of the bitterness of hatred are those who hate. This is a disease that ravages the soul—"

Clara was torn between sadness to see just how powerful the force of hate could be in the souls of men and bittersweet joy at the revelation of yet another dimension of Eliot's sensitive and magnanimous nature.

"Our Master has Himself set the example for us. In the moment of His great suffering He forgave. Can we, who stand in need of so much forgiveness ourselves, do less?"

The congregation departed in stony silence except for one haughty lady who declared to her family, "I suppose he wants us to turn the other cheek. Well, we'll never do that! I don't believe Jesus ever said that anyway."

Clara shook hands with Eliot at the door where he stood receiving the disapproving crowd. She had not allowed herself the luxury of meeting his eyes with her own for some time. Today she looked right into them, and the hurt she found there made her heart ache.

She smiled as she gave him her hand. "The Lord and I are proud of you, Dr. Watson."

"Thank you, Miss Clara, that's enough to make it worthwhile!"

She tried to withdraw her hand, but he held on to it for a moment longer.

How can I possibly endure this, thought Clara, as the tenderness and passion that surged inside her threatened to overflow.

She walked down the church steps, wondering if her legs would hold her up. Annie gave a little jump over the last two steps, and Clara reprimanded her niece, "Annie, that is not lady-like. Do settle down."

By the time they were all seated in the carriage, she had her feelings under control again. John accompanied them on horseback, an old Natchez custom, and in their case, a necessity, with a large family and only one carriage. He sat with an easy grace, delightfully unconscious of his good looks and of the admiring glances of the young ladies that they passed. As they rode along Lucy began to discuss Eliot Watson's sermon.

"Wasn't Dr. Watson wonderful? I thought it was so courageous of him to say those things right out in public when it is so popular to hate Yankees."

"I thought you hated them, Lucy," said Daisy.

"Well, yes, I did during the War when they were our enemies and we were fighting them, but now it's different. We should let bygones be bygones."

"But Jesus said to love your enemies so we shouldn't have hated them ever," said Annie.

"You and Daisy are just too young to understand," said Lucy, and she began to wonder if she did. Dr. Watson's sermon had started her to thinking. I must ask Dr. Shields what he thinks about it, she told herself.

Daisy, who was remarkably observant for her age, looked thoughtfully at Clara. "Aunt Clara," she asked, "why are you not talking any?"

When Clara and the children got home from church, they found to their surprise that Douglas had arrived from Fawnwood, where he had been for the past two weeks.

Mr. Jones, the overseer, was very ill and had had to leave. It was proving to be quite difficult to find anyone to replace him. Douglas was trying out a new man and they were all hoping that Mr. Barton would do.

"I caught the boat home," Douglas explained. "I left Thundercloud for John Henry to use until I get back."

"How is Mr. Barton working out?" Clara asked apprehensively, as she untied the ribbons of her bonnet.

"I let him go."

"Oh, Douglas!" She hung the bonnet on one of the pegs of the mirrored hat rack behind the stairs.

"Well, I guess I shouldn't have let my temper get the best of me, but I couldn't trust him and I didn't like him. The negroes don't like him either. I asked him about some things John Henry had told me, and he said, 'I don't care what they think.' And then he said, 'Mr. Walworth, these niggers is nothing but animals, anyway!' In good conscience, Sister, I couldn't leave anybody like that in charge."

"No, of course you couldn't." Clara winced at the ugly words, and sighed inwardly as she smelled the tell-tale whiskey on his breath.

"Well, if you fired Mr. Barton, Douglas, who did you leave in charge of things? John Henry?"

"Yes. He can handle the situation for a few days anyway. He's done it before."

"He's a good man, isn't he?"

"One of the best."

"Well, I guess you'll have to start looking for someone again."

"Yes, but I'm afraid I've already talked to everybody around here, and let me tell you they're a trashy lot. I reckon you can't hope to find an overseer who is a perfect gentleman, but you'd think you could get somebody halfway decent," said Douglas wearily, rubbing his forehead with his hand.

"Mr. Jones was a gentleman, and honest and kind."

"Well, he was also unusual. I doubt that we can find another man like him. How was Dr. Watson's sermon?"

"I thought it was very good," said Clara carefully. "It was certainly timely."

"How so?"

"Oh, it was about hatred. He said that hate was a disease, and he recommended forgiveness as a cure. Of course, as you know, hate seems to have become Natchez' most treasured sin, so I'm afraid both his diagnosis and his prescription were equally unpopular! The congregation's displeasure was all too evident."

"Well, he ought to have avoided such a controversial subject. He's young and still a stranger here. It's hardly the time to buck the tide. And you know we do have good cause for resentment. It may have been courageous, but I imagine that all he accomplished was to make people madder than ever!"

"Well, I admire him for it anyway," said Clara. "Dinner is waiting. Let's go in."

Lessie was helping Chloe with the Sunday dinner dishes. Uncle Perry and Maybelle had left, and they were alone. She lifted a fluted cup from the foaming water, and held it up reverently between her hands. "It blossoms out just like a flower, don't it?"

"Well, yes, I reckon it does. You and your fancy thoughts! You was mighty late getting home last night, and you got crying streaks in your eyes. That good-for-nothing Sam must be in town again. Comes in like some rat off a barge!" Chloe's eyes and mouth turned grim.

"Aunt Chloe, he ain't good for nothing. Really he ain't." Lessie wished with all her heart that she could explain Sam to people. He wasn't like he seemed. She had found that out. He didn't really mean all those things he said. It was just that he was afraid of people. It was only with her that he wasn't afraid, that he let down his guard and showed all the tenderness that was in him.

"I been hearing about him, all about his drinking and gambling, and his fights. Will you tell me what's good about him?"

Lessie groped for the words. "I admit he's got a real bad temper, and that he hates white folks, all of them, the good and the bad. Of course, he don't know any like Miss Clara and Mr. Douglas or the general or Doctor Watson. I keep trying to tell him how they are, but he won't believe me. But, Aunt Chloe, he's good to me. It's like he's a different person when we're alone. He's just as gentle and kind. I think he acts that other way because he's afraid of folks."

"Hmph!" muttered Chloe.

"And another thing I like about him is the way when he looks at things he sees things other folks don't see. Like he can see how beautiful even the plainest things can be, trees in wintertime sticking up against the sky like rows of porcupine quills, or bare fields after harvest, or empty shacks sitting in the weeds. He sees beauty everywhere. And you ought to see how good he can draw. He can scratch a few lines and do somebody's face so you can recognize it, and it's just them to the life, with all the goodness or the meanness right there. I declare I don't know how he does it! Of course, I know he's too proud, but he just can't help it. It's in his nature. It's hard for him to be colored. Sometimes it's hard for me, too. Grammy Martha used to tell me, 'White folks can do this or do that, but you're black and so you can't,' and I would think why? One day I remember she said, 'The black man is the white man's shadow,' and I thought, but I don't want to be nobody's shadow. I understand how Sam feels, even though I know he's wrong to hate some folks like he does."

"Oh, I expect he hates everybody, including his own self, and for that I don't blame him! He's a gambling man, too, and that always means trouble. You ought to stay away from him."

"But, Aunt Chloe, I love him, and he needs me, and I need him, too. He makes me feel like a real person instead of just a shadow."

"Oh, you and your shadows! What does that talk mean? I never felt like no shadow if I am black as one! What I do know is it ain't hating that makes you feel like a person, child."

"I know that, Aunt Chloe. I know it's wrong to hate people. That's where he's wrong, but, well, you see, there's so much good inside of Sam, and then there's the bad. It's like. . ." Lessie struggled to express it so Aunt Chloe would understand. "It's like flowers in a garden getting choked by weeds!" she finished triumphantly.

"Well, just you watch out you don't get choked." Chloe was always good for the last word.

Lessie sighed. She dried her chapped and cracked black hands and carried a tray full of china from the kitchen to the dining room to be put away. She kept hearing Sam's bitter words. She knew there were lots of white folks who were bitter too. She had heard plenty of whispering and suddenly hushed up conversations. Only today she had heard Mr. Douglas and Miss Clara talking about how some white folks hated the colored people. Why all this should matter so much to her she didn't know. It didn't seem to bother Aunt Chloe, but it hurt Lessie down deep in her soul and made her feel indescribably sad, not so much for herself as for everybody.

CHAPTER TWELVE

THERE was a picnic at Arlington, and the whole family was going. John and the three oldest of his sisters drove over early in the day, and then he brought the carriage back for Clara, Douglas, Ernestine, and Maybelle.

As they rode up the winding driveway, a gay scene lay before them. The grounds, which fell gradually away from the handsome red brick house with its sturdy white columns, were filled with people of all ages milling about under the trees. Massive magnolias and gray-bearded live oaks provided large patches of shade. One of the enormous limbs of an ancient oak grew so low that at one point it touched the ground before it reached up again. Numerous children sat on it like little birds in a row, while some of the more active ones were climbing around in the tree.

Nearby were young ladies and gentlemen playing croquet, others watching or strolling about. On the gallery, surveying the antics of the younger, sat a cluster of elderly ladies, fanning furiously for the day was hot.

Small tables had been placed about the lawn, and near the house was a long table covered with a white cloth. Negro women in flowered print dresses and white aprons, their hair tied up in handkerchiefs, were walking to and from the table, bringing large bowls and platters from the kitchen area.

John turned the horses and carriage over to Uncle Perry, who had been loaned out for the occasion. Uncle Perry loved a party and was speaking to everyone, shaking hands, laughing and joking.

"What a politician that darky is! He ought to run for the new state legislature!" commented one of the guests archly, not troubling to lower his voice.

The nostrils of Douglas' prominent Walworth nose widened, betraying his annoyance. "That fool, Henry Milton! He isn't fit to lace Uncle Perry's boots!" he said to his sister with disgust.

"Deep down I think Henry Milton knows it. That may be why he talks that way. He's just trying to feel superior."

"Well, he has no need or right to insult Uncle Perry!"

"Calm down, Douglas, and don't make a fuss. Uncle Perry has too much sense to let anything like that hurt his feelings. He's much more of a gentleman than Henry Milton, and he's well aware of it. Let's go and speak to Mrs. Boyd."

Douglas and Clara went in search of their hostess.

Maybelle, who was in charge of little Ernestine, led her to where a group of nurses and their small charges had gathered. Aunt Chloe's daughter, Sarah, who had gone to work for Laura Walworth when she had married Will McPheeters during the War, was there with little Sallie McPheeters.

"How do?" said Sarah to Maybelle, moving over to make room on the quilt she had spread out.

"Why, how do, Miss Sarah, ma'am?" Maybelle replied respectfully to the older woman, accepting the unspoken invitation to sit down.

The two little cousins, Ernestine and Sallie, surveyed each other gravely and suspiciously. They had been thrown together at birthdays and Thanksgiving and Christmas dinners, but they weren't really sure they liked each other.

"Where's Lessie? Why ain't she here?" Sarah asked Maybelle with a knowing look.

"She's with that Sam, I reckon," said Maybelle. "That's where she is mostly these days."

"My ma says she don't think about nothing else now."

"That's right," Maybelle agreed, shaking her head and sighing. "She don't hardly talk to us no more."

"Well, she picked a bad one to get mixed up with. He's a gambling man and a drinking man, and I hear he's quick with a knife."

Round-faced, chubby Maybelle shivered and whispered, "Lordy, Lordy!" She reflected to herself that Lessie was mighty brave, crazy maybe, but certainly brave. She couldn't imagine anybody she knew getting involved in anything like that.

A piercing shriek from Ernestine interrupted the conversation. Her cousin Sallie had a handful of Ernestine's wispy brown hair clutched in her little fist and was pulling it with all her might. Ernestine kept screaming and Sallie kept pulling until at last she was persuaded to let go. Nobody could figure out why she had done such a thing. Ernestine climbed, whimpering, into Maybelle's lap and spent the rest of the party there.

John disappeared to a secluded grove at the back of the house where the young men were throwing dice. This was much the greater sport because it was forbidden fruit, and they fancied themselves to be wicked men of the world. A few of them had even been Under-the-Hill. A lad of fifteen or sixteen who had spent an evening Under-the-Hill acquired considerable status with his peers. John and some of his friends had been there recently. They had sauntered down Silver Street, a narrow road which curved from the top of the bluff to the landing below in sinister fashion like a snake going into its hole. They had been as elaborately casual as they could manage to be, a nervous giggle occasionally revealing their true states of mind.

The road itself was pitch dark. The only light for their path had come at intervals from the doors of the noisy taverns which were hidden away behind each bend and dip of the road. As they approached one of these, thin, tinny music in a lively rhythm seemed to shake the walls of the rickety little building. John had seen, silhouetted against the open doorway, a slender negro woman with a long thin neck and small head.

Why, I believe that's Lessie, he had thought, as she looked toward them. She had turned away before he could be sure, and he had decided that it probably wasn't. She shouldn't be in a place like this. Then his eyes had fallen on the man who stood beside the woman. Light skin and an aquiline nose indicated that he had a high percentage of white blood. What a tragic expression his face bore! What caged fury must lie behind it! John was haunted for some time after by that tortured face. How must it feel to be neither white nor black, he wondered?

The woman had reached out her hand to the man in a graceful gesture, and he swept her to him in an enveloping embrace. "Those darkies are certainly passionate," one of John's companions, a chubby boy with a cherubic countenance, had grinned and winked. John had had to restrain an impulse to smash the jolly, insensitive face.

"Come on, let's go," he had said instead, shaking a pair of imaginary dice. "I want to find some of this action!"

His arrival now on the scene stopped the game at the picnic temporarily.

"Well, if it isn't Philippe Laffite!" cried Tom Guillory.

"Yes, you fellows had better watch this pirate! He takes after his grandfather," added another downy-cheeked lad.

"Say, John, old Injun Pete didn't really believe that story, did he?"

John shrugged. "If he didn't, he had me fooled."

"He believed it all right," Tom assured the group. "You know how John can put on an accent. Well, his Cajun was just perfect. He told Injun Pete that he was the grandson of Jean Laffite. He said he'd tried to live down his grandfather's reputation, but nobody'd let him make an honest living and he'd turned to gambling. Pete was absolutely reverent towards him, and John almost had me believing he was Philippe Laffite!"

"Well," said John, his words rising and falling in the Cajun rhythm, "Philippe, he is out of the cash just now. I think he will go to find a partner for croquet. Anybody, they want to come? No? I see, everybody they prefer to throw the leetle dice." He grinned slyly, and abandoned his accent. "You wouldn't like to have some of those good-looking pictures of Mr. Jefferson Davis, would you?"

"We've got plenty of those, thanks. What we're interested in is filthy Yankee lucre, you grandson of a pirate!"

"Then farewell. You play your wicked game, and I'll play my wicket game," John enunciated carefully.

"All right, Walworth, take your Confederate money and your puns! Neither of them is worth a damn! Go and give the young ladies a thrill. That's the reason you want to play croquet."

"But we'll lend you some money if you like."

John shook his head emphatically. "The Walworths have too many debts now. Besides, I like croquet—and young ladies! See you later."

As John rounded a corner of an extensive boxwood labyrinth which hid the dice players from view, he came upon Daisy and Annie engaged in a game of hide and seek. They put their fingers to their lips, warning him not to give them away. He waved silently as he passed them and turned another corner, only to pop back a moment later to give them a playful scare. The girls gasped, but managed to remain silent. "John!" whispered Daisy indignantly. "We might have screamed, and then they would have caught us!"

The table was groaning now. Fried chicken was heaped in wicker baskets, and great china bowls were filled with potato salad, while still others held ears of fresh roasted corn and the fruits of the season were piled on platters. Napkin-covered trays held hundreds of hot rolls. At one end were several large cakes, and nearby sat big vats of ice cream. Annie and Daisy hovered near these, and finally the serving hour arrived. They filled their plates and went to sit with a group of children near the vats.

Clara and Dr. Shields walked by carrying their plates. Dr. Shields was saying, "It's impossible for people in this land of plenty to realize the desperate poverty of a country like China. Even the lowliest field hand over here has a full stomach and medical care."

"I don't think we have so much to eat," murmured Daisy to Annie.

"Aunt Clara is very stingy with the meat," Annie whispered, as she picked up her second piece of chicken.

When the girls had finished, they went over with some of the other children to the vats, which were standing open.

"What kind of ice cream is it?" someone asked.

"It looks like raisin ice cream," said Annie.

"I never heard of raisin ice cream."

"Annie," said Daisy with a sob in her voice, "those aren't raisins. They're flies!"

Clara and Dr. Shields had rejoined their group and were sitting at one of the many small tables.

"Mrs. Shields, you should see Arlington when the azaleas are in bloom!" said Clara. "Did you know that they were brought over from China?"

"Oh, my, I shall look forward to seeing them! The wealthy Chinese have such exquisite gardens, you know, and although we were out in the villages most of the time we did get to see some of them."

A young woman of Clara's age in a much beribboned dress, totally inappropriate for a picnic, thought Clara, approached their table.

"Hello, there!" she trilled. "I'm so glad to see all of you! Do help me with a problem! Wouldn't you just know? Both Edward Butler and John Gaillard asked me to sit with them, and I said I would. Now they're each sitting at different tables! Since I don't want to hurt anyone's feelings, I've decided I shouldn't sit with either of them. Don't you think I'm right, Dr. Shields?"

"Oh, indeed, Miss Frances. Perhaps they could draw straws, but do us the honor of sitting here." Dr. Shields rose gallantly, if a shade reluctantly.

Clara said, "Yes, do join us, Frances," and told herself

sternly that she must not let this small thing spoil the party for her. She noticed with some amusement that Douglas, who had been walking toward them, changed his direction abruptly and joined another group. He couldn't abide Frances, and she was always after him, as she was after every unattached man. She even flirted with the married ones. Old Dr. Shields himself wasn't safe from her. Poor girl, she couldn't get over wanting things to be the way they used to be before the War when there were pretty dresses and gay parties, and plenty of beaux.

People like Frances who refused to face reality were so pitiful. Douglas might try to escape from it, but he couldn't fool himself the way Frances did. It was amazing how many of their friends were like that. Clara wondered if it might not be catching, people fooling themselves and each other that nothing had really changed. Perhaps it was their salvation after all, though. Maybe these people were unable to stand reality. I hope I'll always be able to, no matter how painful it may be, she told herself.

Eliot and Mary Watson sat at a nearby table, and Clara was exasperated with herself for the ridiculous way her heart behaved whenever she glanced in their direction. Her hand trembled when she lifted her fork and, when Eliot stopped by their table to speak, she experienced again that overwhelming feeling which had attacked her on the church steps. It took all her will power just to maintain a calm exterior.

Douglas seated himself with Margarette and Will Martin and his wife's cousins, the Austin Conners, and several other friends. He had intended to join Clara and the Shields, but had spied Frances Mattox heading for their table just in time. How foolish that woman was! And she had once been considered quite an attractive girl. There seemed to be an awful lot of women like that these days.

"Douglas, Scott here has just decided to join us. I certainly wish you and Will would reconsider. The way we see it we're still at war. The Federal government hasn't made peace with us and it looks as though they never will, and so we're just trying to see to our rights and the safety of our wives and children in the same way our pioneer grandfathers did before they had a government to protect them. I really think it's your duty to share in this thing!"

Oh, good Lord, Douglas groaned inwardly, wondering if Frances wouldn't have been better after all.

Will spoke up, "Austin, in spite of what you say, the War is over, and I feel that our best hope for order and safety lies with the government of the United States. Actually, the sort of thing you are doing is apt to prolong our probation. I don't think in the long run any good can come from organizations outside the law."

Douglas added, "As a matter of fact, lasting harm could come from this 'brotherhood' of yours. It could so easily get out of control. I think it's a mistake."

"Well, of course, you and Will have always been Unionists, but I would have thought Reconstruction would have changed that if the War didn't."

"As you know, Austin, I fought as hard as anybody for the Confederate cause," replied Will. "I wasn't too happy about secession, but when the War came I made my choice. So did Douglas. Now, thank God, it's over. There are many inequities, I grant you, and a lot of unfortunate incidents, and I don't like them any better than you do. But I think that exaggerating these things will just make matters worse. Hard as it is, we've got to be patient and let the fever for vengeance die down. I believe things will gradually get better."

"And in the meantime the streets are unsafe for our wives and daughters to venture on alone! Personally I'm sick and tired of darkies running wild in the streets, committing crimes that go unpunished, and making the wildest accusations. Accusations which are not only taken seriously by the government, if that's what you want to call it, but are backed up by that damned Freedmen's Bureau! Let me tell you I don't intend to take it lying down. I'm going to fight back every way I know how!"

Austin's impassioned speech left Douglas feeling rather

less than heroic, but he didn't really approve of those underground activities and he knew he couldn't take part in them.

"I'm sure this talk doesn't interest the ladies," Douglas suggested. "Why don't we declare a truce, Austin? You and Scott have your views, and we have ours, and I doubt very much that we're going to change anyone's mind. By the way, I hear your mare has foaled. I imagine she has a handsome colt. I've always admired that mare of yours. She's got beautiful conformation and such aristocratic manners."

Lucy was eating supper with Gavin Turner. They sat with a sprightly crowd of young people. Flirtation was in the very air about them. Young ladies were listening wide eyed to the least remark of the young men, who, in turn, were each trying to outdo the other in their conversation. They all rather bored Lucy with their chatter, and she found herself thinking, I will be so glad when my friends grow up.

Dr. and Mrs. Watson walked by Lucy and her companions with another couple.

"There goes old 'Idiot Watson,'" said one callow youth whose parents had been particularly disgruntled by Eliot's recent sermon. "I don't see why he doesn't have something to say about the sins of the Yankees. To hear him talk, you'd think we'd burned their houses and stolen their property and taxed the bread off of their tables instead of the other way around!"

"Well, I guess he thinks our sins are more his business than their sins. You know, like the mote and the beam," said Lucy.

"That's just what I mean. None of it is his business. Preachers ought not to get involved in politics. They ought to stick to the Bible."

"Well, he did, you know. Everything he said came right from the Bible. He just said, 'Love your enemies,' at a time when people didn't want to be reminded of it."

"Lucy," whispered Gavin, "don't argue with him. Young ladies shouldn't argue."

"Well, if that's your idea of a lady, then I'm not one!" Lucy turned on him, her hazel eyes flashing as they were so wont to do. "If a lady is a doll that walks and talks and never says or does anything that really matters, I'm certainly not a lady, because I'm flesh and blood—" she paused dramatically, "and fire!"

After supper Margarette Martin said to her husband, "Mr. Martin, I understand the young people are going to put on a show on the gallery steps. Let's go up and watch."

The show was already in progress. A courtroom scene was being enacted, and John, who was one of the players, was speaking. He shouted and whispered, coaxed and commanded, and made gestures so sweeping that he fell to the steps with one of them.

"Who's he taking off now?" asked the general.

John suddenly cleared his throat noisily and at length, and tossed his head back, as if to rid his forehead of an unruly lock of hair, and Will grinned, "Oh," he said, "I guess it's me."

Twilight gave way to dusk, and singing began, spreading from group to group until the hazy gray evening was filled with it. Carriages began to leave one by one. Uncle Perry brought the Walworths' carriage back for Lucy and John and the little girls, the others having left earlier.

As they jogged along in the now black night which had descended upon them, Daisy and Annie fell asleep, one on each of John's shoulders. He looked down at the two little heads, and a deep, sweet tenderness welled within him. He knew that he would do anything to protect his sisters, and he felt so strong and brave that he half-wished for someone to jump out of the darkness so that he might use this power that was in him.

Lucy stared wistfully at the stars. She wished that people weren't so dense. It seemed to her that most of the world's sin and sorrow were due to ignorance and stupidity, and the lack of imagination. But pride and arrogance, she thought to herself reluctantly, but firmly, are probably even worse. She squirmed at the memory of the haughty words she had so recently addressed to Gavin Turner, "I'm flesh and blood and fire." What a ridiculous thing to say! Compared to the stars, what a silly little bonfire I am!

"Look up there at the sky," she spoke aloud to John, "and you can see the beginning of infinity and eternity. How can people on this one tiny piece of the universe ever think they know it all? So many people make up their minds what they think about things at some point in their lives, and then they lock them up and throw the key away and never really think again!"

"Well, Lucy, thinking is unsettling. It's much more comfortable not to. It so often leads to changing your mind, and a lot of people consider that wishy-washy!"

Uncle Perry turned the horses in at The Burn gate. These young folks, he thought, talking about how everybody else thought they knew everything, and all the time acting like they did themselves. They didn't know yet that you had to give a little here and there and bend some with the breeze. He had long ago learned how to get along in the world, and he couldn't understand why Miss Lucy worried so much about things she couldn't do a thing about.

CHAPTER THIRTEEN

DR. Shields sat at his desk writing. The large and cumbersome piece of furniture seemed to fill up the tiny room which he called his workshop. The broad expanse of desk was untidy and burdened with endless stacks of papers and books. Mrs. Shields complained about not being able to dust it but the doctor would not allow anyone to touch it, saying that anyway most of the stacks were in constant use and dust had little time to settle.

Since his retirement Dr. Shields had been engaged in translating a medical dictionary into the dialects of the Chinese villages in which he had ministered. It was a tedious and thankless service that he was performing which would bring him neither fame nor financial remuneration. But the task formed a link between him and the people he had loved that he found very satisfying. Had it not been for his wife, he would have remained in China. Yet he knew she longed for the companionship of people like herself and that she had never been completely happy in the alien land to which he had brought her as a bride. It gave him great pleasure these days to see her enjoying the many friends that she had found in Natchez.

He hunched over his work, bending close to the paper. His eyes were failing him and this spurred him on to try to finish the job before they should give out altogether.

As his pen scratched out the foreign words, his mind was filled with the faces and voices of his Chinese friends. The people in the villages had been, for the most part, simple, ignorant peasants, who had regarded him and his western magic with mingled awe and suspicion. They had accepted his religion as the price they had to pay for his medicine. Still once they had accepted it, they often became very enthusiastic converts. And since, as Eliot Watson had said, certain conditions improved with the embracing of Christianity, notably the treatment of women and children, he found that his best converts came from the younger women with small children. It was a practical sort of faith which they had.

But it was the local Buddhist priest who had offered him the greatest companionship and challenge. He had liked the slim young man from the start, although Soong Jen had been immediately hostile toward him. They were natural enemies, but the forces that eventually drew them together proved greater than those that separated them. They were men of education and above-average intelligence in the midst of uneducated men. They were philosophers by disposition who were required by circumstance to be men of action. Sensitive and compassionate, they had to deal constantly with heart-breaking situations.

Still it had taken a famine and a plague to crumble the wall of prejudice between them. Thereafter they had become devoted friends. Dr. Shields taught Soong Jen all he knew about medicine, and the two spent endless hours discussing theology. Dr. Shields had said in private to his wife that the result of these conversations was that he was now a Buddhist Christian, while Soong Jen had become a Christian Buddhist.

One evening, as the two friends talked, and Dr. Shields puffed away on the pipe that he loved, admittedly, to the point of sinfulness, he had been startled and delighted when Soong Jen had said to him, "Do you suppose, good doctor, that your Christ and my Buddha may be the same person?"

Dr. Shields bit hard on his pipe at the thrill of the thought. "That has occurred to me, too. Of course, I can't accept all I hear about your Buddha, just as you don't accept all I tell you of my Lord, but it may well be that neither of us has gotten our messages exactly right. It's an exciting idea."

Dr. Shields and Soong Jen corresponded often. In fact, without Soong Jen's help, the dictionary would have been an impossibility.

While the old doctor sat writing and remembering, a knock on the door brought him swiftly back across an ocean and a continent.

When he opened the front door of the cottage, he found Eliot Watson standing there. He was not surprised to see the young minister. For some reason he had almost been expecting this visit.

"How do you do, sir? It's a great pleasure to see you. Come in. Come in. How are Miss Mary and the children?"

"Oh, fine, thank you. How is Mrs. Shields?"

"In the best of spirits, and off to call on some friends. She loves a little congenial gossip so well that I often wonder how she endured our years in China. Of course, she gossiped a bit there, too," Dr. Shields smiled. "The ladies seem to do that everywhere, don't they? And the children liked her stories and her chocolate cakes just as much as they do here. She was a great favorite of all the village people, and the mothers always checked out my prescriptions and treatments with her. She was the final authority. Have a seat, Dr. Watson. May I offer you some tea?"

"No, thank you, Dr. Shields. To be frank I've come to you for some advice."

"Well, I think that's the highest compliment one man can pay another! I'm honored, and I only hope I can be of some service. Shall we sit here by the window? It has such a good view of our oak. That old giant out there is popular with all God's creatures. The squirrels and birds love it as much as I do. When I sit and look at it, I find it helps me to think."

"It's rather like Miss Clara's 'Tree of Benediction.'"

"Yes, quite right. I should call mine the 'Tree of Contemplation.' Well, tell me what it is you have on your mind." Dr. Shields selected a pipe from the well-stocked wooden rack beside his chair and poured pungent tobacco from a cloth sack into its bowl, pausing to look at Eliot with an apologetic grin. "Just another crutch for my thinking. I believe you don't smoke."

"No, sir, I don't." Eliot took a deep breath. "Dr. Shields, it's mainly concerning my ministry that I've come to see you. You know, no one expects preachers to have problems, and perhaps they shouldn't, but I seem to have a good many."

Dr. Shields responded with a nod and a sympathetic smile. "I know what you mean. It's a lonely life you have to lead. It has been for me, especially in my ministry in China, where the villagers looked on me as either a devil or a god, both being a lot more responsibility than I cared to have. One slip would have done me in. I couldn't afford to lose their confidence, or as they put it in the East, to lose face. I could never show the least hesitancy, anxiety, or remorse. If a man died because of a mistake I made, I had to bear that terrible burden alone. I'm not a dissembler by nature and I found it awfully difficult to appear absolutely confident in the face of all my doubts and inadequacies."

"I can't imagine your feeling that way."

"Only a fool would not."

"You've succeeded in making me feel better already."

The doctor settled back in his chair and drew on his pipe. "Well, that's good. Now tell me more about these problems of yours."

"Well, I worry about my own faith. It isn't as absolute as it ought to be. I have disturbing moments of doubt and disillusionment, and there are certain elements of it that I can't seem to reconcile."

Eliot paused. Dr. Shields was staring intently at his oak tree. A little frown furrowed his bony brow. He turned abruptly now to Eliot. "You mean truth won't stand still for you? Is that the problem?"

"Yes, that's a good way to explain it, I guess."

Dr. Shields fell silent, drawing deeply on his pipe. After a moment he started to speak, then shook his head. He drew again on the pipe. When he finally spoke, his nasal voice was pulled taut between his passion and his restraint.

"You know, I think faith is the most misunderstood word in our language. Implicit in its very meaning is the willingness to accept without certainty. It's a concept which recognizes the finity of man's mind. Why should it ever require blind obedience to outgrown ideas? One's faith should grow along with one's knowledge. It should never limit man's knowledge, but extend it. I seem to remember you telling Miss Lucy Walworth not long ago that we mustn't be afraid of the truth. By the same logic should we be afraid of doubt?"

"I did say that, didn't I? I guess I just don't practice what I preach," Eliot smiled.

"In this case it might be better for you to practice than to preach. If you start preaching doubt in the place of dogma, you may end up being tried for heresy," chuckled Dr. Shields.

Eliot's smile turned wry. "Which leads me to another one of my problems. I keep wondering how much I ought to say publicly on controversial questions."

"Like your recent sermon on hate, you mean? Well, it was pointed, but very gentle in its thrust. It didn't deserve the reaction or the criticism it received. If I were you, I'd be proud of it."

"Thank you," said Eliot. "Your good opinion means a great deal to me. But you know, I feel there's still so much more that needs to be said, and yet I know if I say anything more I'll lose my congregation. They're already annoyed with me, and they might shut me out altogether. Still I feel it's cowardly not to speak out on some of these matters."

Dr. Shields surveyed the anxious young man before him, wishing that he knew what to say.

"Tell me, Doctor, am I a coward?"

The sallow, wrinkled face broke into a smile. "No, I don't think you're a coward."

"Then can it be right for me to keep silent and give them a chance to forgive me before I say anything else unpopular?"

Dr. Shields looked out the window. His answer was long in coming. Finally he shook his head.

"You've asked me a question I simply can't answer. What's right for one man may not be right for another, and this is something you'll have to decide for yourself. It's really a question of deciding what God wants you to be, of determining in what capacity you can serve His purposes best. Your dilemma is one we all face at some time or another in our lives. It's a matter between you and your God. Ask His help. He'll let you know what He wants you to do."

Eliot was silent and after a moment Dr. Shields asked, "Well, now that I've disposed of that problem by dodging the issue, is there anything else on your mind?"

Eliot hesitated. "No, I guess not." He sighed. "There are some other problems, but I guess no one else can solve them for me. It is a great help to me though, Doctor, to have your understanding and sympathy."

When Eliot had gone, Dr. Shields returned to his chair by the window. He sat there for some time chewing on his pipe, sending up tiny puffs of smoke from time to time. He wondered what had made Eliot Watson look so unhappy. It wasn't just the problems they had discussed. There was something else disturbing him.

It's unusual for a young man of such high ideals to have such a strong sense of compassion as well. I only hope that in forgiving sinners he won't be tempted to forgive the sin itself. Lord, how difficult You've made it for us to be good! Even our virtues become vices if we don't watch out! We need that young man here in Natchez. Why couldn't I have told him that? That's what he wanted to hear. And how else can God speak except through those we love and trust?

No, that's not entirely right. Very often He speaks to us

through those we don't like at all, and who don't like us. When you get right down to it I guess you can learn a lot more from your enemies than your friends, if you have the will and intelligence to listen, which most of us don't. Of course most of us don't listen to anything we don't want to hear no matter whom it comes from. I believe it was easier for me to preach the gospel to the ignorant peasants of China than it is for Eliot Watson to preach it to the pious people of Natchez.

CHAPTER FOURTEEN

LESSIE didn't appear in the kitchen at the usual hour. She had not spent the night in the room she shared with Maybelle, but it was not the first time that had happened.

"That Sam ought to be whipped," declared Aunt Chloe with a disapproving frown.

"Way Sister Chloe talks you'd think Adam gave Eve the apple." Uncle Perry spoke with good humored sarcasm.

"May the Lord take me tomorrow if the serpent wasn't a male!" was Chloe's quick retort.

The clock on the shelf ticked away the morning and still Lessie didn't come.

Finally Maybelle gave voice to their mounting fears. "I hope she's all right."

"Well, she had better get herself home or she'll be in trouble, all right! " said Chloe harshly.

Uncle Perry was silent, remembering his two young sons who had run off years before the War. He had never seen them again. Most of the time he put them out of his mind, but every now and then he wondered about them and relived the agony of losing them.

The news was brought by Eliot Watson around noon. He asked to speak to Douglas, who had returned again from Fawnwood to interview a candidate for the still-vacant position of overseer. They conferred briefly in the back parlor of The Burn and then the minister left.

Clara was standing at an upstairs window watching him leave when her brother called to her. She knew something was terribly wrong. She gathered her strength to meet a crisis and refused to let herself speculate as to the nature of it.

Lucy and Daisy and Annie followed her down the stairway.

"What did Dr. Watson want?" Lucy asked her father, her curiosity outweighing her better judgment.

"I want to speak to your aunt privately," was Douglas' curt response. "Come into the parlor for a moment, please, Sister," he added.

She stepped into the parlor and he closed the door.

"What is it, Douglas? What has happened?"

"I don't know how to break it gently. Something terrible has happened. Lessie has been murdered in a brawl Under-the-Hill."

She felt as though he had struck her.

"Oh, no! Oh, Douglas, no! There must be some mistake!"

"I'm afraid it's true, but they've asked me to come and identify the body. Dr. Watson is certain that it is Lessie."

"I can't believe it. I just can't believe it! Gentle little Lessie! Oh, Douglas, it just can't be!"

"Well, I guess I'd better go and then we'll know for sure."

Suddenly she did know for sure. It had happened. It was Lessie.

"How did it happen, Douglas?" she asked him now.

"There was a quarrel and some threats between this high yellow, Sam, and another man. Sam pulled a knife and started for the other man, and—and Lessie threw herself between them."

"Oh, dear God! Was she—was she—killed instantly?"

"I don't know. I'll go now and take Uncle Perry with me. I think we should wait to tell the children and the other servants until we get back. I'll stop by Judge Harris' and bring John home with me."

When Douglas, Uncle Perry and John returned with

confirmation of the appalling event, The Burn was shaken to its foundations.

John in particular was shaken by it. He had had no trouble believing it. He knew it was true the moment he heard it. The face that had haunted him, that man, had done this terrible thing. That had been Lessie he'd seen that night Under-the-Hill. He was struck with horror by the deed itself, and at the tragedy of beautiful, young Lessie, and she was beautiful he suddenly realized, with a knife plunged into her. And somehow he felt a strange sympathy at the plight of the murderer himself. He couldn't help but think what that poor, tortured soul must be going through. He would never forget his face and he would pray for that man for the rest of his life.

Clara kept thinking that she should have followed her instinct and checked up on Lessie's mysterious activities. Of course Lessie might have resented that and probably would have lied to her. She mustn't be like Douglas, thinking everything was her fault. Looking back with regret and dwelling on mistakes did no one any good. Still, if only she had said something.

Lucy was stunned. She couldn't believe it. As mature as she was in some ways, she was still standing on the brink between childhood and womanhood, and she found it impossible to realize that Lessie, who was her contemporary, was at the center of this passionate controversy with its ghastly ending. Things like that didn't happen to people you knew! But, then, she guessed she hadn't really known Lessie. There had been another Lessie that they hadn't known.

Aunt Chloe, red eyed with weeping, kept muttering to herself and anyone who would listen, "Told her that man was no good! But would she listen? I told her. I told her and I told her. Just wouldn't listen to nobody! I knowed it would happen. I knowed it and I told her."

On the morning of the funeral Clara went down to the garden, and filled her basket with blossoms from the white rose bush. Fortunately there were a lot of nice buds that morning. She planned to make a spray to put on Lessie's casket. The white rose had always had a special importance to their family, and last spring she had realized that it also meant a lot to Lessie.

On the day before Easter Lessie had come to her with a request, "Miss Clara, I wonder if you'd let me have a few blooms from the white rose? I wouldn't need more than a half a dozen. I want to do something for our church for Easter Sunday."

"Why, Lessie, of course, but you can't do anything with a half-dozen roses that'll show up at all in church. Take all the white rose blossoms, and as many other flowers as you need."

"No'm I just want the ones off the white rose, but if it's all right I'll use all of them. I'll show you when I finish."

Clara couldn't imagine what she was going to do with them. On Easter morning, when Lessie brought her a tall cross made of two rough, weathered boards which she had twined about with the thorny stems and fragile white blooms, she caught her breath. Its beauty left her speechless.

"Lessie, it's exquisite!" she cried finally, wishing she could find the words to do it justice. "It's true art. It appeals to the eye and the mind and the heart."

"I knew you'd like it," Lessie beamed shyly. "I hope the others will. It's not so showy, but it seems just right to me someway."

In many ways Lessie reminded Clara of Naomi. Rebecca and Clara had taken turns giving the children lessons when they were in Alabama during the War, and they had taught Lessie to read and write but the girl had been filled with longings and talents beyond her opportunities. Most of the negroes seemed contented with their lot. As so many said, the majority were probably better off under some sort of paternalistic system, but you couldn't say that of the Naomis and the Lessies. And the same was undoubtedly true of the embittered "man of color" who had slain Lessie, from all Clara had been able to learn about the quarrel and the stabbing. The man whom Lessie's lover had tried to kill had been white. Although Clara sensed that the quarrel was about Lessie, this was a subject forbidden for a lady to mention and she did not, except to ask Douglas, "Did Sam have any justification?" To which he had rather grimly replied, "Yes, I think he did."

All the Walworths except for little Ernestine attended the funeral. Clara was hesitant about allowing Daisy and Annie to go, but Douglas had insisted. "They might as well make acquaintance with death. They're old enough to understand. I think we all owe it to Lessie to be there. She's been a part of our family, and her great-grandmother before her."

As he spoke, Douglas allowed himself briefly the awful memory of cursing Mammy Martha in one of his drunken rages. No one had heard his tirade but little Lessie. He had never known for sure whether his harsh words had brought on the stroke which paralyzed his wife's old nurse shortly after that, but it was an agonizing possibility.

He had come to the bedside of the stricken old woman and taking her hand had cried over and over, "Mammy Martha, I didn't mean it!" The black eyes held suffering and what else? He searched their depths frantically for forgiveness.

Lessie had touched his arm. "Mr. Douglas, she knows you didn't mean it, and I know it, too. Please don't misery yourself like this. I don't think what you said done this. I really don't." Her words and her compassion had been a balm to his tortured spirit.

"Thank you, child, thank you so very much," he murmured in humble gratitude.

He looked back into the unfathomable eyes once more and knew that he would have to live with only the hope and comfort that Lessie had offered him to lighten this new burden. His sins were great and he knew it. Why couldn't he control his drinking? He was weak, weak! Not the man his father was! And why couldn't he control his temper? Especially when he really couldn't bear to hurt people?

He couldn't understand how he could say the terrible things he did.

The family dressed in their best Sunday clothes for the funeral, wishing to do Lessie proud. Seats had been reserved on the front row for them, and when they were ushered into the shabby, unpainted little church, the chattering stopped and a respectful silence fell.

A tall, neatly dressed black man with a shiny bald head and steel-rimmed spectacles rose, a worn leather-bound Bible tucked under one arm. He bowed graciously to them. "We wish most especially to make our visitors welcome on this occasion of our shared grief, and are most honored by their presence."

Douglas and Clara nodded their acknowledgement and formed the words, "Thank you," with their lips.

The service began with a prayer, which the congregation participated in with a fervor that must have been equal to that of the Early Church, thought Clara, remembering the biblical accounts.

As the minister prayed, the people kept up a rhythmic accompaniment. They swayed and hummed and occasionally cried, "Amen." There was a highly emotional atmosphere, but it was not without its own discipline. They seemed to have a feeling for when to cry out and when to vary the cadence of their humming. There was in it, Clara knew, a nostalgia for another way of life, not quite forgotten, and the ritual had a certain beauty and dignity. There was awareness of the sacramental nature of life and reverence for it. If there was ignorance, there was also the wisdom of humility.

The minister turned to the Walworths. "We would be pleased to have a few words from our distinguished visitors."

Clara saw Douglas' look of dismay. The man, who had once addressed the Polymnian Society of Harvard University with a stirring oration, who had run successfully for the Mississippi State Legislature on a platform of preserving the Union at a time when feeling ran high for secession, could no longer bear to think of speaking in public.

John whispered, "Father, may I speak?"

Douglas nodded in great relief.

John rose, bowed to the minister, and then to the congregation. He stood there in his grandfather's gray frock coat facing them silently for a long moment, his eyes searching for something or someone in the crowd. Finally he began to speak.

"First, let me thank all of you here for welcoming us so kindly. My family and I join you today in mourning the tragic and untimely death of a mutual friend, whom we all loved and whom we will miss very much. She had many special qualities and talents. I'm sure we all have good reason to know how thoughtful and kind she was, and her artistic eye and clever hands created bouquets which were more than just bunches of flowers.

"She has died a heroine. Her brave deed saved a man's life, and perhaps a man's soul. Somewhere right now," again he looked searchingly into the crowd, "there is a man whose whole life could be changed as a result of what she did for him. He must be lost indeed not to be touched by her courageous and selfless act, and I hope for her sake that he will be saved.

"In conclusion let me say Lessie's presence in this world made it both a happier place and a more beautiful place. Our loss is most assuredly heaven's gain."

There was a stillness in the church, and black eyes gleamed with the pride which was buried deep in the hearts of the men and women who were at such a disadvantage in the sophisticated world into which they had been catapulted. The profound respect with which the handsome young white gentleman spoke of Lessie reflected respect for them all, and they were so hungry for it.

As John returned to the seat next to his father, Clara thought, I'll never be any prouder of him, no matter what he does.

"We will close our service with the singing of our sister's favorite hymn," said the minister.

The piano struck a chord, and voices sweet and strong filled the frail little building with soul-stirring melody.

"Swing low, sweet chariot,
Comin' for to carry me home."

Low keyed and in melancholy harmony, wailing and moaning came from everywhere. They were crying for more than Lessie, thought Clara. They were crying like the Jews for their lost world, their native land. They were adopted children, and they still didn't feel at home.

Both Daisy and Annie began sobbing softly, and Clara held tightly to each one's hand. She glanced at her brother and saw that his lips were pressed firmly together and that his eyes were bright with tears.

"Swing low, sweet chariot,
Comin' for to carry me home.
I looked over Jordan
And what did I see?
Comin' for to carry me home . . .
A band of angels
Comin' after me
Comin' for to carry me home."

The words of the spiritual conjured a touching picture of Lessie, riding triumphantly up to the gates of heaven to be received into glory.

"Swing low, sweet chariot,
Comin' for to carry me home."

The tears ran unchecked down Clara's cheeks, and Lucy dabbed furtively at her eyes with her white-gloved hand.

At the conclusion of the service, a line began to form, and it was indicated by the minister that the Walworths should come first to view the body before the casket was closed. The viewing of the body was a necessary part of the ritual, required as a matter of respect. Holding on to her little nieces' hands, Clara paused briefly beside the coffin. There was nobility in the still, small, black face, and she was moved from her own personal grief to a wider more objective one. What a shame that all the beautiful secrets of Lessie's heart should be lost to the world forever.

The afternoon heat was intense, and Aunt Chloe sat in the shade of the chinaberry tree to shell peas.

Daisy had been "talking to the trees," and when she saw Aunt Chloe sitting there, she ran to join her. "May I help, Aunt Chloe?"

"Lord, child, you sure can." Chloe scooped up as many of the unshelled peas as her gnarled brown hands could hold and dropped them into Daisy's held-out skirt.

They sat in companionable silence, their fingers busy and their thoughts wandering.

Daisy looked up into the wizened old face, lined with living, and somehow reassuring. Chloe had a practical wisdom, which accepted life as it was and rejoiced in it. Clara had gone to her for advice more than once when she felt her inexperience in dealing with Douglas' children, and Chloe was always ready with an answer. "Lord, Miss Clara, you use to do just that way yourself, child. That's nothing to bother about."

"Have they ever caught the man that murdered Lessie, Aunt Chloe?" asked Daisy.

"Lord, no, child. He took out of here on the next boat. They'll never catch him."

"What do you think it's like in heaven, Aunt Chloe?"

"Why, like what the scriptures say. The streets paved with gold and jewels."

"I hope there are some flowers there, or else Lessie won't be happy."

"Why, Lord, Miss Daisy child, that's just what she said once. 'I hope heaven will be like a garden, and I can be a bird, flying and singing.'"

CHAPTER FIFTEEN

DOUGLAS' interviews with the applicants for the position of overseer at Fawnwood proved fruitless. Both men wanted more money than he was able to pay.

He and Clara sat on the back gallery until late into the night discussing the situation.

"Douglas, what about just letting John Henry be the overseer? That's really what he's doing anyway, isn't it, when you're not there?"

"Well, I think he might be able to handle the labor, but of course he couldn't keep the books or any records. And although I'd trust him with my life, I couldn't leave any money with him because of the other negroes. They wouldn't hesitate to steal from him or even murder him."

"Why don't you take John with you sometime? I know he's awfully young and he wouldn't be much help to you now, but at least he'd be somebody to talk to, and he could learn something about farming. Eventually he could really be some help to you."

"Well, I've thought about doing that, but it's almost time for his regular classes to start. I want him to finish school and to continue his studies with Judge Harris and get his degree. I don't want him to end up trapped down there with me in that God-awful quicksand!"

"Perhaps we ought to sell Fawnwood."

Douglas gave a sardonic laugh. "What do you think we could get for it? Enough to pay the mortgage maybe? No, Sister, there's nothing to do but stick it out and hope that things will get better. I don't mind it that much. I get a lot of reading done and writing. I didn't tell you, but I've submitted some articles to the *Natchez Courier.*"

Oh, Lord, she thought, if only they would accept them! At least some of them. It would mean so much to Douglas. But she was sure that they wouldn't. She had read some of Douglas' essays from school and it seemed to her that they were awfully wordy and dull.

"Well," continued Douglas, "one bright spot in the picture is the crop this year. I don't know when I've seen a better stand of cotton. I just wish I had a few more hands to harvest it. I really need to get started on that, too. I've got to go back with or without an overseer. I think I'd better count on leaving in the next few days, maybe day after tomorrow, if I can get myself lined up. I've spent so much time dealing with Lessie's death and burial that I haven't gotten all my business attended to."

"Did you order the marker from Mr. Samuels?"

"Yes, and I've already paid him for it, too. Let me know if he doesn't put it up, or if it isn't right."

"It still doesn't seem possible that it all happened."

"Did you know that she was involved with that man?"

"No, I didn't, but I suspected something. She had begun asking for afternoons off. Then she stopped for a long time and I didn't think any more about it. Then she started again, more frequently, and she may have taken some time off without asking. I should have talked to her. Oh, if only I had!"

"I doubt that it would have made any difference. She wouldn't have listened to you. She didn't listen to Aunt Chloe."

"But Aunt Chloe is so much older and so fixed in her opinions. I can see why a young person might not listen to her."

"She was fascinated with that man, damn him—excuse

me, Sister, but damn him—and she wouldn't have listened to anybody."

"Well, I suppose you're right. Oh, what a tragedy it all was! So unnecessary! And I hate all the gossip about it, and having Lessie's reputation tarnished. If there was ever a pure and good person, she was."

"Justice doesn't always prevail in this world." Douglas looked off pensively into the darkness. He was sombre, but somehow at peace, thought Clara. He was really more at home with tragedy than with rejoicing. Then his inner and outer selves seemed to be more in harmony. But he hadn't always been that way, or had he?

At any rate he had not had too much to drink since the episode in early June, at least not that she knew about. She was fairly sure that he did some heavy drinking at Fawnwood.

The Fawnwood harvest was a disappointment. The crop had been as good as any they'd ever had, and Douglas even thought that he might make enough money to finance next year's crop. Then a spell of hard rain had come before he could get it picked. If he hadn't been so short on labor he might have gotten the fields cleared in time. Now the fluffy white gold had turned into a soggy, heartbreaking mess.

Douglas returned to The Burn sober, but wrapped in gloom.

"Well, Douglas, I think it's wonderful that we made 110 bales of cotton. We can at least pay this year's debts and the taxes and the mortgage payments," said Clara.

"But you count on the good years to make a little extra. It just makes me sick to think about it!"

"I know," murmured Clara, soothingly, "I don't blame you. It's a shame. Well, I have some news."

"I hope it's good. I don't think I want to hear it if it's not."

"Oh, it's very good news. Laura has had her baby, another little girl! Her name is Clara and I must say I'm pleased about that."

"Well, that is good news. Is Laura doing well?"

"Just blooming. Motherhood definitely agrees with her."

"I hope the new baby is prettier than little Sarah, or Sallie, or whatever they call her. She's the scrawniest and homeliest little tyke I think I ever saw."

"But she's a smart, lively little creature, and I like her even if she did pull Ernestine's hair! No, this baby looks just like Laura, and she's already beautiful, even as brand new as she is."

"Well, I'm sure you're very proud of your namesake."

"Oh, indeed I am. It's the first I've ever had, excusing the calf at Fawnwood!"

"Well, you'll be happy to hear that that little Clara is doing quite well, growing and thriving."

"Good! I am pleased to hear that."

"By the way, I've taken your advice and made John Henry the temporary overseer at Fawnwood. He was awfully pleased with his new title. I hope it will work out all right. I've paid all the hands and laid in supplies for the winter and I'll go back every couple of weeks until Christmas and check on things. There aren't any messages for me from the *Natchez Courier* are there?"

"No. There hasn't been anything. Why don't you call on them? It's much harder to say no to someone face to face."

"Well, perhaps I will."

The days had grown shorter as autumn replaced summer. As winter came on the weather was cooler, and occasionally cold. The humid climate of Natchez made the hot weather seem hotter and the cold weather, colder, so that although the thermometer seldom dipped below 50 degrees, winter could be very unpleasant.

Douglas spent a lot of time in his room writing, and seemed almost happy.

Clara missed the garden. On all but the rawest, rainiest days she bundled up and walked about in it seeking its solace. Her life went on as usual, but Eliot was more and more in her thoughts. He had made his peace with his congregation, and he had preached no more sermons about hate. He had gained steadily in popularity, but there was a sadness in his eyes at times which Clara found hard to bear. Often, as she paced restlessly in her forlorn and barren garden, feeding the hardy little birds who had chosen to stay the winter, she imagined herself comforting him. In fact, she day dreamed so much these days that she sometimes wondered if she hadn't made up that brief moment in the garden last summer. Perhaps after all it had meant nothing to Eliot.

On the very worst days, when sheets of gray rain descended relentlessly on The Burn, or when the north wind whipped viciously against it, she took comfort in the crackling fires which warmed its big drafty rooms, sitting with her sewing, or reading to little Ernestine by the hour. She held classes for the older girls, and she began to give piano lessons in order to help out with the mortgage payments on Fawnwood. Altogether she stayed quite busy, and the year drew on to its close.

CHAPTER SIXTEEN

CLARA and Chloe were planning Christmas dinner. They surveyed the contents of the basement storeroom, Clara making notes as they talked. Ernest was coming with his family from Memphis and would be staying with them for several days, and Laura and her husband, Will McPheeters, and their children would be coming over for dinner on Christmas day. Christmas night they would have an Open House for family and friends.

"If you think we have enough to spare, I'd like to take a ham and some preserves to the Orphanage for their Christmas dinner," Clara was saying.

"Well, I ain't sure what we'll eat for the rest of the winter, but I reckon we can live on chicken. We've done it before."

"Now, Aunt Chloe," said Clara, "you know you don't begrudge those little orphans their Christmas ham."

"Miss Clara, just suppose you had to embroider the same design over and over, year in, year out. I gets tired of cooking chicken."

Clara laughed. "Well, I think that about completes the menu. Let's give the puddings another good stir and then we'll take these dried fruits and nuts and get started on our fruit cakes."

"Now don't tell me. I know I got to make extras for the orphans," Chloe grumbled. This was part of the game. She pretended to be very outdone, but she got as much pleasure from their charity as Clara did.

The rich, deep red of wine-filled glasses lent a Christmas note against the heavy white damask cloth which it had taken three people to iron. Plum and fig puddings, bedecked with holly and resplendent on silver trays, decorated the table, and there were bowls of jellies and nuts and crystallized fruit.

Having the family together was well worth all the trouble, Clara thought, as she looked around the long table at the faces that she loved.

It was a special treat to have Ernest with them this Christmas. They saw so little of him now. She was glad to see how well and happy he looked. He obviously adored his pretty and flighty little red-haired wife, Mary, and she him. If Rebecca had only lived, perhaps Douglas could have been that happy too.

Clara glanced from Ernest to Douglas, who was seated at the opposite end of the table. How much they looked alike, the two handsome bearded men. But in spite of their strong resemblance, her brothers' differing personalities were reflected in their outward appearances—Douglas, dignified and remote; Ernest, always laughing and always in motion.

Laura sat next to Douglas, exuding the deep, earthy contentment with which motherhood seemed to fill her, and her Will gazed at her with a worshipping look from across the table.

The younger children were having a marvelous time together at a side table. The Christmas spirit has even touched their little pagan hearts, she told herself. John, the bon vivant, was in his element. Only Lucy seemed a little wistful. Lessie's tragic death seemed to have had a lasting impact on her. Other than her frequent visits to the Shields, she didn't go out much. She spent most of her time reading or writing, seeming to live in her own little world. But Aunt Chloe said she would "outgrow" it, and Clara hoped that it was indeed only a stage of development.

Douglas finished carving one huge turkey stuffed with oyster dressing and Uncle Perry brought another. Then came sweet potatoes in orange shells, green peas with chestnuts, cinnamon apples, and Aunt Chloe's famous rolls. When everybody had been served, Douglas raised his voice above the chattering. "I have something to tell you all. I've accepted an offer to become the editor of the *Natchez Courier.*"

His announcement electrified the gathering. Of all the family only Clara had had the slightest inkling of Douglas' interest in the newspaper; and she, too, was amazed that anything had come of it, especially anything like an editorship!

"How splendid!" cried Ernest. "I had no idea you were considering anything like that, although with your interest in politics I can see how a newspaper would provide you with an excellent vehicle now that any public office is out of the question."

The others agreed that it was indeed wonderful and that Douglas was well suited to the job. No one mentioned Fawnwood, but Douglas addressed that question. "I've made it clear to the owner that I do have other responsibilities, that I will have to be away from time to time to see about the plantation. He found this an entirely satisfactory arrangement. It is, after all, a small paper, and being published on a weekly basis will not require an inordinate amount of my time. Of course my salary will be quite inconsequential, but I guess it's better than nothing."

"Indeed it is." Ernest lifted his glass. "Let me be the first to toast the new editor of the *Natchez Courier*!"

After everything had been passed again and Uncle Perry and Maybelle began taking the empty dinner plates back to the kitchen, Ernest rose, glass in hand.

"Brothers, sisters, nieces, nephews, Walworths all, I've composed a little poem. Anybody who wishes to leave the room at this time has my permission. Otherwise, I'm afraid you'll have to listen to it!"

"Why, we love your poetry, Ernest!" said Clara.

"How long is it?" demurred Douglas.

"Oh, it's quite short."

"I'm glad to hear that."

"After all blood is thicker than water, and so's wine," declared John, reaching eagerly for his glass. The wine was a special Christmas treat which he and Lucy had been permitted to share.

"Well, get on with it," urged Douglas.

Ernest grinned amiably. "All in due time. Could we ask Aunt Chloe and the other servants to come and hear it, too?"

Aunt Chloe was sent for and she and the others gathered in the doorway to listen.

Running his fingers through his thick and wavy hair, Ernest bowed to Clara at one end of the table and then to Douglas.

"To our hostess and to our host
We raise this Merry Christmas toast.
To John Periander and his spouse,
Our pa and ma who built this house,
Who reared us all, a goodly brood,
Let's drink a toast of gratitude.
To Uncle Perry who's served us well
We offer thanks, and to Maybelle.
Last, but not least, our glasses we raise
To one who's known us all our days,
Spanked and scolded and loved us, too
And cooked this scrumptious feast for true.
To Aunt Chloe we here-by say,
'We love you' on this Christmas day!"

Cheers and applause followed. Aunt Chloe stood in the doorway listening, her eyes wet. When they lifted their glasses to her, she hid her face in her apron, overcome with emotion.

Uncle Perry led her away, heaving and sobbing and murmuring, "Miss Sarah would be so proud. Mr. John, too. Lord, let them look down and see."

Ernest's toast had moved them all, and more than a few tears salted the fine red wine.

Then Douglas lifted his glass in solemn salutation. "To the many Walworths who have gone before us, leaving us the treasured heritage of a good name and a good example."

And John rose next, exclaiming, "To the Walworths, dead or alive!"

After the puddings had been doused with brandy and set aflame, then served with a hot sugary sauce, they sat at the table talking for over an hour, enjoying the warmth and camaraderie of their reunion.

Clara felt at peace with the world. Seeing Eliot at church that morning, she had told herself, he's a friend, a man that I like very much, and that's all. My infatuation with him is ended. This had given her a tremendous sense of achievement. All through the busy day she didn't think of him at all.

The parlors of The Burn glowed that night with leaping fires and the softness of candlelight. Clara had not had the lamps lit, preferring to let the candles shed their shimmering magic on the waxed fruit and holly with which she had decorated the rooms.

The women guests were gaily dressed in holiday colors. If most of their gowns had seen many Christmases, it wasn't noticeable in the candlelight.

The aroma of the punch, a spicy mulled wine, pervaded the house, mingling harmoniously with the pungent fragrances of the cypress logs and the huge cedar Christmas tree, which reached all the way up to the fourteen-foot ceiling.

Someone was playing Christmas carols on the piano, and a group had gathered around to sing.

Douglas was standing in the double doorway between the parlor and the dining room receiving congratulations on his new job as editor of the *Natchez Courier.* He seemed quite thrilled over the appointment. Clara was so happy for him, and she tried to banish an uneasy feeling that it might have come too late.

She stood nearby talking with some of their guests. Her

eyes, searching the room looking for someone to replace Lucy at the punch bowl, met Eliot's burning gaze. He looked quickly away, but she knew that he had been watching her. She steadied the cup of punch she was holding, putting both hands firmly on it, and tried to concentrate on what was being said.

Margarette and Will Martin's daughter passed by, and Clara put a hand on her arm. "Ellie dear, will you help Lucy with the punch?"

CHAPTER SEVENTEEN

HOW can I have allowed this to happen, Clara kept asking herself? There was no longer any use in pretending or denying. The feelings she had tried to disown had come back with renewed force and were consuming her. Although not so much as a word had been exchanged between them, she knew that Eliot was in love with her and she had responded to his unspoken love with her total being. She hadn't sought it, hadn't done anything to encourage it. She had even avoided him when possible. Still she knew that somehow she was wrong. Among other things she felt disloyal to Ross, who was becoming just a bittersweet memory. Even her memories of him were blurring. It was a fact that he no longer lived in her imagination. Time had healed all too well. She knew though that Douglas was right. You couldn't live forever on a package of letters tied with white ribbon. But you couldn't take what didn't belong to you either. Eliot belonged to Mary whether she was the right wife for him or not. He had thought so once. He must remember that and return to her, and she must return to her letters. She tried reading them over, but they had become just words with no power to move her. The new love had emasculated the old. She struggled against the dawning realization of what it was necessary for her to do. On her knees she had asked God to help her. Now He was speaking to her, and she was trying hard not to hear.

Oh, all right, dear Lord, you win, she finally answered Him one bleak January day. I'll destroy my love.

From that moment she started ruthlessly to strip away the beautiful illusions and distortions that create the portrait of romantic love, and she began once again to be free. But there was an emptiness within her, a sense of desolation in the place of the intense joy and pain that had made her feel so alive, and the days dragged cheerlessly by.

One morning as she picked up her mending basket, her life seemed suddenly unbearable. She put the basket away, told Daisy and Annie they would have no classes that day, and asked Uncle Perry to saddle Mac. Uncle Perry was startled by this request since he had not known Miss Clara to ride for many years, really not since the War. She had ridden every day as a little girl when she and Ernest had spent many happy days on horseback, exploring along the river bluff which marked the end of their property in those days. Clara had often thought what a mistake her father had made to set his house so far from the river, foregoing the beautiful view of it for the convenience of town. Clara and Ernest liked to ride along the river's edge, frequently taking a picnic lunch. Ernest would bring his gun, and they shot quail and rabbits and squirrels. Clara was a good shot, always bagging her share. Then one day she wounded a baby squirrel. Ernest had caught the pitiful creature and mercifully dashed his brains out against a tree. It was a moment she would never forget, and Clara didn't shoot the gun again.

There was no good place to ride along the river now, so she headed Mac eastward toward Linden, and the country of open fields which lay on the other side of it. It was a cold clear day and Mac was glad to be out in the open air with a chance to stretch his legs. He galloped swiftly down the road sending clouds of dust behind them.

Clara rode like one possessed. No horse could have gone fast enough for her that day. On and on they went until Mac, no longer in his prime, began to slow his pace, panting and heaving. Clara, realizing that he was exhausted, directed him off the road into a field. She dismounted by an elm tree and looped the reins about a branch.

She stood for a while looking across the empty fields. Then she flung herself to the ground where she lay face down screaming, striking and kicking at the earth. Her shrieks rent the stillness of the deserted countryside, and the patient and silent earth absorbed the violent stabbing of her anguished feet. At length she rolled over on her back and lay looking at the sky. "Dear God," she murmured, "after all these years I've had a temper tantrum!"

After that ride Clara resumed the routines of her life. Although there was no happiness or pleasure in it, her rebellion against it had passed.

Most of February was cold and wet. It rained day after day, and they all developed colds that they couldn't seem to get rid of. Douglas was particularly susceptible to them. He had had a bout with his lungs when he went North to school, and several serious recurrences during the War. Now he contracted a severe case of bronchitis and was too ill for several weeks to go to his office or even to do much work at home. It was most unfortunate since he had really just gotten started at his new job, but it couldn't be helped.

When a pale and thin Douglas returned to the newspaper office, he came back home after a few hours utterly exhausted and thoroughly irritable. He drank too much for the first time in months. There was the usual unpleasantness, but he apologized to everyone the next day and promised to do better. He had not touched any whiskey since and they all breathed more easily.

The crocuses began popping up, and the robins arrived, although the weather was not noticeably warmer. One sunny day in early March, Clara and Annie walked down through the garden. Clara stopped to break off some dead foliage from the Cherokee rose bushes which lined the way. Suddenly Annie, who had run ahead, called excitedly,

"Aunt Clara, the white rose is blooming! Come and see!"

Clara hurried to her niece's side and there cradled in Annie's hand was the first blossom of the season. A little shiver ran through her. Every spring that this old bush bloomed again it seemed more and more of a miracle.

Daisy came running from the yard and joined them, pressing her face joyfully into the blossom.

"Tell us again about the white rose, Aunt Clara," begged Annie.

"All right. Let's sit down over here under the Tree of Benediction."

Clara seated herself on the bench and the little girls snuggled beside her. She hugged them to her. Mercy, how she loved them!

"Once upon a time," she began, "The Burn had a Scottish gardener. He didn't just have Scottish ancestry; he had lived in Scotland, and he spoke with a very heavy brogue. He came to Natchez to help the people here with their fine new houses to lay out gardens. He designed and engineered the terraces behind The Burn. He loved the little brook that ran through the property then, and he planned the garden around what he called 'the wee burn.' So Grandma and Grandpa Walworth decided to name their house The Burn."

"It's too bad the stream dried up," said Annie.

"But the name will make us always remember it," said Daisy.

"Well, tell about the rose now."

"Perhaps I should let the rose tell you herself. If she could speak this is probably what she would tell you:

"I was given by the old Scottish gardener to my little mistress, Lucy Walworth, in 1848 when she was only six years old. She planted me and worked me, and watered me herself. I loved her and I did my best to grow and bloom for her. Several happy years passed. Then one summer evening my little friend brought her dolls and sat near me in the garden playing with them. The dolls were dressed in new outfits that she had just made for them. The little dresses were quite well designed and sewn with tiny neat

stitches. It grew late, and her mother called her, but before she left she laid her cheek on one of my flowers and whispered to me, 'I hope there'll be lots of these to put on my birthday cake next week.'

"I tried my hardest, and then I waited for someone to come and pick my roses, which they did finally, but instead of the happy faces I had thought to see they were weeping. The Yellow Fever had struck Lucy and she never came to our garden again.

"After Lucy died I continued to bloom for the family, who loved me because I had been hers. Her grieving mother tended me herself, and came each morning to gather my roses. No one but me ever saw the father's tears, but many times my petals glistened with them.

"The years went peacefully by until I began to hear loud talk and argument among the gentlemen. Then our garden began to tremble at the distant sound of cannons. We flowers, having our roots in the earth, felt before anyone else the awful vibrations of the War.

"One evening as the big round sun was bidding us good day I saw one of the daughters of the house and with her a young soldier.

"They walked about the garden hand in hand. Finally they stopped near me and he commented to her that I was a beautiful rose.

"'Yes,' said the girl, 'that's my sister Lucy's rose. She planted it herself. She died of Yellow Fever when she was just eleven years old so you can imagine how very special this bush is to all of us.'

"The soldier stooped and picked one of my blooms. Handing it to her, he said, 'Pin this over my heart, and when I come back you'll find it there.'

"But he never came back, and my flower lies with him in a soldier's grave.

"When the Union soldiers came to The Burn all of us flowers were crushed to the ground beneath their heavy boots. We were trampled until not a green blade was left standing. I sank into the earth, and not until the cruel war had passed did I show my green leaves. The first thing I saw was Lucy's mother, whom I knew at once in spite of the way the years of war had aged her. She was walking with one of her daughters, and when they saw me peeping above the ground, the mistress cried, 'Look, look! Here's Lucy's rose! It's living! Oh, thank God, it's living! We'll build a new

garden around it. It will be the spirit of the garden.'

"And now visitors who come to our garden always gather about me, exclaiming, 'See the old white rose, the spirit of the garden!' Of course, I'm not as young as I used to be. I sometimes think that I cannot bloom another spring, but each year when I awaken from my winter of sleep my blossoms are greeted with such joy that I say to myself, 'I have not lived in vain. They all love me!' And then I know that I must go on blooming as long as I am loved."

"That's a good story," said Annie, and Daisy wiped the tears from her face with the skirt of her gingham apron.

"Aunt Clara, could we see little Lucy's dolls again?" Annie loved to see the things which had belonged to Lucy and been lovingly put away. And so they went up to the storeroom. Clara unlocked an old trunk and lifted out the little stuffed dolls with china heads. They exclaimed over them and the dresses made by Lucy, sewn with such dainty stitches.

They spent the morning in happy reminiscence. Clara opened a big tin box which contained old diaries and letters, pictures, and mementos. She showed them some letters that Lucy had written in a small neat hand, one to her big brother Douglas when he was away at college.

"Here's a picture of Lucy," said Clara. "You know she looks just like Daisy," cried Annie, and Clara smilingly agreed, hiding the little stab of pain she felt as she looked from the living child to the faded daguerreotype.

Eliot sat in his study, his half-written sermon before him, his thoughts far from its subject. He couldn't seem to get on with it. The state of his marriage was so much on his mind that he couldn't think about anything else.

His love for Clara he knew was both the cause and the effect of an unsatisfactory marriage. He and Mary had been so happy once. What had happened to them? It had been such a gradual process that he couldn't think when or how their estrangement had come about.

For one thing they seemed to have no common interests. Mary was wrapped up in the children and in the running of the household, and this was natural enough. She was extremely feminine, and her interests were, too. Of course, this absolute femininity was one of the very qualities which had attracted him to her. He had found it charming and ingenuous. As he reviewed the early and happy days of their life together he realized how much of the gulf that existed between them was his fault. He had shut her out. With sudden resolution he went to the door and called, "Mary, would you come here? I need some help with this sermon. Will you listen to it, and give me the benefit of some of your common sense?"

That night after everyone was tucked away, Clara opened her desk and lifted out a bundle of letters. She took them with her to bed. She untied the white ribbon that bound them, and lying propped against her pillows, she read them one by one.

"When I think I cannot endure this miserable war any longer, I call to mind the picture of you standing there in the garden of The Burn in your white dress, looking like one of the blossoms on your sister's bush. Then, Clara darling, I confess I take the rose you gave me from my pocket and I kiss it as though it were you. Somehow this helps me to go on."

She could no longer see the words for her tears, but they were tears of relief.

Part III

1878-1930

CHAPTER ONE

CLARA was in the garden feeding the birds. "Soon it'll be spring," she told them. Then you'll be able to feed yourselves, and you'll leave me."

"Aunt Clara, I'm going to call on the Shields."

Clara smiled. How many times had she heard Lucy say that? The old couple had meant so much to Lucy since their return to Natchez. That must have been ten years ago. No, it was exactly nine, Clara decided, because it was the same year that Eliot Watson had come.

"Tell them hello for me," said Clara.

As Lucy walked the short distance between The Burn and the Shields' house, she drew her heavy gray flannel cloak close about her. It had been a mild day, but was turning cold. She pushed open the gate which leaned so under its burden of vines in the summer, but now swung quite freely to and fro.

Humming softly to herself, she went up the short walk and onto the little gallery of the cottage. She started to lift the iron knocker, when the door suddenly moved away from her. A very tall man whom she had never seen before stood in the doorway smiling at her.

"Oh," she put her hand to her throat, "you—you startled me."

"I am Edgar Poague," said the tall man, as though that explained everything, and they stood there for what seemed a very long moment. Finally he stepped aside. "Won't you please come in?"

"Thank you," said Lucy. "I am . . ."

"Why, Lucy dear," said Mrs. Shields, "do come in. I'm so glad you've come to see us. I want you to meet the son of one of my old friends. He's here visiting us. This is Dr. Edgar Poague, Miss Lucy Walworth, the young lady you've heard us speak so much about. Have a seat by the fire, my dear. The doctor has gone to town, but he should be back any minute. Let me get us some tea."

Away she went and there they were. The clock in the corner ticked loudly in the ensuing silence and the fire hissed and crackled. Dr. Poague sat awkwardly on the tiny love seat and tried to arrange his long legs comfortably.

Why should I be frightened of this man, wondered Lucy? No person had ever awed her before. Bravely she made herself meet his eyes in spite of the fluttery way she was feeling inside, and she found this even more disturbing though oddly pleasant.

"Are you from Virginia, Dr. Poague?"

"Yes, but I'm living now in Louisiana, practicing medicine. I'm on my way home for a visit, and my mother asked me to stop by to see her dear friend, whom she's not seen for so long. I only arrived this morning, but I already feel as though I've known the doctor and Mrs. Shields always."

Lucy smiled. "Yes, they are like that."

Dr. Poague was a large, rawboned man. His shoulders were wide, his arms and legs long, and his hands and feet big. He looked a little bit like the pictures she had seen of Abraham Lincoln. Dr. Poague rose as Mrs. Shields entered, and took the tea tray from her. "Let me have this," he said. He stood there filling up the little room with his bigness.

"Oh, thank you, Edgar," said Mrs. Shields. "Will you just put it here for me on this chest?"

"That's a handsome chest. Leather, isn't it?" asked Edgar, scrutinizing the chest which was to serve as a tea table.

"Yes, it's pigskin. The Chinese use it so much."

"What a fascinating life you and Dr. Shields must have led!"

"Yes, it has been. As I look back I realize it more than I did at the time. I hated it at first. I used to cry myself to sleep every night! Everything was so different; the language, the customs, the thinking of the people. Things that are so important to us meant nothing to them, and the other way around. I was lonely. I was homesick. And I wanted desperately to go home. I told Dr. Shields that I had nothing in common with those sly, slant-eyed people, who always seemed to be laughing at me! The exasperating man just smiled and said, 'My dear, there is at least one thing we have in common. We're human beings.' Maybe that's when I began to change my attitude. Anyway I finally stopped expecting that everyone would be like me and think as I did, and, of course, you know what happened. I began discovering all sorts of things we did have in common. It seemed as though the people had changed, and they had. I had changed them by changing myself, the sort of miracle that any ordinary person can perform. There's Dr. Shields now." Mrs. Shields rose, but Edgar was already at the door.

"Well, Lucy," Dr. Shields' face beamed with pleasure at the sight of her, "I couldn't have planned things better. I had intended to bring the doctor here to call on you. You asked me to look out for a teaching position for you next year when you've finished your course at Oakland, and Dr. Poague has been telling me about the great need for teachers in the towns where he's practicing. The area is rather backward, but I thought you might like the challenge of it."

"Oh, yes," said Lucy somewhat uncertainly. It seemed almost too much of a challenge, and she could imagine with what disapproval her family would view such a step.

"Of course," said Dr. Poague, "Miss Walworth's family might not think it proper or wise for such a gently reared young lady to leave home, and she, herself, might find the rural atmosphere tedious."

"My family allows me to make my own decisions," said Lucy recklessly, "and I'm sure that a person with any inner resources needn't find life boring anywhere." How pompous that sounded, thought Lucy. Why did I say that?

"Well, a young lady such as you is much needed there, I can assure you. When I get back to Louisiana I'll talk to my good friend, William Murray, who has done so much to improve our schools. One of the biggest problems, of course, is the widely scattered population and the difficulty of building good roads in that swampy country which poses something of a problem to my profession, too. My buggy is forever getting stuck in the mud on rainy nights when somebody is desperately sick twenty miles away. I lost a woman patient just the other night because I couldn't get there in time." The look on Edgar's face betrayed his intense involvement with the welfare of his patients. For all his huge frame he was gaunt and spare, and Lucy suspected that he gave unstintingly of himself to others. He places too much strain on himself, she thought.

"I must go," said Lucy finally, glancing through the long narrow window at the darkening winter sky. "I'm afraid I've let the time slip by."

"I'll walk you home," said Edgar. When he fetched her cloak and placed it gently around her shoulders, the most delightful sensations rippled through Lucy. Why, it's just like the poets say, but I never dreamed it could happen to me, she thought, very much surprised at the stirrings within her.

Tall as she was, Lucy found herself fairly skipping to keep up with Edgar's long strides. She asked him a few shy questions about new techniques in medicine, a field she knew little about, and he responded with an almost boyish enthusiasm, becoming so wrapped up in his subject that he didn't notice how rapidly he was walking. When they arrived at The Burn, Lucy was quite out of breath. "Won't you please come in? I'd like for you to meet my family."

"I'd like very much to meet them. I mustn't keep the Shields waiting for supper, but I think I might come in for a moment."

They found Clara and Douglas sitting by the fire in the library. "This is Dr. Edgar Poague. He's visiting Dr. and Mrs. Shields. His mother and Mrs. Shields were girlhood friends."

"How do you do, Dr. Poague," said Clara. "How nice for Mrs. Shields to have you here. She still misses her old friends. Sit here near the fire. You too, Lucy dear. It's gotten rather chilly outside."

"Is your home in Virginia, Dr. Poague?" asked Douglas.

"Well, yes, it was, but I'm practicing medicine now in Madison County. I cover a lot of countryside in my horse and buggy. Barcus and I have deepened the ruts in those roads by a good many inches I'm sure."

"Do you call him Barcus because he's willing?" asked Lucy.

"Exactly so, Miss Lucy!" exclaimed Edgar. "I see that you are a fan of Mr. Dickens, too."

"I'm well acquainted with that country you practice in, Dr. Poague. I farm in it," said Douglas, adding with a smile, "I hope your Barcus likes a muddy track! I expect you know William Murray. He's an old friend of mine."

"I certainly do. I'll tell him I saw you. The smallness of this world never ceases to amaze me. I'm always running into someone I served with in Stuart's cavalry during the War. There were a lot of men from Natchez. I remember a Colonel Martin. Do you know him?"

"That's Uncle Will!" cried Lucy.

"In fact you and I may have met before, Dr. Poague," said Douglas. "I served with my brother-in-law, Will Martin, under Jeb Stuart's command myself during the first year of the War."

"We must have just missed one another then, because I didn't join Stuart until the summer of '62, but I was with him all the way to Yellow Tavern."

"His operations were most effective."

"Yes, they certainly were. Stuart was our 'Swamp-Fox,' fighting on his home ground and making the most of it! He knew every thicket and bog like the back of his hand!"

"An apt comparison! Stuart had much in common with

Francis Marion. And wasn't he a colorful figure? Those plumed hats he wore made him look quite the Cavalier, although he was actually very much of a Puritan."

"He was a showman, Major Walworth, and the men loved it! As you know, the boredom of camp life is much worse than the hardships. General Stuart's ruffles and plumes enlivened our spirits!"

"His death was a bitter blow to our cause."

"Yes, one always wonders what would have happened if Stuart had lived, or if Johnston hadn't been killed at Shiloh, or if Lee hadn't gone to Gettysburg, but I guess it's better not to dwell on the 'if onlies.'"

"Unless you include in your fantasy the problems that would have faced us if we'd won our independence."

"That's something nobody ever thinks about. Well, tell me, what's become of my friend, Martin?"

"He became a general after joining the Army of Tennessee. We both served under Joe Wheeler. Will had some heroic adventures. He's practicing law now and is very active in community affairs. He did everything but lay the rails for the 'Little J.'"

The "Little J" was a nickname for the newly built railroad which connected Natchez with Jackson and Columbus. It had finally been built over the impassioned protests of the steamboat companies and citizens, who abhorred the commercialism which a railroad would bring.

"That sounds very interesting. I'd like to hear more about it. I have to leave tomorrow, but perhaps I'll get a chance to call on him before I go." Dr. Poague got to his feet. "I've enjoyed meeting you and Miss Clara, and talking to you. We seem to have a great deal in common. I hate to rush off, but I'm afraid the Shields may be waiting supper for me. I do hope to see you again." At the door Dr. Poague turned to Lucy. "Goodbye, Miss Lucy. I'll write you about that matter."

Dr. Poague was, of course, considerably older than Lucy, and no one considered the possibility that a romance was in the making. Lucy wasn't sure herself. She only knew that she very much enjoyed being in his company and that the prospect of seeing him again played a large part in her decision to go to Newellton. The doctor kept his promise. A letter came from him, telling her of a position that needed filling in a little town near Milton.

"But, Lucy," said Clara, "surely you can find something right here in Natchez if you want to teach. Why must you insist on going off into the wilderness? A girl as bright as you would be welcome anywhere. In fact your talents will be wasted in Newellton. You'll be surrounded by ignorance and illiteracy."

"That's just the point, Aunt Clara," said Lucy. "Because there is so much ignorance they need me, and I want to help them. And as for leaving home, I think that may be best for everyone. Father and I get into such arguments. I can never seem to let well enough alone, and I end up making matters worse for everyone." Lucy sighed and sadly shook her head.

Clara reached out and placed her hand over Lucy's. "Now Lucy, that isn't so. Perhaps you do make it harder on yourself. I know it is hard for you, and I know how much you want to do something that you feel is worthwhile. And," Clara smiled, "if you weren't my niece, I would probably say what a wonderful thing for a young woman to do! Since you are, however, I just don't want you going off alone to a jumping-off place with no friends or family to look after you."

"Dr. Poague will be right over in Milton. He knows the family I'll be staying with, and he says they are quite nice people."

"Well, I don't know what your father will say."

Surprisingly Douglas made no violent objection. "If you're sure in your own mind that it's what you want to do, then I think it's all right for you to try it for a year. But mind you don't go into it unless you plan to stick it out the whole year. It wouldn't be right to leave your post. As far as your safety is concerned, I feel sure Dr. Poague will see to it that you are in the care of the right sort of people. But these people won't be able to discuss Socrates and his method or Aristotelian ethics with you."

Lucy started to say, well, Dr. Poague is very intellectual, but thought better of it.

"I know, Father, but I still want to go, and I promise to stick it out the whole year."

One October afternoon after Lucy had gone to Newellton, John returned from Judge Harris' office where he was now working as a clerk. He noticed a buggy and a pair of horses hitched up in front of The Burn. "Wonder who the callers are?" he murmured to himself.

As he walked through the front door, he saw little Ernestine coming down the stairs. Striking a pose he launched into Romeo's soliloquy. "But soft what light from yonder window breaks? It is the East and Juliet is the sun!"

Ernestine seized the bannister and moaned dramatically, "Romeo, Romeo, wherefore art thou Romeo?" Then she ran down the rest of the stairs to greet him and he swooped her off the floor in an enveloping hug. When he set her down, she smoothed her dress and hair, protesting, "Mercy, John, you forget I'm thirteen now."

"But you've only been that old for a week. I'm not used to it yet. And I don't care what Father says, I'm going to keep calling you 'Birdie.' It suits you better than Ernestine. What's up? Who are the visitors?"

"Cousin Alice Gordon and Leila. They drove up from the country to do some shopping, and they're having tea with Aunt Clara and Daisy and Annie in the garden right now. I'm on my way to join them."

"I guess I'd better go with you and speak to them."

They found the ladies sitting in the summer house. "The fairest flowers in the garden!" John gestured toward the group with his winning smile.

"How nice to see you, John," said Alice Gordon as he stooped to kiss her.

He turned to the dark-haired young lady seated next to his sisters. "Well, Leila, I hope we're still kissing cousins. You're certainly growing up. I don't even know you anymore. Where in the world are your freckles? I miss them. You must be wearing bonnets or putting on powder!" In between sentences he placed a kiss on Leila's blushing cheek.

"Don't pay him any mind, Leila," said Annie. "He's a terrible tease! Just be glad you're not his sister!"

"I'm rather glad of that myself," said John, and the hint of appraisal in his voice, and in his sparkling blue eyes, made Leila blush again and drop her own lovely brown ones.

When the visitors had gone, John commented, "Well, that little chicken is hatching out very nicely."

"I'm afraid you embarrassed her with all your foolishness!" said Clara. "We got a letter from Lucy today. It's on the table in the hall."

John found the letter on the console in the hall beneath the portrait of his grandfather. "I wish you wouldn't look at me like that, Grandpa," he said to the stern face with its steely blue eyes. He picked up the letter and began to read.

My dearest family,

Your letters have come duly to hand, as Grandpa Walworth would say, and the candy came duly to mouth, only not mine! My landlady ate most of it! Mrs. Bates is quite a dear, but an absolute gourmand. She reminds me very much of Mrs. Miller from our Evergreen days; always cooking, forever making cakes and pies for her church, and I'm certain she eats half of them herself! She and Mr. Bates, who is just as lean as she is fat, have been very good to me and almost smother me with kindness. I have to plead "homework" to stay alone in my room, which is not as cozy as I would like. The wind whistles in all around the windows, and I have one small braided rug beside my bed, which is scarcely big enough for one foot. I am very glad that I brought my own quilt. The mattress is lumpy, but the bedding clean, and I am really not too uncomfortable. Of course the meals are delicious, although I live in horror of growing to look like Mrs. Bates!

I think that I am going to like teaching. My students are an odd mixture, all ages, and from all walks of life. Some of the children come from such poor homes that they have no decent clothes, no shoes, and many times no lunch. The ignorance is really appalling, much worse than I had expected it to be. I have had to concentrate on reading, writing, and arithmetic, although Ihope to get around to some history soon.

I have had some problems of discipline with several of the bigger boys. They try to bully the smaller children and have been impudent to me, but are beginning to show me more respect as they see I have no notion of letting them run over me. It may be that my famous "will of iron" will prove to be of some value at last!

Dr. Poague was here last Sunday and took me to services at the Presbyterian Church. I hope the sermon we heard was not the preacher's best effort, but I fear that is the case. Dr. Poague has been so kind. He has a lot of patients in Newellton and is here quite often.

Write, please, whenever you can, and let me know the news about everyone. I miss all of you so very much, and I will admit to being homesick, but I am not sorry that I came. I know it is a good experience for me, and although I came to teach, as they say, it's I who have learned the most!

Please don't forget to write.

Much love to all,
Lucy

John walked out to the back gallery where Clara had taken her sewing. "What's this Dr. Poague like?" he wanted to know.

"Why, he's very nice, a charming gentleman, rather on the serious and dedicated side. Why do you ask?"

"It just struck me that I might wake up one day and find that he's going to be my brother-in-law."

"Oh, I don't think so, John. He's much older than Lucy. He's just looking after her because she's so young and away from home."

"Well, I think Lucy would be apt to like an older man. He sounds like just her type. I'm glad you think well of him."

CHAPTER TWO

BY the end of Lucy's first year in Newellton it became obvious to the family that the relationship between Lucy and Edgar Poague had blossomed into a full-fledged romance. Within another year they were married. Edgar bought a little house for them in Newellton and Lucy continued to teach. Edgar was as large of mind and spirit as he was of frame and he and Lucy were so congenial. Only Lucy's recent miscarriage had marred their complete happiness. Lucy had gone back to her teaching which seemed to give her great satisfaction. But Clara cautioned her that at the first signs of her next pregnancy she must stop teaching immediately. It could not be good for her to be on her feet all day.

John had obtained his law degree and joined his Uncle Will Martin's law firm. According to John, business was a little slow. "I think our problem is that we have more talent than Natchez people have the money to pay for," he told the family one night at the dinner table.

Douglas looked thoughtful. "I know you're joking, John, but there's a lot of truth in what you've said. You could probably do much better in your chosen career somewhere else. You might try Cleveland, Ohio. You know you have a lot of relatives there. Or you could go to Memphis and stay with your Uncle Ernest and Aunt Mary."

"I know, Father, I've thought about that, and someday I may go seek my fortune elsewhere." He waved a roll in the air. "But you know, 'man does not live by bread alone.'" He took a bite of the roll and smiled ecstatically. "However, I do think I could live on Aunt Chloe's rolls."

Although it seemed no time at all to Clara since they had come as little children to live at The Burn, Daisy was twenty-four now and Annie twenty-three. The right young man did not seem to have appeared for either of them. Daisy had become a pretty girl, quietly charming and demure with an intensity of spirit, which burned within her and illuminated her. She had beaux and suitors enough, but Annie was a belle, and the parlor at The Burn had seen more than one desperate swain seeking Douglas' permission to marry his daughter.

"Annie, you must be leading these young men on," said Douglas sternly after one of them had left.

"Why, Father, I'm just polite to them." Annie's round blue eyes were all innocence.

"They are both beautiful girls," said Clara to herself as she waved goodbye to Daisy and Annie one summer evening in 1882 on their way to a dance. John was driving them and she cautioned him to drive carefully.

"Aunt Clara, even if I wanted to, I couldn't make these old fellows go at more than a slow trot," John called over his shoulder.

Ernestine stood beside her on the gallery. At seventeen she was an awkward, gangling girl who read a lot and kept her own counsel. She and Clara had a special rapport, and she followed her aunt about the house like a little shadow.

That shade of apricot became Daisy so well, thought Clara, and Annie looked adorable in her new gown, even though it hadn't come from Paris. Myra McGowan, who was Annie's "bête noire," always wore gowns from Paris.

Clara had heard the girls talking as they dressed for the party. "You know, Daisy, sometimes I wish Father were a scalawag like Mr. McGowan. Then you and I could wear Paris dresses."

Daisy laughed, "Yes, and then everybody would hate us the way they do poor Myra."

"But she does look so elegant. I still think it's mighty inconvenient to have a conscience."

"And, of course," Daisy admitted, "Father does carry his pretty far, resigning from the paper just because his publisher didn't like what he wrote."

As she watched them drive away, Clara thought of Douglas. He was moping in his room, which he had done ever since his dramatic gesture of resigning from his post as editor of the *Natchez Courier.* Although she would have to agree with Daisy that Douglas' exacting conscience had not helped the family fortunes, she was, in fact, rather proud of his uncompromising stand against the publishers of the *Courier.*

Ever since the War, Douglas, and others like him, had been politically emasculated. The Republican party, based on a coalition of negroes and carpet-baggers, had held undisputed control of the state until the Democratic party's return to power in 1875. But that Democratic victory was achieved by fraud, intimidation, and every kind of unsavory means, repugnant to men like Douglas. Unfortunately it seemed that these same tactics were their only hope of staying in power. Reconstruction, with its wild swings between tyranny and anarchy, had bred a system of politics within the state which was crudely pragmatic. White fear of a return to negro and carpet-bag rule kept some of the worst white men in office, men who cynically exploited this fear.

Douglas, finding the situation hopelessly frustrating, tried to avoid local politics by concentrating on the international scene, and he wrote long articles on the Franco-Prussian War. But the time inevitably came when local issues could not be avoided; when, in his position as editor of the *Natchez Courier,* it became his duty to take a public stand in an election where all choices seemed equally odious to him. After days of soul searching, he arrived at a resolution of his problem which failed to satisfy his publisher.

Clara was not too surprised when Douglas told her what the publisher had said. "He claimed I 'damned the Democratic candidate with faint praise' and 'gave aid and comfort to the enemy'!"

"And what did you say?" she asked him.

"I just said that I had told the truth as I saw it, and that I could never do otherwise."

"And then you resigned?"

"Why, yes, I did. How did you know that?"

Clara laughed, "Somehow I knew."

But it was no laughing matter, and, in the days that followed, she saw him growing increasingly depressed and bitter in the idleness and boredom that engulfed him. Was he doomed to fail at everything, she wondered, he to whom so much had been given, for whom so much had been hoped, of whom so much had been expected? He who had been prepared so painstakingly for success was totally unprepared for the failures that besieged him. His confidence had always been a fragile thing. Now defeat and discouragement were destroying it. As usual, he refused to discuss his personal problems, and Clara felt powerless to help him.

The party was at D'Evereux. It was their cousin Ellie Martin's birthday and Mrs. St. John Eliot, their mutual great aunt, was honoring her favorite niece with a dance.

As they rode out toward D'Evereux, Annie commented to Daisy, "Aunt Anna has never had any dances for us on our birthdays, or for Margaret Martin either. She just thinks Ellie hung the moon."

"Well, you know, Ellie has been awfully sweet to Aunt Anna."

"Well, I wish I'd been nicer to her myself. Since Aunt Anna and Uncle Eliot didn't ever have any children, she'll probably leave all her things to Ellie, too."

Daisy chuckled, "Well, maybe it isn't too late. Try being especially nice to her tonight."

"Yes," said John. "Maybe she'll leave you a spoon."

"Well, she ought to. After all, I'm named for her."

"Oh, but you know she doesn't like your being called Annie. She says she really doesn't consider that you are named for her."

When John turned the carriage into the driveway to D'Evereux he said, "Do you remember when we stayed here for a month after the Yankees took Elmo away from us?"

"All I can remember is us leaving from here to go to Alabama," said Daisy. "I don't remember much about it, just you and Lucy singing 'O Susannah!' and then us all riding and riding in that carriage."

"Elmo looked exactly like D'Evereux, didn't it?" asked Annie.

"It was identical to D'Evereux. Mama loved Aunt Anna's house so much that she built ours just like it. You know I think to this day when Father sees D'Evereux something inside him hurts. Well, here we are."

John jumped to the ground in a quick agile movement and handed the reins to a courtly negro man who said, "Fine, thank you, Mr. John, how are you?" in answer to his, "Good evening, Prentice, how are you?" Then he held out his hand to Daisy, who stepped lightly from the carriage. They both stood waiting for Annie, who was having difficulty with her skirt, which was drawn tightly across the front, but was quite full in back and had a train. The blue satin was caught up on each side with bunches of pink rosebuds. When Annie had landed safely, John offered an arm to each of his sisters, and they went up the wide steps of the gallery together.

Shafts of light from the long windows lay across the gallery floor, and the wrought-iron balcony above the doorway cast a lacy shadow. Music and laughter poured from the open windows, and excitement mounted within the girls as they made their entrance.

Their hostess, Mrs. St. John Eliot, stood in the doorway greeting her guests. The austere and regal lady had been a widow for many years now.

John kissed her lightly on the cheek. "Everything looks and sounds like much fun, Aunt Anna."

"That's because I invited no one but young people."

"Aunt Anna, you look so beautiful! I love your dress!" said Annie in her most ingratiating way, darting her eyes wickedly toward Daisy, who added, "Oh, I do, too."

"Thank you, young ladies. Do go and get some punch to cool you off. The dancing has just begun."

D'Evereux was exquisite in every detail, from the beautifully carved woodwork and ceilings, from which crystal prismed chandeliers hung like huge diamond pendants, to the tasteful furnishings. Anna Conner Eliot had found the stylish Victorian furniture of the period too heavy, preferring instead the grace of old-fashioned Chippendale, Adam, and Duncan Phyfe. As a result, her home had a classic and timeless elegance.

The twelve-acre estate, complete with lake and swans, had been the scene of many a brilliant ball. One of these had been in honor of the great statesman, Henry Clay. Douglas had described this gala affair to his children and told them of his meeting with Mr. Clay. "I never met a man who was so easy to talk to. The agility and breadth of his mind were phenomenal. He seemed to understand what you were going to say before you finished saying it."

Daisy and Annie began to chat with some friends. In a few moments their group was joined by Myra McGowan, stylishly clad in a close-fitting black-and-white-striped taffeta, undoubtedly of Paris origin.

"Oh, Annie, you look lovely! What a sweet dress!" Myra's eyes swept swiftly over Annie, who was her most serious competitor.

"Thank you, Myra, you look nice, too." Annie was boiling inside. When Myra had left them, she muttered murderously to Daisy, "She looks like a zebra."

"Well, Annie, you know it's hard to tell whether Myra is really mean or just tactless."

"It's not hard for me to tell!"

In the next moment Annie was led away to the dance

floor. Daisy stood with the group of girls who were left, all entertaining the same frightening thought that perhaps they would not be chosen to dance. Daisy, glancing toward the waltzing couples, noticed that most of her beaux were already dancing. It was with great relief that she saw a fat figure with a toothy smile approaching her. "Milton, how nice to see you," she cried, so much more cordially than usual that Milton was quite overcome. He decided that he would ask Miss Daisy again to marry him. It looked to him as though she might have changed her mind. And she wasn't getting any younger. She was well over twenty.

John had immediately sought out Sally Duncan. She was a vivid brunet, good company, and an excellent dancer. They spun about the floor, making a strikingly handsome couple. John enjoyed Sally more than any girl he knew, except for the times when he was in love, as he frequently was. Right now his heart and his imagination were free, and it was good to be with Sally again. As they danced he said so, and she casually returned his compliment. "It's good to see you, too, John."

They collided suddenly with another couple and John found himself looking into Leila Gordon's serene dark eyes. "Well, hello!" said John. "Please forgive this unwarranted intrusion. I'm afraid my feet move faster than my brain!"

They whirled away and John smiled at Sally, "It's hard to believe that was my little cousin, Leila. She keeps growing up on me! I can't seem to think of her as such a young lady."

CHAPTER THREE

THE year 1884 brought two important letters, a visitor and an engagement. One letter came from Lucy in May of that year bearing the happy tidings that she and Edgar were anticipating the birth of a child in November. She was, she knew they would be glad to hear, resigning from her teaching immediately.

Another letter came in June addressed to Douglas from a Mr. Sidney Deeson of Deeson, Mississippi. Mr. Deeson owned a plantation in the rich floodlands of the northern part of the state, the area known as the Delta. The letter informed Douglas that an overseer, a former employee of them both, had been found by the police. The man had forged checks on their accounts and Mr. Deeson was sending his step-son, Wallace Wilbourn, to discuss the matter of prosecution.

Young Wallace stayed overnight at The Burn and had dinner with the family.

"He's a very nice young man," thought Clara, "but underneath those polished and courtly manners, I believe he's extremely shy." His sensitive, sharp-featured face should have been dominated by a pair of unusually beautiful and appealing, though melancholy, brown eyes. But to Clara's great amusement they were completely overwhelmed by a waxed handlebar mustache. It was the very latest style, but she noticed that he was quite self-conscious about it. "At least I guess that's it. I know if I were wearing one of those things, I'd be self-conscious."

He arrived an hour or so before supper with a huge basket of fresh vegetables. To Maybelle's delight the butterbeans were already shelled. She had taken over the cooking with Aunt Chloe as advisor and helper when there was a party, or a Christmas dinner, or the like. The old woman could hardly use her hands at all now. "It's the rheumatiz what's got me, and sometimes I think I'd prefer the devil," she told them.

When they were seated at dinner, Douglas said to his guest, "I certainly envy you your Delta land. They tell me that cotton grows there like a weed!"

Young Wallace smiled. "Yes, sir, and the weeds grow well, too."

"Well, the vegetables most certainly do,"' said Clara. "These are very superior butterbeans.

"Oh no, Miss Clara," returned the young knight from the Delta. "It's not the vegetables. It's the Natchez kitchens that are superior."

After dinner Douglas and Wallace retired to the back gallery to talk about their problems. Douglas poured them each a glass of brandy and asked, "What are we going to do with this bad-check artist, Mr. Wilbourn?"

"I don't know. I really hate to prosecute him and after all it won't bring us back our money," said Wallace, trying in vain to keep his fingers off of his mustache.

"No, punishing the poor devil certainly isn't going to help us any. It's too late for that. But it seems to me we have some obligation to society to see that he doesn't cheat anybody else."

"That's true. That's very true. But I doubt if a year or two in jail will accomplish that. Then, of course, when he gets out, he won't be able to get a decent job. He has a nice wife and four little children. Drinking is his worst crime. If he could stay sober, perhaps he wouldn't be tempted to cash bad checks."

Douglas stirred uncomfortably in his chair. "Drinking never made a man dishonest."

"No, sir, but it might help."

"Well, you're certainly right that a jail sentence would aggravate the problem for his family, who are, after all, innocent. Actually, if he could get a job he might be able to pay us back at least a part of the money. I wonder if there's some kind of work we could let him do, but keep an eye on him."

"Mr. Walworth, let me talk to my step-father again. I believe I have an idea about how we could employ him."

As the girls made ready for bed that night, Daisy said, "Annie, do you know what?"

"No, what, Daisy?"

"I have a funny feeling that I've met the man I'm going to marry."

Annie's mouth dropped open in amazement. She blinked her eyes and gave her head a little shake as though to clear her thoughts. Finally she spoke firmly. "Daisy, you're out of your mind. You just met him. You said, 'How do you do,' and he said, 'How do you do,' and that's all you even said to each other."

"I know." Daisy smiled in a maddening way. "But we like each other."

"Well, I'm glad you didn't say, 'We're in love.' I think being in love is awfully silly."

"Well, it isn't."

"Daisy, what you need is a good night's sleep. In the morning you'll laugh at this nonsense."

In the morning Daisy and Wallace found an opportunity for a chat after breakfast. They strolled about the yard and sat in the garden on the bench that circled the Tree of Benediction, and he said that he would come again soon.

Several days later John requested the use of the family carriage to drive Leila Gordon home. As the Gordons lived in the country, it was Leila's custom to spend the night in town with a friend when she went to a party. "I saw Leila at the supper at Stanton Hall last night and I told her I'd be happy to drive her home. We don't see enough of that branch of the family, and I intend to make an effort to see more of them," he explained to Douglas and Clara.

John began journeying back and forth frequently to call on the Gordons. One day when Douglas had their horse at Fawnwood and the ladies needed the carriage, John decided to ride the mule.

"That's not a very dashing way to call on a fair lady," observed Annie.

"That would never stop Don Quixote. I'll just tell the Gordons that he's come to call. I think it's actually a much more interesting way to arrive than by some more conventional means!" And off he blithely rode with a broad grin on his face, brandishing a small switch like a sword.

Both families watched and waited. The Burn household wondered. Was it really serious this time? John whistled about the house and went his usual merry way.

"I think everyone in town will know about it before we do," said Annie in exasperation.

Clara and Douglas discussed the possibility of John's marriage to Leila with mixed emotions. They loved Leila and her family, and the fact that she was a cousin did not trouble them at all, but, horror of horrors, she was a Roman Catholic. The rivalry and misunderstanding between Catholics and Protestants was intense in Natchez. The members of these Christian bodies would sooner have accepted the Jewish faith than each other's.

"I do wish Leila weren't a Catholic," sighed Clara. "It's too bad for a couple to be separated in their churches, and, of course, John could never become a Catholic."

"Perhaps she might give up her church."

"Now Douglas, you know better than that!"

"You know I know better than that!"

"Well, I'm going now to call on Dr. and Mrs. Shields. I've been wanting to read them Lucy's last letter. They seem to take such a genuine interest in hearing about her. I may discuss this problem with them. They are both so wise and sensible."

"That's a good idea. Dr. Shields might even talk to John about it."

The Shields welcomed Clara with their usual enthusiasm. "What warm people they are," thought Clara; and then as she looked around their little parlor, "How charming and cheerful this room always looks. It has a personality like theirs."

"I brought a letter from Lucy, which I thought you might enjoy hearing. She says in it how much she misses her teaching, what it has meant to her and how grateful she is to you two for putting her on to it."

"How is she? Is everything going well so far?" Mrs. Shields inquired anxiously.

"Oh, yes, she says that she is feeling fine and having no problems."

"Oh, how glad I am to hear that! I've been so concerned that Lucy and Edgar might be denied the pleasures of a family as the doctor and I have been. Of course, we've had so many other blessings that I certainly shouldn't complain."

"Well, now that we know what it says," Dr. Shields smiled, "do read the letter to us!"

Clara laughed, "I guess I have told you most all of it."

After she had read the letter and discussed it in detail with the old couple, Clara brought up the subject of John's latest romance.

"There's something else brewing in our family," she began.

Mrs. Shields, who always seemed to know everything that went on, interrupted eagerly, "You mean John and little Leila Gordon?"

"Yes. It appears to be fairly serious, although you never can tell with John. He's had other romances, and nothing ever came of them. Still I have a feeling that this time it's different. Although we couldn't possibly love her more, Douglas and I are somewhat concerned about the idea of a marriage between John and Leila."

"The consanguinity troubles you?" asked Dr. Shields.

"No, no, it's not that. Leila and John are only second cousins once removed. It's not that. Leila is a Roman Catholic."

"That doesn't seem like such a terrible thing to me."

"Well, of course, it isn't and I'm sure her religion gives her great comfort, but that's just the problem. She would certainly not be willing to give it up, and, of course, John could never become a Catholic. I've always felt that it is very unfortunate for a married couple to attend different churches. But the worst part is that, as you know, John would be required to agree that their children would be brought up as Catholics. He would have to sign a paper to that effect."

"How do you know that John wouldn't want to become a Catholic or have his children be Catholic?"

"Because he's been brought up as a Protestant. There are so many differences in doctrine and in practice that would be alien to him. And surely, Dr. Shields, you don't believe that any man should give up the right to teach his children what he believes."

Dr. Shields sighed, "'Alien' is a rather strong word to describe the differences between two sorts of Christians. Leila's background is so similar to John's that I don't see how anything she believes could be that foreign to him. I do, however, find the idea of signing papers regarding the spiritual instruction of one's children objectionable personally. It's a great pity, isn't it, that all organized religion tends to become so dogmatic and rigid? Of course, we always seem to notice it more in the other fellow's religion. I do sympathize with your concern for John's happiness, and I know that that is your main concern. Still, it seems to me that it is really his decision. Only John himself knows how much these things will matter to him. I wouldn't worry too much about it. He and Leila are both sensible young people. If they love each other enough, they can probably work out their differences satisfactorily."

That evening after supper when Douglas and Clara were alone for a moment on the back gallery, he asked her, "Did you talk to Dr. Shields about John and Leila?"

"Yes, Douglas, I did, and he didn't seem to think the religious differences would matter so much. In fact, he made me feel ashamed that it mattered so much to me."

"Perhaps he should speak to the pope or the priests. They evidently think it matters very much."

"Well, Douglas, regardless of how we feel, the fact of the matter is that the decision is really John's. We're going to have to accept whatever he decides as graciously as we can."

Douglas frowned thoughtfully. "Well, Leila is a precious child. There's no denying that."

About a week later the family sat at breakfast on the back gallery of The Burn. John was late as he usually was. They had finished their blackberries and cream. Maybelle was removing the bowls and bringing plates for the scrambled eggs and sausage which Uncle Perry had brought on a big silver platter. Suddenly sounds reached them from within the house. "What in the world?" said Douglas. "Who's that playing the piano at this hour?" Then as they recognized the tune, they all fell into helpless laughter. It was Lohengrin's wedding march, played very badly by John.

"What a relief!" cried Annie, dropping her biscuit and her butter knife with a little clatter. "I couldn't have stood the suspense a minute longer!"

Aunt Chloe came running out of the kitchen, her hair as white as the kerchief tied around it. Her mottled brown skin was pulled tightly over her bones now, and her once full lips were compressed into a narrow line by a lifetime of disciplined expressions and, in recent years, a good deal of pain stoically endured.

"Praise the Lord! Is that the wedding march I hear? Oh, the good Lord is going to let me see my boy married!" And then, of course, she began to cry. It was the delightful inconsistency of her nature that no amount of physical suffering could bring tears to her eyes, but the least stirring of her emotions always brought them in a great flood.

After breakfast Clara walked down to the garden. Douglas followed her.

"John seems very happy," he said.

"Yes, and he doesn't seem to mind being married by the priest or signing the papers about the children."

"Of course, he may mind it more later, but it would be hard to convince him of that now."

"I think they're going to be very happy, Douglas. At any rate, I hope and pray so."

"Well, I hope and pray so, too. Sister, if it's agreeable with you, I'd like to give them a piece of The Burn grounds to build on."

"I'd like nothing better, if that's what they want to do."

John and Leila were delighted with the offer and began making plans to build a cottage on the south side of The Burn.

CHAPTER FOUR

YOUNG Edgar Poague was born at The Burn in November of 1884. He arrived two weeks before he was expected and his father was still in Louisiana. However, as Clara told Aunt Chloe, Douglas had done quite enough pacing the floor for both him and Edgar. "Of course, I know he kept thinking of Miss Rebecca when Ernestine was born," she had added. Actually Clara had been extremely concerned herself about both Lucy and the baby. She was vastly relieved that it was all over at last with little Edgar safely into the world and Lucy recovering satisfactorily from the delivery. They hadn't told her yet that there must not be any more children, and Clara dreaded doing it. However, she knew that Lucy would accept this bitter disappointment philosophically and make the best of it. She responded to the experiences of life in such a positive way. Lucy had always had great intelligence and strength. But the joys of love and fulfillment had made her a warmer and gentler person. And the pain of her sorrow and disappointment had left her a legacy of maturity and serenity. How thrilling it was to watch another person develop and grow in spirit!

Clara cuddled little Edgar in her arms, cherishing the warmth of his tiny body against hers. He was sleeping blissfully through all the racket of the hammering and hollering of the workmen next door. The house would be ready for John and Leila to move into after their marriage next spring. The rooms were small but well proportioned, and there were to be galleries across the front and the back of the house.

The Burn itself was none too quiet these days. They had a house full of people. Edgar had finally arrived to join his wife and baby and Wallace Wilbourn was visiting again. He kept coming back to Natchez on one pretext or another, and Daisy's incandescent quality was more noticeable than ever.

Clara heard Daisy calling to her, and reluctantly she laid the baby down in the little crib by her bed. Although it had held all of Douglas' children, she associated it especially with Ernestine.

She went to the stairway. "Yes, Daisy, what is it?"

"Wallace and I were talking about going for a drive. Do you think it will be all right for us to use the carriage?"

"Why, certainly. Go right ahead. It's a lovely day for a drive. But be sure to take some sort of wrap with you."

Daisy and Wallace drove over in the carriage to the river bluff to watch the sun set. It was a glorious sight. The broad horizon beyond the widely curving river was ablaze with constantly changing color. Even the mud-brown river itself was transformed by it. They sat watching the sky, compelled by its transience.

"You know," said Daisy, "you keep thinking it will never be just this way again, and you wish you could stop time for a moment to get a good look. It goes so fast you can't remember it. Sometimes I think life is that way. It's so beautiful, and we go rushing through it without appreciating it. We're so preoccupied the most precious moments go unnoticed. Some people don't even realize they're happy until it's too late."

"Are you happy?"

"Oh, yes!" Some of the sunset glow was in her eyes. Wallace thought what a special sort of beauty she had, fragile and yet strong, hauntingly tender and heartbreakingly vulnerable. He felt suddenly afraid for her and fiercely protective toward her.

The sky was quieting now, its tumult over. Pale streaks of color, subtly blending together, were all that remained of the magnificent event, but this was, perhaps, even more beautiful. It provided a restful contrast, a new mood.

Daisy felt completely at peace. Being near Wallace made her feel happy and whole. He had not actually asked her to marry him yet, but she knew that he would.

John and Leila married on Valentine's Day and moved immediately into their new house. Leila and Clara spent hours planning and supervising the planting around it. "We won't even be able to see the house by the time they get through!" John protested.

Wallace Wilbourn came to visit again in March and this time he brought a small package with him. After supper, in the moonlight under the Tree of Benediction, he took Daisy's slim little hand in his and slipped a small horseshoe shaped ring set with diamonds on her finger. "It's my lucky piece," he told her.

"And mine," she said.

Plans began to be made for a September wedding. The ceremony was to be at The Burn in the garden. Lucy's wedding dress trimmed with the lace from their mother's wedding gown was brought down from the garret and fitted to Daisy, who was not as tall as Lucy.

Annie was to be maid of honor and her dress was being made of white organdy embroidered with forget-me-nots.

The arrangements for the wedding were well under way when a dreadful thing happened in Natchez. The Yellow Fever struck again. The citizens of the town, lulled by some years' respite from the fearful monster, could not, at first, believe what was happening. The death of its first victim chilled the hearts of all. Buried memories of former epidemics rose from their graves to haunt those who had survived. The paralyzing force of fear brought all normal living to a standstill. Natchez was sealed off from the rest of the world.

Daisy's wedding plans were cancelled. Wallace couldn't get in and she couldn't get out. Her disappointment was added to the general depression. Douglas drank heavily and lectured everyone incessantly. Clara strove to maintain sanity and some degree of cheer.

Keeping busy and being out of doors were two things that seemed to help. As usual, she spent as much time as possible in the garden. One morning found her weeding the flower beds. She gave her whole attention to the job, not thinking, just doing, and it brought her a wonderful sense of well being. She was taken completely by surprise when a breathless voice cried, "Miss Clara!"

"Wallace, how in the world did you get here?"

He took several deep gulps of air before replying. He had obviously run to the point of exhaustion. "The ship," he pointed toward the river. "I came on a ship and rowed off her to shore. I've come to get Daisy and we have to hurry. We'll need your carriage to make it. Where is she?"

Without further questioning Clara motioned him to sit on the bench beneath the Tree of Benediction. "Sit there and catch your breath. I'll get her right away."

She ran up to the house and finding Ernestine on the back gallery sent her to get Daisy. "Find Daisy, Ernestine. Tell her to go immediately to the garden. Wallace is there and wants to talk to her."

Ernestine's eyes followed her aunt in amazement as Clara kept right on going toward the kitchen. Then, realizing there must be a need for great haste, she fairly flew upstairs to Daisy's room.

Clara pushed open the kitchen door. "Oh, Little Doug, I'm so glad you're here!" Little Doug, Aunt Chloe's grandson, was a strapping six foot three. He worked for them now that Uncle Perry was too feeble to do much. Aunt Chloe's other grandson, Periander, was working in New Orleans. "Will you hitch up the carriage right away? Maybelle, please, come with me to Miss Daisy's room. I need your help to get a few things together for her. And, please, don't anybody mention anything about this to Mr. Douglas."

Ernestine burst into the room which Daisy and Annie shared. "Wallace is here, Daisy! He's waiting for you in the garden!"

"Here!" squealed Daisy. She glanced into the mirror, nervously patting her already smooth brown hair. "Do I look all right, Annie?"

"You look beautiful and it's a great waste because they say love is blind anyway."

"You'd better go, Daisy. I think he's in a hurry," urged Ernestine.

Daisy stood silent and still for a second. Then she left the room without a word.

"What's it all about, Ernestine?" demanded Annie.

"I don't know," replied Ernestine. "Aunt Clara just told me he was here and to get Daisy. She was very excited and in a big hurry."

At that moment Clara and Maybelle entered the room with a suitcase.

"Help us, girls. We need to pack some things for Daisy if she decides to go with Wallace. He's rowed off a ship to get her. I'm sure he wants to take her away from the Fever. There won't be room to pack anything but a few necessities. Everybody get busy."

Clara pulled open a dresser drawer filled with monogrammed linens and tucked and lacy clothing, fragrant with the scent of lavender and lemon verbena, and began to sort things out.

Maybelle gestured toward the ivory satin wedding gown on a dressmaker's dummy in a corner of the room. "Ain't it a pity she can't wear it? She looked so beautiful in it. Just like a queen."

"Maybe she'll decide not to go," said Annie.

"Well," declared Clara, "it's up to her. If she wants to go with Wallace now, I want her to. She'll be much safer out of Natchez with the Fever raging the way it is."

"I think it's so romantic, Daisy being rescued just like a Walter Scott heroine," Ernestine sighed.

"Oh, Ernestine, you think everything is romantic," snapped Annie.

"Sister, is that you?" Douglas suddenly opened his door and called across the hall.

They all looked from one to another in alarm. In his present condition there was no telling what attitude Douglas might take toward Daisy's departure.

"What shall we do, Aunt Clara?" Ernestine whispered anxiously.

Clara's decision was swift. "I'll go and talk to him. Annie, you and Maybelle take the suitcase down the stairs. Act natural about it and he probably won't even notice. If he does, I'll just have to tell him." Then she started across the hall. "Yes, Douglas, what is it? Would you like something to eat?"

"No, I certainly do not want anything to eat," he replied irritably. "How many times do I have to tell you I'm not hungry! All I want is a cup of hot tea, and, please, tell Maybelle I didn't say lukewarm. She evidently thinks that's the way I like it as she always brings it that way. There she is now. I'll tell her myself"

"Now, Douglas, wait a minute. If your tea must be such a special temperature, I'll make it myself. I'm going to bring it boiling, too, so be careful or you may scald your tongue," she retorted with an unusual amount of sharpness.

"You'd like that, wouldn't you?" he muttered, slamming the door.

"How lucky!" she murmured to Ernestine as she joined her in the hall. "Now he's going to sulk a while, and we'll have time to get Daisy off."

Daisy ran into Wallace's arms. They held each other close, overcome with the happiness of being together again. But Wallace's mission was urgent, and there was no time to waste on sentiment. "Daisy, you've got to come with me. I've rowed off the ship to get you. There's not time to pack or anything. Just come. The captain will marry us. Come with me, darling."

Daisy felt a sudden panic at the thought of such an abrupt departure from her home, her family, her friends, and her maidenhood. If only she had a little time to think. Of course it was what she had been longing for, but this way she felt so unprepared.

She nearly said, I can't go, but a picture of the look on Wallace's face if she said that flashed through her mind and stopped her. Then she knew without any question what she must do now and always.

"Of course I'll go, Wallace. Anywhere you say, but isn't there really any time to pack just a few things and say goodbye?"

"Scarcely any time at all, Daisy."

Annie was coming toward them with a coat and a little valise in her hands, and the look on her face nearly shook Daisy's resolution.

"Annie, you'll come soon to visit us. It isn't as if I were going so very far away. We'll be able to see each other often."

"Why, of course," said Clara, joining them. That had been an anxious moment upstairs and she was still so nervous that she had to hold her hands together tightly to keep them from shaking.

"Daisy, we really must go." Wallace took the suitcase from Annie with one hand and Daisy's arm with the other.

"Little Doug is ready to drive you. Goodbye, darling." Clara put her hands on Daisy's shoulders. "Take care of yourself. Get in touch with Lucy and tell her we're all right. Just as soon as you can, get some word to us."

"Aunt Clara, what about Father? Shall I leave without saying goodbye to him? I can hardly bear to do that."

"I think it's best, Daisy. He's not himself. I'll explain."

"Daisy, we've got to go right now. The boat won't wait."

"Oh, Aunt Clara, goodbye, and thank you for everything. Goodbye, Annie, remember you're coming soon. Goodbye, Ernestine, keep Annie company for me. I love you all." Daisy kissed each one and climbed into the carriage, blinded by her tears and choking back the sob that would keep rising in her throat. As rich and fulfilling as her new life might be, she knew she was leaving a part of herself behind.

As they rounded the bend in the road and The Burn could no longer be seen, a white beacon on its hill, she whispered to herself, goodbye, little Daisy. I'll miss you, too.

CHAPTER FIVE

CLARA lost count of the funerals she attended. There were sometimes three or four in one day. Eliot Watson was thin and haggard and on duty twenty-four hours a day. When he wasn't holding services for the dead, he was praying over the dying and comforting the living. Fires burned in the streets at night and road blocks were everywhere, enforcing the quarantine. The Fever thrived in the hot and humid weather that continued without a let up. About all one could do was pray for the first frost that would put an end to it.

Dr. and Mrs. Shields fell ill at the same time. When she heard the news, Clara took Chloe and went to the little cottage, where they found the old couple, in their raging fever and delirium, trying to help each other.

"It's a pitiful sight, Miss Clara. I'm sure glad we come. I can look after them. I'm a good nurse even with my rheumatiz."

Clara answered a knock at the door and Eliot Watson stared at her in disbelief. "What in the world are you doing here? You must go home. You'll take the fever."

Clara stood back to allow him to enter. "That isn't the way you get it. If it were, you'd have died of it long ago."

"That may be, but I don't think it's wise for you to take the chance."

"They're here alone and both desperately sick," said Clara. "I've brought Aunt Chloe. She's an excellent and experienced nurse. She's with them now."

"I want to see them. Will they know me?"

"They didn't know me," replied Clara. "They are both quite delirious."

Eliot gave Clara his hat and, Bible in hand, headed for the sickroom. He nodded to Chloe, who stood back respectfully as he walked first to the doctor's bedside. The emaciated form on the bed was an appalling sight, and the deep-set eyes burned with an eerie light in a yellow face that was already skeletal.

At the sight of Eliot, Dr. Shields struggled to rise, crying out shrilly, "Oh, thank goodness you've come! There's so much work to do! There are all these bodies to be buried, and then we have to burn the houses! We must destroy their homes to save the people! It's got to be done! Help me! Help me to save them! Help me to explain what has to be done!" He spoke with a desperate urgency and Eliot assured him that he would help him. Dr. Shields grasped his hand with surprising strength and clung to it. "This is God's will, you know, for us to be working together to save the people instead of against each other. We must never forget this lesson! I want you to know that I have the greatest respect for you, Soong Jen. You are my friend—my brother—not one truth, many—many—" At this point the doctor became incoherent, and in a moment he had lapsed into unconsciousness. Eliot murmured a prayer. When he turned to Mrs. Shields, he found that her soul might now be floating over her beloved Blue Ridge Mountains.

He left her to Aunt Chloe's ministrations and joined Clara in the parlor. He walked to the window and stood looking out at the big oak tree in silence for several minutes. Finally, he turned to face Clara. "She's gone," he told her, "and he doesn't know me. He thinks I'm someone named Soong Jen, some sort of Chinese priest, Buddhist, I guess. He wants me to help him stamp out the plague."

"His heart never left China any more than hers ever left Virginia," said Clara.

"That's true," agreed Eliot, and she noticed that his voice was dry and cracking with fatigue, as well as grief.

"Let me fix you some tea," she urged him, yearning to comfort him.

"No, thank you. I must go," he said, and then he slumped into Dr. Shields' armchair. "In a moment," he added with a sigh.

Clara seated herself on the love seat. The ticking of the clock was like music in the silence that united them. Finally Clara spoke. "I hope that Mrs. Shields' soul is floating over those mountains of hers right now. She was a wonderful person. To think of her going as a bride, just a child really, to a country as strange and backward as China. I don't see how she did it. I don't think I could have."

"You could, and you would have done just as she did."

I might have, Clara thought, if you had asked me to marry you and go to the ends of the earth. If that had been possible, I would have.

To Eliot she said, "Perhaps, I might have gone, but I could never have adapted to it as well as she did."

"They were a most unusual couple." Eliot spoke without realizing that he was putting Dr. Shields into the past tense along with his wife. "I've always been so fond of both of them. I don't suppose they have any family left, do they? What should be done about services for her? Will you handle the arrangements?"

Clara looked thoughtful and replied slowly, "No, I don't think there is any family left. There was a nephew, but he has been committed to a mental institution. The other Shields family here are distant cousins, but I don't think there are any close relatives. I suppose I'm as close to them as anyone. I'll be glad to make the arrangements. The services should be held at the graveside, I guess."

"Yes, I have several scheduled in the morning. Of course, we don't know the outcome of the doctor's illness yet, but from what I saw in there it is most unlikely that he will recover. In fact joint services can probably be held."

"I'll keep you informed about the situation," said Clara.

A silence fell again between them and the clock resumed its ticking.

"Are Mary and the children all right?" Clara asked.

"Yes, thank you, they're fine. I sent them to North Carolina to stay with Mary's sister as soon as I first got word there was Fever in Natchez. I have to be so involved in it I felt it would be dangerous for them."

"I'm sure that was a wise thing to do. I was delighted when Wallace took Daisy away, and I'm grateful that Lucy and the baby hadn't come. She was planning to come for the wedding, you know. The only problem is not being able to hear anything from them. I do hope the Fever isn't breaking out up there. Of course, Lucy hasn't even fully recovered her strength yet. I'm awfully glad that Edgar is a doctor."

Clara glanced toward the hall that led to the Shields' bedroom. "Perhaps I ought to see if Aunt Chloe needs some help." She rose reluctantly. She could have sat there forever. She would have asked for nothing more in life than just to sit there in that little room and talk to Eliot Watson. She felt sure that no physical consummation of their love for one another could have brought them any closer than they had been in those few moments together.

Eliot pulled himself up out of the armchair, and she picked up his hat and handed it to him, observing his drawn face and the dark circles under his eyes. "There's nothing more you can do here. Aunt Chloe and I will take care of everything. I'm sure you're needed in many other places, but I do hope you can get some rest. You look exhausted and I know you are."

He gave her a look that dissolved her heart.

"I'll try to," he promised, and taking his hat, he left the cottage.

As he walked down the steps of the little gallery, he reached up and caught the overhanging branch of Dr. Shields' Tree of Contemplation, holding to it for a moment, as though he needed it to support him. Then he walked resolutely on his way.

CHAPTER SIX

AT last the epidemic waned. The immediate family had been spared, but they were saddened by the deaths of so many friends and relatives.

Jane Conner also died during the epidemic of complications from a broken hip suffered in a fall.

Laura and Will McPheeters were expecting their fifth child, and Douglas muttered, "As soon as we get one new addition safely into the family, we have another one to worry about."

"Well, Douglas, Laura never seems to have any difficulty having her babies," Clara tried to soothe him.

"Yes, but she's older now, and I can't help but worry about her. And the next thing you know, John and Leila will have a piece of news for us!"

"Well, Douglas, I don't want to distress you any more than you already are, but I've been suspecting that. I think they just haven't told us yet."

"Of course you know that if that's indeed the case, no one will be more pleased than I."

"I know, Douglas."

The letters, which began to come now from Daisy, assured them of her happiness and well being.

Annie was desolate without her. They had been so close all their lives and Daisy's marriage had left a void in her life which it seemed impossible to fill. Winter came early, its gray skies and damp coldness sending chilly drafts through the wide hallways of The Burn.

A letter came from Daisy:

Deeson, Mississippi

Annie dearest,

Hallelujah! The Lord be praised! Wallace and I have at last moved into our little house! Of course, Mr. and Mrs. Deeson have been lovely to us, sending breakfast to our room every morning, and doing everything for our comfort and pleasure, but there is nothing a young couple needs so much as a home of their very own. In fact I am just now beginning to feel married.

"Wilbourn Manor" is amazingly well furnished with odds and ends from Mrs. Deeson's house, and we think it is very charming, though unpretentious. Of course, I am only joking about the name. It's not the sort of house to give a name!

Tell Aunt Chloe I have a good soul in my kitchen, but she should have seen us trying to make charlotte russe for our first dinner party! And tell Aunt Clara that I have been busy setting out shrubs and wishing I were she instead of me. I followed her instructions as far as I could understand them, but they are even vaguer than Aunt Chloe's recipes. Will you tell me what does "not too deep" mean? Or worse yet "until the soil feels right"? Well, Mose and I did the best we could. My plants are now in the bosom of the earth and the hands of the Lord.

At this point, Annie shook her head. "Daisy will always put off her responsibilities on the Lord as if He had nothing else to do."

The letter ended by saying:

I do miss you most dreadfully and am perishing for some sisterly chatter. Now that we are settled in our little nest I want to make my happiness complete by having you visit us. Why don't you come now and stay with us for the rest of December? Wallace and I are planning to spend Christmas at The Burn so we could all make the trip back together. Wallace says The River Queen *is due in Natchez and will be leaving headed for Memphis on the twelfth. See if you can get a berth on it. It could make a stop for you at Commerce Landing and Wallace would meet you there.*

A few days later Douglas and Ernestine drove Annie to the boat docks Under-the-Hill and put her on board *The River Queen*. The boat, like all the floating palaces, as they were fondly called, was glamorous and gaudy, bedecked with gingerbread outside. Inside, its white walls had panels of ruby-red damask, and its floors were thickly carpeted with red velvet. White-coated stewards were everywhere. One of these lifted Annie's suitcase from Douglas and led the way down the long cabin. This enormous, central room, which served as both hall and lounge, was known as the saloon. Between the tall, thin Gothic columns that supported the vaulted roof were doors to the individual staterooms. The ceiling held a dazzling succession of huge crystal chandeliers to light the room at night, while stained-glass skylights provided multicolored illumination by day.

Annie, feeling very stylish in her new navy suit and little ermine hat, shivered with the pleasure and excitement which she was trying so hard not to show. She didn't want people to think that she was unaccustomed to travel. After the War none of them had been able to afford steamboat passage, and she had not been on one since she had been old enough to remember it. This trip was an extravagance. She would not have been able to make it, but for Aunt Clara's gift of her savings from the music lessons which she continued to give.

The steward put Annie's bag in the stateroom and departed with profuse thanks when Douglas tipped him generously. One of the most difficult things for Douglas to accept about his poverty was his inability to be as generous and as expansive as he wished to be.

"Now, Annie, let me show you how to lock this door."

"Oh, Father, really! I know how to lock a door."

"But this works a little differently. I want to be sure you know how, and I don't want you to forget to do it. And be sure you find some nice older woman to talk to. I really don't like your traveling alone."

A warning whistle blew, and Douglas and Ernestine

kissed Annie quickly. They hurried through the saloon to the deck where a negro band was playing, and a chorus of deck hands was singing:

"De Coonjine, jine de Coonjine,
De Coonjine, jine de Coonjine,
Roll dat cotton bale down de hill
De Coonjine, jine de Coonjine."

This was part of the colorful embarkation of a steamboat. What had begun with the spontaneous singing of the dock workers and deck hands had become a tradition and was now planned entertainment for the passengers. Douglas threw a handful of coins into the hat of one of the musicians, and he and Ernestine descended the gang plank minutes before it was raised. Annie ran to the side of the upper deck to wave to her father and sister, who stood watching. A bell clanged, two sharp whistles blew, and the ship pulled away, steam belching from its two tall chimneys.

"I hope she'll be all right," Douglas muttered. "I don't approve of a young girl traveling alone."

"Annie likes adventure," said the gawky young girl at his side, her eyes following Annie and the boat longingly.

"That's just what I'm afraid of," Douglas replied.

When the great boat and the little blonde figure were lost from their view, they climbed into the carriage and went home.

In spite of Douglas' fears, Annie's trip up the river proved quite uneventful. She spent the day on deck watching the river traffic—other steamboats, barges, and flatboats loaded with cotton bales and cargo of all kinds, and little fishing boats from which friendly fishermen called and waved to the passengers of *The River Queen*. She never opened the book she had brought to read.

At dinner she was seated between two elderly ladies, one with an imposing diamond brooch, and the other with an equally imposing bosom. Annie thought, Father would be so pleased! But the meal was sumptuous, and the captain himself came over to ask her how she was enjoying the voyage. When Annie climbed into her bunk that night, after carefully locking the door, she looked back with pleasure over a most delightful day.

The boat made a stop especially for Annie at Commerce Landing and she waited on the deck with her luggage ready to disembark. It was with much relief that she saw Wallace standing on the dock waiting for her.

"I can hardly believe I'm here," she told him.

"How was the trip?"

"Just marvelous! Those boats are palaces sure enough, and all the people looked terribly rich and fashionable, and the food was fabulous!"

"I'm afraid I couldn't bring the buggy," Wallace apologized, picking up Annie's suitcase. "It rained hard last night, and the buggy just couldn't make it over these roads so I've brought the wagon. It isn't very fancy, but it's a lot safer."

As they jogged and sloshed through the water-filled ruts, Annie said, "I'm beginning to see what you mean."

"It gets worse," Wallace warned her.

"Absolutely impossible," murmured Annie.

But it did get worse, and at several points Wallace was forced to get out and prize the wagon wheels up out of the sticky soil.

Their progress was agonizingly slow, and it was dark when they arrived at the white frame house set back in a grove of trees. Daisy came running out to greet them, and the sisters fell upon each other, laughing and crying at once.

Annie was exhausted from her long ride through the mud and she had a splitting headache, but she was eager to spend the evening talking to Daisy. She had months of stored-up conversation. So many things had happened which there was no use talking to anybody else about. Then to her utter disgust she was told that she must hurry to dress for dinner. Wallace's best friend, a young doctor who had lived with the Deesons since he was thirteen and been educated by them, was coming to dine with them.

Annie behaved almost rudely during dinner, saying little to anyone and practically nothing to the pleasant young doctor who was trying so hard to make a good impression on the little Natchez beauty. She excused herself after dinner, saying her headache was worse, which it truly was, and she went miserably to bed.

The following morning she apologized to Daisy and Wallace. "I felt so awful, but I acted worse."

"Well, it was thoughtless of us not to realize how tired you'd be," they assured her.

To everyone's surprise, Dr. Brooks arrived after breakfast to take Annie on a horseback tour of the plantation. Although Annie had thought the night before that he was just about the dullest man she had ever met, she began reevaluating him as they rode along together over the endless open fields of the flat delta country. He chatted and joked easily with the negro workers that they passed, speaking their language, using their own expressions, not with condescension, but with an obvious rapport. Annie noticed that they responded enthusiastically to his warmth, grinning and bantering back.

One of the workers, a hulking, jolly black man, had only one eye. "What happened to his eye?" she asked Dr. Brooks.

"His wife stabbed him with an ice pick."

Annie gasped, "Why, how awful! Was she convicted of it?"

"Oh, no. Lily was really sorry after she'd done it, and the consequence of the whole affair is that she's become a much better wife. And the other women were so impressed they steer clear of Jasper now. Actually I think Jasper misses them more than he does that eye."

"Mercy me!" Annie exclaimed.

"Oh, Jasper and Lily's goings on are really nothing. You should hear about some of the others. But they're not so very different from us, you know. They just act the way they feel and don't cover up or pretend the way we do."

"I'm afraid Aunt Chloe would call them 'black trash.'"

"Have you ever seen a cotton gin, Miss Annie? Let's hitch up our horses here and I'll show you how it works. Then I expect we'd better get back to the house. It's getting time for lunch, and besides it's turning colder, and I wouldn't want you to get chilled."

Annie and the doctor cantered back to the house. The horses were eager to get home, and the day was cold enough to make the exercise welcome to their young riders. Annie's curls shook loose from the bright red knit scarf she wore, and her cheeks were rosy from the exertion and the weather. "Goodness," she said as Dr. Brooks helped her to dismount, "I must look a mess!" She tried to tuck a stray curl back into place, smiling mischievously at the smitten young man, whose approving eyes spoke to her like the magic mirror, "You're the fairest one of all."

At lunch Annie reported everything they had seen and done. She raved especially about the gin. "What a marvelous invention it was! I never realized before. I never really saw one work."

"I hate the ugly monster," said Daisy. "I don't like machines of any kind."

"Oh, Daisy, don't be so unprogressive," said Annie. "Machines are a boon to mankind. I can hardly wait to see what they'll come up with next. Of course, the cotton gin has been around for a long time. You'd think there'd be something new in farming machines."

"I don't believe they'll ever be able to replace a good negro," said Dr. Brooks, smiling, and Wallace nodded.

"Nonsense!" Annie responded. "They will, too, one of these days. You wait and see."

As Annie saw more and more of the young doctor, she found she liked him more and more, although he wasn't tall or dashing or handsome. He was of medium height and stockily built with blunt features, but his blue eyes were kind and twinkled often, his laughter was deep and hearty, and he had a force and vibrance of which she was keenly aware.

One evening shortly before she was to leave, they were sitting by the fire in Daisy and Wallace's modest parlor. He began to tell her about himself. His father and five older brothers had been killed in the Civil War, and he and his mother were left propertyless and penniless in the wake of Sherman's sweep to the sea.

"When Mother heard that Sherman had said, 'War is Hell,' she said, 'Yes, and he's the Devil!'

"Well, there we were, Mother, not well, and I, not quite thirteen, without a dime between us. Friends offered to take us in, but there was no employment for me in Huntsville, so I left Mother there with her friends, and made my way over here where the fields weren't stripped barren. I got a job picking cotton on the Deesons' place. Mr. and Mrs. Deeson sort of adopted me. They took me into their home and I worked wherever they needed me so I could send some money to Mother. The Deesons educated me along with their own five children. I've always been interested in medicine. Whenever the doctor came over from Rosedale, I'd help him set bones and bandage wounds. He'd tell me what to do when he wasn't there. I reckon I practiced as much before I got my degree as I have since. Anyway, the Deesons sent me to school at Vanderbilt. I got a part-time job so I could keep on sending Mother a little money. I went from there to Bellevue Hospital in New York for my internship. I already knew that I was no city boy, and I had made up my mind that the Delta was the place I wanted to live. I figured I'd go back, save a little money, and buy some land to farm. Then I'd send for Mother," he paused, "but she—she died before I could send for her. I'm glad I decided to come back here. I feel at home in this country. I like cotton farming. I like working with colored labor. People are always saying how they're shiftless and good for nothing. It's true that if they don't like you, they sure can drag their feet, but they can work hard when they want to. We can learn a lot from them. Why, they can be happier with nothing than white people can with everything their hearts desire! I've wondered a lot about why that is. I believe their secret is that they don't take themselves or life too seriously."

He paused and glanced hesitantly at Annie, whose big blue eyes were fastened intently on him.

"I believe a man can make a fortune in the Delta, Miss Annie, if he doesn't mind being stuck in the mud. There's an awful lot of that, but it grows mighty good crops."

"Have you bought any land?" asked Annie.

"Not yet, but I'm going to. I'm saving every penny I can lay my hands on. I've got a piece of land in mind and I know just how I'm going to work it. I've got a lot of plans."

Some men would have spoken of their dreams. Her father would have. But Dr. Brooks didn't dream. He planned. His enthusiasm was dynamic. He had a zest for life which matched her own, and Annie was much attracted by it. She had an intuition that he was about to propose to her. When instead he changed the subject abruptly, she felt mingled disappointment and relief.

CHAPTER SEVEN

ANNIE returned to The Burn a few days before Christmas with Daisy and Wallace. They made the trip to Natchez on the train. The recently completed railroad ran from Memphis to New Orleans.

Wallace marveled at the accomplishment it represented. "What an undertaking it was to cut through all those virgin forests and lay down rails in these swamps with the river continually changing course! They say that once it inundated four miles of newly laid track! Then another time one of the bridges they'd just finished was completely washed away. Of course there's quicksand everywhere. I don't see how they ever did it, but here we are speeding along. A lot of people think the railroad's going to put the steamboats out of business."

When Wallace went out to the platform for a smoke, Annie, who had noticed that Daisy was very quiet, and that her face wore an anxious expression, asked, "Daisy, what is the matter with you? Does the motion of the train make you sick?" Her eyes widened. "You're not—?"

"No, I feel fine," Daisy blushed. "It's nothing like that. It's just that I'm worried about seeing Father. You know I haven't seen him since I left home to marry Wallace."

"Well, I don't see that you did anything wrong. You already had his permission to marry Wallace, and Aunt Clara knew that you were going."

"Yes, but you know how he is. His pride is so easily hurt, and if he's drinking he could be terribly rude to Wallace, and bless me out, and Wallace might get mad, and it would be an awful mess."

"Now, don't worry about it yet, Daisy. Sufficient unto the day is the you know what."

"Did Father get very upset when he found out I had gone?"

"Well, yes, at first. But he was mostly rather martyrlike about it, sort of, 'Oh well, nobody ever consults me anyway.'"

John met them at the station in the family carriage. Daisy's heart leapt at the sight of the familiar lean figure and the handsome face with its chiseled features, which bore a broad smile of welcome. Her apprehension was gone for the moment in her excitement and in the sudden realization of how much she wanted to see her family. It returned, however, on the ride to The Burn. She asked John anxiously, "How are Father's spirits?"

John's blue eyes danced with mischief, but he thought better of his joke and answered her gently. "They're fine, Daisy, and he's longing to see you."

Daisy's relief was evident. She began to chatter gaily, questioning John about Leila's health and when their baby was expected and about their friends and the latest gossip. She still dreaded the first meeting with her father, but not nearly so much.

When they arrived at The Burn, Uncle Perry and Little Doug met them at the gallery steps to take over the horses. Wallace jumped out of the carriage to shake Little Doug's hand, saying, "Here's a man who knows how to drive horses. If it hadn't been for you we'd never have made that boat!" This pleased Little Doug tremendously. He was good with horses and he knew it. "Thank you, Mr. Wallace," he said, smiling broadly, "I'm mighty glad we made it."

Uncle Perry helped Daisy out of the carriage, shaking with his palsy, but otherwise looking remarkably well and more distinguished than ever. None of the negroes on the plantation at Deeson had anything like his aristocratic style.

"How wonderful to see you, Uncle Perry! You haven't changed a bit, I'm glad to see!"

"You neither, Miss Daisy. Welcome home!" He beamed fondly at her and then turned to assist Annie. "Have a nice trip, Miss Annie?"

"I certainly did. Just wait 'til you hear about my steamboat ride!" Annie cut her eyes at Wallace. "And my wagon ride! They were both very interesting."

"It sure is good to see you, Miss Daisy, ma'am," said Little Doug. "You, too, Miss Annie. Been right lonesome round here."

Douglas and Clara and Ernestine came running into the hall, as John flung open The Burn's front door. Daisy hugged her Father hard and knew from his answering embrace that all was well between them. He stood back and looked at her. "My child, are you as happy as you look?"

"Oh, yes, Father!"

Douglas and Wallace shook hands heartily and the difficult moment was over.

Daisy looked around. "Where's Aunt Chloe?"

"She's in bed today," replied Clara. "These damp days are so bad for her rheumatism and she just couldn't get up. You'll have to go over to her room. She's dying to see you. I always have to read your letters to her at least twice. When you say how happy you are, she just cries and cries."

"I'll go right now," said Daisy, and off she went to the kitchen wing, where she found Maybelle in the kitchen. Giving her a hug she thanked her for her part in the wedding. "How's Aunt Chloe, Maybelle? I hear her rheumatism is worse."

"She ain't too good, Miss Daisy. She has good days and bad days, but mostly bad lately. She's wanting to see you, though."

"Well, I can't wait to see her. It's so wonderful to see everybody. You don't know how I miss you all."

"We misses you, too, Miss Daisy."

When Daisy joined the family in the parlor, after a tearful reunion with Aunt Chloe, Clara was telling Annie, "Gavin Turner has come by almost every day to ask about the news from you. He wants to take you to Susie Koontz's party on Christmas Eve."

Annie made a little face. "I can't stand that Gavin Turner. He's more of a priss than any girl I ever saw!"

"Isn't that Lucy's old beau?" asked Daisy.

"Yes, and she couldn't stand him either. He ought to marry Myra McGowan. They'd be a perfect couple. By the way, how is Myra?"

"Enjoying your absence," murmured Ernestine. "She's had all the beaux to herself."

"Well, let's talk about something pleasant," said Annie. "When do Lucy and Edgar and little Edgar get here?"

"They're not coming until Christmas Eve."

Christmas Day was wonderfully like all Christmas Days. Everything was familiar, from Eliot Watson's Christmas sermon to the waxed fruit decorations at The Burn.

Now that the family was scattering, these traditions assumed a new importance, which the family all felt deep inside.

Aunt Chloe sat in the kitchen in a ladderback chair, a queen on her throne, receiving homage from the other servants and from the family. She shed a few tears and reminisced about Miss Sarah and Mr. John and Christmases past. She told the story about Ernest's toast to her. She recalled the Christmas at Elmo during the War and the one in Evergreen when they had had wild duck and quail and cornbread served with blackberry wine.

She insisted upon holding little Edgar, although Lucy protested, fearing Aunt Chloe's rheumatic arms might not be equal to the task, and she pointed out his resemblance to various Walworths, although it was obvious he was the image of his father. "If the Lord takes me tonight, I'll go a happy woman," she said.

Shortly after Christmas a letter arrived for Annie from Dr. Brooks, telling her of his purchase of a small piece of land with a house on it, and asking her to marry him. Annie read the letter over and over.

The house is small and not in very good repair, but I plan to fix it up gradually. I wish I could offer you a palace, and maybe I can some day. You certainly ought to have one. I don't know how I have the nerve to ask you to share such a modest existence, but I do offer you all the love in a man's heart.

Annie couldn't make up her mind. One moment she thought she wanted to marry the doctor. The next she was positive she didn't want to. She liked him, but was she really in love? What was love anyway? What concerned her most was the life that she would be forced to lead in the Delta. It would be so different from anything she had known before. She would have to leave her family. There would be no congenial friends, though, of course, she would have Daisy. Then, too, she kept remembering how primitive and inconvenient and inaccessible everything was. Her long wagon ride through the mud to get to Daisy's stood out vividly in her mind. The more she thought about it, the less she knew what to do.

One bitter cold morning she opened the door of her room, which was comparatively warm with the fire going, and went into the hall. She shivered as she stepped out into the icy air of the unheated hall, and the memory of Daisy's snug little parlor and of herself sitting by the fire with Dr. Brooks flashed through her mind. She thought, I believe I could be happy with Dr. Brooks even in the Delta, and I know I'd be warmer!

She followed the curving path of the stairway to the downstairs hall and opened the door to the library, where Little Doug was putting another log on the fire. Clara sat with her sewing, and Ernestine, with her copy of Dickens.

"Aunt Clara, I've decided to marry Doctor Brooks."

"Why, Annie, my goodness! You're announcing this earth-shaking piece of information as though you were telling us you'd decided to take a walk."

"Well, I've thought about it a lot, and I've decided that it's what I want to do."

It was almost time for the wedding. The out-of-town guests and those who had driven in early from the country were sitting on the gallery chatting. The Burn shone from its bronze chandeliers to the wide plank floors, and bouquets of flowers were in everything that could hold water. The nervous bridegroom paced the floor of the guest bedroom at John's house. He certainly would be glad when it was all over. Weddings were bad enough for a groom anyway, but when they were in a place where you didn't know anybody and everybody was Cousin Somebody, it was bad indeed. He also had the impression that nobody thought he was good enough for little Annie, especially the dozen or so unsuccessful suitors he kept running into. Then there were the gimlet-eyed ladies who kept asking him about his family. He wished that he had listened more carefully to his mother when she had tried to tell him about those things.

Over in Annie's bedroom a crisis was taking place. Annie had just burst into tears, as she was about to put on her wedding dress. She declared that she didn't want to get married after all. Clara and Daisy, in a state of shock, looked helplessly at one another.

"What shall we do, Daisy?" asked Clara.

"I guess there's nothing to do but call it off. She mustn't marry him if she doesn't want to," said Daisy, attacked by sudden pangs of guilt. Had she, perhaps, influenced her sister unduly in her longing to have Annie near her?

"I'll talk to Douglas about it." Clara crossed the hall to her brother's room and he opened his door immediately at her knock. One look at her face convinced him that something of the most serious nature had happened. "What in the world is the matter, Sister?"

"Oh, Douglas, what shall we do? Annie has begun to cry, and she says she doesn't want to get married."

"Is that all? Sister, you're usually so much more astute

than I, but I believe I understand my Annie better than you do."

He walked swiftly and purposefully to the door of Annie's room. "Annie, it's your father. I want to talk to you."

Daisy opened the door slowly, glancing apprehensively at her father. "Now, young lady," he spoke in his severest voice to Annie, who was wiping her eyes and sniffling from her tears, "dry your eyes and put on that wedding dress! You shall not treat a fine young man that way!"

"Yes, Father," replied Annie meekly.

A few moments later a radiant little bride appeared on her father's arm and walked happily to the side of her husband to be. Later, when Annie said her goodbyes to the family, she put her arms around her father's neck and whispered softly, "Thank you, Father." Douglas hadn't known such a gratifying moment in years. It seemed to ease some of the hurt inside him.

After the wedding guests had gone, Clara suddenly realized how tired she was. She excused herself and went up to bed, leaving Douglas talking to Ernest, who had come down from Memphis for the wedding. Daisy and Wallace and Lucy and Edgar were chatting away with each other and with Ernest's wife, Mary. Ernestine was listening attentively first to one conversation and then the other. John had taken Leila home early, and Laura and Will had had to leave, too. Clara smiled to think how horrified both her mother and Jane Conner would have been to see Laura and Leila attending the wedding in their condition and she knew that some of their guests had probably disapproved. Both Laura and Leila had asked Clara what she thought about their coming, and she had told them, "If you feel like it, I certainly don't see anything wrong with your coming to Annie's wedding, and I know she wants you to be here."

Clara peeped in at little Edgar on the way to her room. There he lay sound asleep beside his parents' bed in the crib that had held Ernestine and the others before her. What a marvel a baby was, a tight little bud of a person, waiting to unfold! She loved him fiercely already without knowing what he would become.

She tiptoed out and went toward her room, passing the room that had been Daisy and Annie's for so many years. The Burn was going to be lonely and sad with both of them gone! But Ernestine would still be there. Douglas and I are lucky to have her, Clara murmured to herself. Although, of course, we must be ready to let her go, too, when that time comes.

CHAPTER EIGHT

IN the years after Annie's wedding, Ernestine was a great comfort to Clara, but Clara was concerned about her future. Ernestine didn't have the physical charm of her older sisters. She was tall and too thin, and, worst of all, her eyes had never been right. They had been weak since her illness as a baby and were badly crossed. Yet with her keen intelligence and subtle wit, her extensive knowledge of history and the classics, and her discriminating taste, she would have graced an eighteenth-century salon. What could the town that Natchez had become hold for this kind of delicate and carefully cultivated plant? Who was left in the new Natchez to appreciate such a rare specimen?

Natchez' decline had been going on since the War. There had been the big jolt of the War itself, and the tremendous adjustment to a new set of circumstances. But the long-term effects on the people and the town were just now becoming fully evident. These had been so gradual that at first you didn't notice them, and by the time you did you had gotten so used to them you scarcely paid any attention to them.

By 1888 Natchez was divided, like Gaul, into three parts. One group was made up of the remnants of the old society, anachronistic ladies and gentlemen who lived like gentle ghosts within their crumbling mansions. In trying to preserve their golden past they had forever lost touch with the vitality which had characterized those days. Then Natchez had been engaged in living; now it spent its time remembering. It offered no opportunity to enterprising young men and they had left it. Naturally there was a large negro population. So many of the big plantations had reverted to swamps, and displaced field workers had poured into Natchez. There was also a type of white person who had multiplied at an alarming rate and who existed in a separate world from that of the old families. These people were, for the most part, employees of a paper mill, which was Natchez' main industry.

The older girls had left just in time, thought Clara, but what could be done about Ernestine? She might go to visit her sisters, but their life in the country was even more isolated than that in Natchez. They hadn't the money for travel. There seemed to be no answer to the problem. Of course, thought Clara, I've lived an old maid's life here and found a large portion of happiness, but I had Douglas' children. Ernestine doesn't have that strong link with life. All she has for company are her father and a maiden aunt and their eccentric friends. There isn't any gay, young group for her to be a part of. There are precious few young men to choose from for a beau much less a husband.

There was really only Bert Dunscomb, the scion of one of Natchez' finest old families. The good blood ran thin in poor Bert's veins, and he was a dreadful bore, but Ernestine endured him patiently, and he took her to parties. One day a young man came to call on Ernestine. He was the son of people Clara knew to be coarse and uneducated, but he appeared to be a gentleman himself, though lacking somewhat in polish and charm.

Maybelle brought them tea and some little sandwiches in the garden, and Clara sat with the young couple making what she was afraid was very stilted conversation. The young man was good looking with a splendid physique, dark curly hair, and lively gray-green eyes, but his personality had an abrasive edge to it. He's acting like the new horse in a pasture, and I guess that's just what he is, she thought. She couldn't help but wonder what such a young man saw in Ernestine. They didn't seem to be the same type at all. Of course it was true that opposites often attracted and balanced each other.

"As I was telling Miss Ernestine about this picnic, the plan is that all the ladies will bring a box lunch. I'm hoping mine will have some fried chicken in it." He winked at Clara, and she winced at the undue familiarity. "And my favorite kind of cake does happen to be chocolate. You know, Miss Ernestine, it wouldn't hurt to pack that little fan of yours there to keep away the flies!"

"Well, I hope the weather will be good for the picnic, and that there won't be many flies. You were too young at the time to be able to remember it, Ernestine, but there was a picnic at Arlington a good many years ago—," Clara paused. She had just caught a glimpse of her brother standing on the back gallery. He had been at Fawnwood for several weeks. He had gone by boat as he did more and more often now. It was a longer, but less strenuous trip that way. One could never tell exactly when he would return. It all depended on which boat he caught, and even then they never operated on any definite schedule.

"Why, there's your Father! He must have just come in."

Her anxious eyes met Ernestine's, as Douglas started down the gallery steps toward them. Her worst fears were realized when he reached them. He had been drinking and was in one of his moods.

"Well," said he, a crooked, mocking smile on his face, "so we are having a tea party."

"Yes, we are. Do come and join us."

Ernestine rose to greet her father, then turned to the young man standing beside her. "Father, this is George Grubbs."

George eyed the older man in a cooly appraising manner, enraging to Douglas. Their mutual dislike was immediate and evident. Douglas' eyes narrowed, his nostrils flared, and his mouth tightened. "Are you by any chance the son of Mabel and Matthew Grubbs?"

"Yes sir, I am."

"Then I will ask you please to leave my house. You have no right to be calling on my daughter."

"Oh, Father!" breathed Ernestine, horrified by this rudeness.

"Douglas," gasped Clara. "Remember this is my house, too."

"Well, then suppose you remember that this is my daughter!" Douglas turned a terrible look upon her. His words and his look left her speechless.

"Never mind," George spit out the words. "I'm going, and I'll never come back." Without a glance at either Clara or Ernestine, he departed.

"I'll see him to the door," said Ernestine with quiet dignity. Risking her father's wrath, she followed the figure of the young man who had come to call on her. Douglas ignored her, concentrating his fury on his sister, who had betrayed her trust in allowing a Grubbs to call on his daughter.

"They are the worst kind of trash and you know it! What could you have been thinking of? They aren't the sort of people I want my daughter to associate with!"

"Oh, Douglas, he only came to call. Ernestine has so few young men to go out with. Surely there couldn't be so much harm in her seeing him."

"Well, you are unbelievably naive, Sister, if you think you can turn young people loose together like that and not run the risk of a serious attachment. Do you want Ernestine to be a part of such a family?"

"I trust Ernestine's judgment."

"What does she know about him? I could tell you some things about Mabel and Matthew Grubbs that would make your hair curl. Why, the servants would be as shocked as I am at your allowing this!"

"Oh, of course, they would. They're worse than you are."

When Douglas had finally gone to bed that night, after haranguing both of them all evening on the evils and dangers of associating with ill-bred people, Clara and Ernestine sat in silence by the fire for some time, too exhausted from their emotional ordeal to go up to bed. At last Clara rose, and went to her niece. She sat on the arm of her chair and leaned her cheek against Ernestine's soft, mousy, brown hair. "I know there's a lot of truth in what your father says. I've always tried to respect his wishes about his children, and I mean to continue to although if it ever comes to a choice between my respect for his authority and your ultimate happiness, I'll have to choose your happiness."

"It doesn't matter, Aunt Clara. George Grubbs doesn't mean a thing to me. I don't find him attractive at all. I guess I'm just as much of a snob as Father! I don't care about going to the party with him. What matters to me is that Father behaved so awfully! Of course he wasn't himself. He would never have done such a thing if he hadn't been drinking."

"That's true. It's only when he's drinking that he lets all that bitterness spill out. He's a lonely and unhappy man. It's a shame he didn't marry again, but he loved your mother so much. She was so perfect for him, he could never see anyone else, although as you know there have been plenty of ladies who have set their caps for him!"

The next day Douglas paid a call upon George Grubbs to apologize for his behavior. George was not at home, but his father was. Mr. Grubbs was as drunk as Douglas had been the day before, and, shouting vile language, he jerked open a drawer, from which he drew a pistol. Brandishing it wildly, he ordered Douglas to leave, which he did, mortified and sickened by the whole affair, but unable to rest until he had made an apology to George. He went home and wrote a note, which George returned unopened. There the matter was formally ended, but Douglas would remember it with shame to the end of his days. Although he felt that he had been right, that Ernestine should never have received such a person, he also felt that once even a Grubbs had become a guest he should have been treated with respect and courtesy.

Ernestine continued to go to parties with Bert Dunscomb, and she and Clara went calling together upon the charming, haunted folk of Natchez society, but she spent most of her hours in the stimulating company of the world's great authors. In spite of Clara's concern, Ernestine didn't seem discontented. Certainly she didn't complain. But beneath the glasslike surface of her disciplined life there were longings and a quiet agony of spirit.

CHAPTER NINE

AFTER the distressing incident with George Grubbs and his father, Douglas embarked on a period of humility and sobriety. If only it would last, thought Clara. But, of course, it wouldn't. After his drinking and his tensions had built up and reached the point of explosion, these peaceful interludes invariably followed. They might last as long as six months, although more often it was from two to four. Well, the thing to do was enjoy it while it lasted, she had remarked to John, and in his optimistic way he had said, "Well, maybe it will last this time."

John and Leila usually came over from their house next door for dinner at least once each week. Little Doug and Maybelle served them now. Aunt Chloe had died in the year following Annie's wedding. That was the same year that John and Leila's daughter Madeleine was born. Uncle Perry had died a year later just a few days after a telegram had come from Dr. Brooks with the message "Young Douglas Brooks presents his compliments. Both he and Annie doing well."

One day when Leila and John were having dinner at The Burn, John mentioned that he had heard in town that morning that old Mr. Smith, the editor of *The Natchez Democrat,* had just died.

"Well, it was time for him to go in more ways than one.

He was too old to be trying to run the paper," said Douglas.

"Why don't you apply for the job, Father?" asked John.

Douglas put down the piece of fried chicken he had just picked up. He stared at his plate, looking thoughtful.

"You're so well qualified for the position, better than anyone else I can think of. You have experience in the field. You did a fine job of editing the *Natchez Courier.* I think you should approach the publisher about it right away."

Douglas looked up, and Clara noticed there was a definite gleam of interest in his eyes. How clever of John to have thought of this! She said, "I think it's a wonderful idea, John! You're right. Your Father is the very man for the job!"

"Well," Douglas said hesitantly, "there's still the problem of Fawnwood. It seems to take more of my time than ever."

"And we don't make that much out of it. I'd be in favor of trying to sell it," said John.

"But what would we live on, the money from the sale?" asked Clara.

"And the interest, or if we sold it for cash we might buy some rental property in Natchez," said John, being his most persuasive.

"I don't know how much we could get for it," demurred Douglas.

"Why don't we find out?"

"We'd have to discuss it with Ernest and with Laura and Will. I don't know what they would think about selling their part."

"Then let them go down and run it," said John. "You've been saddled with that responsibility long enough, it seems to me."

Clara couldn't imagine selling her father's beloved Fawnwood. It seemed such a part of the family. But she had to admit that John had a good point about Douglas having had to bear the responsibility of running the place for all the rest of them. That wasn't fair. If Douglas wanted to edit *The Natchez Democrat,* he should certainly be given the opportunity. She would give him all the encouragement she could. And it certainly was a comfort to have John grown up and taking charge of things like this.

"Why don't I ask Laura and Will to come by for tea tomorrow afternoon? We can see what they say, and then, Douglas, you can write to Ernest about it."

"But Father should go ahead and inquire about the editorship," insisted John. "We'll go to Mr. Smith's funeral tomorrow, and then we'll look into it."

Clara decided to go to see Laura that afternoon and talk things over privately with her before Douglas brought up the question of selling Fawnwood at tea the next day.

She found Laura on the back gallery of her home with two of her older daughters and her three-year-old son. The oldest girl, Sallie, was now twenty-five, a tiny, homely girl with a peppery disposition. Sallie was not generally popular, but Clara had always liked her. Her namesake, Clara, was the image of her beautiful mother, and as sweet and lovable as she was pretty.

"Girls, I need to talk to your mother privately for a few minutes," said Clara after she had chatted with them briefly and gotten a bear hug and sticky kiss from little Laurance. "How about taking Laurie for a walk in the garden or somewhere?"

Just as Clara had imagined, Laura was shocked by the idea of selling Fawnwood.

"I know how you feel, Laura. I feel the same way. But I want Douglas to have this chance. I think it would mean so much to him."

"But can't he do both? He did when he was the editor of the *Natchez Courier.*"

"He isn't as young as he was then, Laura, and, besides, I think he finds it really irksome. After all, he's borne the whole responsibility of operating Fawnwood for years now. If you hate the idea of selling it so much, maybe you and Will could take it over."

"Now, Clara, you know that's impossible. There aren't enough hours in the day for Will to take care of his practice as it is!"

Laura finally came around, although grudgingly, and Clara felt that at least one hurdle had been passed successfully. It would take some time to hear from Ernest, but somehow she sensed that he would not stand in the way. Of course Ernest had never really understood or accepted what little they told him about Douglas' moods and his drinking. On his visits to Natchez, he saw Douglas at his happiest and best. He had no idea of the seriousness of Douglas' problems, which was also true of almost everybody outside of the immediate family.

The publisher of *The Natchez Democrat,* who lived in New Orleans, responded favorably to Douglas' inquiry and asked him to meet him in New Orleans for an interview.

Douglas was gone for a week. He stayed in the home of a Harvard classmate to whom he had written with the hope that they might get together for an evening. The classmate had insisted that he stay with him.

The week seemed to last forever to Clara and John and Ernestine, anxiously awaiting the outcome at home. Douglas returned at the end of the week perfectly sober and in excellent spirits. He felt sure he had the job. Clara couldn't believe that he was the same man who had left a week ago. He had a confidence that he hadn't shown in years, a buoyancy.

He had had such a delightful time in New Orleans, in addition to the success of the interview. He had enjoyed being with his old classmate and his wife, who was quite attractive. Through them he had met the daughter of one of his professors at Harvard, an authoress, who now lived in New Orleans. Her name was Jeannette Haderman. She had written several novels, and he brought home with him an autographed copy of one of them, which was entitled *Dead Men's Shoes.*

When the letter came from the publisher of *The Natchez Democrat* making the official offer of the editorship to Douglas, everybody was quite excited and happy about it. Clara was so pleased that Douglas had gotten the job, but now she began to wonder if he was equal to it. If it didn't work out he would be so disappointed. Well, that was always the risk in doing anything. She would just say her prayers and join in the general rejoicing.

Another letter came, this time from Memphis. Ernest had never thought what a burden the operation of Fawnwood must have been to Douglas all these years. He would be glad to sell his interest and would rely on Douglas' judgment as to the value of the land and the handling of the sale.

Since Douglas really needed to go back to New Orleans to wind up his contract with the publisher, he told John and Clara that he would look into prospective buyers for Fawnwood while he was there. He would stay at a hotel this time, so as not to wear out his welcome with his friends, and he would probably stay two weeks.

"I don't see that it's necessary for your father to stay two weeks in New Orleans just to accomplish his business," Clara said to Ernestine. "I think the reason he plans to stay that long is because he enjoyed himself so much when he was there before. How wonderful it is to see him getting a little pleasure from life!"

CHAPTER TEN

JOHN met the train from New Orleans and brought his father home to The Burn. Clara and Ernestine were having their tea on the back gallery when they arrived.

When they heard the carriage and the men's voices, they both tensed, and Ernestine gave voice to the constant, nagging fear they lived with, "Do you suppose Father is all right, Aunt Clara?"

Clara sighed, "Oh, I do hope so!"

"Yoo-hoo," called John, and they both relaxed.

Douglas was fine. He had had a very good time. The contract was signed and he was to begin work right away. He also had a prospective buyer for Fawnwood.

Clara thought, I must be dreaming. Everything is just too good to be true.

Douglas told Clara that he would like to invite John and Leila, Laura and Will McPheeters, and Margarette and Will Martin for tea the next day. She said to Ernestine later, "I guess he wants to get the family together to discuss the offer on Fawnwood."

"Well, then, why did he want to ask Aunt Margarette and Uncle Will? They don't have anything to do with Fawnwood."

"Your father sets great store by the general's opinion. I'm sure he wants to see what he thinks about it."

The family group gathered in The Burn garden. Everybody was congratulating Douglas and asking him about the New Orleans restaurants he had gone to.

Margarette Martin was especially anxious to hear about the Oysters Rockefeller which were served at Antoine's. "I've heard that they are simply delectable, baked in the shell with spinach, flavored with anisette. Hortense Dunbar said they were named for Mr. Rockefeller because he took such a fancy to them. When he asked the waiter what the dish was called, the clever man replied with a courtly bow, 'They are Oysters Rockefeller!'"

"Yes, I did order them. I was told that I must try them, and I found them very delicious. I was also told the same story about Mr. Rockefeller that Hortense Dunbar told you."

Leila turned to Ernestine, who was sitting next to her. "If I were you, Ernestine, the next time Cousin Douglas goes to New Orleans I'd make him take me with him. You and Cousin Clara should both go!"

Douglas, who had started to say something to Will Martin, looked around at that, and clearing his throat, addressed the group. "I think before I go back to New Orleans, we may have a visitor from there. I've asked Jeannette Haderman to come to visit us at The Burn. In fact the purpose of this party today is to announce our tentative engagement. I have asked her to be my wife."

If Douglas had suddenly sprouted wings and begun to fly about the garden, he could not have elicited greater amazement. They all sat in utter astonishment, open mouthed, but incapable of saying a word.

John was first to recover the power of speech. "Why, Father, that's simply wonderful!"

Will Martin shook his head. "Douglas, you certainly had me fooled. I had no idea that you had gone a-courting."

"Well, it has certainly been a whirlwind courtship!" exclaimed Laura.

"Yes, indeed!" echoed Will McPheeters.

Margarette Martin and Leila, as well as Clara and Ernestine, were still speechless.

"When is the lady coming?" asked the general.

"In a few weeks."

Margarette Martin, who had never in all her life remained silent for so long a time, finally found her tongue. "Why did you call it a tentative engagement?"

"Because Jeannette wanted it that way until after her first visit."

"Oh, I see."

Clara was groping amid the chaos of her thoughts for the right thing to say. Should she say it was wonderful when she wasn't at all sure that it was? Should she say she was happy for him when she wasn't sure that she was? She didn't know the woman or anything about her except that she wrote books and Douglas found her interesting. He had only seen her on two brief visits. He couldn't really know her himself. And what did she know about Douglas? Well, something had to be said.

"My goodness, what a surprise!" she said finally.

It's my turn now, thought Ernestine. I must say something, too, but what?

"Is your fiancee the same lady who was the daughter of your history professor?" she asked her father.

"Yes," he replied. "It was such a coincidence that she had decided to come to New Orleans to live and had looked up my classmate, who had been a very good friend of her father. Baron Haderman was one of my favorite professors, a fascinating man. He was from Bonn, Prussia. His uncle was Count Jean Rapp, who was created a peer of France by Napoleon Bonaparte for gallantry in battle. Professor Haderman, as we always called him, was educated at the University of Heidelberg and at the Polytechnique in Paris. The political problems in and around Bonn drove him to this country. He was a brilliant man, and he certainly made history come alive for me."

"His daughter must inherit her literary talent from him," said Will Martin.

Douglas radiated happiness these days and everybody

seemed delighted. Clara was dismayed by her own mixed emotions. She had some legitimate doubts about the wisdom of her brother's marriage to this woman on such short acquaintance and about the permanence of his rebirth, but she had to admit that mingled with these doubts were feelings of resentment and envy. She was ashamed of herself for thinking such a thing, but it did seem unjust to her that Douglas had been given another chance at happiness, while she had been cheated of fulfillment twice. A sense of no longer being needed blew on her like a winter wind. The children were grown, and Douglas' marriage would mean that he no longer needed her, either.

Furthermore, she realized the marriage was going to create a difficult situation at The Burn. Douglas no doubt intended to bring his bride there to live. Of course, The Burn was his home, but it was also Clara's and she had been mistress of it for over twenty years. Who would be mistress now? Clara didn't believe that she could turn the household over to anyone else and continue to live there. Should she leave The Burn? That would be almost unthinkable, shocking to everyone. Clara could hear her brother accusing her of martyrdom if she should even suggest it. She lay awake night after night, pondering the question. There seemed to be no graceful way out.

Clara's longing to live began to throb within her again, and the sight of Eliot these days made her pulse quicken. The love she was supposed to have vanquished valiantly on the field of honor, stirred now in her soul and in her senses. It was disturbing, yet sweet beyond words. She felt she couldn't bear to live with it, or without it.

By chance she was seated next to him at a dinner party at Green Leaves.

Garlands of fresh flowers, and china, hand painted with birds by Audubon himself, graced the table.

"Your table looks like a garden," Clara told her hostess.

Eliot smiled. "That is the highest praise she can give, you

know. And how does your garden grow these days, Miss Clara?"

"Entirely too well! I'm such an intemperate gardener, always planting more than I can comfortably take care of. I can never seem to resist a new plant!" As she spoke, Clara was thinking, that's one place I'll always be needed—in my garden—I can never leave it. But one shouldn't say never. Perhaps that's just what I must do.

"Well, I can think of no more fortunate plants than those tended by your love."

Eliot's eyes held hers briefly, but significantly. The look in his eyes and the awkward and extravagant compliment combined to awaken all the unspoken things between them.

Clara took a small sip from her wine glass, and, drawing a deep breath, replied, "Thank you, Dr. Watson, I do try to keep the weeds out."

Next Sunday the family was surprised by Clara's announcement that she wouldn't attend church with them. "There's so much to do in the garden, and I feel that I can worship the Lord just as well there."

"Sister, I can't believe that you would not attend services with the family even for the sake of your precious garden! Surely you don't put it before the Lord."

"Douglas, that's a matter between me and the Lord, and I will not discuss it any further."

After spending several Sundays in the garden, Clara rejoined her family at church.

Dear Lord, she prayed, as she entered the Walworth pew through its little swinging door, please help me not to act the way I feel, and to feel the way I act. When she had seated herself she focused her gaze with some determination on Mary Watson in her front pew with two of the five Watson children. The eldest daughter, who was the image of her father, sat with her husband and their children directly behind Mary. Another daughter, who closely resembled Mary, sat with her family in the third pew. The oldest son did not live in Natchez. He was a mixture of his father and mother, as were the unmarried son and daughter who were sitting with their mother. They were all beautiful children. Mary had grown matronly, but she was still quite pretty, and she was really a very fine woman in her limited way. Clara smiled at herself. Well, she was limited!

Clara glanced at Douglas sitting beside her, his face glowing with his happiness. She felt a sudden rush of warmth and love toward him, and she knew that she was genuinely happy for him. But still a tiny, miserable, hateful creature deep inside of her nibbled and gnawed.

CHAPTER ELEVEN

THE time came for Jeannette's visit and Clara and Ernestine made elaborate preparations. They spent the days before she arrived housecleaning intensively, and planning a party to introduce her to the family's friends.

"I thought we might serve a champagne punch for such a special occasion as this," Clara suggested.

Douglas hesitated. "No, Sister, I'm afraid we can't do that. Jeannette is very active in the Woman's Temperance Movement, and she is opposed to any sort of drinking."

"Oh, I see. Well, all right, we'll just have a plain fruit punch," Clara replied. Goodness, but life was full of surprises these days. One wondered what would happen next.

"How interesting," murmured Ernestine. Later she said to Clara, "I can't help having a little private chuckle over Father's engagement to a member of the Temperance Movement. Well, she certainly ought to be a good influence on him!"

On the day of Jeannette's arrival they filled The Burn with flowers. "I think our bouquets are just beautiful! I do wish Lessie could see them. Wouldn't she have had fun helping us?" Clara said to Ernestine. Then she added, "I forget you're too young to remember much about Lessie. She loved flowers so and she had such a way with them. Well, The Burn looks marvelous now, but look at us! We'd better do something about our own appearances. What shall we wear? I don't mind telling you I'm nervous as a cat about meeting this lady who's going to be my sister."

"Well, I'm nervous as two cats, as Annie would say, and my wicked stepmother-to-be from New Orleans probably is, too. I suspect we'll all be glad when this first meeting is over."

But if Jeannette was nervous she certainly didn't show it. She was friendly and pleasant, and all of their friends seemed charmed by her.

She was an attractive woman, Clara had to admit. She was intelligent, very intellectual, and vivacious and dynamic. She was a good-looking woman, too, not exactly pretty, but stylish looking. She was certainly not like Rebecca either in temperament or appearance, except for her coloring. She did have dark eyes and hair, matched with a fair and creamy complexion.

Her obvious devotion to and admiration for Douglas seemed sincere. She was constantly quoting him and referring to the greatly improved quality of *The Natchez Democrat* with Douglas at the helm. She took a great interest in the paper, and Clara heard her telling General Martin, "Douglas and I both feel very strongly that it is important for the *Democrat* to give more of a picture of what is going on in the world than Natchez papers have provided."

Jeannette and Douglas did appear to be quite congenial. They discussed his editorials and his editorial policies endlessly, and Jeannette spent a good deal of her time with him at the newspaper office.

One morning at breakfast Clara reminded Jeannette that they had been invited to tea at Rosalie that afternoon.

"Oh my goodness, I completely forgot about that!" exclaimed Jeannette. "Dear Clara, could you possibly make excuses for Douglas and me to those very kind people? A gentleman is calling on Douglas this afternoon to show him a new printing press, and I am so anxious to see it! Unless, of course, you think it is really necessary that I go."

Clara assured her that it was not "necessary," but she didn't especially enjoy having to make the excuses.

At dinner one day Jeannette praised the oyster soup. "It is very nearly as good as that at Antoine's and, of course, I think theirs is the best in the world! Tell me, Clara, do you really use this exquisite, fragile china every day?"

Clara replied that they did.

"But aren't you afraid it will all be broken up, especially with servants handling it?"

"Little Doug and Maybelle are much more careful with it than I am. We've always used our good china. Of course some pieces have been broken through the years. After all, though, why have it if you don't use it?"

"I'm sure you're right. I just have such a strong, practical streak in me that I can't help but worry about such lovely things being broken!"

It was obvious that Jeannette was not comfortable with the servants, nor they with her. She had some very advanced theories about equal rights for colored people, but she couldn't seem to get along with them on a personal basis.

John, who was always irreverent about everything, made the mistake one day of joking about the Temperance Movement. Jeannette did not smile and observed rather sharply, "It is a matter of the utmost seriousness, and we cannot afford to make light of it!" However, she went on to chat of other things and seemed to bear him no grudge.

Taken all together, the visit proved to be a success, and before Jeannette left, she and Douglas announced to the family that they were planning to be married on the ninth of December, three months away.

It was not until Jeannette returned to New Orleans that Ernestine finally broke through the crust of pretense which had covered their true feelings about Jeannette. She asked Clara, "Do you really like her, Aunt Clara?"

"Why, yes, I like her," replied Clara. "Don't you?"

"Yes, I like her," said Ernestine with a small whimsical smile. "But not very much."

Their pent-up resentments bubbled to the surface now like the juices in a pie when the surface is pricked.

"She really can be irritating. I never thought of myself as frivolous until I met Jeannette. She's so absolutely practical all the time."

"And she's just too plainspoken. Of course I don't like hypocrites, but it seems to me there's something rather egotistical about speaking your mind so frankly about everything. A little bit of equivocation from her now and then would have been quite refreshing. It would have shown a lack of absolute certainty that she's right about everything!"

Clara laughed, "She really does have plenty of self-confidence, doesn't she? But she also has a lot of character and sense, and she's certainly made a new man of your father. I think he's truly happy for the first time in years."

"Yes," agreed Ernestine reluctantly. "That's true, I guess, but that annoys me too, the way she's taken him over so completely. I don't like to see him become a puppet with her pulling the strings!"

"I don't think Douglas will ever be that, Ernestine. I think he's just very much in love right now. And I believe Jeannette is really in love with him."

"Well, maybe so, but, Aunt Clara, I don't think I can stand to live with her."

"Nor I," sighed Clara.

As Douglas' wedding day approached, a plan began to take shape in Clara's mind. One evening, as they sat on the back gallery after supper, she said to her brother, "Douglas, what would you think of our arranging an apartment for Ernestine and me here at The Burn? Then you and Jeannette could have your own household, and we could have ours. I think everyone would be so much happier that way instead of all of us trying to live together. Of course we could move somewhere else if you think that best."

Douglas looked as shocked as Clara had expected him to, and as hurt.

"This is your home, Sister. I wouldn't consider your ever leaving it."

"Well, Douglas, I don't want to leave. I just want to allow

us all a little privacy and independence. I feel sure Jeannette would like it that way, too. You know, no household can have two mistresses, and by all rights, as your wife, she deserves to be in charge of hers, but it could be awkward with me hanging around."

Douglas frowned thoughtfully. "Perhaps, as you say, it might be difficult for us all to live together. If you'd be happier in your own quarters, why don't you look into how it might be done?"

And so The Burn was split in two. A small kitchen and a bath were added to one side of the house, and out of the original rooms Clara and Ernestine derived a parlor and a bedroom. They would do most of their entertaining in the garden. It would be a new way of life, but they would adjust to it. When Jeannette Walworth moved into The Burn, Clara knew that she had done the right thing.

CHAPTER TWELVE

AFTER Jeannette's visit, Ernestine said to Clara, "I can't wait for Lucy and Daisy and Annie to meet Jeannette! I want to hear what they think of her, especially Annie, who will say exactly what she thinks!"

As it turned out Lucy and Ernestine were the only two of Douglas' children who were able to attend his wedding. Daisy had given birth to little Clara Walworth Wilbourn earlier in the year about the same time that John and Leila's son, John Gordon Walworth, was born. Neither Daisy nor Leila felt sufficiently recovered to make such a strenuous trip, and Annie couldn't leave young Douglas Brooks, who had the croup.

"Now, Ernestine, we must not influence Lucy in any way," said Clara. "Let's let her form her own opinion of Jeannette. Besides, we may even like her better than we think. We ought to keep our minds open."

"I promise you, Aunt Clara, that I'll keep my mind open, and my mouth shut. That will be the fun of it, to watch Lucy forming her own opinion of Jeannette!"

As soon as Lucy arrived at the hotel in New Orleans she began to quiz Clara and Ernestine about Jeannette. "But what is she really like?" she asked in exasperation. "I have the feeling you're keeping something from me. Do you really like her?"

"Yes, we do, Lucy, and if you'll hurry and get dressed you

will soon see for yourself what she's like."

"Jeannette is quite attractive, don't you think?" Ernestine asked Lucy later in the evening.

"Yes, she seems very charming, and Father is simply radiant! You all had told me, but I had to see the change in him myself to believe it."

"Well, she has Lucy completely fooled. I must say I am disappointed in Lucy's judgment," said Ernestine as she and Clara made ready for bed.

"It may be our judgment that is at fault. Did you ever think of that?"

"Well, the first moment Jeannette saw me, I could see she identified me as the enemy. I could see it in her eyes. I did wonder then if I had done something wrong, but that was the last time."

"I hope I haven't influenced you to dislike her so."

"Oh, Aunt Clara, I'm just joking! She isn't all that bad. And she does seem to make Father so happy. I do find her a little irritating at times, but she's really a good sort. She could certainly be a lot worse!"

Clara felt relieved. She didn't want to prejudice any of the children against their father's new wife.

Douglas and Jeannette spent their first Christmas together in New York visiting Jeannette's brothers and sisters, so it was not until the following June that Annie finally met Jeannette. She came to visit her father, bringing young Douglas Brooks with her. To Ernestine's secret delight Annie took an instant dislike to Jeannette, who was obviously not overjoyed to have a two-year-old house guest.

"Douglas is really a very good child, too. I don't know what she would have done if Daisy had come and brought little Clara, who shrieks and screams day and night loud enough to wake the dead—the way they say I did," Annie protested indignantly to Ernestine, who was busy weeding the garden. Like Clara, working in the garden gave her great satisfaction.

Ernestine sat back on her heels and removed her big brimmed straw hat to fan herself.

Annie was sitting on the bench that went around the Tree of Benediction, watching little Douglas, who was dividing his time between chasing butterflies and climbing up onto the bottom step of the flight that led to the next terrace so that he could jump down.

"It's obvious she doesn't understand children," Annie continued. "She looks at poor little Douglas as though he were some sort of wild animal. I think she's actually terrified of him."

"Well, she's awfully strict with John and Leila's little girl. When Madeleine toddles over from next door, she always calls immediately for me or Maybelle to take her home," said Ernestine.

"I thought everybody liked her so much."

"Well, Annie, we do like her, and she is very good for Father."

"I think she is sour as a pickle, myself."

"She does take herself rather seriously."

"I should say she does! She thinks she is the goddess of wisdom!"

"Well, to tell you the truth, Annie, it's a comfort to have you say so. Aunt Clara and I, and John and Leila, too, although they're very careful what they say, feel the same way. But we are all afraid that maybe it's somehow our fault that she acts the way she does."

"Your fault! I don't see how you stand her. I can't wait to go home!"

Annie was exaggerating, of course. Didn't she always? But her candor was like the cool glass of water that Ernestine wished she had right now.

"And I'm not sure she's all that good for Father, either," Annie went on. "I guess she does help him with the newspaper. It's really all she seems to think about."

"Well, of course, that and world affairs, and then we must not forget the Temperance Movement," Ernestine mimicked Jeannette's tone of voice at her most evangelical.

"Ernestine, I had no idea you could be so naughty!" exclaimed Annie with relish. "Do it some more!"

"Well, I could, but we might get caught, and do you have any idea how serious that could be?" Ernestine continued with her imitation of Jeannette.

Annie began to giggle and Ernestine, abandoning her role, joined in, as did little Douglas.

"My goodness, what sort of fun am I missing?" asked Clara when she found the three of them laughing away in the garden.

"We're making sport of our stepmother," chortled Annie, wiping her eyes. She had laughed until she cried.

"Annie, you're incorrigible!" said Clara, but she laughed in spite of herself, and suddenly all the resentment and jealousy she had felt vanished. She felt a pang of sympathy for Jeannette. Why, bless my soul, I believe I'm beginning to like her, she thought in amazement.

CHAPTER THIRTEEN

ERNESTINE was pulling weeds in the garden again and thinking about how much fun she and Annie had had there just a month ago. She really missed Annie and little Douglas. If only Daisy could come for a visit, but she was already expecting another child.

She was working in a freshly dug bed where Clara had planted several new rose bushes. A particularly stubborn weed refused to yield so she took her hoe and began to chop the soil around it. When she reached down deep into the turned-up earth to get at the root, her hand came in contact with a smooth hard surface.

"Whatever is it?" she muttered. "It feels like a piece of metal." Her curiosity excited, Ernestine dug away at the surrounding earth. "It's a cannon ball!" she exclaimed in amazement. "What in the world is a cannonball doing in our garden?" As she sat there puzzling over her unusual find, it suddenly dawned on her how it had gotten there. The Yankees must have fired it from their gunboat when they shelled Natchez during the War!

How lucky it was, she told herself, that Grandma and Grandpa Walworth and Aunt Clara and Aunt Laura and the servants and The Burn itself weren't all blown to bits! I guess it's harmless after all these years, but maybe I'd better not touch it.

Ernestine ran up to the house and into the hall, where Jeannette was preparing to leave for her daily visit to the newspaper office. When Ernestine told her about finding the cannon ball and how she thought it happened to be there, Jeannette was beside herself with excitement. What a marvelous story for the newspaper! She would get an engineer to come out right away and make an assessment of the situation. She hurried off, and within an hour had returned with an engineer and a photographer.

Meanwhile, Leila had come over with her children, Madeleine and the baby, Gordon. Clara and Ernestine sat with them on the back gallery of The Burn, discussing Ernestine's discovery.

"I suppose it's perfectly safe after all these years for us to be sitting here," said Clara a trifle uncertainly.

Maybelle was hovering about nervously and was delighted when Clara suggested that she take the children for a walk. They adored the gentle and jolly young woman and Maybelle adored them.

Off they went, the rotund Maybelle with her slim little charges on either side of her, all of them happy to get away, albeit for different reasons.

Little Doug was hovering, too, but his reason was curiosity, and he laughed as Maybelle scurried off with the children. "Miss Maybelle don't like the idea of that bomb. She may be too scared to come back! Dinner might be late today," he chuckled.

When Jeannette appeared with the photographer in tow in addition to the engineer, Clara's first reaction was that it was an awful lot of fuss to make over a twenty-five-year-old bombshell. They were probably buried all over Natchez. Certainly plenty had been fired on that infamous occasion, she thought, as she and Leila followed Ernestine and Jeannette and the engineer and photographer down to the garden.

Suddenly she thought of Douglas, his controversial role in the bombardment, and his assumption in his own conscience, whether rightly or wrongly, of the responsibility for it. This would bring it all back. Clara wished they could push the dirt back into the hole and cover the miserable shell up and forget it! Certainly Douglas would not want a big to-do made over it.

Ernestine was standing by the hole and pointing into it as she talked to the engineer. The photographer took a picture and prepared to take another.

"Jeannette," said Clara, "have you talked to Douglas about this? Are you sure he will be pleased with all this publicity? Douglas is very conservative, you know. I'm afraid he may not want anything so personal as his daughter's photograph in the newspaper."

Jeannette either didn't hear her in her preoccupation, or she ignored her. Clara tried again. "Jeannette, I don't think you should go too far with this until you talk to Douglas."

Jeannette turned around and said, "Clara dear, I know you mean to help, but I am quite busy. Of course, I won't publish anything without consulting Douglas."

Well, that was all she could do, thought Clara.

The engineer told them that it was entirely possible that the bombshell could still explode, that it must be removed by experts most carefully, and that the family should not be at The Burn when it was done. John and Leila's house, being as close as it was, should be empty, too, when the shell was removed. He would arrange to have the job done and would report back to them as soon as possible.

Shortly after the departure of the engineer and the photographer, Douglas arrived home for dinner. Jeannette took the lead in telling him all about what had taken place—from Ernestine's discovery to her plans to write a story for the paper. He appeared to accept it all remarkably well, Clara thought. He even agreed with Jeannette that they should publish a story about it, although he was reluctant to include a picture.

"You know," said Jeannette, "I never knew that Natchez was bombarded during the War. Of course I knew about the siege of Vicksburg and the shelling there. I didn't realize that Natchez was fortified as well, although I did know that the city was occupied. Was much damage done?"

"Surprisingly little," replied Douglas. "Most of the shells became embedded in the walls of houses or in the ground just as this one is. Very few actually exploded. No one knows exactly why. The best guess is that the shells were defective."

"Were many people killed or injured?"

"One child was killed. A good many were injured."

"Who was in charge of the fortifications here?"

Clara shuddered inwardly. Would Jeannette never hush? Why must she keep asking questions? She tried to think of a way to change the subject. "We didn't really have any fortifications here like Vicksburg. Ours were homemade breastworks and a couple of cannons. The siege of Vicksburg was a terrible thing. I'm glad we didn't have to suffer in Natchez the way those people did. Of course the occupation was not exactly a picnic, especially toward the end. That was when we all moved to Evergreen, Alabama," Clara rattled on, hoping to distract Jeannette from her line of questioning.

"I was in charge," said Douglas quietly. "And I very foolishly allowed my men to fire on a group of pillagers from the *Essex*. They retaliated by shelling the town."

Well, Douglas had managed to silence her at last, thought Clara. Jeannette was speechless, at least for the moment.

Maybelle and the children returned from their walk at this opportune moment, and the conversation was permanently interrupted as Leila and the children told everybody goodbye and took their leave. Clara assured Maybelle that they were all perfectly safe, and Jeannette asked her if she would please get dinner served.

The newspaper story caused a mild furor in the little town and Ernestine found herself the center of attention for once in her life, but she was so unused to it that it made her quite uncomfortable. Clara was pleased that almost everyone seemed to have forgotten Douglas' role in the shelling and she noticed that those who did remember had differing versions. Douglas did not seem troubled by all the discussion about it.

It was not until a couple of months later, as Clara watched the autumn winds set the scattering leaves skipping and swirling in their dance of death, that she told herself there was no doubt about it. Douglas was having one of his moods, his first as far as she could tell, since his marriage to Jeannette. But he wasn't drinking. You certainly had to hand it to Jeannette and her Temperance Movement. Douglas hadn't touched any spirits since their marriage.

He had been out of sorts for several weeks and was pessimistic about everything. Jeannette was worried about him and had talked to Clara about it.

"I just don't know how to handle him when he's this way. He's so sensitive about everything. He's neglecting the paper shamefully, but when I try to help him with it he gets upset with me."

"Yes, I know," sighed Clara. "I know how you feel. You want so much to help him, but he won't let you."

"I've kept hoping that soon he would just snap out of it, but instead it seems to get worse and worse."

"Maybe you should take a little trip somewhere, go to visit in New Orleans, or go to Memphis to see Ernest. Ernest is always so good for Douglas."

"I tried that. At least I mentioned to him that I would like to go to see my family in New York, and he just said, of course, I should go if I wanted to, but that he didn't feel like going anywhere himself."

I'm afraid I was no help at all to Jeannette, thought Clara now. The task of cheering up Douglas and restoring some of his confidence in himself seemed as difficult as putting the falling leaves back on the trees.

As Clara mounted the steps to the back gallery, Jeannette came out of the house. "Clara," she called softly, a look of utter consternation on her face. She put a finger to her lips and beckoned to Clara with her other hand.

They met at the head of the steps.

"Douglas has been drinking," said Jeannette.

"Oh, Jeannette, I am sorry."

They had a bad two weeks. Douglas drank every form of alcohol that he could by any means lay his hands on and shouted every kind of abuse that he could think of at the women of the household and the servants and even John.

Then one morning he woke up very ashamed, very apologetic, abjectly humble. In a few days he was back at the paper and had resumed his normal routine. Life at The Burn went on, as the second year of Douglas and Jeannette's marriage began, much as before on the surface. Jeannette had a new humility, which was not unbecoming. Douglas struggled to do his duty and fulfill his responsibilities, but the confidence and *joie de vivre* that had characterized the early days of his editorship and his marriage were gone. His disappointment in himself hung like an albatross around his neck.

CHAPTER FOURTEEN

IT was hard to believe that Jeannette and Douglas had been married for three years. His episodic drinking continued to be a problem, but Clara admitted that but for Jeannette it might have been worse.

The winter of 1893 was unusually cold and rainy. John's children had had one cold after another since early December. Now in February they were sick again, and Leila was quite worn out with nursing them.

Ernestine had a croupy cold, which went into pneumonia, an alarming development, although Will McPheeters assured them that she had a relatively mild case. Still Clara couldn't forget Ernestine's severe illness as a baby and what a frail child she had been. She had always worried more when Ernestine got sick than when the others did.

Clara was bringing a tray from Ernestine's room to the kitchen when John came in the front door. Observing that he was hatless, she reprimanded him, "Goodness, John, it's raining cats and dogs outside! You shouldn't be out in this weather without a hat!" Then she saw the expression on his face. "What's the matter? What's happened, John?"

"Oh, Aunt Clara, it's the children! They were quite sick all night so this morning I went and got Uncle Will McPheeters to come to see them, and he says they have scarlet fever!"

Clara tried not to show the terror that froze her heart when she heard those last two words.

"I'm not really supposed to be here. We're in quarantine now. But I just had to talk to you. I won't come any further, and I'll leave in a minute. How is Ernestine?"

"She's better, I think. Oh, John, how is Leila?"

"She's, well . . . she's . . . well, she is not too well. I've worried about her. She hasn't had any sleep for days, and she won't eat anything, and—and—oh, Aunt Clara, she's just this side of hysterics, I'm afraid!"

"Aunt Clara," called Ernestine hoarsely, and she came to the door of the back parlor, which had been turned into a bedroom. "I'm ever so much better. Maybelle can look after me perfectly well. She can bring me my soup and tea and keep me mustard plastered. I want you to go over next door and help nurse those children. John and Leila need you much more than I do."

"Ernestine, you must not come out in this drafty hall! Get back in your bed this minute! I promise that I'll come and talk this over with you, and then we'll decide what I ought to do."

"I don't want you to leave Ernestine, Aunt Clara, and if you come to our house you'll have to stay. You'll be quarantined, too."

"This will take some thinking about, John. I need to talk to Ernestine and to Will McPheeters. You go on back to Leila and the children. I'll either come myself or send Maybelle. Either way, just know that you have all my love with you and my prayers. God bless you, John, darling, and Leila, and your precious babies!" She tried to convey the overflowing love she felt for him with her words and her eyes, but it seemed so inadequate.

John's blue eyes filled with tears, and quarantine or no she held out her arms. He buried his face against her shoulder and his sobs reverberated through her. In a few moments he straightened up with a long shuddering sigh. "I'd better go now," he said.

Clara decided to go to John and Leila. She packed up

some things and left Ernestine with a heavy heart.

"Promise me you will be careful and stay put in this bed. Maybelle will take good care of you, I know, and your Uncle Will is coming by every day to check on you for me. I hate to leave you, but I believe you're right. They need me even more next door."

"I'm going to be saying my prayers, Aunt Clara. I only wish I could do something more. I love John and Leila so, and I couldn't love those children more if they were my own."

"I know, Ernestine. I know how you feel, but there's very little more that anyone can do. Love and prayers do help."

Clara had never seen sicker children. She arrived in the midst of a terrible scene. Will McPheeters had ordered that the children be immersed in tubs of cold water to bring their soaring temperatures down. Leila was hysterically protesting that she couldn't put them through such torture. John was sorely torn between the professional advice of his uncle and the motherly concern of his wife.

"It does seem like a very extreme measure, Will," Clara demurred. "Won't it be a terrible shock for those feverish little bodies to be put in that cold water?"

Will McPheeters sighed, "Convulsions will be a worse shock, Clara, and we are dealing with life and death here."

"Then we must just do it," said Clara. She gathered up little Madeleine in her arms and murmured soothingly to the child. Then she knelt beside the tub of water and leaned over it, lowering the fiery little body still clasped in her arms into the cold water. The child's shrieks of agony were like a bayonet ripping through her heart. "Tell me when it's enough," she said to Will.

After the ordeal of the cold baths, the children were bundled in quilts. Leila rocked Madeleine while John held Gordon. Clara, who was completely soaked, changed into some dry clothes and made a pot of tea for herself and Will. He had insisted upon staying, which they all appreciated so much.

Will was such a gentle and patient man, ideally suited

by temperament to his profession. Clara didn't think that Laura had ever been as much in love with Will as he was with her, but they seemed to have had a very happy marriage. Will was one of those men who grow more attractive with age. His gray hair was quite becoming, and he had acquired more self-assurance and ease of manner. His professional reputation was of the highest order, but he never seemed to make much money. Clara often wondered how many of his patients never paid him.

"What do you think?" she asked him now, and he knew she wanted the truth and not reassurance.

"I think we may lose them."

"My God!" Clara moaned. "Oh, my God!"

"Leila said something to me about sending for the priest. I guess I ought to ask John about it first."

"Yes, I think you should, although we must send for one if Leila wants it."

John found the idea quite disturbing. "I don't want the children to be frightened," he said.

"It will comfort Leila, John," said Clara, "and the children won't understand enough about it to be frightened."

The priest came. He anointed the little Walworths with the holy oil and murmured the prayers which would ensure their salvation. The rites made John uneasy, but it obviously was a relief to Leila to have had them performed.

Several hours later Clara sat rocking little Gordon, hoping that he could feel the love in her arms. She laid her cheek against his damp curly head. How infinitely precious he was! Suddenly he seemed to relax. The labored breathing stopped. Oh God, the breathing had stopped! John walked back in to relieve her. She looked up into his blue eyes. Would they ever be merry again? He held out his arms and she handed him the body of his dead child.

Joint services for Madeleine and John Gordon Walworth were held on a beautiful springlike day in 1893, the first sunny day in over a month.

Oh, thought Clara, how Madeleine and Gordon would

have loved this day! How they could have frolicked in it! I've had a lot of griefs, but I believe this one hurts the worst of all. And yet with all my years and all my tears I find I've grown stronger than I used to be. I don't have to wonder anymore if I can stand it. She glanced at Leila, supported by John's arms, very nearly prostrate in her grief, and wondered if she would be able to endure this blow.

Unfortunately Clara's misgivings appeared justified. Leila went into a complete shell, refusing to leave the house, or even to see anyone other than the immediate family. Spring gave way to summer and summer was well under way, but she could not let go of her grief.

"I feel so sorry for Leila, and I know she can't help it, but it does make it so hard on John," Ernestine remarked to Clara one morning as they were cutting some roses in the garden.

"Yes," agreed Clara. "It is an unhealthy situation. If only there were another child that Leila had to think about. It would help if there were someone who was dependent upon her. When my mother lost her children there was always another child or children to help her to go on living."

Clara fell silent as she began to clip the blooms on her sister Lucy's rose. When she had finished she said to Ernestine, "I believe I'll take these over next door, and tell Leila that I'd like to go with her when she goes for her daily visit to the cemetery." Leila seemed pleased that Clara wanted to go with her and that she had brought the blossoms from the white rose.

Clara rearranged the blossoms in their container which she had set between the two small graves. Then she stepped back. "They won't last long in this heat, of course, but somehow I just wanted to bring them."

She sat down on a nearby stone bench, and after a while Leila joined her. "Thank you for coming and for bringing the blossoms from the white rose."

"My first experience with death was when my sister Lucy died. I wasn't even born when my older brothers died."

Clara rose and went to stand by three little graves in another part of the lot. She read the names on the headstones out loud. "John Walworth, Charles Walworth, Horace Walworth. You know, Horace is the little blond boy in the portrait that hangs in the parlor at The Burn."

Leila came to stand beside Clara. She looked at the little graves as if she had never seen them before. Finally she said to Clara, "Each one of these holds a Gordon or a Madeleine. I never thought about what tragedies Aunt Sarah and Uncle John lived through—and Cousin Douglas—and you. I guess I have a lot to learn. But I'm not strong like you."

"You're stronger than you know, Leila. We all are. God gives us the strength to stand whatever we have to."

"Well, I'm going to try. I'm really going to try. I don't know if I can ever be happy again, but I'm going to try."

Oh, thank you, God, thought Clara and she glanced at the white roses, dying in the heat of the morning. They had done their job.

CHAPTER FIFTEEN

DURING the years following Douglas' marriage, Clara and Ernestine often played a game together of "When My Ship Comes In." When their ship came in they planned to go to Europe. They spent hours talking of the places that they would go and the things they would see.

They wanted to see the paintings by the master artists of the world that hung in the Louvre and in the Florentine galleries, the Gothic cathedrals of Europe, the frescoes and sculpture of Italy and Greece, and the magnificent ruins that were the echoes of ancient civilizations. They read prodigiously about all these things. They pored over the family's collection of steel engravings, although these extremely handsome copies of the world's masterpieces were mere shadows of the richly colorful works they represented.

Douglas, with Jeannette's inspiration and help, continued to edit *The Natchez Democrat.* John invested the money from Fawnwood in some rental property which provided a small but steady income. The Burn, with its extensive acreage, was located in the heart of town, and they began to sell off portions of it. As the family gradually climbed out of the debt which had plagued it ever since the War, Clara and Ernestine were able to put some money aside for the realization of their dream.

One April afternoon in 1898 Clara approached John about the idea of their going abroad.

He had walked over from next door with his four-year-old daughter, Mary, to have tea at The Burn. Leila was at home with their newborn baby daughter, Alice. Ernestine had gone calling on some friends, and Douglas and Jeannette were in New Orleans for a few days.

Clara fixed Mary some tea with plenty of milk and sugar in it, gave her a cookie to go with it, and lavished upon her all the attention that she felt a little girl with a new baby sister needed.

"How do you think Father is these days?" John asked her.

"Oh, I think pretty well. He seemed to be looking forward to the trip to New Orleans. What do you think?"

"I think he's been in extremely good spirits lately."

"Your Cousin Madeleine has written to Ernestine again asking her to come and visit her in her villa in Florence," Clara remarked as she handed John his cup of tea.

"Well, I think she ought to go. She needs to get away from Natchez, to get out in the world more."

"I think she should go, too, and I told her so, but she says she won't go unless I go. I doubt if your father would approve of her going alone anyway."

"Why don't you both go?"

"Well, I wonder if it would be too much of an extravagance? Even though we would be visiting Madeleine most of the time, it would still be quite expensive. Our transportation alone would cost an awful lot."

"Nonsense! It wouldn't really cost that much. And even if it were a sacrifice financially I still think you ought to go. It's too good an opportunity to pass up, and I can't think of any two people who deserve it more!"

"Of course it would be such a heavenly treat for us to go to Europe and see some of its treasures. And I'm sure we'd be royally entertained by Madeleine and her husband. It sounds as though they lead the most fascinating life."

Cousin Madeleine was the daughter of Clara's first cousin, Anna Cartwright, who was the daughter of Sarah Walworth's sister, Mary Wren. Anna had married a Frenchman several years before the Civil War and gone to live in Paris. She had died recently and Madeleine, who divided her time now between Paris and Florence, was apparently anxious to maintain some ties with her mother's family. She and her mother had visited in Natchez when she was a child and Madeleine and Ernestine had hit it off rather well then. Surprisingly, shy little Ernestine had been able to bridge the gap of language and culture with more alacrity than the other children.

"Well, I really think you and Ernestine ought to go. And you ought to go now. Ernestine is thirty-two. She'll never be any younger. While I'm not suggesting that she should go husband hunting, you never can tell. She might meet someone. Even a shipboard romance would make her life a little more interesting."

"Well, I wouldn't count on that, John. Ernestine is rather retiring you know. She's not the sort who could strike up a casual acquaintance with a gentleman very easily."

In June of 1898 Clara and Ernestine's ship finally did come in. It was not a great ocean liner, but a smaller sort. Still it was large enough to get them to the land of their dreams.

The trip was all they had hoped it would be and more. They planned to spend three months in Europe starting with a tour through France and the low countries.

In the museum in Amsterdam Ernestine reveled in the luminous canvases of her favorite painter. She wrote home on a postcard:

The quality of a Rembrandt has to be seen to be believed! His paintings have such depth and spirituality. Even the great cathedrals don't make me feel the reverence that they do.

She and Clara loved the little villages of the French and Dutch countryside, and the sturdy, friendly folk who inhabited them. They ate with zest the peasant soup and the bread and cheese. The tidiness of the farmland impressed them, and they were fascinated by the cleanliness of the Dutch people, who scrubbed their streets as well as their floors.

They were warmly welcomed on their arrival in Florence by Madeleine and her husband, whose name was Enrico Luserna di Campiglione, but who was best known to his intimates as "Kiki."

The Natchez ladies found Madeleine and Kiki charming and hospitable, although they were rather shocked by the freedom of continental society. Madeleine and her friends had such a different way of life. They were kind and warm-hearted, and they were unusually attractive people. But it seemed to Clara that they were too self-indulgent, while she was certain that they would find her principles prudish and narrow. Was it wrong for them to live the way they did? If it was not wrong for them to live in such a casual manner, then why would it not be all right for her to do so? And of that one thing she was sure; it would be wrong for her. But why must I follow the hard path? Why must I deny myself when others can so easily do as they please? It seemed terribly unfair and illogical, but there it was.

Cousin Madeleine's villa was situated on a hillside in the outskirts of Florence. Clara and Ernestine's suite of rooms overlooked the distant city. It lay like a lovely mirage far below them. Between were the silver olive groves, descending the hillside and punctuated by dark-green cypress spires.

A soft blue veil of space hung between them and the red and gold city, the walls of most of its red-roofed buildings washed with sunny yellow. In the center of the city the dome of the cathedral rose to crown it, and the tall bell tower of Giotto stood guard beside.

"It looks like a magic kingdom," said Ernestine. "And I feel like the princess in a fairy tale!"

There on the balcony off Clara's room they were having their breakfast of rolls and coffee.

"I'd love to paint this view! If only I had the talent!" sighed Clara. "If we stayed here long enough, do you think we might absorb some? There's bound to be something in the atmosphere!" She lifted her cup and took a sip of the thick, fragrant liquid that was much like the chickory coffee back home. "Florentine art is so unbelievably prolific."

"That's true," agreed Ernestine. "And when you think how exhausting it is just to go and look at it, imagine all the energy it took to create it—and the dedication as well as the talent."

"Well, what exhausts me most is trying to speak French all the time," replied Clara. This was the language which Madeleine and Kiki and their friends most frequently used. "I certainly envy the ease with which you do it. Miss Fortescue would be proud of you. Everybody says your accent is so good, too."

Miss Fortescue, an Irish governess whom Douglas had employed to teach his daughters, had lived with them for several years. Clara had felt this to be extravagant and unnecessary, but she had to admit now that Miss Fortescue had enriched all their lives, and especially Ernestine's.

"Miss Fortescue was very good with grammar and vocabulary, but I've learned the accent on my own," said Ernestine. "I've picked up most of it just from hearing the language spoken since we've been here."

Soon after their arrival they went up to Paris with Madeleine and Kiki to attend a ball. Madeleine maintained her mother's town house there, and she and Kiki went back and forth from Paris to Florence, as did so many of their friends.

Since Clara and Ernestine's wardrobes were rather modest, Madeleine had wanted to give them each a new gown for the elaborate occasion. Clara had urged Ernestine to accept this kind offer, although she herself had refused. After all, Ernestine had had so little in the way of beautiful gowns and she was still young enough to enjoy wearing a glamorous dress.

When Clara started to get ready for the ball, a maid

arrived with a billowing cloud of golden satin in her arms. It was one of Madeleine's dresses, which she was lending Clara for the evening. Clara hesitated. Her deep sense of dignity and identity told her to refuse politely and wear her own dress. But Clara knew that pride could be false and selfish. Madeleine wouldn't really understand her refusal, and perhaps everyone would be more comfortable if she were dressed in their fashion. So she sent her thanks and put on the shimmering gown.

When she viewed herself in the long gilt mirror set into the wall of her room, she caught her breath. She hadn't tried to be beautiful for years. She hadn't even thought she could be. Could this golden princess really be she? The dress was masterfully constructed, seeming to add inches to her height while subtracting them from her waistline. She chuckled, why, I look like one of the goddesses in the museum!

The lavishly carved door that separated her room from Ernestine's opened, and Ernestine swept in, her thin, awkward figure greatly enhanced by the skillful cut of the emerald-green velvet, designed and made especially for her.

"Oh!" Ernestine started, as she beheld Clara in Madeleine's dress. "Aunt Clara, I thought I was beautiful until I saw you."

"And so you are! So are we both. I wish everybody at home could see us."

"I wish Annie could." Ernestine's eyes were mischievous. "She'd be just the color of my dress, wouldn't she?"

"Yes, Annie always did want a Paris gown."

"Well, Annie didn't need one. She was always beautiful in anything she put on, and she still is! Come, Cinderella, I'm sure our pumpkin is waiting. Let's go to the ball."

"Mon Dieu!" cried Madeleine. *"Comme vous êtes belles!"*

And if Kiki had been gallant before, he outdid himself now.

The ballroom was walled with mirrors and dazzlingly lit by exquisite crystal chandeliers. Everyone was gorgeously dressed and bejeweled, and Clara and Ernestine knew that Cinderella's ball could have been no more splendid than theirs.

The ladies had sensed a polite condescension toward them by most of the Europeans they had met since their arrival. Everyone was so kind, and yet the superior attitude was unquestionably there. This was exceedingly irritating to Clara, although she knew it was petty of her, and she tried to conquer her annoyance. But Ernestine found it amusing.

During the ball, a distinguished gentleman—tall, handsome, and silver haired—inquired of Ernestine, "How do you like Paris?"

"Oh, it's beautiful! The city is very cleverly laid out, and all the buildings are so well proportioned. I think it must be the most beautiful city in the world!"

"Ah, yes. And what do you think of us Europeans?"

Ernestine paused, her small owlish face brightened with a whimsical smile, and she said, "You're very much like the people in Natchez. You know, we think we are at the center of the universe."

The gentleman's courteous expression gave way to a delighted smile, and Ernestine knew that she had found a friend.

He took supper with their party. When he met Clara, he told her, "I've enjoyed so much becoming acquainted with your little niece. Now I see that her charm is a family trait." After supper he confided to Madeleine and Kiki, "I have found your American visitors quite beguiling. I will be in Florence next week. I do hope you will allow me to call on them."

On the way home Madeleine said to Clara, "*Ma cherie,* you have made quite a catch. That was Le Comte de Meurigny, a widower, very wealthy, and prominent socially. You should set your cap for him."

"He's Ernestine's conquest, not mine," replied Clara. "But I think he's very charming, and I hope he will call on us."

He did call, appointing himself a guide for Clara and Ernestine. He planned to take them to see all the things they mustn't miss. They would see the Pitti Palace and the Boboli Gardens, the palaces of the Medici, and the paintings in the Uffizi Gallery, and they would spend several days seeking out the widely scattered works of Michelangelo. Henri, as he insisted upon being called, made a perfect guide. He loved Florence and its treasures, and his knowledge and enthusiasm about everything appeared limitless.

"Although Florence is such an ancient city, it has the vigor of youth," he told them as they strolled its stone streets, Ernestine on one of his arms and Clara on the other.

"Here past and present live together. The Renaissance, of which one might say Florence is both mother and child, still lives here, and will never die as long as the city stands.

"You know it is very interesting that the Renaissance movement, which was so richly creative, awakening the most exciting new ideas in every field, began, in fact, with a rediscovery of the past. In the Dark Ages man had let himself become imprisoned in the present. Renaissance man learned to free himself through the use of memory and imagination. And so, perhaps, with our memories and our dreams, we, too, can conquer the tyranny of time!"

"And of place," added Ernestine thoughtfully.

They were just entering the Piazza Santa Maria Novella, and Clara exclaimed with delight over a large flower market.

"Look!" Ernestine pointed to a long building opposite the church of Santa Maria Novella. "It's decorated with Della Robia medallions! How lovely!"

"Yes, isn't it? It's an orphanage."

"Flowers for your ladies?" inquired a beaming, fat woman, beautiful with the hearty joy of living and loving that was written all over her broad face.

"But of course," replied Henri, and he bought them each a bunch of violets.

"In a moment we will go into the church. You will see

it contains many treasures. The facade is a mosaic of green and white marble, quite handsome, and while this is a Gothic building, it has much of the Romanesque about it. To the right there behind the wall is a cemetery where many of the great Florentine families are entombed. Do you see the two obelisks at each end of the square? These have been used as posts for coach races since 1563. I will take you to see one. You will find it entertaining."

While Henri attended to some business in town, Clara and Ernestine spent the afternoon browsing in the quaint shops of the Ponte Vecchio. They looked at the silver and the linens, and they bought some books and pictures from a little bookbinder with an aristocratic face and long snowy hair. They spent a delightful hour with him. He showed them his rare editions, including a copy of Elizabeth Browning's sonnets, which she had autographed for him, but this he said he would never sell.

"She was a great artist and a great lady. She and Mr. Browning came here often. What a privilege it was to be in their presence! My shop would glow for hours after they had left." The little bookbinder even invited them to have tea with him, but they declined, promising to return soon.

Henri had arranged to meet them for tea in a small pastry shop near the Ponte Vecchio. Outside the shop, which overlooked the river, were tables covered with red checked cloths and on each a tiny vase holding fresh flowers. The sun was beginning its descent, and the promise of a spectacular sunset was in the sky.

"You two look very pleased with yourselves," said Henri. "I do hope you haven't had too much fun without me."

"We did have a very good time, and a charming gentleman, a perfect stranger, invited us to tea," said Ernestine.

"*Mon Dieu!* I mustn't let you out of my sight again. Tell me, who is my rival?"

"The sweetest little bookbinder you ever saw." Ernestine held up a package. "We bought some books and a folder of prints from him, and in return he entertained us all afternoon."

"Yes," said Clara, "he showed us an autographed copy of *Sonnets from the Portuguese,* and he told us that Elizabeth and Robert Browning were often in his shop. In fact, he talked so much about them that I feel as though we spent the afternoon with them, too! He was really quite an interesting little man."

"Your bookbinder must be Pietro Ficino. It's said that he is a descendant of a famous Florentine family. What books did you buy from him?"

Ernestine unwrapped the package and handed him one of the books, a beautifully bound collection of nineteenth-century French verse.

"I admire both of your Brownings, although I understand her better. I hope you will like our poetry," said Henri, turning the pages of the book of French verse with obvious approval.

A sly twinkle lit the gray-green eyes behind the spectacles, as Ernestine recited softly in excellent French:

"O Lac! rocher muets! grottes! forêt obscure
Vous que le temps epargne ou qu'il peut rajeuner,
Gardez de cette nuit, gardez, belle nature,
Au moins le souvenir!"

Henri was rendered speechless by this performance. He found it touching beyond words that a little American girl could so accurately, and with such feeling, quote one of his own favorite verses.

"You know Lamartine so well?" he asked in wonder. "How about de Vigny?"

Ernestine nodded. "So noble and gallant, but awfully depressing."

"De Musset?"

Ernestine nodded again. "I love de Musset, especially the lines where he says that a happy memory is more real than happiness itself."

Henri murmured, *"Un souvenir heureux est peut-etre sur terre plus vraie que le bonheur!* Well, certainly it is more lasting." He drew a wallet from the inside pocket of his gray and white pin striped morning coat and produced several snapshots from it. "Here are my memories." There was a picture of a dark-haired woman wearing a pearl necklace. "This is my wife." And then there were pictures of two young boys in ruffled shirts, one of whom was brunet, the other blond. "This is my son Jacques and this is my son François."

"She is beautiful," said Ernestine.

"What fine boys!" said Clara. "Jacques looks like you, and François like his mother."

"Yes," said Henri, "that is what everyone said." He looked off into the sky, all pink and gold now, his eyes seeming not to see it. "There was an accident. The train went off the rails. They were all three killed instantly. I comfort myself that they never knew anything."

Henri took Clara and Ernestine one evening to a concert in the Boboli Gardens. In this exquisite setting, in the hands of master musicians, the music soared to majestic heights and probed to the tenderest depths. By the end of the concert tears had come to Ernestine's eyes, and she was quite overcome and grateful for the darkness. She thought, as much as I love words, there aren't any that could say to me what that just did.

She was trying to blink away her tears as unobtrusively as possible when Henri offered her his handkerchief, commenting with a smile, "I hope they are tears of happiness."

"Oh, my goodness, yes! Oh, yes, I don't know when I've enjoyed myself so much!"

"You can never imagine what a treat this has been for Ernestine and me," said Clara. "We hear very little really good music in Natchez. Of course, before the War, artists from all over the world came there. I remember hearing Jenny Lind. That was a thrilling experience! But I've never in my life heard such great music as we have tonight."

Henri had to return to Paris, and sadly they bade him goodbye.

"I shall be back soon, and we'll continue to explore. There's so much left to see. I don't say *adieu,* but *au revoir.*"

After Henri's departure they went with Madeleine and Kiki to Rome for a few days.

At first sight of the Coliseum, proud even in its ruin, and so appealing to the imagination, Ernestine cried, "I love it! It reminds me so of Natchez!"

Perhaps their greatest delight in Rome was Michelangelo's Sistine Chapel ceiling.

"It's incredible!" marveled Ernestine. "An absolute orgy for the eyes! The paintings are beautiful, and he has changed the shape of the ceiling with them just as Henri said!"

They sat on the wooden benches that were placed against the walls so that the ceiling could be seen from every angle.

"How ridiculous we must all look," said Clara. Every head was turned up, and people walked across the floor without taking their eyes from the compelling ceiling. "You know," she told Ernestine, "I believe it's the most comprehensive artistic achievement I've ever seen. Think of the audacity of a mere human being to conceive it!"

"I know what you mean. And he's the same man who made Moses come to life out of a block of marble!"

"Look at the scope of this! He's spread the whole epic of man on this ceiling!"

"It is glorious," Ernestine murmured. "You know, I can actually feel Michelangelo's presence. It's as if he's up there shouting down to me, and even though my neck hurts, I can't look away. He won't let me!"

When they returned to Florence, they found a letter from Natchez telling them the disturbing news of another outbreak of Yellow Fever. John's wife, Leila, wrote that she and their two little daughters had gone to the country to escape it, but John, who had recently been made postmaster, felt it his civic duty to remain in the town and assist the health officers.

On the heels of this distressing information came a wire:

John died tonight of the Fever, a hero's death. Conscious to the last he sent you both his love.

Signed, Douglas

The first wire was followed by another. Jeannette had the Fever.

Clara and Ernestine felt that they must go home. Douglas and Leila needed them, and there was no way that they could enjoy the gaiety of their surroundings with their hearts in mourning. In spite of the protests and persuasions of Madeleine and Kiki, they took the next ship home, bringing with them bright memories, candles for a winter night.

CHAPTER SIXTEEN

AFTER their return from abroad, the years went by like weeks. Clara could hardly keep up with them. Douglas was unwell and retired from his position as editor. After the tragic deaths of his son and his wife from the Fever, his drinking became more of a problem than ever.

One night in October of 1904 he went to bed early. Before the morning broke, he died in his sleep.

Lucy, Daisy, Annie, and Ernest, with his wife, Mary, came immediately, and The Burn welcomed its children home, united in their grief.

It had been some time since Clara had seen Ernest. She was startled to see how much older he looked. Although he claimed he was fine, she didn't think he looked as though he felt well. Of course Douglas' death had been a shock to him. He had always been so devoted to his older brother. His pretty Mary still looked and acted like a little girl. Clara guessed she always would. Some people were like that. She was quite lovable, and Ernest, and everybody else for that matter, petted and spoiled her.

Ernest and Mary had three children now, a boy, named Ernest, a girl named Mary but called "Mamie," and another little girl named Clara. Ernest still worked for the printing company although he said he was thinking of retiring soon, if only he could afford to. He had been managing the firm for years now and he made a good salary, but he had an expensive family and he had never been able to save anything.

However, in spite of her misgiving about her brother's health, Clara noticed that his blue eyes still twinkled with fun, and he obviously relished seeing the many friends who came by The Burn to pay their respects the night before the funeral. Several of his boyhood chums had stayed quite late, talking about old times. Clara thought they would never leave. She was glad to see Ernest enjoying himself so much, but she felt cheated not to have the opportunity to have a real chat with him.

The day of the funeral the family gathered at The Burn for dinner. There was just the family now, but that added up to quite a lot of people. It seemed as though everybody was trying to talk at once, and important conversations kept being interrupted.

Clara had seated Ernest in Douglas' chair, at the head of the table, opposite her end of the table. It had seemed the right thing to do. Now she wished she hadn't because, if he weren't so far away, she might have had a chance to talk to him at last. However, she thought, perhaps not. He was sitting between Laura and Margarette Martin, and Clara noticed that as usual Margarette was doing most of the talking. It was a good thing her chatter was entertaining!

She had put Wallace Wilbourn on one side of her and Dr. Brooks on the other. They were enjoying this good visit with each other immensely. Daisy and Wallace had moved to Memphis after his mother's death, and while they did some visiting back and forth, the Wilbourns and Brooks did not get to see as much of each other anymore.

Lucy, who was seated next to Dr. Brooks, joined in their conversation from time to time, always with some apt comment. What a fine-looking woman she had grown into, and how well she had met the challenges and vicissitudes of her life. Clara didn't worry about Lucy anymore. She seemed in full command of her life. How long now had she been a widow? Edgar must have died over a year ago. He had retired for reasons of health from his strenuous practice in Louisiana about ten years ago and accepted a job teaching at the Virginia Military Institute in Lexington, where he had grown up. Lucy and Edgar had been quite happy there. The academic atmosphere had suited Lucy perfectly. However, after Edgar's death, she and young Edgar had moved to Memphis, where Daisy and Wallace were living, and she seemed to like it there very much. She had rented a little house down the street from Daisy and they saw each other practically every day.

Clara had asked Lucy about Wallace's job, and Lucy had said, "Aunt Clara, Wallace is about as practical as Daisy! He'll never make much money, but they don't seem to care. He hated farming and is glad to have gotten away from it. I think he likes his job, and he and Daisy have such nice friends in Memphis. It's a better place to raise children, too, because of the schools. As a matter of fact, it wouldn't surprise me to see Annie and the doctor move to Memphis one of these days when the children are older, although they seem quite happy on their plantation now."

Clara looked down the table at Annie. Yes, Annie seemed to be blooming and thriving in the country. She had worried about Annie's marriage at first. Of course Annie's last-minute jitters had proved not too serious, but Clara had wondered nevertheless if Annie would be able to adapt herself to a life of isolation and the lack of comforts and niceties.

She remembered Annie telling about her arrival in Deeson with Dr. Brooks following their brief honeymoon in New Orleans. "Before we went to see it, Dr. Brooks explained to me that the house we were going to live in wasn't all he wanted it to be, but in my most pessimistic moments I had never pictured anything quite like it!

"It was the dingiest house you ever saw. It had a hideous red tin roof that glared at me. There wasn't a single tree to protect the house from the sun. The lawn was a desert of dirt with a few scrawny bushes scattered around it.

"The doctor said, 'I know it's in terrible shape now, but

we'll have plenty of labor to repair it after we get the cotton in.' And I said weakly, 'Oh, I'm sure it'll be just fine,' but I was absolutely appalled. I didn't see how we could ever do anything with that miserable house.

"He went off to talk to some of the tenants, and left me there to look around. I just walked from room to room in utter despair. All the floors slanted so badly I felt as though I were walking on a ship in a typhoon! Every last window sill was rotten. The only sound feature of the whole house was that roof!

"I walked back out onto the front porch and sat down on those sagging, splintery steps and cried like a baby. Then you know, Aunt Clara, while I was sitting there feeling so sorry for myself, I remembered something Grandmama Conner said to me when I was a child. In fact I could actually hear her saying it, as plain as I'm hearing you now. She said, 'Your forebears were pioneers, Annie, and they didn't expect life to be easy!'"

Clara smiled. "That sounds like Mrs. Conner."

"Well, I told myself, whatever my forebears did I can, too! I dried my eyes and decided I'd better try to wash my face with some cold water before the doctor came back to take me to Daisy's. I found the water pump by the kitchen door. It was rusty and so was the water, but I splashed it on my face anyway and patted it dry with my handkerchief so the doctor wouldn't know I'd been crying. Then I started planning what I was going to do with that ugly house."

Annie had oozed with pride and satisfaction. "You wouldn't know it now since the carpenters and the painters and I have taken it in hand. I'm not through yet, but it's already beginning to look attractive."

Clara had found it hard to believe that this woman of purpose and determination was her spoiled little Annie. She was so proud of her. Of course, Clara guessed she probably still threw a temper tantrum from time to time. Maybe she even hid under the bed still during the thunderstorms that she had always been so afraid of. But in most ways it looked as though Annie had grown up.

She glanced across the table to Daisy. She still had that glowing look about her, and Lucy had reassured Clara that all was well with her. Why did she have an uneasy feeling about Daisy and Wallace? She guessed it was because, as Lucy had said, they seemed such babes in the woods.

Suddenly she realized that Dr. Brooks had asked her a question. "Oh, you'll have to forgive me! I've been sitting here gazing at your wives and noticing how happy they both look. What did you ask me?"

"I just wondered if the white rose bloomed this year?"

"It has never been more loaded with blossoms! Each year Ernestine and I wonder if it can bloom another season, and each year it says, 'Of course I can!'"

All the way down the long table Ernest heard Clara's comment, and he said to her, "It looks as if Lucy's rose will outlast us all. It's like the family. The blossoms of one season die, but the old bush keeps putting out new blooms." He turned to Laura. "Here you are a grandmother again. I have three children, Lucy has one, Annie has three, Daisy four, John two, all of them blossoms for another season."

As soon as they had finished dinner, it was time to leave for the funeral. The cars arrived and Clara divided the family into them, taking care that she and Ernest should ride in the same car. Why did she keep thinking that she would never see him again?

CHAPTER SEVENTEEN

AFTER the services were over, they left the cemetery, where they had said their last goodbyes to Douglas, supposedly. But of course, thought Clara, that was not the case. She had said goodbye that morning in Douglas' room after Maybelle had come to tell her that Mr. Douglas did not answer her knock. That was the terrible thing about the death of those you loved—the not being able to find them. Douglas was not there; only the tired, worn-out body which he had used lay in his bed. There was no use clinging to that, or to a coffin, or a grave. You had to find them somewhere else.

They were rather quiet on the drive back to The Burn. Ernest and Mary, Wallace, and Dr. Brooks had left directly from the cemetery to return to their various obligations, and Leila and her little girls were in the McPheeters' car.

As they drove the short distance from the cemetery to The Burn on the narrow streets that had been built for buggies, a general feeling of sadness and loss was with them all. To Lucy, Daisy, and Annie the loss was not of their father only, for they saw with the eyes of outsiders now that Natchez seemed to be dying, too.

It has lost all contact with the reality of the world outside, thought Lucy. When Edgar died, she had decided that she and her young son should not try to live at The

Burn, that they should have their own home; and she had decided not to live in Natchez. Now she realized how right she had been. Natchez was living on the memories of what it had been for one brief hour of history. The town had begun to wither, blighted by the War, before it had come to the fullness of its bloom. It was no place to rear a young son.

The sight of The Burn, rising serene and unchanged on its hill, lifted them out of their dejection. The long, black funeral car turned in at the gate, and proceeded in its sombre pace up the curving drive. It was a lovely fall afternoon, crisply cool. Squirrels scampered about the leaf-scattered lawn, and the tall trees cast long shadows.

"I feel as though Father should be there on the gallery waiting for us," said Daisy.

Little Doug had lit a fire in the parlor for them, and one in the dining room, and Maybelle had left a cold supper.

The ladies visited, catching up with one another's news.

"Do you still like living in Memphis, Daisy?" asked Clara.

"Oh, I really do! Our new house is in such a nice neighborhood on a quiet little street. All our neighbors are charming, congenial people, and there are lots of playmates for the children. Wallace likes it so much, too. You know, he never did like farming. He felt as Father did about it. He only did it because he thought it was his duty. Of course I miss Annie, but we are close enough to visit frequently, and now I have Lucy right down the street. I can't tell you how wonderful that is!"

"For me, too," added Lucy. "It has meant so much to me to be near both Daisy and Annie. You know Daisy and I often go down to Brooksland to visit Annie in her little kingdom there. She rules over it quite efficiently, too. Her beds are usually full of guests, and there are always a dozen or more people at her table, which is laden with the largest assortment of fresh vegetables you ever saw, along with the best cornbread and fried chicken, and ham that Dr. Brooks cures himself. Annie plays Pied Piper to an antlike trail of pickaninnies all day, and she's mother confessor to every darky on the place, as well as to the ministers who come to preach at the church Dr. Brooks built. They have a different young man each week, and they stay with Annie and the doctor. She claims she even writes their sermons for them, although I must say I certainly wouldn't want to claim some of them!"

"Well, I do try to help them. They're so young and inexperienced, and when they say they don't know what they ought to talk about, I just make a few suggestions. I advise them to forget all the big words they learned at school and talk to people in a way that they can understand, and I recommend that they tell stories just as Jesus did with His parables. It's so much more effective to tell about the Good Samaritan than to say we ought to be kind. Everybody likes to hear a good story."

"Can't you hear Annie teaching them how to tell Bible stories? She'd have the whale swallow Jonah's whole family!" laughed Ernestine.

"Laugh if you like, but several have written me to say how much I've helped them, and they all end up with good churches, too."

"You ought to hang out a sign—'Miss Annie's Post-Graduate Academy for Promising Young Theologians,'" Daisy suggested.

"Well, I'm afraid I couldn't collect enough tuition to pay for the sign." Annie laughed and then added, "But seriously, I've been reading the Bible a lot lately trying to help these young men with their sermons. You know it's really a marvelous book!"

"You don't say!" said Lucy at her driest.

Annie ignored Lucy's sisterly sarcasm and continued, "There's just one thing about it. I wish that once, just once, it would say, 'And then God laughed.'"

"Annie, you never did have any reverence," protested Daisy, smiling affectionately at her sister.

Clara nodded thoughtfully. "That's a very interesting point, Annie. It doesn't ever say that God laughed. And yet I feel sure that He must."

"Perhaps when you finish with the sermons, Annie, you might try your hand at rewriting the Bible!" Lucy chuckled. "As Ernestine says the stories couldn't help but come out better when you got through with them!"

"Have you heard anything from Madeleine and Kiki, Aunt Clara?" Daisy asked.

"They've been urging Ernestine and me to pay them another visit. We'd love to go, but I've written them that it's their turn to visit us and that we won't come until they do."

"Gracious!" exclaimed Lucy. "Whatever would you do with them?"

"Why, we'd treat them just as we would any other visitors," said Ernestine, "and they'd love it, especially Kiki. They are the sort who find a way to enjoy life wherever they are."

"Ernestine," said Clara, "do your imitation of Kiki for them. You know, Ernestine is as talented at mimicry as John was. I found that out the night we got home from the ball in Paris. She recreated the whole party for me just as John used to do."

"Please, do Kiki, Ernestine. I'm consumed with curiosity about him," urged Lucy.

"Oh yes, please," added Daisy and Annie.

"After supper," promised Ernestine. "We really should eat now, I think. I'll just go back to the kitchen and bring things out. Maybelle has left us a salad, and Margarette Martin brought over a stuffed ham, and then we have Ruth Britton's chocolate layer cake. Everybody has been so kind."

"I always thought when I was a child that baking a cake was such a funny way of expressing sympathy," said Daisy.

"I didn't," said Annie. "I was always happy to get the cake." Then irrepressibly, "And I still am."

"It's good to have our Annie around," smiled Clara. "There's nobody else who says such deliciously frank things."

"Lucy told me the other day that I was too frank. I'm afraid she often disapproves of me!"

"Absolutely," agreed Lucy. "I always was itching to give you a good spanking, and every now and then I still get the urge."

When they had taken their plates out to the kitchen and returned to the parlor, Ernestine regaled them with her imitations of Kiki and Madeleine, the little bookbinder, and many other friends and acquaintances of the trip, but she did not "do" Henri.

"Who was the man who took you two under his wing and showed you all the sights?" asked Daisy. "He sounded so charming. 'Do' him, Ernestine."

Clara looked quickly at her youngest niece, but Ernestine merely smiled and said, "Oh, he's much too complex a person to take off successfully. I'm not equal to it."

Daisy looked from her aunt to Ernestine, her beautiful and expressive eyes thoughtful. She possessed an acute awareness of the inmost feelings of others. Observing Clara's protective reaction, she wondered if Ernestine's heart was as untouched as they all believed it to be. Then she suggested, "We're so tired anyway, and since we do have tomorrow to be together, why don't we go to bed now?"

"We really should," said Clara. "But one more day is just not enough when we see each other so seldom. Much as I love having all the children, when they're here we don't have the chance to visit like this. Not that I want you to leave them home next time," she hastened to add.

Clara was brushing her hair. Just a few strokes, not the usual hundred, she told herself, for she was so tired. Death, with the illness that went before it, and the sad and solemn rites that followed it, was an exhausting business.

There was a knock at her door, and when she called, "Come in," Lucy entered in her kimono.

"Aunt Clara, may I come in for a minute?"

"Of course, Lucy. Sit down, dear."

Lucy sank down in the small velvet-cushioned rocking chair which Clara offered her. "I just don't see how I'm going to be able to go to sleep. I can't seem to get Father off my mind. I keep wishing he hadn't had to die feeling that he'd been a failure. He had so many disappointments, but the worst was in himself!"

"Oh, I know, Lucy. He was always trying so hard, too hard, and he suffered such a lot. Only God knows how much. When he married Jeannette, he seemed to be happy for the first time since he came home from the War. For a while it looked as though he might stop drinking but that didn't last long. I suppose, Lucy, that your father could qualify as a typical tragic hero. You might say he was a Don Quixote, tilting at windmills. However, I've never been sure it was fair to dismiss things like honor and chivalry as 'windmills.'"

Lucy nodded. "Nor I. But Father took those sorts of things too seriously. Then when he couldn't live up to them, he let it destroy him. He longed so for perfection." She paused, and added with a wry smile, "Maybe he'll find it now."

The daughter's eyes met the sister's, and they shared the unspoken thought that if anyone could find anything wrong with Heaven, it would be Douglas.

Lucy stood up. "How selfish I'm being keeping you up like this when I know how tired you must be! But I do feel better, if that's any comfort to you. You've always had the most wonderful genius for untying the knots in a person."

She stooped and placed a light kiss on the top of Clara's head. "I'd better let you get some rest. If the Rock of Gibraltar should crumble, then what would we all cling to?"

Lucy had seemed quite cheered by their conversation, thought Clara, as she slipped gratefully into her bed and snapped out the light. She found she could not sleep though, however tired she was. As she lay staring into the darkness, the tragedy of her brother's life seemed suddenly to overwhelm her. Oh God, she prayed, let him be happy. Please let him be happy. And then the releasing tears came, and she fell asleep.

CHAPTER EIGHTEEN

WITH the passing of the years Clara's chestnut-colored hair turned as white as Lucy's rose, and her quaintly angular face bore that stamp of serenity and dignity that age brings to the disciplined.

She had known it in her bones that Douglas' funeral was the last time she would ever see her brother Ernest. Sure enough, he had died the following year. When Laura died three years later, Clara said to Ernestine, "Now I'm the last rose of summer, left blooming alone! It's a lonely sort of feeling. I've been so close to Laura these past three years. We had so many shared memories to enjoy with each other. After Will's death, and with her children grown, we had more time to spend together. I'm going to miss her terribly."

"Well, you'll always have me," Ernestine told her with the soft little chuckling laughter which was one of her charms.

In somewhat the same way that age had been kind to Clara, it was also becoming to Ernestine. She wore thicker spectacles now, and loose-fitting dresses, and sensible shoes on her long narrow feet. Her shoulders stooped a little, and she was thinner than ever. Yet she had an indefinable elegance about her. She was shy and retiring, as she had always been, but the unexpected, sparkling humor and wit were there for those who listened.

There were times when Ernestine wondered if she had not been foolish when she had refused Madeleine's invitation to stay with them. After the wires had come about John's death and Jeannette's illness, and she and Clara had announced their decision to go home, Madeleine had come to Ernestine privately. *"Ma cherie,* I know Clara feels she must go to look after Douglas, but you could stay."

Ernestine's heart had leapt within her. To stay in this wonderful place! To see Henri again! It was a great temptation. She refused, but Madeleine had seen her hesitation.

"Think about it for a little bit before you say no. Do your packing if you must, but be thinking. If you change your mind, we will be so happy."

When Madeleine left her, Ernestine sank into the nearest chair and tried to compose her thoughts. If only there were time to think. It was such a big decision. She wanted to stay, but she was afraid to. She admitted candidly to herself that one of the main reasons that she wanted to accept Madeleine's invitation was to see Henri again. But what am I to him she thought? Just a plain little American spinster of whom he is rather fond. From the moment she had seen the picture of Henri's wife she had known that she didn't have a chance. And Henri was so handsome himself. She was a skinny, little, cross-eyed woman, and Henri was one of the handsomest men in Europe. It was an impossible dream she had and she must get over it. But when she thought of going back to her narrow life in Natchez, it seemed almost worth while to take the wild chance and stay. Impulsively she started for the door between her room and Clara's. She put out her hand to open the door, and then she drew it back.

But how can I tell Aunt Clara? How can I possibly say, I'm staying here. You go home, and take care of my father for me. Go, and travel across the seas alone. You, who have spent your life rearing your brother's children, now must go home and spend the rest of it taking care of him.

She knew she couldn't do that.

That all seemed so long ago, but often Ernestine woke

in the morning from a dream in which she and Henri had strolled the streets of Florence. Sometimes he had bought her a bunch of violets. Sometimes they went into the little bookbinder's shop, and Pietro Ficino would say, "I haven't seen such a happy couple since the Brownings were here." Then there were times when they had tea beside the Arno, watching the sun set behind the Ponte Vecchio. On these mornings she went humming down to breakfast.

After breakfast, which she and Clara usually ate on the back gallery, weather permitting, Ernestine took the flower basket and shears from their accustomed place by the back steps and went down to the garden to cut the roses before the day got too hot.

Always a little dark-haired girl with luminous eyes was waiting for her. John's youngest daughter, Alice, had been Ernestine's special pet since their return from Europe after his death. She had been just a baby then. As soon as she could walk, Alice had begun to run over to The Burn to see Aunt Ernestine. Ernestine read to her and taught her to read, almost before she could talk. She showed her the steel engravings and the bookbinder's prints. She taught her about the many beautiful things that were to be seen in the world, describing in detail the Rembrandt paintings, the statue of Moses, and the Sistine Chapel ceiling. She told the wide-eyed little girl how Michelangelo had lain for days flat on his back on a high scaffolding to paint the famous ceiling. She raved about the clean Dutch people who scrubbed their streets. She painted a vivid picture of the red and gold city of Florence, where the Renaissance was born and would live forever. She told her about Pietro Ficino and the Brownings, reading their poetry to her, and some French verse. As the years flew by, they read together the works of Charles Dickens, Jane Austen, and Walter Scott, Milton and Keats, Wordsworth and Tennyson. They devoured Shakespeare's plays. They studied the epic poems of Homer and discussed the ideas of Plato and Aristotle. They talked endlessly about the heroic deeds and noble spirits that were the gift of the past.

And they talked about John. "Tell me about Papa," Alice would beg, and Ernestine would tell her about John's jokes, and how he could imitate people, and sometimes she would tell one of John's favorite stories just as John himself had told it. "He knew how to make people laugh, and no matter how many worries or problems he had, he could always find something to laugh about!" Ernestine told her.

She had always been extremely close to her brother. Lucy had been so much older and Daisy and Annie had always had each other, but there had been a special kinship of the spirit between Ernestine and John. He had nicknamed her "Birdie" when she was a small child because, as he said, "She looks just like a little bird, so tiny and alert, always hopping around on those little sticks of legs!" Everybody had picked it up, and Ernestine had been Birdie to all the family until her thirteenth birthday, when Douglas had declared she was getting too old for such a silly name. Henceforth she should be called only Ernestine. It was hard to change, but the family had respected Douglas' dictum, all except John, who refused to give up the old name entirely. "What I wouldn't give to hear him call me 'Birdie' again," Ernestine said to Alice. "He often told me that I was his favorite sister, and whenever he called me 'Birdie' I believed it."

She told Alice about the little brother and sister who had died of Scarlet Fever and about her own aunt, little Lucy, who had planted the white rose and looked after it herself, and who had died of Yellow Fever. She told her about her grandmother, the beautiful Rebecca Conner, and about the family's adventures during the War.

"It's a wonder her poor little brain isn't addled!" said Clara to Ernestine when Alice had left after one of their sessions together.

"Her mind is a bottomless pit!" declared Ernestine. "I don't know enough to fill it up, but I want her to know enough to want to know more. She's already told me that someday she's going to live in Florence and write novels. I said, 'Oh, Alice, when you're a famous writer I'll be so proud of you!' She just shook her head and said to me, 'But you won't be there.' Of course I knew what she meant, but I asked her, 'Where will I be?' She looked at me, started to speak, then changed her mind, and raising those big dark eyes of hers she pointed solemnly to the sky. She was too polite to say that I would be dead and gone. Of course I don't intend to be!"

"You'll be around, but I may not be. I do hope I will, though. It's such an interesting world, isn't it? And the only sure way to see into the future is to live into it."

CHAPTER NINETEEN

UNHAPPILY Clara told herself she had seen into the future all too well with regard to the trouble in store for Daisy and Wallace.

Although Wallace had a good job, his salary was modest, and it looked as though he was in danger of losing his valuable land in the Delta.

Wallace's mother and her second husband, Mr. Deeson, had had some unfortunate dealings which resulted in the loss of much of their property to a Mr. Scott. Then, after Wallace left the plantation and went to Memphis to live, his brother not only let the place run down, but borrowed heavily against a future crop without realizing that Mr. Scott was influential in the bank from which he had received the loan.

Annie was horrified and said to Daisy, "I don't see why Wallace allows this sorry state of affairs. I wouldn't stand for it and neither would the doctor. And I certainly wouldn't for a minute let Mr. Scott get away with another one of his dirty tricks!"

"I know, Annie," responded Daisy. "But Wallace is a lot like Father about things. He just won't stoop to fighting the man on his own terms. And I love him for it. Do you remember the first time I met Wallace how he insisted on giving that forger another chance? I loved him for that then, and I love him for being like this now."

"Well, I think you're crazy!" declared Annie with her usual frankness.

But the great tragedy which was to come upon them was not then fully evident. Little by little, year by year, Wallace began to show signs of a creeping paralysis which gradually disabled him until he was eventually totally helpless.

Daisy took in boarders and struggled to keep her family financially afloat after Wallace was forced to give up his job. Then she herself, always of delicate health, and now so overburdened, developed tuberculosis and had to be hospitalized. The two older sons, Frank and Brooks, left high school and went to work to support the family. They took turns bathing and shaving their father before they left to go to their jobs. Their sister, Clara, looked after the youngest boy, Doug, and taught a kindergarten class. Lucy had begun teaching again after Edgar died, but she lived so near that she was able to help run the household during the long months that Daisy was in the hospital. Daisy's tuberculosis was finally arrested, although she remained quite frail. Unfortunately Wallace required more and more nursing. Annie and Dr. Brooks, who had prospered with their cotton farming, helped where they could financially, as did Clara and Ernestine. However, Daisy and Wallace were proud and wouldn't accept much.

Meanwhile World War I came and went. Lucy, Daisy, and Annie sent their sons to it and all came safely home.

When he returned from the War, young Edgar Poague, who had worked for Dr. Brooks on his plantation before the War, bought a piece of land to farm for himself. He wanted Lucy to come and keep house for him. Lucy was torn. She hated to leave Daisy, but she felt her son needed her, too. And Annie and the doctor had moved to Memphis so Daisy would have Annie near her now. Lucy finally decided to go to the Delta with Edgar at least for a while. She had been there scarcely a year when she died suddenly following a brief illness. The devoted family reeled from this unexpected loss.

Clara said to Ernestine, "Lucy has lived away for over forty years and hasn't even visited often in the last twenty, but I feel utterly bereft. We kept in such close touch with our letters. I'll miss those letters full of wit and philosophy, bringing her strength and her adequacy to me across the miles."

A few months after Lucy died Annie persuaded Daisy to join her in a pilgrimage to The Burn to see Clara and Ernestine. Daisy protested that she couldn't leave Wallace, but Annie insisted. She and Dr. Brooks hired nurses for Wallace for the week they would be gone and made all the plans. Daisy's children urged her to go and finally with some reluctance she agreed to make the trip.

It was June, and they sat in the garden at The Burn late in the afternoon, Annie and Daisy sipping tall glasses of iced tea with sprigs of mint. Clara and Ernestine had theirs hot as always, regardless of the weather.

The day had been sultry, but a breeze had sprung up. Now that the sun was going down, it was very pleasant in the garden. Over in the east the new moon was hanging in the sky like a little crescent-shaped cloud and could be seen peeping through the thick foliage of the trees.

Some friends had come to call, but they were gone now and the family was left together. Clara was telling them about all the new things she had planted.

"Aunt Clara, what will you do when you give out of ground to plant?" teased Annie, still beautiful, although her golden hair was gray now, and her figure stout.

"Why, I expect I'll have to plant myself, but I don't want to do that yet. Life is so beautiful, and I love to live it. I want to see the Sistine Chapel again and look down on Florence from the hills and spend at least a week in the Louvre. Ernestine and I are saving our money to go again now the War's over. A Mr. Von Haglundt has been here visiting. He's from Berlin, a perfectly delightful man. We've enjoyed talking to him so. He has such an extensive knowledge and understanding of art and music, and of history, too."

Daisy stiffened, her cheeks flushed, and she spoke sharply for her. "I don't see how you can even be polite to a German."

Clara started at the bitterness in her voice. She was shocked that Daisy should have this attitude.

"Why, my dear child, you mustn't let yourself harbor that kind of resentment! You have a heritage of tolerance, you know. Even during the Reconstruction days your father and I made every effort to forgive and forget. I can't help but remember a sermon that Eliot Watson preached many years ago on that very subject."

"Why, I remember that sermon, too, Aunt Clara," said Annie. "He said we shouldn't hate the Yankees."

"He said we shouldn't hate anyone."

"Yes," said Annie, "that's right, and Mrs. Bedford Smith said afterward that she didn't believe Jesus ever said to turn the other cheek. I remember it all so well. While Dr. Watson was talking, I was thinking about one time during the War when we were at Elmo—I don't know how I remembered it, but I did—I still do—you and I, Daisy, got caught in a thunderstorm. We must have been way over at the end of the grounds near the road. Some Yankee soldiers were running past, and when they saw us, they climbed over the fence and picked us up in their arms and wrapped their blue capes around us and took us into the house. I think that's why I've never been able to hate the Yankees."

"Well, that was different. There were two sides to the Civil War, but the World War was launched in cold blood by the Germans for no reason but a lust for power!"

"Well, that's the way it may look to us, Daisy," said Clara. "Still I find it's quite rare that there aren't at least two sides to every question. Besides I don't think we should place the blame for the sins of his nation on an individual. But let's not argue about it. We have so little time to be together."

"Well, I don't object to Germans, but I still don't like Yankees in spite of what Annie says!" Ernestine commented, only half in jest.

The women laughed together, releasing the tension of their disagreement.

"The trouble with you, Ernestine, is that while you've been to Europe, you've never been to Boston," said Clara. "You sound like my Uncle Will Wren, who was your great uncle. He wrote a letter to your father when he went to Harvard, which he began, 'Poor Douglas,' instead of 'Dear Douglas.' I don't know how well you all remember him, but he was what you call a character. I have the letter upstairs in that big tin box. I must show it to you."

"Speaking of Dr. Watson, how is he, Aunt Clara?" asked Daisy.

"Why, Daisy, I thought I wrote you that he died. It's been two years now."

"I don't remember it. Is Mrs. Watson living here?"

"Oh, yes, I see her quite often. She comes frequently to have tea here at The Burn with Ernestine and me."

"She says that Aunt Clara is her dearest friend," said Ernestine.

A tiny twinkle appeared in Clara's eyes and then gave way to a wistful look. "How nice that she should feel that way. I'm very fond of her."

After supper Clara brought the big tin box downstairs and set it on the marble-topped table in the parlor. The ladies dived into it, exclaiming over the contents, as delighted as pirates discovering gold doubloons.

"Look here!" cried Annie, holding up some papers. "It's an oration which Father made when he was at Harvard. Nobody makes 'orations' anymore, do they? They only make speeches. The heroic quality seems to have gone out of everything."

"Why, Annie, that sounds much more like me than you!" protested Daisy.

"Oh, well," grinned Annie, "I only feel that way about words. I'm not heroic enough to enjoy living without electricity and plumbing. But do listen to this passage from Father's oration."

O Mr. President, may the accursed word disunion never agi-

tate our beloved country again. I believe every true American will offer up the same prayer. Though I may offend some who hear me this night, I speak it from the depths of my heart when I say I scorn the one as a traitor to his country, who would have this sacred Union severed.

"I never realized he felt so strongly about the Union."

"Well, look here," said Daisy. "It's a list of men elected to the Mississippi State Legislature in 1859 with their political affiliations: Whig, Democrat and so forth. Father is listed, 'Patriot.' Imagine feeling the way he evidently did about the Union, and then having to fight against it!"

"It was an agonizing decision for him," agreed Clara. "As it was for so many others. The issues were confused, and so were our loyalties. Here's that letter from Uncle Will that I told you about."

Way down in the Piney Woods
4 miles from whare
I was this 6th Jan. 1851

Poor Douglas,

I just got to town and find your mama scribbling to her darling away down east so I just thought that I would sit down and let you know that I am still one of the American citizens and hope long to be. Now that being fully understood I will tell you that I have long looked for a letter from the first Walworth *but alas I have looked in vain—but I suppose that hard study and having letters to write to so many you have forgotten your Poor Old Uncle, but if this should in the least remind you of him I hope you will let him know it.*

Sue and the children are all well, fat, and saucy and the finest lot of youngsters in these diggins.

As your mother will write you all the news about here I will wish you good night.

From yours till death etc. etc.
Will Wren

P.S. Christmas gift to you and a happy new year.
N.B. You need not charter a ship to send my presents to me, but can remit by telegram.

N.N.B. I want them sent by the fastest line as I go home in the morning.

"Show them how he addressed it, Aunt Clara," said Ernestine. The letter was addressed:

This are rit 2 mi deer nephue
who are 2 a Kolidge way down too
Massachusetz naimed
Douglas Walworth
2 Caimebrige

While they were laughing over that, Clara handed another letter to Ernestine. "Why don't you read this out loud to them as you did to me the other night when we were going through these things?" She turned to Daisy and Annie. "It's a letter your great-grandfather Wren wrote to your father when he was at Harvard. Although Ernestine never knew Grandpa Wren, she sounds exactly like him."

Ernestine cleared her throat, adjusted her spectacles, and began to read with great solemnity:

Natchez, Mar., 1851

Dear Douglas,

Your welcome letter of the fifth of last month came duly to hand, for which I thank you and by which I feel gratified to be informed of your well being and comfortable condition and situation.

I suppose by this time you have become fond *of the fashionable dish of pork and beans. Beans make excellent, healthy food cooked in almost any way, provided all the* wind *is boiled or baked out of them to prevent the cholic.*

"He was joking, wasn't he?" Annie inquired amid the prevailing laughter. "Read on, Ernestine. I can't wait to hear the rest!"

You say you have good health, gained in weight and knowledge of human nature and science, and that you maintain your integrity as a southerner notwithstanding Yankeeism, beans, and cold weather. All this is gratifying to me and I hope I shall never hear otherwise of you. I am very much pleased with the letters you send to your friends here which give us regular accounts of your well-being and well-doing, and I do most fondly hope never to hear anything of you to the contrary. If your mother were to be informed of your falling off, or committing any impropriety, or submitting to any temptation I believe it would almost destroy her. Her whole soul seems to be wrapped up in her son Douglas, her eldest son who is to be a leader and examplar for her other children. You have a noble little brother, Ernest, a little gentleman of sterling principles and unbending purposes, who should never have a pernicious example from his elder brother, the hope of the whole family.

You also have a band of lovely, aimiable, lady-like, little sisters who are smart and intelligent, whose hopes are centered in their dear Douglas, on whom they depend in a great measure for respectability.

You are my eldest among many smart, promising grandsons, to whom they will all look for character pattern and respectability, and I have no doubt but that they will be happy in contemplating their forerunner as a worthy examplar.

Daisy interrupted, "'Poor Douglas' indeed! Father must have felt that absolutely everything in the world depended on him and that he had to be perfect!"

"Yes," murmured Annie, "and he thought everybody else had to be, too. What else does Grandpa Wren say, Ernestine?"

If you should so far from home, under so many surrounding temptations, seen and, perhaps unseen until too late, escape them and come home at the end of your college course, pure and unscathed, with a tolerable proficiency in learning, I shall esteem you as a jewel worthy to be applauded and rejoiced in by a large, wide spreading, respectable connection. For this purpose you must watch and pray with out ceasing; for the enemy never slumbers but is always ready to take advantage of the least opportunity. The first, smallest error or sin that you may consent to is the most dangerous. A youth commits a sin, which at first alarms him a little, but finding that it has not killed him or made his sick, he is readily induced to repeat it and repeat it, till alarm or remorse is banished. He goes into deeper error with the same result, and before he knows where he is, he is in the sink of iniquity from which he cannot extricate himself. He is gone from home, family, and happiness or the least respectability or usefulness. God grant my dear Douglas that this may never be your unhappy lot. Write to me Dou-

glas. I will answer your letters. We dine at your father's today and you will be spoken of though not seen by us.

All join in love to you

Your affectionate and
anxious grandfather
Woodson Wren

"He has a Post Script, which lightens things up again."

P. S. After dinner. We had a very fine Turkey, well cooked and suitable fixings to taper off with—But no Beans—While at dinner I told Ernest I was writing to you, and asked him what I must say to you for him. He put his finger up to his shirt collar and said, "Tell him I am wearing a dickey." And he was as stiff about the neck and shoulders as if he had had a crick in the neck. Had to turn his whole body to get his head around. After dinner he and your father and your cousin William from Cleveland and myself, went down into the yard and took a game at marbles. Ernest beat all of us.

"You read it perfectly, Ernestine," said Daisy. "I don't remember Great-Grandpa Wren, but I've heard Aunt Clara and Father talk about him so much that I feel I know exactly what he was like."

"He was a real old dear, wasn't he?" inquired Annie.

"Yes, I thought he was," replied Clara, "but he was also extremely opinionated and obstinate, and he had a terrible temper. I remember he got into a fight on the church steps one day. My mother and father were humiliated. Your father was, too. The Conners and Grandpa Wren never got on too well, and they all thought it was very gauche of him, which, of course, it was. But he never cared what anyone thought of him and I adored him."

"Who wrote all these?" Annie lifted two huge stacks of letters written in a thin spidery hand.

"Those are all from your grandmother to your father when he was at college," said Clara. "She must have written him almost every day."

Ernestine laughed. "Listen to the first two sentences of this one."

My Dear Douglas,

This is Tuesday morning and here I am writing to you. It is one of the most pleasant occupations I have and another is reading letters from you.

Daisy shook her head. "I don't see how Father ever found time to study, what with reading and writing all those letters!"

Clara had been sorting through some papers. "Here's a combination letter from Uncle Will and my brother Ernest. They used to have so much fun together. John was a lot like both of them."

Dear Douglas: Ernest and I now write you a letter.
One line will be good the other will be better.

"That's in Uncle Will's handwriting. The next lines are in Ernest's."

I took my gun the other day
And tried a black bird for to slay.
The gun went off, the bird it flew.
What I write to you are true.
On Monday I'll be eleven years old
The weather here is mighty cold.

"Now Uncle Will's."

Ma gives Ernest a birthday dinner
I wish you were here you Sinner

"Ernest's."

On Monday I'll have a turkey cooked
Some 'taters, bread, and a pot of soup.

"Uncle Will's."

On Monday I intend to work
For E. S. Russell as his clerk.

"Ernest's."

I hope that Uncle Will succeed
For of money he stands in need.

"Uncle Will's."

Ernest says no more he'll write
So now we bid you good night.

Youre muther sais as how she will rite sum to you and send it along with this 'ere so u kan anser both 2 gether when you chuse and direck as abuv. Yourn in grate trouble,

Erny and Unkle Will

"I'm beginning to see what you mean about Uncle Will being a character," said Daisy. "No wonder Grandpa Wren was so worried about his grandchildren!"

"Here's a paper Lucy wrote about the religions of the world. Our dear philosopher! If only she could be with us tonight," Clara said, and every heart in the parlor ached with loss. "But in a way, she seems to be, and all the others, too. Here's a letter she wrote me shortly after her marriage."

"Oh, let me see it!" cried Daisy.

"Read it to us, Daisy," urged Annie.

Dearest Aunt Clara,

As I sit here in my new home, which is beginning to look quite livable, filled with such happiness as I never would have believed possible, groping for the words to express my gratitude to you for the beautiful wedding and reception, I am suddenly overwhelmed with the realization of how infinitely much more I have to thank you for.

It has been such a long time since you came into the confused and war-wrecked world of a lost little girl, and put the pieces back together. Your love and guidance have seen me through so many problems and crises ever since, and what a trial I have been, opinionated and contentious, always certain in my unbounded egotism that I could touch the stars! You will be glad to know that I no longer expect to touch them, although I do keep on reaching, out of habit I guess.

Daisy's voice faltered, and for a moment she was unable to go on.

I would never dare mention this longing for the stars to Edgar, or he would try to get me one. How did I have the good fortune to find a man like him? Perhaps, after all, I do hold a lucky star in my hand.

The unpacked boxes are looking at me reproachfully so I will get back to them now, but I will write again soon. Thank you, dear, dear aunt, mother, teacher, counselor, and friend. You have been all these to me.

Edgar sends love and his thanks, too.

Ever your devoted niece,
Lucy

The wire from Douglas about John's death was there,

and the newspaper clipping with his picture. Ernestine picked it up. "How handsome he was, and such a lot of fun! I miss him so." Then she sat thoughtfully, reading the telegram.

"Oh, Ernestine, here's the picture of you and your bombshell," exclaimed Annie.

"Why, Aunt Clara, I had no idea you'd saved that. What a terrible picture of me! But it is extremely good of my shell!"

"Here's a poem," said Daisy, "that Father must have written. It's on the fly leaf of his War Diary, dated 1862."

The peace of the valley has fled
The calm of its once happy bowers
Is disturbed by the rude soldier's tread
While the gore of its brave gilds the flowers
Those young hearts that beat but to love
Are blighted, forsaken, and dead.
The peace of the valley has fled,
The peace of the valley has fled.

The vine 'round the cottage door twines
Its tendrils neglected and stern
From the door way the widow will gaze
For a form that will never return
He sleeps far away 'mid the slain
His broken shield pillows his head
The smiles of his children await him in vain.
The peace of the valley has fled,
The peace of the valley has fled.

They read the letters, poems, compositions and newspaper clippings eagerly, suddenly seeing a father, or a grandfather, or a sister in a new perspective, just as human beings, each with his own strengths and weaknesses, hopes and fears, fulfillments and disappointments.

Clara had spoken to Annie privately earlier in the evening, after their conversation in the garden. "Annie, I was so surprised to hear Daisy speak with such bitterness. It was so unlike her."

"I know," Annie sighed. "But, Aunt Clara, you can't imagine the strain she's under. Wallace's condition is so pitiful. It has been for a long time, of course, but it gets worse and worse. It just breaks your heart to see him! And Daisy anguishes over her children not having the advantages and the opportunities that she wants for them. Then you know she's far from well, and she drives herself much too hard. I worry about her so." The tears stood in Annie's blue eyes.

The next morning Clara asked Daisy to help her cut the roses. Ernestine, whose job that usually was, had to go to town on an errand.

"It's so nice out here this morning, Daisy, why don't we just sit here for a moment, and let the Tree of Benediction rain its blessings on us?"

"All right," said Daisy. "I do love this old sentinel." She touched the bark of the tree with her slender fingers. "You know it was right here that Wallace asked me to marry him. I was so thrilled. It was the most wonderful thing that had ever happened to me." She looked off into the garden with unseeing eyes and a tragic expression on her face.

Clara yearned to comfort her, and yet she could seem to find no words that might help. She thought, Daisy's suffering is really worse than Wallace's. God gives strength to those He afflicts. When you only imagine what it's like, it's unbearable. Daisy, with that vivid imagination of hers and her acute sensitivity, is undergoing absolute, unrelieved torture. I must find a way to tell her that.

"Daisy, dearest," she said aloud, "you're going to have to stop putting yourself in Wallace's place. You won't be able to stand it. God is giving him some kind of strength to endure his agony. You must believe that. Do for him whatever you can and leave the rest to God. If you go to pieces, you won't be any help to him or to your children."

These words from Clara seemed to unlock a door inside Daisy. Great sobs wracked her frail form, and she held her face between her hands. Her grief seemed to have no end and was terrible to see, but Clara thanked God in her heart for this expression of it. How long has she held this inside of her she wondered? She sat silently waiting.

At length Daisy's sobbing became less violent, and finally it subsided completely.

"Daisy, I'm going to cut some roses, and go up to the house. You stay here for a while. Come on up when you feel like it. I'm so glad you had that good cry. You know, along with laughter, I think tears are the best medicine in the world."

As she sat there resting, spent from the outpouring of her grief, Daisy thought, I believe this is the most beautiful spot in the whole world right here. She looked up at the branches that spread over her protectively. She could feel them blessing her. They really did send down grace and mercy and peace. Then she looked about her in the garden. She seemed to see a happy little figure running here and there, her brown braids bouncing behind. The child picked a white blossom from a bush and held it cupped in her hands. Who was she? To which generation did she belong? It doesn't matter, thought Daisy. She is myself.

CHAPTER TWENTY

ERNESTINE was packing her books. Her back ached from reaching and stooping, but she scarcely noticed that. It was the turmoil within her, threatening to sweep her over some kind of precipice, that occupied her attention. She tried to concentrate on the job of selecting her most precious volumes from the rows and rows of shelves. These would go with her to Annie's.

Of course I'm not leaving forever, she told herself, and then the sinking, drowning feelings came flooding back worse than ever. There was no use trying to fool herself. She would never be able to come back. She couldn't live here alone. She had tried it briefly over the strenuous protests of the family and had found it so terribly lonely. She had not yet admitted to anyone else that she wasn't coming back. It was easier to say she was going for a visit with Annie in the house in Memphis which Annie, widowed now for a little over a year, shared with her bachelor son Douglas. And after all, that was the truth. It would always be a visit because when she left The Burn she would never be at home again.

She placed a beautifully bound book of French verse carefully in one of the boxes, and then she stood looking at Aunt Clara's mahogany secretary. It seemed to her to be alive. How could she leave it? "I will send for it—if I don't come back," she answered herself, and then she went to the desk and lifted out the packages of letters in their white ribbons. "But these I will take with me now."

"Miss Ernestine, your lunch is ready."

"All right, Susie, I'll be right there after I wash up," she told the young black woman, Little Doug's wife, who had taken Maybelle's place. Oh, not her place, that was impossible! That was what had made everything especially difficult, losing Maybelle and Aunt Clara both within a matter of weeks. She would just as soon go herself. Thinking about that at night alone in the house was one of the reasons she had decided to leave The Burn. Also she knew it wouldn't do to get peculiar, the way so many of her old friends had living alone with only memories, wonderful as memories were. But the main reason she was going to Annie's was that she knew somehow that Annie not only wanted her, but needed her. Daisy's death had been such a blow to her, and now with Dr. Brooks gone, too, she must be very lonely. Her two daughters, Margaret and Clinton, were married and did not live in Memphis, and a bachelor son didn't provide much company.

"I guess we need each other, Annie and I. We're all that's left of the family." She was talking to herself again as she had found she was doing so often these days.

Susie served her lunch on the back gallery. She nibbled at it, looking down at the garden, which was suddenly miraculously filled with people. Her father was there and her grandmother Conner and the Grandma and Grandpa Walworth that she scarcely remembered, and her mother, whom she did not remember at all, but had only heard about and seen pictures of. Lucy was there and Daisy and John and Leila. Even her little Aunt Lucy was there, and Aunt Clara was in the midst of them looking much younger than she had in years. She knew they must be ghosts, but they seemed very much alive.

Susie was speaking to her, and they vanished. Only the empty garden remained and it needed weeding and pruning. It was a shame not to keep it better, but she couldn't do the work anymore, and good help was hard to find. Little Doug worked full time at the paper mill now and just helped her when he could.

What about the white rose? Aunt Clara's last words, almost, had been about it. It had been hard to understand a lot of the things that she had said, but the part about the white rose had been very clear. She had said, "The white rose should be planted by Lucy's grave. Put it in your will, Ernestine. I should have put it in mine."

If she never came back, what would happen to the little rose? There would be somebody to take care of it at the cemetery. She would ask Susie to see if Little Doug could come over tomorrow and transplant it for her.

After lunch she got out the old tin box and went through it. She took a few things out of it and then carried it back to the attic.

Then she went to her room to lie down for a little while. She realized suddenly that she was awfully tired. Her back ached and her head did too.

She was really nervous about going to Memphis. Added to the trauma of leaving The Burn was her apprehension about the new and strange environment that she would have to adjust to.

One thing, though, she was looking forward to getting to know all the great nieces and nephews who lived in Memphis. She had missed John's daughters so much since they had grown up and married and moved away. In fact, the cottage next door had been rented to strangers since Leila died, and it made her sad to look over there.

Daisy's grandchildren all lived in Memphis, and Annie had told her about Daisy's granddaughter Louise, who looked so like Daisy. The child had only been three years old when Daisy died. She must tell her all about her grandmother and about Aunt Clara and Brother John and Rebecca Conner. Ernestine always referred to the mother she had never known as Rebecca Conner.

Oh, there was so much to tell her! She would describe to little Louise the Rembrandt paintings and the Sistine Chapel ceiling and the Renaissance city. She would read

Dickens to her and Shakespeare and she would tell her about Odysseus and Penelope, and Socrates and the little slave boy. She would try to share with her all that she had learned about the wisdom and beauty of the ages just as she had with Alice. She dropped off into a fitful sleep and dreamed the wildest kind of dreams. First she and Henri were walking the streets of Florence, but they were paved with vanilla wafers instead of stones.

Then she saw Aunt Clara standing in the garden, but instead of her arms there were branches reaching out from her in all directions like the Tree of Benediction.

Then one of the blossoms on the white rose bush had a face like the first Lucy Walworth, then it was like Daisy's, and then it was like them both yet different.

She woke with a start and looked at the little clock on her dresser. It was already nearly four o'clock! She had invited guests for tea at four-thirty, a sort of farewell party because she didn't know when she would see her friends again. She would really have to hurry!

Ernestine dressed herself hastily, which she was unused to doing, putting on her sensible shoes, a simple navy blue dress, and the long ropes of pearls and her little pince-nez glasses that gave her such a look of distinction.

She started down the stairway. As she rounded its sudden curve she thought, this is one of the last times I'll ever do this, and a lump arose in her throat.

She found Susie in the kitchen starting the tea.

"Goodness, Susie, I let the time slip up on me! Everybody'll be here in a minute. I'm glad to see you've got things started. I'll get out the tea cups."

She went into the dining room and carefully took out the yellow china tea cups. Then she brought them back to the kitchen two by two.

"I feel like Noah loading the Ark," she said to Susie.

"Yes'm," grinned Susie. "Miss Ernestine, is those vanilla wafers all you plan to serve with the tea?"

"Yes, Susie. I don't think it really matters what we have to eat."

Well maybe it did to some people, thought Ernestine, but Maybelle wasn't there to bake the wafer-thin molasses cookies that Aunt Chloe had taught her how to make.

The party turned out to be a success in spite of the scarcity of refreshment. Old Natchez was assembled in the garden of The Burn, and they had a fine time together reminiscing about the past, as always, and gossiping about each other's eccentricities, which increased every year.

"How long do you plan to be at Annie's, Ernestine?" somebody asked.

"Oh, I'm not sure yet. I'll just have to see," replied Ernestine vaguely. She looked up at the house, and a picture of it boarded up, sitting silent and bereft as an abandoned nest in a winter tree, arose before her. She pushed the vision resolutely out of her mind.

After everyone had gone Ernestine went to Aunt Clara's desk and took out the things which had come from the old tin box. One of these was a story which Annie had written based on the story Aunt Clara used to tell them as children. It was entitled "The Legend of the White Rose."

Ernestine read it to herself and had a good cry. She finally got herself together, patted her eyes dry, polished her little glasses and picked up her pen. In her tall, slanting script she added this new ending to the story:

The white rose looked about the moonlit garden, and then at the empty house, brooding on its hill. The other flowers were silent. They knew how much she missed the family.

Finally the old rose sighed softly and confided, I am so glad you have asked me to tell my story for tomorrow I am to leave you. My friend the mockingbird told me he heard I am to be moved and planted by the grave of that little girl who loved me so long ago. I am old for such a change, and my roots are deep in this garden. Still I hope I shall continue to bloom, and scatter my petals. Goodbye, old friends, my blessing I leave with you in our garden.

Please do not forget the old white rose, who will forever bloom for those who love her.

Douglas Brooks helped his little aunt into the car. "I

know how hard it must be for you to leave The Burn, Aunt Ernestine," he said solicitously.

The fragile, white-haired woman met his eyes in a level gaze. "Leave The Burn? Oh, I could never do that! I'm taking it with me—right here." She pointed a finger toward her heart. Then she murmured something in French which he couldn't understand. She said, *"Un souvenir heureux est peut etre sur terre plus vraie que le bonheur!"*

The 1930 Packard slid smoothly down the drive. It paused at the gate. Ernestine did not look back, but Douglas Brooks did.

The Burn had a lonesome look about it.

Genealogy of the Walworth Family

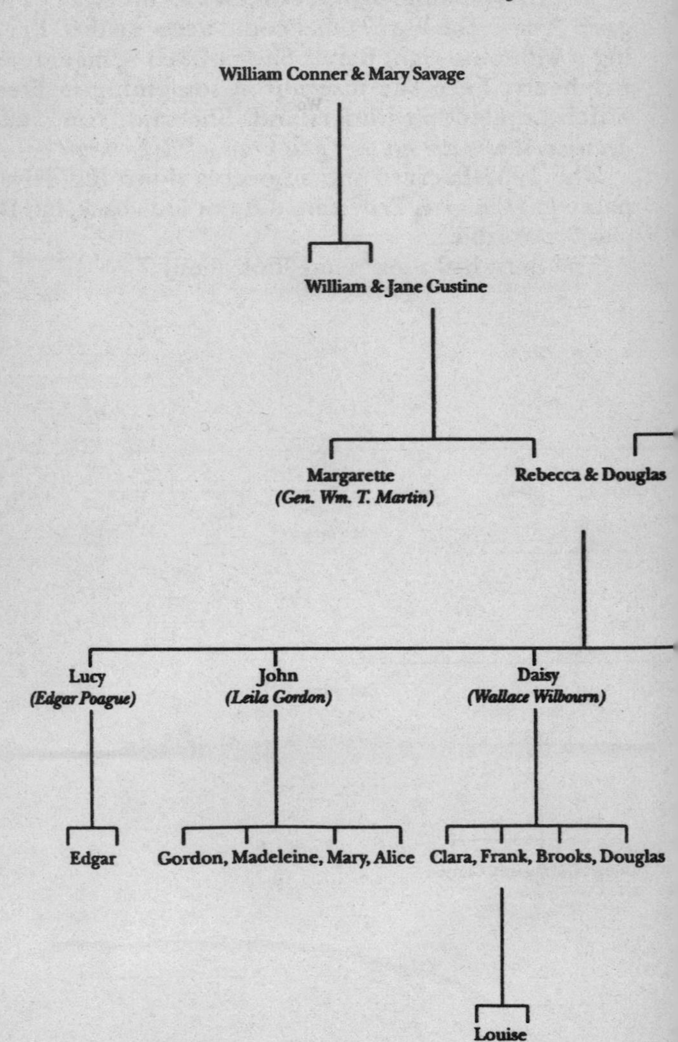

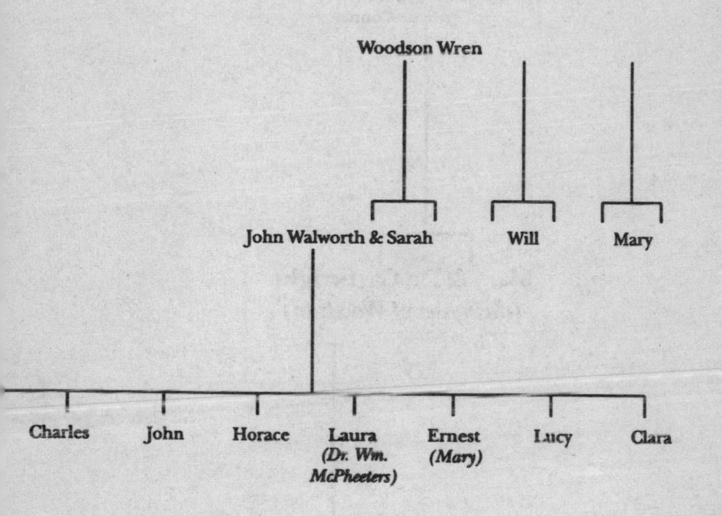

Woodson Wren
John Walworth & Sarah
Will
Mary
Charles
John
Horace
Laura
(Dr. Wm. McPheeters)
Ernest
(Mary)
Lucy
Clara

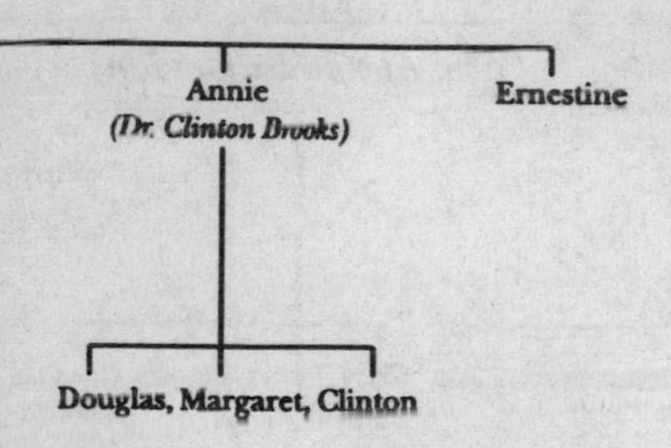

Annie
(Dr. Clinton Brooks)
Ernestine
Douglas, Margaret, Clinton

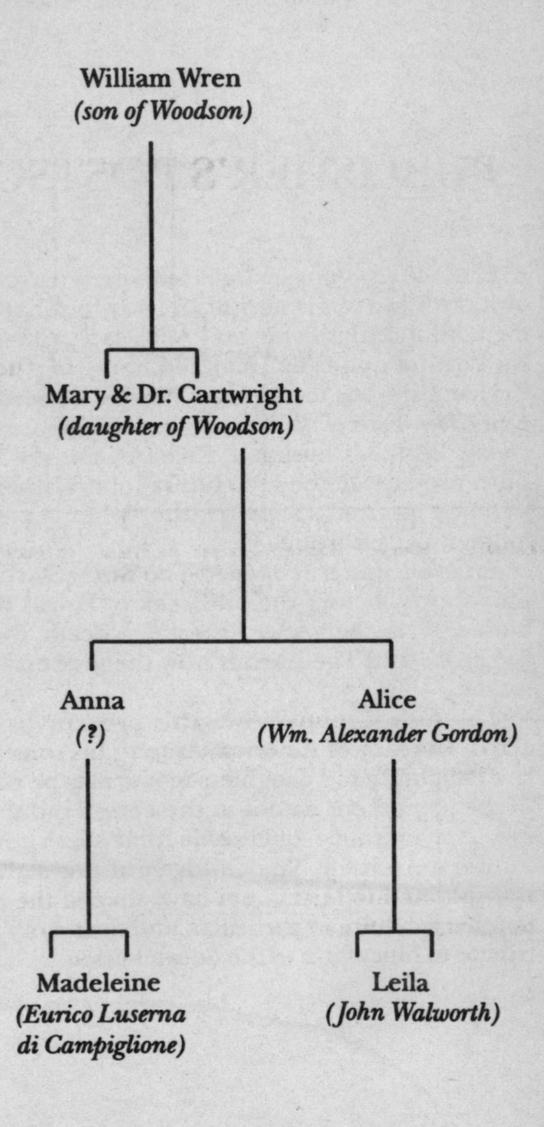
William Wren
(son of Woodson)
Mary & Dr. Cartwright
(daughter of Woodson)
Anna
(?)
Alice
(Wm. Alexander Gordon)
Madeleine
(Eurico Luserna
di Campiglione)
Leila
(John Walworth)

PUBLISHER'S POSTSCRIPT

Ernestine's young charges both grew up to carry on her own tradition of giving stories away to others—Louise as the author of this book, and Alice as a professional novelist. Writing under her married name of Alice Walworth Graham, she was to produce: *Natchez Woman, Indigo Bend, Lost River, Vows of the Peacock, Shield of Honor,* and *Summer Queen.* With her husband, Richard, she still lives on The Burn property in the little house John Walworth built as a wedding present for her father when he married her mother, Leila Gordon.

Ernestine never reopened The Burn. She died in Memphis shortly before the outbreak of World War II and is buried in Natchez. After Ernestine's death, the family sold the home and The Burn is now the property of Natchez' mayor.

The rest of John Walworth's progeny have scattered across the face of America. Among his sons and sons-in-law, daughters and daughters-in-law, may be counted some of the prominent names in the cotton industry, in banking, in politics and—quite aside from Alice's contribution—in literature itself. The children of this stalwart Yankee transplanted to Mississippi have shaped the character of Southern culture in particular, and their story is as much a tribute to him as it is to the South herself.